CAPERS IN THE SAUCE

Laura Lockington was born in Kent but, via interludes in Cornwall, Florence and London, has now settled in Brighton. She has been married, more than once, but vows never to do it again — at least not unless too many vodka martinis prevail over her better judgement. She has had a varied career, working at various points in TV, film, theatre and interior design, but in 1999 abandoned the rat race to write her first novel, *Capers in the Sauce*. She has now grown out of clubbing and taken up cooking for friends instead, but is a firm believer in one's inalienable right to behave disgracefully when necessary.

Praise for *Capers in the Sauce*

'Reading this book is like going to the most outrageous, wonderful party and somehow avoiding the hangover. Pure pleasure.' Katie Fforde

'A cool Nancy Mitford' Julie Burchill

'A rollicking romp by the original good-time girl' Louise Rennison, author of *Angus, Thongs and Full-Frontal Snogging.*

CAPERS IN THE SAUCE

Laura Lockington

ARROW

Published by Arrow Books in 2001

3 5 7 9 10 8 6 4 2

Copyright © Laura Lockington 2001

Laura Lockington has asserted her right under the Copyright, Designs
and Patents Act, 1988 to be identified as the author of this work

First published in the United Kingdom in 2001 by Century

Arrow Books
Random House Group Ltd
20 Vauxhall Bridge Road, London SW1V 2SA

Random House Australia (Pty) Limited
20 Alfred Street, Milsons Point, Sydney,
New South Wales 2061, Australia

Random House New Zealand Limited
18 Poland Road, Glenfield
Auckland 10, New Zealand

Random House (Pty) Limited
Endulini, 5a Jubilee Road, Parktown 2193, South Africa

Random House Group Limited Reg. No. 954009
www.randomhouse.co.uk

A CIP catalogue record for this book
is available from the British Library

Papers used by Random House
are natural, recyclable products made from wood grown in
sustainable forests. The manufacturing processes conform to
the environmental regulations of the country of origin

ISBN 0 09 941677 8

Phototypeset by Intype London Limited
Printed and bound in Great Britain by
Bookmarque Ltd, Croydon, Surrey

This book is dedicated to the memory of
Joan Helen Deering
1917—1996

To all the people who still miss her, don't worry. I have it on very good authority that she is in the great kitchen in the sky, a G&T in one hand, a cigarette in the other, imparting wisdom, advice and laughter. We all, one day, will meet up again.

With love and thanks to:

Polly Marshall, the princess of the apostrophe's and whose encouragement and enthusiasm was invaluable. To Tony Glenville, for fashion advice and giving such great copy. To Steve Devine for inspiration. To Mark Williams, for endless cups of tea and vodka when necessary, and to all the other Brighton stars for help and support. Cheers.

Chapter One

Always start off on the fifth floor at Harvey Nichols. To have a drink. To try and get into that 'hey, yes let's go, let's go spend that money, and cane that plastic' frame of mind. And today's reason? I've got two hours and a credit card to buy a drop-dead outfit for a party.

The casual way that I've mentioned the word party won't have given you any clue as to the horror that this particular party will involve. I have to keep taking deep breaths as I think about it. The party (oh God) is next week, and I, for once, am not leaving it to the last minute. I've booked a facial, leg wax and haircut. And manicure. I thought about a pedicure too, but on balance decided against it. I mean, who is really going to be studying my feet? I know that the royals seem to be rather fond of the odd toe-suck, but other than an encounter with Prince Andrew in the bathroom, I can think of no justification for forking out even more money than the damn party is going to cost me already.

So, on to the outfit. How do I want to look? Arty, smart, creative, sexy not tarty, not mutton dressed as lamb, and above all (the eternal cry of the over-thirty) comfortable. I can't cripple myself as I did when I was younger . The agony of the stiletto, or the jeans that could only be done up whilst lying flat on your back with a shoelace threaded through the zip, is long gone.

On the other hand, I don't want to look like Eleanor Bron or as though I work in middle management at the Halifax. I'm sick to death of black velvet and strappy little dresses that look like the nighties I wore as a child and bloody cashmere twinsets. I want something different. I want something yummy. What will Zena be wearing? Something bloody gorgeous, I bet. Zena always does. She has that knack of throwing things together, designer and high street, that somehow just work. She also has that big blank look that blondes (natural) with huge blue eyes have. Somebody said once that the reason Zena looks constantly surprised is because when she catches sight of herself in the mirror she expects to be dark.

I realise I am automatically wandering over to a rail of clothes that has a lot of black velvet on it. Exasperatedly I pull out the mobile and entreat Monty to come shopping with me. Even though it's a weekend I can tell he's in the office from the noises in the background, girls squealing, faxes whirring and phones ringing.

'What's the point of having a fashion journalist as a best friend if they don't go shopping with you?' I complain when he refuses to come and play.

'No point at all, but I simply can't. The collections are frantic, and I'm off to Paris in the morning and—'

'OK, OK, I understand, but help me. Where can I go? You know if I buy something by myself I'll end up looking like Edith Sitwell on acid, I've got proper money for this you know.' I realise I'm beginning to sound panicky, but I'm desperate.

'I could bring something back from Paris for you,' he offers. 'I get back on Thursday and the party's not till Friday.'

I am seriously tempted. Monty has exquisite taste; designer friends and he knows what size I am. He also understands what bits you want to cover up and what can be safely revealed. He, unlike most gay men, seems not to possess the secret misogynist streak that makes them want to dress all women like Barbie dolls or their mothers. Accepting would also get me out of this shopping hell.

'How much?' I ask, ever aware of the precarious state of my bank account.

'How much do you want to spend? Don't forget I'll get loads of discount.' His voice fades a little and I hear him shouting across the office, 'I don't care if it's her last show and her brother *was* shot, I wouldn't sit in the sixth row for *God*, let alone some jumped-up Italian with wobbly tits.' His voice comes back to me: 'Look, leave it to me. I'll get you something and bring it round on Thursday evening. You can cook me dinner.'

'Thank you. If it's ghastly I shall give you rissoles.'

'In that case I shan't dress.'

We hang up, and released from making a buying decision I go back to the fifth floor and order a large vodka. The waiter who looks like an extra from *The Beach*, manages to imply that he is only serving drinks to supplement his real calling of high art and spills the tonic on to the table. Grabbing a napkin I'm starting to mop up the sticky mess when I suddenly hear my phone bleeping in the bottom of my bag. Frantically I scrabble through the junk found in all women's handbags. Finally finding my phone I whisper hello into it, as I am very aware of disapproving looks all around me. I too hate people who have long, loud conversations on a mobile in a restaurant, but this is Harvey Nicks, for God's sake, I expect the bloody thing was invented here or something.

'Hello it's John here,' comes a very tetchy voice, 'and you are holding up the entire project. When are the lights going to be delivered? It is clearly stated in the contract you know. We're all waiting for you here in bloody Sidcup.'

I interrupt him to tell him he has the wrong number. Again.

He sounds exasperated, and then amused.

'Sorry, I keep doing this to you, don't I?'

'Umm, you keep shouting at me, too,' I say, glad that I'm not the cause of his horribly important sounding project being delayed.

He laughs, apologises and hangs up.

I feel obscurely let down. After all, I'm sitting in Harvey Nichols and the call should have been from someone extremely glamorous like Jade Jagger or Jimmy Choo, not a builder in Sidcup that I don't even know. I keep my phone in my hand and want to call someone, someone to share the day with, someone that I can beguile, to come and drink the late part of the afternoon away with. I run through the possibilities. I crunch on a salted almond from the little frosted glass bowl on the table and absent-mindedly reach for another. Sarah? No, too far away for such short notice though I make a mental note to winkle her out at a later date, I never get to see much of her because she's always so damn busy. What about Paul? A very sweet guy I used to work with . . . No, he's just got himself a new boyfriend, known to us secretly as the child bride because of the vast age gap between them, and they're no doubt spending a romantic day together *à deux*. Realising that I've eaten the last of the almonds, I dab my finger into the little greasy bowl for the last of the salt and suck it. Got it. Steve. Steve can always be winkled out for a drink, no matter what he's doing.

I press in his number and wait for him to reply. When he answers he sounds pissed off. I'm going to have to charm him, which means hard work: when his black moods descend it takes spoonfuls of sugar to lift him up but I decide it's worth it and launch into the attack;

'Steve? it's Liv, fancy a drink?'

'Hello, trouble, you know I can't. I've got to finish these illustrations or I won't eat for the next week . . .' He sounds determined, but I know better.

'You don't eat anyway. Go on, you know you want to really, and I haven't seen you for ages. I could buy you a bottle of wine and listen to you explain to me why Damien Hirst is the most overpaid wanker in London.'

Steve is an artist and takes Damien's success personally. Steve also has a bit of a thing about sharks.

'Look, I'll meet you at the Casa in half an hour, and I promise to get you home early,' I say in my most wheedling tone.

'The last time you said that I got home at seven in the morning and Connie didn't talk to me for three days,' he objects. True, but hardly relevant.

'My God, that woman bears a grudge, it's her Irish background. Is she there now?'

'No, she's gone to Paris with some new designs.'

Connie is an Irish dyslexic textile designer who looks like a large Flemish milkmaid. She has absolutely no sense of humour and refuses to believe that Steve and I, who shared a flat together for years, have no romantic yearnings for each other. (I think we once did, but nothing came of it and we are left with a comfortable mateyness that she feels excludes her. She's right.)

'Well, the coast is clear, what are you whining about?' A

firm tone usually works with Steve. 'Besides, we can talk about Zena's party.'

It works instantly. He barks down the phone, nearly puncturing my eardrum, 'Party – what party?'

I interrupt and repeat 'Casa, half an hour,' and hang up. He'll be there, if only to talk about Zena.

I feel that I should clear up any possible misunderstanding about Zena. I love her. Everyone does. People stand up when she walks into a room, just to be near her, to join in with her, to keep up with her. She's a whirlwind of adrenalin with no artificial stimulation. She's fun. She looks terrific (she looks perfect all the time). But, there's a mystery. Something is missing from her, maybe. She can be vague to the point of blankness.

I've known Zena for years, but feel I don't know her any better than the first day I met her. I realise that I've never seen her cry, or lose her temper. She's generous and kind, but also prone to doing things for people that really shouldn't be done. She arranges things, sometimes beautifully, sometimes with catastrophic results. She once arranged a private plane so we could all go and 'surprise' her brother, Kirk, on his honeymoon. You can imagine how thrilled Kirk's new wife, Katie was to see a troop of bedraggled, worse for wear party-goers yoo-hooing at her on the beach. I mean, it was a nice intention, but just not thought through. A bit like this up-coming party.

The party is, you see, for me. I have finally left my job (where I did nothing but moan about it for years), split up with the love of my life, and decided to set up on my own. Zena is convinced that all I need is contacts, so she has arranged this party with the express intention of getting me some peachy clients and finding me a new man. I begged her not to, but oh no. She really believes that the interior design world will be falling over themselves to snap me up. She's invited a lot of aristocracy, a bit of TV media, and quite a few journalists. Then she became worried, and invited loads of friends as well. I just know it's going to be a nightmare, as my kind of interior design has really taken the form of gussying up places; I'm definitely not in the 'Let's make over the East Wing for Lady Mary' type. I also told her, she says that I bleated it at her, that I don't want a man, new or otherwise.

I wander through Soho to get a table at the Casa, and am, as usual, struck by the sheer volume of people. Does no one have a nine-to-five job any more? Are they really all runners for film companies or are they doing some creative research for a thrusting new ad agency?

The Casa is fairly crowded, even at quarter to four in the afternoon, and the pale winter sun shines through the heavy wooden venetian blind in the front window that is meant to screen the famous from the curious. In reality, of course, it just accentuates them, in the way that a darkened window of a limo makes you stare more into the depths, hoping to catch sight of someone well known.

I see that William Magpie, the white-haired editor of *Review*! is hogging a chesterfield with a bottle of champagne stuck into an ice bucket and is leering down the cleavage of a young hackette. He lifts a hand holding a cigar and makes a half-wave in my direction. I make a half-wave back, and scuttle towards a table as far away as I can get from him. He truly is a horror, and I've no wish to be stuck with him.

The hackette, who is backing further and further away from him, throws a glance of appeal at me. I can see William sliding an arm along the back of the couch, ready to drop down over her shoulders. I am half smiling though, because although he is a horrible, lecherous old man, he's so much a caricature that I find it hard to believe that anyone can take him seriously. All that hand holding and knee rubbing went out with the ark, but I suppose amongst the new young it might well be mistaken for an archaic form of chivalry. The hackette looks again in my direction, while William starts to stroke her hair. She looks like she's going to get the giggles, and I see her excuse herself and disappear towards the Ladies.

Ah, the Ladies at the Casa, that's a fascinating subject that deserves a footnote in the history of modern London. The rows, the making-ups, the deals, the lies, the tears, the sex, the drug taking, the sheer drama of it all. It also has one of the best noticeboards in London. Underneath it is a stack of blank postcards, a large cocktail glass full of pencils and a packet of drawing pins. I can spend ages reading the board; it's like looking at some crazed anthropologist's notes on women's lives *circa* 2001.

'*If ANYBODY knows where Charlie is, come and see me, I'm sitting at the bar drinking sea breezes wearing a Philip Treacy hat*'. '*Does anyone have the private number of Gino's in New York, desperate to book a table there*'. '*David is descended from thieves and whores, don't touch him with a bargepole*' (this particular card had many added scribbles, like '*yeah, damned right*' and '*Bastard*', and a particular current favourite of mine – '*Does colonic irrigation hurt?*' The replies to this go from the seemingly helpful to the truly obscene. I hoped that the hackette who had fled from William was finding some solace there.

Ben, the one truly gorgeous waiter at the Casa, brought over a bottle of house white and two glasses.

'Livia, nice to see you. Paying cash? Or shall I put it on your tab?'

I decided to be grown-up and go for the cash. Some of my tabs at the Casa have been beyond alarming.

As he pocketed my money, Ben rolled his eyes in William's direction and hissed at me, 'He's been here since eleven this morning and he's as pissed as a fart. God knows how I'm going to get rid of him.'

'Anyone else in?'

'Liam's upstairs playing snooker, Caroline has just left and I have no idea who all the rest are, just Eurotrash dodging jobs, I should think . . .'

Ben has a very low opinion of the members of the Casa, which is why he is courted by most of them.

I took off my Nicole Farhi coat, made a mental note of where I'd slung it – I'd once had a divine leather jacket pinched from the Casa, when I was too pissed to notice that it'd gone – and settled down to wait for Steve. I'd just had my first sip of wine when a hand on my shoulder made me jump. William was swaying slightly to the side of me. How the hell had he got there? For an elderly pissed man he moved like a panther.

'My dear girl, how lovely to see you, may I – ' he waved at the spare seat opposite me, and began somewhat unsteadily to lower himself into it.

Oh God, think quickly.

'The thing is, William, I'm meeting someone, and well, it's a bit delicate, you know, umm, we need to sort a few things out.'

William looked delighted. Anything that had a whiff of secrecy was to be cherished: with a bit of luck it might pad out his very tired gossip column in *Review!* He leaned over me and I was treated to the full frontal onslaught of his boozy breath, as he tapped the side of his nose with one finger.

'Say no more, m'dear. Height of discretion, Gentleman always. Specially with m'friends. Shall leave you to it.' He slurred the words, turned with surprising agility and started to weave back to his own table, using the backs of chairs and sofas as support, then sank down into the green leather chesterfield and shuffled around a bit. Bastard, he's watching the door to see who's meeting me!

A few minutes later the double doors from reception opened and Steve walked in. I stood up, waved and as he walked nearer to me, flung both arms around him and kissed him on the lips. Steve disengaged himself, looking very surprised.

'Christ, what are you on? I've never seen you quite so desperate. What have you—'

I interrupted him.

'Shut up, you're my ploy to get away from creepy William.'

His eyes lit up. 'Great! All my life I've wanted to be a ploy. But I have to say that kissing you is a bit like incest. Very unsettling.'

'Don't think that I enjoyed it either,' I said tartly, pouring a glass of wine and offering it to him. 'Have this to get over the shock, and look like you're entranced to see me.'

'It'll take more than a glass of white wine,' he grinned.

'Bastard.'

We both laughed. Our relationship flourishes on rudeness to each other.

Steve settled himself down and started to take off his many jackets and coats. Being one of the thinnest people I know, he wears layers of clothes, to protect himself from what he calls ' the interminable cold of perfidious Albion'. As he sat he started to search for his cigarettes and lighter, and I pushed mine towards him, even though he only smokes Camels. It's easier in the long run to offer your own, rather than go through the agony of watching him contort himself trying to search through his clothes. He is known as Mr Eleven Pockets.

I don't fancy Steve – we've been friends for so long that sexual attraction would just seem silly – but there's no denying he's nice to look at. He's got a full smiling mouth, over-styled hair, cheekbones that you could balance a cup and saucer on, and the most beautiful hands, that are usually black as he sketches mostly in charcoal. His eyes swept the room, and then did a double take at a stunning Chinese girl.

'My God, how *does* Connie stand it?' I giggled.

'Stand what?' he asked with mock innocence. The thing with Steve is that he's not even a flirt. He really insists that he is searching for love. Or lurrrve, as I scathingly pronounce it. Generally speaking his girlfriends are very beautiful and very affected, with absolutely no charm. I suppose he thinks that he has enough to make up for their lack of it. Most of them drift away, but this time Connie had settled in with him and things had suddenly become complicated because of that dreaded thing – the joint mortgage.

Swiftly we drank our way through the bottle and caught up with each other's news: his new commissions (book cover illustrations); his mother's move to Dorset; the lack of vision of any major art gallery; the waste of grants to the arts, the lack of talent in modern art and his preoccupation with Damien Hirst.

'Get over it. He's done and dusted anyway,' I said brutally.

He gave me an old-fashioned look, and went to the bar. I saw him chatting to Ben, but was too far away to hear what they were laughing about. He came back smiling, holding another bottle of wine.

'Ben tells me that William has paid for this and wishes us every happiness.'

11

'Oh God,' I sighed. 'It's going to be all over the place now that you and I are an item, and I only said that to get rid of him.'

'Quite a laugh really, as long as Connie doesn't find out. Besides, everyone knows you're not my type.'

'Your type, as we know, only has two things in common – living and breathing. Oh, and an IQ of eighty.'

The second bottle was well on the way to being finished, when he tackled me on the subject of Zena's party.

'What are you going to wear?' That is one of the nice things about Steve, you can really talk to him about what you are going to wear, and he'll be interested. I explained about Monty and Paris. He brightened.

'That's where Connie is. Do you know where Monty is staying? They could have dinner together or something.'

I looked at Steve and just didn't have the heart to tell him that Monty loathed Connie, and would rather dine out with a crocodile. What must it be like, I wondered, not to know that your partner was universally disliked? Steve knew that I wasn't keen, but he probably put that down to my not liking his girlfriends in principle. I remember once, drunkenly, pleading with him to find a girlfriend that we could all have dinner with, without stuffing our mouths with napkins to stop us laughing and he, quite crossly for him, demanding to know when was I going to stop being professionally heartbroken and go out with someone. Anyone, in fact. When I found a man who knew that Smeg was a brand of kitchen appliance and not a sexually transmitted disease, I'd muttered.

Finally, when both bottles were dead, we decided to go in search of somewhere to eat. We walked arm in arm through the cold dusk, Steve chanting 'Soho was their play-ground, dawn was their sunset' to stony-faced people lining the streets, and after some argument (he wanted Chinese, I wanted Indian) we settled on a Thai noodle bar. We sat at a window table and giggled at the impossible names of dishes that Thai menus always have.

'Are you going to have the Lum Now Luk Fung or the Two Yuk Lim Tow?' Steve enquired.

'Whatever. As long as it comes with alcohol.'

'Right, well I'll share the Fuck Lung with you and we can have a side order of Yukky Toes.'

'What would you say to a little wine?'

'I should say, good evening little wine . . .'

We both collapsed, and under the indifferent eye of the impassive Thai waiter struggled to regain control.

The broth that we'd ordered came very quickly, and it was delicious. Hot and clear with strong bites of ginger and coriander. As I looked around the busy restaurant and through the window to the even busier street outside, I saw a taxi stop and a laughing couple get out, hand in hand. The man paid off the cab driver and the woman put up her collar against the cold night air. The man turned to her and protectively put his arm around her shoulders. I sighed. Steve looked up and caught the look on my face. We mock glared at each other for a moment, and then continued our conversation.

We have a rule, you see, that I'm just not allowed to start talking about him. The man who broke my heart. The man who, of course, is married, and who I was a fool to even start talking to, let alone start sleeping with. I'd met him at one of those classic London dinner parties, you know, all supposedly beautiful people who do nothing but boast about the rising price of their houses. Christopher had been invited as a touch of bohemia, as I had too, I suspected. We sat next to each other and flirted outrageously all evening. He had

13

put his elbows on the table, ignoring everyone else and then swivelled around to look at me.

'You really do have the most beautiful eyes: they are like two spoonfuls of the Adriatic on a summer's morning,' he had drawled, giving me a lazy smile. I had succumbed, that very night in the back of a taxi, then further still back at my flat.

Steve, good friend that he is, allows me to sink into a melancholy mood sometimes. Tonight, though, I was determined not to slip into it. I kept telling myself that I was out, in London, with a friend and having a good time. I kept repeating the mantra in my head, and with a stout heart agreed to go to Pete's new bar after our meal.

Pete, I should explain, is one of my best friends. We've known each other for years, ever since we met at one of Zena's famous summer parties, and like Steve, he's someone I can't do without. That said, I had quoted for the interior design of his new place and hadn't got it, so I was curious to see what he'd chosen (and secretly hoping, of course, that it would be horrible).

We walked to the bar and pushed our way in. Pete was bellowing orders to some waiters and fought his way through the crowd towards us. He gave us a bear hug and I was engulfed in his huge arms.

'Well well well, if it isn't Livia out on the town for the night, Gawd help us. What are you doing with this starving piss artist?' People looked around approvingly. Normally only the rich and famous were insulted by Pete and they obviously couldn't work out who the hell we were.

Pete, all curly dark hair and wickedly twinkling eyes, was even more rotund than the last time I had seen him, and his face was dripping with sweat. He dragged us towards the bar, shoving people out of his way and tipped two girls unceremoniously off their bar stools to make room for us, simultaneously thumping his fist and calling for a bottle of champagne. The overworked bar staff grinned indulgently and produced the bottle and three glasses. Pete was loud, vulgar and bullied them to death, but he gave them great bonuses and turned every night into a party. His rude banter was famed, and part of what attracted people to the bar was the hope that they, too, would be admitted into the inner circle.

Looking around, I noted the décor of the bar and saw with a pang that it was nothing like the proposal I had given him. This was all steel and primary colours, although I was smugly pleased to see that it was already starting to look a bit scruffy.

Pete saw my wandering eyes, and lowering his voice, said, 'Livia, it was just too expensive, you know. It's not that I didn't like it, but you're too classy for this, it has to be cheap and cheerful, like me. It doesn't matter that it won't last – neither will I.'

'What do you mean?'

But his attention was elsewhere. A ravishing young boy had just walked through the door and Pete pointed to him and boomed across the bar, 'Have that boy washed and brought to my tent immediately!' I saw the boy blush with pleasure as he moved through the crowded room towards a group of his friends, and noticed that all the gay boys in the bar looked as though they'd been in a Gap TV ad. They were dressed in that sort of clean-cut American, slightly preppy look, even though, frankly, some of them were a little too old for it. They probably got all their furniture from IKEA, too.

The noise level in the bar was becoming deafening, and

Steve was having to shout as he nagged Pete about naming the place, 'You can't keep calling it the Bar for ever.'

'I won't have to.'

'Liv, do you remember that Dutchman we met in Italy last year, the one with the *lithp*?' Pete bellowed in my ear.

'Yeth, I do. Why?'

'Well, he came in here the other day, looking for us. Either of us! He'd love to have a little party . . .' Pete was laughing his head off, remembering the awful Dutchman who had attached himself to us last year on holiday. He'd been after both of us, and was convinced we would 'par-tay' with him. I shuddered at the memory.

Things were starting to get a bit hazy. My trouble is, that once I start drinking I either have to go for it in a big way, or I have to cop out early and reduce the devastating effects of a hangover for the following day. It was tempting to stay, but what remained of my common sense — and the fact that tomorrow was a working day — persuaded me to leave. I'd got to meet a client the following morning, one who was proving to be very tedious indeed about some details of his flat I was doing for him.

Steve and Pete were well on the way through yet another bottle, and as I started to gather my coat and belongings Steve surprised me by giving me a huge goodbye kiss on the lips.

'Got to keep up appearances, you know,' he winked. 'After all, we are an item now. Shouldn't I be seen attentively squiring you into a taxi?'

'What the bleedin' hell is going with you two?' demanded Pete.

'Livia and I have succumbed to our secret yet all-pervading lust for each other,' said Steve, rather smugly.

'William Magpie has a lot to answer for,' I smile, kissing Pete goodbye.

As I pushed the door open, the rush of cold night air made me realise how much I'd had to drink and gave me a bad case of hiccups. Luckily a vacant taxi was just outside, and falling into the back of it I asked for Warwick Avenue between hiccups. I love being in the back of a London taxi at night, it feels so secure and faintly luxurious. The huge crowds on the pavements gradually disintegrated as we left Soho and soon I was home.

The taxi driver kept the cab running whilst I was fighting the front door with my keys. What a shining dark knight of the roads, I thought, but I finally made it in, flicked the lights on and threw my coat on to the back of the sofa.

I made a deal with myself: I would go to the loo, make a mug of Earl Grey, take my make-up off, clean my teeth and then, and only then, would I check my answerphone. Even now, three months after the break-up, the unreasoning hope lingers that he may have called me, begging me to reconsider. Christopher was famed for his amorous phone messages, and they became a large part of our affair. I missed them, even now.

But you can tell I'm not expecting him: my flat's starting to look neglected, the flowers are drooping in the vases, there's a heap of interior design trade magazines that have succumbed to gravity and spread themselves out of the office door and into the hallway, and a stack of washing up.

As I wiped off my make-up I managed to avoid looking too intently in the mirror by squinting. Actually, you can't look directly into the mirror in my bathroom: the reflected colour of the walls prevents it. I'd painted it last week in a frosted lime green and metallic silver, and realised too late that it was a ghastly mistake – it made everyone look like a sick cat with a liver complaint. I waved my hand in front of the starfish (another mistake) and the lights dimmed. That was better.

I moved into the bedroom, still hiccuping, and quickly undressed, putting on my comfort nightdress of red flannel. I made the tea and curled up on my favourite chair, a large squishy thirties cube, covered in shocking pink velvet. Blowing on the hot tea, I pressed the flashing red button of the answerphone.

There were three messages: 'Liv, it's me (*why* do people say that on a machine? Do they all assume that they have such distinctive voices, or that you only ever have one person calling you?) how long do you cook sea bass for? I'll try your mobile, bye.'

'Liv, it's me again, your mobile's off, I bet you're at the Casa, I've just taken it out the oven and the damned thing still looks raw, shall I just call it hot sushi? Call me when you get in.'

'Livia, where the hell are you? The chocolate thing is runny as hell, it looks disgusting, like baby poo. Will it thicken if I put some flour in it? This is meant to be a seductive dinner, you know, not a meal with the Borgias. Call me, I need help.'

I was smiling into my tea. Molly is a notoriously bad cook, and was trying to seduce a photographer that she'd recently met. She figured that he must be bored with eating out all the time with stick-thin models (yeah, right) and was trying to woo him with home-cooked pleasures. I glanced at the time on the VCR to see if it was too late to ring. Past midnight. I made a mental note to ring her in the morning and staggered into the kitchen to drink a pint of water to dispel the incipient hangover and try to get rid of the hiccups. Listening to Molly had made me smile much more than any of Christopher's anguished messages ever had. I snuggled into bed, kicking the duvet into place. Maybe I really am getting over him, was my last thought before I passed into blessed oblivion.

Chapter Two

I'd already pressed the snooze button on the alarm clock twice and knew I couldn't delay getting up any longer. Mornings are never my best time, something I inherited from my mother, normally a loving, charming woman who was a snarling beast in the early hours. I'm the same. No matter what the day holds in store, I've never been one of those people who fling the covers off the bed, and whistling happily are lathering in the kitchen, ready for a big breakfast. I have to break myself in gently: a bit of Radio 4, cups of tea while staring moodily out of the window, a hot shower and then I can face what humanity is going to hurl at me.

At least I had the luxury of *not* going into an office and dealing with bloody Julian any more. (Julian had been my boss at JJM, a corporate interior design company, and as bosses go, he wasn't *too* bad. But you know how it is, sometimes you just want to do things your way.)

I stood under the hot shower, closing my eyes to the colour of the bathroom, and let the water stream over me. I could hear John Humphries grilling some poor soul on the radio, and stepping out of the bathroom, swaddled in towels, I started the day's preparations.

The washing up had to be tackled, I decided. I didn't have to meet Mr Abraham at his flat till eleven, which gave me enough time to whiz around my flat clearing up. I flung old newspapers, junk mail and rotting food into a bin liner and ran outside to put it in the bin. It was a cold, sunny day and I was heartened to see that a few brave green shoots were pushing up through the London earth in the front garden. I waved at Mrs Grieg from opposite, who sat at her window for about twenty hours a day (she'd once said to me that it was better than watching anything on telly).

The kitchen wasn't too bad once the washing up had been done. I often used my own flat to try out different themes and colours, but the kitchen had stayed the same for years. It was a deep French blue, with wooden fittings and a caulked floor; one wall was completely taken up by a Provençal dresser that held my eclectic collection of china. I sprayed the herbs growing on the windowsill and topped up the kettle for another cup of tea.

I had always longed for a large kitchen with room for a table and chairs in it, so I'd knocked through a wall when I'd first moved in, losing a bedroom but gaining my heart's desire. The large, old elm table had wonderfully intricate carved legs and sat eight people comfortably. The only draw-back was that people could see exactly what you were doing when you were cooking. Dropping food on the floor and casually throwing it back in the pan had to be done surreptitiously. As did cooking anything that you were trying to pass off as your own, when it was patently coming out of a packet. But it was great for the sort of entertaining that I like to do.

The best times round that table had been the long lazy Sunday breakfasts that had drifted into Bloody Marys when Christopher had spent the weekend here. We used to read the papers, go back to bed, make love, share a bath together, lazily dress and then invite some friends over, and I would

21

cook. Usually a large roast lamb smothered in garlic and rosemary, or a chicken stuffed with lemons and tarragon. And all the while I would be looking over at him with a cat-that-had-swallowed-the-cream smile. Occasionally he would look up, and hold my gaze and smile that sweet private smile that always made me feel so bloody special, and somehow blessed.

We would all sit round that table for hours, opening more wine, arguing, laughing, playing silly games and drinking coffee. Not any more.

The drawing room needed a bit more attention, it was really a room that worked best when there was order to it, as most theatrical sets do. What people just don't get when they come to decorating (good thing too, or I'd be out of a job) is that a room is a stage for your own life. You have to be bold and set a scene. You have to create a style that works for you.

I loved my drawing room, but maybe it was time for a change. The walls were scarlet, a sort of Cardinal Richelieu colour, raspberry sorbet, or cranberry red. (A very flattering colour, loads of TV interviews and photographic portraits had been done in my flat for that very reason: it looks rich without being overwhelming. I also got a location fee each time, which with my finances, was very welcome indeed.)

The floor was a mishmash of Persian and Afghan rugs (mostly fake, but a few antiques in amongst them). The furniture was old, covered in throws of fake fur or purple velvet, and I'd hung twenty-two pictures on one wall. (Always hang pictures together if you want to create a feeling of sumptuousness.) Books lined the wall opposite and heavy, ornate French mirrors reflected everything back into the room. I had put in a nineteenth-century French overmantel, and in the winter had wonderful log fires: apple logs were the best, imparting a heavenly smell. I noticed a lot of dripped candle wax on the surfaces and decided to ignore it. I only had time for a quick tidy and hoover before I went to meet Mr Abraham.

When the phone rang, I decided to take it in my bedroom, talking and putting on make-up at the same time. It was Molly.

'I was just going to call you,' I said, 'how was the dinner? Did the chocolate poo ever thicken?'

'Not only did it never thicken, I think it's clogged up my sink for ever,' she sighed. 'I can't get rid of the bloody stuff and I'm sure I've got fish poisoning. Still, if I have I can't go to work, can I?'

I was squinting into the mirror, putting on mascara with one hand.

'Did he stay the night?'

'Don't be daft. Why is your voice funny?'

'Putting on make-up. Lipstick now . . .'

'Oh. Well, no it was a disaster. He said he'd call, but I think he's just trying to get more work out of me. He was flying to New York today, so he left early and I sat up finishing the wine.'

Molly is the art editor of a fairly high profile, glossy, monthly magazine. It's not *Vogue* but it's got pretensions. I sprayed some Mitsouko down my neck and started to brush my hair.

'That's why you feel rough, then, it's not fish poisoning at all.'

A deep sigh. 'The thing is, Liv, I really, really like him, and I was wondering, well, if umm . . . You know I think he needs to get to know me properly away from work, and well, if I wasn't under pressure to cook . . . And well you,

you're such a fantastic cook, if you were to invite him to dinner, I'm sure, well . . .' she tailed off lamely.

'How the hell can I invite someone to dinner I don't know?' I objected.

'I've thought about that. You know I said I'd do your brochure for you – you will need one you know, *and* cards, by the way – I thought you could ask him to do the photographs for it.' She sounded triumphant.

'Very clever,' I said sourly.

We spoke for a few more minutes, and agreed that if she was taking the day off work, I would stop by after my meeting. I promised to think about cooking dinner for her photographer and said goodbye. I was halfway through the front door when the phone rang again.

Rushing back into the flat, I grabbed it. It was Douglas MacPherson, my decorator from Mr Abraham's flat. This didn't bode well.

'Problems, Doug ?'

'Aye.'

Oh God. Please not anything drastic. When I was working for a company, problems could be shared and didn't seem quite so awful. But now that there was just me dealing with everything, my heart sank into my boots every time there was a setback.

'Look, Doug, I'm just on my way over now, I'm meeting Mr Abraham there in about half an hour. Can it wait?'

'No, and you'll not be meeting him here unless you can swim.'

'What!' I shouted. 'I'll call you back on the mobile.'

I ran out of the door and frantically waved for a taxi, whilst punching in Doug's number. He answered immediately.

'What the hell has happened?'

'Well, young Roger managed to spike a pipe last night. It seems he didn't like to tell anyone, so we're under about two inches of water.'

Young bloody Roger indeed. Oh God. OK, think. Take Mr Abraham shopping, buy him lunch, keep him out of the way, sleep with him if necessary and leave Doug to clear the mess up. I willed the taxi along faster, and as soon as the flat was in sight ran out of the cab and up the steps to a scene of near-biblical disaster.

Thank God the flat was on the ground floor. The water was gently lapping at the skirting boards, with a silvery cascade gently streaming down the steps leading to a patio. I balanced like a stork on one leg, on a huge bag of cement, trying very hard to keep my temper and my suede boots dry. Doug had already started to do something miraculous to stem the flow, and his minions were clearing up as much as they could. But it was still going to be impossible to let Mr Abraham in to view the progress we had made. I decided to wait outside, and whisk him off as soon as he arrived, while Doug promised to clear up and phone me the moment it was OK.

I stood outside trying to work out what this delay was going to cost me. I had a deadline, and if I went over it, there would be penalties to pay. This flat meant a lot to Mr Abraham: he had inherited it from his mother and I don't think it had been touched since the 1940s. It was rather wonderful in a high Jewish rococo sort of way, but he didn't think so. His ambition was to move into a flat that looked as though he was sitting in a bowl of porridge. Beige, beige and a bit more beige everywhere.

I had tried to guide him towards Lutyens's style (black floors and eau-de-nil walls, which would have suited the flat brilliantly) but he was stuck in an early seventies time warp.

Ideally he wanted a shag pile carpet too. Or maybe he just wanted a shag. I had rather gathered that although his beloved Mama had a place in his heart, the reason that he'd never married was that she was a bit of an ogre. And apparently he had a brother that he had fallen out with in 1980 and hadn't spoken to since.

I spotted Mr Abraham's hat before anything else. No matter what the weather, he always sported a homburg, worn at rather a jaunty angle. He was a dapper little man of indeterminate age, and the first time I'd met him I'd assumed that he was gay, or maybe denying it. But now I wasn't so sure, although he was certainly very fussy, a bit of an old woman. He walked briskly towards me carrying a furled umbrella and swinging a briefcase, and then held his hand out, ready to shake mine.

'Miss Hunter, rather cold, surely, to be waiting outside?'

'Not at all, Mr Abraham, I didn't want to get under Doug's feet. There are so many contractors in there today, the electricians are in testing everything, so the power keeps going on and off, and the guys from the planning department are going round with Doug, so it's rather crowded. I thought we might go shopping this morning, we really must choose the bathroom suite, and the carpets, you know . . .' I tailed off, guiding him towards the kerb, straining my eyes for a cab.

'I thought we might pop into Harrods as well, to look at bedroom furniture. You know if you really want to move in on that date, we must start ordering things now.'

'I see,' he said uncertainly. 'Well, I suppose we could. I have absolutely no wish to go to Harrods, though, I don't want to shop in a souk.'

I could have kicked myself. He had already made his feelings clear on that 'Fayed chappie'.

'No, no of course not. I quite agree. How about Peter Jones to start with, then maybe a spot of lunch?'

There followed an exhausting couple of hours during which we looked at every single shade and type of beige carpet that has ever been made. I could feel my jaw starting to ache as I held in the yawns. I took him to a trade bathroom display shop and he became very excited at the possibility of a beige bath as well. Whilst he was staring entranced at the double delights of matching bidet and lavatory (beige), I phoned Doug.

'How's it going?' I hissed.

'Still very damp, but passable. I was just about to call you. Oh, and young Roger's turned up . . .'

There was a question mark in Doug's voice.

'How sheepish is he?'

'Oh, I think ye'll be in for a spot of grovelling,' Doug's amused Scots voice buzzed in my ear.

'Well, it's up to you, Doug, but give him a bollocking at the very least.'

'Aye.'

I whisked Mr Abraham off to lunch, and sat nodding sympathetically over a large glass of Chablis while he extolled the virtues of his late lamented Mama. She sounded a dragon. He hinted that at one point he had become attached to a woman that Mama had thought unsuitable.

'Do you mean she was the sort of woman who ate the wrong end of the asparagus?' I enquired.

'I mean that she was the sort of woman who ate *all* of the asparagus.'

I snorted with laughter. After a couple of glasses of wine, he was a much jollier man.

Suddenly he looked thoughtful. 'I've been meaning to ask you, do you think that I should have a housewarming party? Just a few friends, of course, nothing too fancy. I think Mama would have wanted me to.'

I was fairly taken aback. I mean, I just couldn't imagine him playing the host or, to be truthful, having many friends. I had to respond quickly, he was actually looking a little nervous.

'I think it's a super idea,' I said warmly, 'and if you need the number of a caterer or anything I'd be very happy to pass it on to you.'

He looked quite shocked.

'Oh no. No, I thought that you'd do the honours, I mean it's part of your job really, isn't it. Besides, you could use the flat as a showcase and invite some prospective new clients. I, of course, would be delighted to tell them how happy I am with your work, and I would foot the bill for the evening. But I really do think that it's much more your sort of thing.'

I groaned inwardly. How the hell could I tell him that his flat was the last place that I'd use as a showcase. Somebody else offering to give a party for me – maybe he'd offer to find me a new boyfriend as well. I stifled a giggle.

'Umm, yes, of course,' I said weakly, despising myself for being such a coward.

'Good,' he said briskly. 'I shall furnish you with the addresses of anyone that I want to invite and leave the rest to you. Time for the bill, I think . . .'

We parted outside the restaurant and, reeling slightly at the thought of organising a housewarming party for him, I decided to walk back to his flat and view the mess.

London was cold, the streets were crowded, mostly, as far as I could see, with seemingly happy couples. When you've stopped being part of one, you see them everywhere, and after my trying day with Mr Abraham I wanted to run between them and break them apart. Bitter and twisted, that was me right now, I muttered, much to the astonishment of an elderly lady walking her dog. It sounded like a cocktail. Yes, I'll have the bitter and twisted on the rocks, please. Cheers.

I stopped off to buy some groceries, and caught myself looking forlornly into my wire shopping basket in the supermarket. One salmon steak, one bunch of watercress, should I go the whole hog and buy *one* croissant for breakfast in the morning? I was so fed up with missing Christopher, God knows what I was like with my friends. I mean, if you're bored with yourself, what must it be like for your mates? I gave myself a stern talking to and then threw an enormous bar of chocolate into the basket as well.

The light was fading as I approached the flat, and I saw young Roger hanging around outside, kicking an imaginary stone on the pavement. He started to stammer out an apology.

'Look, Roger, mistakes and accidents happen, but for God's sake, when they do, *tell* somebody, don't just go home thinking that it'll all have gone away by the morning. It won't. It never does.' I stopped short when I saw his face. His bottom lip was wobbling. Doug must have really given him a hard time.

'Go on, it'll be OK.'

He looked tremendously relieved. I went through the door and found the guys packing up for the day. Doug and I toured the site, and then he left, offering me a lift.

'No thanks, Doug, I need to measure a few things. I'll lock up, I've got keys, night-night. And Doug, thanks.'

When the front door closed I walked around the flat in the gloaming. The floors were still slightly damp. There was no trace of the once formidable Mrs Abraham now. All the gilt and crystal, the Bakelite, the curtains had been disposed of. The walls had been ripped out, the kitchen and bathroom removed, there wasn't even a whiff of chicken soup left.

The flat was large and silent, without a trace of personality in it. I wondered if she knew, or minded, what was being done to her home. All the interior doors had been removed and it gave the place a strange, slightly surreal look. Her son, though convinced of his love for her, had demanded that she be completely erased. Every picture, ornament and piece of furniture had been sold.

As I walked into what had been the kitchen, I saw a spoon that had been left on a windowsill. Obviously not by the builders as they relied on the café and sending young Roger out several times a day on tea and bacon sandwich runs. It was an elegant, silver, rat-tailed coffee spoon, and I could imagine her stirring many spoonfuls of demerara sugar around and around her cup, whilst quizzing her son on his love life. I stood looking out of the dark windows, twirling the spoon between my fingers, then walked over to one of the many floorboards that had been prised up, and dropped it beneath the floor. There would be something of her here, after all.

After taking the measurements I needed, I walked home, carrying my shopping, feeling rather gloomy.

When I turned into my street I started to scrabble for my keys in my bag, and almost bumped into my next-door neighbour, Joe.

'Hello, Liv,' he smiled. 'There was a delivery for you when you were out, looks like another load of paint. I shoved the box in the outside cupboard. If you need a hand with it, give me a shout.'

Joe is a large rugby-playing type, he's tremendously kind, and often helps me lug bits of furniture around.

'Thanks Joe. You're either off to commit a crime, or going to work out,' I observed looking at the gym bag swung over his shoulder.

'Come on, give it a try . . .'

As well as playing rugby, football and any other sort of outdoor activity, Joe is constantly trying to get me to join a gym. He really doesn't understand that I'd rather chew my own arm off, although it would be completely obvious to a stoned three-year-old that I'm just not that type. I stuck my tongue out at him.

'Have you got any spare paint?' he asked, grinning persuasively at me. 'I'm thinking of repainting my flat.'

'My God, has the world ended? Yeah, of course I can let you have some. I don't recommend this lot, though, it's the delivery of porridge for Mr Abraham.'

'What?'

'Well, OK then, beige, if you must. But let me know what colour you want. Unless you want frosted lime, they keep sending me freebie tins of it.'

'Maybe not. Can I come in and pick your brains later?'

'Sure, but bring your own carrot juice.'

I let myself in and dumped the shopping in the kitchen. Resisting the urge to pour myself a glass of wine – I've learned from experience that alcohol when I'm feeling a bit down just makes it worse – I made tea, lit the fire and curled up on the sofa. A night mindlessly watching TV would suit me fine. I settled back to watch the flickering flames, and in a semi-hypnotic state was gazing into the fire thinking fairly melancholic thoughts when the phone rang. It was Zena.

'Hello, darling, now you're not sitting, brooding over Christopher, are you?' she asked in her voice so husky it just stopped short of asthma. 'Because if you are, I have the perfect antidote. I'm just about to leave to go to a private view of the most fantastic paintings over at Hoxton. They're sending a car for me, so I could easily just *swoop* by and pick you up.'

Zena was always going to private views, first nights, screenings, and they invariably sent a car for her.

'Zee, honestly, I'm pretty shattered, you know, and I've just lit the fire . . .'

'Well, if you're sure.' She sounded doubtful, but the nice thing about Zena was that she instinctively knew if you just needed a bit of persuading, or you really wanted not to go somewhere. She didn't push, but then again, she didn't have to. Usually people jumped at the chance of being with her.

'Honestly, I'm bushed. But bring back a catalogue, unless they're wildly expensive.'

She gave a little chuckle. Of course they would be wildly expensive, but then Zena never paid for things like that.

'Well, OK. The party plans are coming along nicely, by the way, nearly *everyone* has accepted, I'm a bit worried that we'll have too many. Have you planned what to wear yet?'

I explained about Monty buying me something in Paris, and she thoroughly approved. I told her about Mr Abraham, and she positively cooed.

'But he sounds an absolute *poppet*, you must invite me to it, you will, won't you?'

No doubt Mr Abraham would fall under her spell, and she'd have him choosing bright pink over the porridge in a trice. The phone made a little bleep in my ear.

'Oh damn, must go darling, that's my call-waiting sound,' she explained. 'It's a wonderful invention, isn't it? See you very soon, and you take care of yourself, my darling.'

I sighed as I put the phone down. What must it be like

to be Zena? Always popular, her beauty carried around like a fur coat thrown casually over her shoulders. Life must be just peachy, I thought.

I decided to cook myself some dinner, and eat it from a tray in front of the TV. I made a silver foil parcel for the salmon steak and was just shaking some soy sauce over it, when the phone rang again.

'Hello, Liv? It's Molly. Where have you been? I've been waiting for you.'

Bugger, I'd completely forgotten that I'd agreed to go and see her that afternoon. I explained about the water in the flat and taking Mr Abraham out to lunch, which mollified her.

'Shall I bring a bottle of wine round, then?'

I hesitated. Molly and I together had never been known to drink just one bottle of wine, and I really did want an early night.

'I thought you'd got fish poisoning and – or a hangover?'

'Miraculously cleared up. He called me!'

I laughed and decided that a dose of Molly's cheeriness might just be what I needed.

'Well, OK then, come over, but just the one bottle, OK? I have to get an early night. Do you want to eat?'

'Ooh, yes please, then we could plan the dinner party.'

Great. Just what I wanted, another bloody party to have to think about. Hanging up, I went back into the kitchen and retrieved the salmon steak out of its little parcel. It would have to stretch to two, so that meant a stir fry. I started to chop vegetables and was rootling around in a cupboard looking for noodles when the phone went again.

It was Steve. 'Liv, it's me, thank God you're in. I'll be with you in about twenty minutes, I'll bring some wine.' The phone went dead.

Hmm, definitely not a quiet night in, then. I went back to chop even more vegetables, and dragged some prawns out of the freezer. I was just pounding the garlic and chillies in the pestle and mortar (the part of cooking I really enjoy), when the intercom buzzed. I wiped my hands and went to answer the door. Molly came charging in, black hair falling over her face and her cheeks pink from the cold. She looked exactly the same as she had done at school when we both bunked off games and slipped into town to hang out at record shops, trying to look cool. She went straight to the fridge and started to unload an off-licence carrier bag.

'I know that you said only one, but two never hurts, and you can always keep the other one, and my God that cheese smells!'

'Chuck it,' I said laconically.

She opened a bottle and poured us both a glass of wine. I told her all about Mr Abraham, and as she was hooting with laughter the intercom buzzed again. It was Steve. He looked dreadful.

'Beetroot mixed with sour cream,' I muttered.

'What?' Steve and Molly looked puzzled.

'The colour of your eyes,' I explained, looking at Steve. 'I can tell just by looking at you that you had a night and a half after I left you with Pete. You've probably got half of Colombia still up your nose, and you're going to expect some sympathy. Well, forget it. It's all self-inflicted and quite frankly, I don't want to know. Not that I'm jealous or anything . . . I mean, I have fun every single bloody night, don't I?' I let my voice trail off into wistfulness.

'Ever considered joining the Samaritans, Liv?' Steve said, rubbing the top of my head. 'That kindly tone would work wonders with would-be suicides. They'd be hurling themselves off high buildings in droves.'

He slumped into a chair at the table, and Molly sympathetically pushed the bottle and a glass towards him.

'Oh Lord, am I in trouble . . .' he began.

'Just try saying "No",' I said teasingly.

'No, no. See I can say it, it's the *doing* it, I can't do. I've got the willpower of an ox. Oxo cube, that is. Oh Lord am I in trouble . . .'

Molly was giggling and pouring out more wine for us all.

'Why Steve, what's happened?' she said with mock innocence.

'It's all Livia's fault. She left me in a bar with Pete, with easy access to excess.'

'Oh, have something to eat, it's only a hangover,' I said, plonking a plate of food in front of him. 'You'll feel better once you've got something halfway solid inside you.' I was horribly aware that I sounded like a school matron. I'd be asking about the state of his bowels soon, if I wasn't careful. It had been so long since I'd had a real humdinger of a hangover, I wasn't very sympathetic.

'If only that were true. You don't understand – I'm in trouble,' said Steve, picking up a fork and starting to eat anyway as he began his tale of woe.

It seems that after I'd left the Bar, Pete had become very nicely thank you, and so had Steve. They had ended up in one of those illegal after-hours drinking clubs that proliferate in Soho, and after being fleeced at pool had met up with a few mates. Steve met a girl, beautiful, called Mimi (Molly and I snorted at this) and they had got on so well that they had decided to further their conversation back at Steve's. Nature had taken her course (along with copious amounts of recreational drugs and drink), and Steve, being the gentleman that he is, had escorted her downstairs and hailed a taxi for her, at 2.30 this afternoon. He had then thought,

I'll pop round the corner to the local shop, buy some cleaning stuff, and some flowers, go home, clean, tidy and wait very guiltily for Connie's return. But that's when the trouble had started. He was locked out.

By this point, Molly and I were shrieking with laughter.

'So, let me get this right,' said Molly. 'You've been trying to get in all afternoon, to clear up your sordid little mess, and you can't. Is that right? And when does Connie return?'

'Tomorrow, and it's not sordid,' he said rather sulkily. 'But, it is well, it's umm, let's just say she was a very physical girl. The flat is a complete and utter mess.'

I wiped away tears of laughter. Steve's adventures exasperated me, but at least they were funny. He *always* got in trouble, and he *always* involved me and Molly. Steve and Molly were my oldest friends. Molly and I had gone from school together to art college where we had met Steve and immediately formed an unholy trinity that had lasted over the years. Ever since our first term together, Molly and I had helped Steve out of scrapes, and it seemed our fate to carry on doing so. *Carry On Painting*, starring Steve Devlin, Molly Green and Olivia Hunter.

'Come on,' I said, 'let's be grown-up here. Paint the picture for us, we have to *see* the scene: are we talking about random items of clothing hanging from the light fittings?'

'Yes. We are,' said Steve gloomily. 'We are also talking about cocaine powder on every conceivable flat surface, used condoms, empty bottles, a large mirror unscrewed from the wall, some sketches I did of her, and well, umm, and a large bowl of slightly soiled fruit and vegetables . . .'

'What!' Molly and I screamed together.

'Don't ask . . .'

'Connie's going to *kill* you,' said Molly gleefully.

'What sort of vegetables?'

'Shut *up*.' Steve glared at me. 'What *am* I to do?' He walked to the fridge, for another bottle of wine. 'I haven't slept for thirty-six hours, my life is in ruins and you want to know about vegetables.'

'Break in, or get a locksmith,' I suggested.

'What do you think I've been doing all afternoon? I can't break in, we're on the fifth floor, remember, and well, the locksmith is a bit of a problem.'

'I would think you've enough problems, without creating a problem with a locksmith,' said Molly.

Steve put his head in his hands, half laughing and half crying.

'The locksmith said that he needed an electronics expert, because of that ridiculous security system we had installed, and the electronics expert said I needed proof of identification before he broke in for me, and all my sodding ID is in the sodding flat. And if that isn't enough, they also want the police there, just in case I'm a burglar. Hand me that knife, I might as well stab myself through the heart right now.'

The intercom buzzed and, still doubled over with laughter, I went to answer. It was Joe. He came in carrying tins of beer, and we filled him in on the details. I think Joe was a little shocked. He's a clean-living boy, and my rackety friends, although amusing him, leave him a bit bewildered.

'Explain the bit about the vegetables again,' he asked.

Steve banged his head down on the table, and Molly and I screeched with laughter.

'I've always found courgettes a real turn on,' said Molly, between giggles.

'No, no it's cucumbers for me,' I said weakly.

Joe opened a beer and looked hopefully round the kitchen

for some food. Being such a healthy sort, he was always starving.

'Dinner's all gone, I'm afraid,' I said, 'but I think there's some cheese in the fridge unless Molly chucked it.' Looking disappointed, Joe gave up his foraging and we all sat at the table. Molly started to talk about the new love of her life, the photographer.

'He's called Guy,' she began excitedly.

'As in the gorilla?' I asked.

'Yes. Ha ha. Anyway, Livia has promised to cook dinner for him, and I think Joe should come as well. Joe could make eyes at me and that might make Guy see me as fanciable. But, for heaven's sake don't ask Steve, we don't want riff-raff here.'

'Charming, thank you,' said Steve, putting on a mock injured face.

Joe was intrigued. 'Do women really think like that then? You know, planning things?'

'My dear boy, you have no idea. They're like spiders, weaving and scheming, and these two are the twins of evil,' Steve told him.

Molly and I hit him.

'What's so fanciable about him?' asked Joe, suddenly intrigued by the dark complexities of the female mind.

I groaned. 'Please don't even begin to answer that Molly, we'll be here for hours, and even then Joe won't understand. Let's just say that it's chemical, shall we?'

Molly ignored me. 'He has the most gorgeous eyes, a sort of blue-green, with yellow flecks, and a wonderful smile and I think he's really a bit shy, you know, he sort of blushes easily, and his hair has that little curly bit that sort of flicks into his neck. He's funny and kind, and . . . well, he's just gorgeous all over and he smells divine.'

'He's got curly hair, he goes red and he smells nice, is that it?' asked Joe in amazement.

Steve staggered to his feet. 'I am beginning to feel unwell . . .' he announced.

'Go and lie on the sofa, and get some sleep. We'll deal with everything later,' I said, and he wandered off to the drawing room.

Joe and Molly decided to finish off the wine and beer, while I tidied the kitchen and went to throw a blanket over Steve. He had fallen asleep immediately and was looking like an exceptionally naughty choir boy. I drew the curtains and made sure that the fire was out. Then I turned the lights off in the drawing room but, as I was about to close the door on him, I heard a slight whimper from the sofa. Crying in his sleep wouldn't do him any good, I mused. He really was for it, this time. Connie was going to go ballistic. Humming happily, I went back to join the fun in the kitchen.

Chapter Three

I dreamt that there was a helicopter hurtling around in my room, and woke with a start to find Molly sprawled beside me on the bed, snoring loudly. I felt dreadful. My head was thumping and my mouth was so dry that my tongue was sticking to my teeth. I padded out to the kitchen and ran the cold tap, filling a pint glass and gulping it down. Where were the bloody aspirin. I searched the kitchen cupboards with no luck.

I was just stumbling into the bathroom in search of medicine, when I stubbed my toe on a very large object in the hall. I cursed under my breath, hopping up and down on one foot. What the hell was it? I turned on the lights and a very large, abstract modern painting leered at me. It was leaning against the wall. My memory, feeble as it was, started to come back to me as, trying to avoid the lights in the bathroom, I desperately fumbled for the painkillers. Eventually I found them and swallowed three, with more water.

The painting had arrived late last night with Zena, who'd brought it from the private view. Molly had persuaded Joe to smoke some Thai grass that Molly had found in her pocket, when the intercom had buzzed. We had all jumped, thinking it might be Connie back early from Paris; giggling, we'd gone to wake Steve up, to make him answer it. Steve had proved impossible to wake and, hearing the buzzer again, we'd all summoned up the courage to answer the door ourselves. Zena had waltzed in (reducing Joe to a gibbering slave) with a bottle of champagne and this picture.

After that, it got a bit hazy. I do remember Joe offering, stammeringly, to be Zena's personal trainer and then turning bright red. He squired her down to her waiting car and came back, stuttering about her. Molly and I had exchanged weary glances and opened the brandy. The rest of the night was a complete blank.

I went back to the kitchen and put the kettle on for tea. I looked in the fridge for some orange juice, but there was nothing. My head splitting, I sat at the table waiting for the water to boil, and noted the number of empty bottles. No bloody wonder my head hurt. I promised myself a detox and a long walk. In fact, I promised God I'd never drink again, as long as he took away this frightful pain. I made the tea and noted resentfully that it wasn't worth going back to bed; not that I could, with sleeping beauty stretched out in there anyway.

I wandered into the drawing room, and drew back the heavy curtains. The rain was splattering against the windows, and the trees waving wildly in the street. I gave a sudden jump as a voice said 'Turn the bloody lights off.' It was Steve, who I'd temporarily forgotten, curled up on the sofa, wrapped in a crumpled blanket.

'Coffee, please, and painkillers, I've got a bastard behind the eyes,' he complained.

'I'm not surprised,' I said rather primly. 'And get off my sofa – you look like a tramp.'

'I feel like a tramp.'

I went back into the kitchen to make tea and coffee, and started to collect the bottles and put them into a bag. I know that really I should take them to the recycling place, but I also know that it's just not going to happen and I've given up pretending that it will. The clanking of glass woke Molly up.

'Stop that infernal noise,' she shouted from the bedroom. 'Something has crawled into my mouth and died. Where am I, who am I, and what's the time?'

'You're in my bedroom, on my bed, and your great fat snores made me think a helicopter was attacking us all and I'm pleased to say you're going to be late for work. Oh yes, and it's raining,' I called back, adding, 'Coffee's on, aspirin is in the bathroom. Don't turn the lights on in there without sunglasses though, it's just too cruel. I'd avoid looking in the mirror, too.'

I spooned coffee into mugs for them, and made tea for myself. Then I sat at the table and listened to the little moans and movements from various parts of the flat. Molly was virtually sobbing in the bathroom, and I could hear Steve stumbling and cursing his way down the hall. He came into the kitchen wearing his blanket like a shawl.

'Hardly a pashmina, and hardly the time for a fashion statement, I'd have thought. Besides, they are *so* nineties.'

'Liv, what are we going to do?' he moaned. He'd obviously woken up enough to remember the vegetable girl disaster.

'I really, really hope that that is a rhetorical question, as *we* are going to do absolutely nothing. *You*, however, are going to have to do something,' I said sternly and, I hoped, firmly.

Molly came into the kitchen dripping from the shower and wrapped in my dressing gown. She slumped down and picked up her mug.

'I can only feel my head, the rest of my body is numb.

Liv, *why* did you let me smoke that grass? You know what it does to me.'

'Yes, I do and that's why I don't smoke it,' I said a trifle smugly. 'And I feel just as awful, even without it.'

'You can't do. You simply can't. I feel like a jellyfish with a migraine.' She clutched her head. 'Oh God, what must Zena have thought of us?'

'Zena was here?' Steve sounded alarmed.

'Yes, oh sleeping one, we did try to wake you, but it was like trying to resurrect the dead,' I said. 'And believe me, you have much bigger worries than missing Zena – like Connie, remember? What time is she due back?'

'Of course I bloody remember, I can't think about anything else.'

'And?'

'And I don't sodding well know what to do, do I?'

The phone rang. We all just stared at it. Eventually I picked it up. It went dead. We all stared at it again.

'It's Connie from Paris, she knows you're here,' said Molly, adding, 'Oh God is she going to kill you . . .'

Steve told her to shut up. We were staring like zombies at each other and the phone. We looked like a group of people waiting for a séance to start.

'Come on, let's pull ourselves together,' I said briskly, beginning to feel that we could be stuck like this all day.

'I don't think I can, I can't feel my fingers,' sighed Molly. The phone went again, and she snatched it off the wall. 'Livia Hunter's phone, how can I help you?'

I could only hear her side of the conversation.

'What?'

'Why?'

'I see, thank you. Oh God, did I? Sorry. No, of course we don't, don't be ridiculous. Bye.'

She turned to us. 'It was Joe. He's put some artichoke and milkthistle capsules through the letterbox, we have to take four each with water, he says they'll ease our pain. Apparently I tried to snog him last night, and do we want to go swimming.' There was a rude noise from Steve at this point. 'Oh yes, and when can he meet Zena again?'

I put the kettle on once more and went to pick up the capsules from the doormat.

'How long do you think they take to work?' whimpered Molly, who was slumped across the table.

'No idea. They taste disgusting though, don't they?' I was trying to decide if toast was going to make me feel any better.

'Please, please help me,' Steve interrupted my deliberations. 'What am I to do? Connie's back this evening. That gives me about seven hours to think of something, and you two are talking about bloody hangover cures.' He was definitely rattled now. His hands, I noticed, were shaking slightly as he lit a cigarette.

'Well, you have a couple of choices, as far as I can see. You could wait outside for Connie, grab her keys, run ahead of her and clear up. Or you could, well, you could break down the front door with an axe, and say that you've been burgled,' I said brightly.

'Thanks. A lot.' Steve glared at me.

'I've got it,' Molly announced. 'Listen, you could phone Connie in Paris and tell her you're going to meet her at the airport. You take her straight to a restaurant, or something, where Livia is waiting, hiding in the loos. You steal Connie's keys, slip them to Liv, Liv runs to your place, tidies up, and then slips the keys back to you. Problem solved.' She sounded really pleased with herself.

'Forget it,' I said shortly. 'If you think I'm touching his

bowl of vegetables or hiding in any loos you are out of your mind. No way.'

Steve completely ignored me. He was staring intently at Molly. He leaned forward and kissed her. 'I think I love you. Thank you.'

I could feel my voice getting shrill. 'Hello, can you understand English? I am *not* going to do it. I am not going to touch your smelly remains of an illicit love fest nor am I going to lurk in the Ladies somewhere just to—' I was interrupted.

'Rubber gloves.'

'What?'

'I'll buy you some rubber gloves, that way you won't actually have to touch anything,' Steve cajoled.

'*No.*'

'Please . . .'

'Look, it'll all go horribly wrong anyway, Connie'll want to go straight home and change or something, and, and well, she's bound to see me in the restaurant, and how on earth are you going to steal her keys? And I don't want to. And, even if I did I'm not doing it on my own.'

Steve knew I was weakening. 'You wouldn't have to, after all it was Molly's idea, I'm sure she'll help. Won't you?' he appealed to her.

'Only if you promise to come to dinner, without Connie, when Guy is here and be really, really nice to me, and tell Guy how fantastic I am.'

'Done, shake on the deal.'

I always knew that I'd have to sort the mess out, and my head hurt too much to argue any more.

'Right, well, I'll leave you two to work out the plans, I'm going in the shower. I take medium in Marigolds, and you owe me big time,' I said. I had an awful feeling about this.

It was a recipe for disaster, I was sure. I stayed in the shower for a long time; the hot water eased my head, and I thought I'd stay out of the way while Molly and Steve sorted the details out. Oh God, I must still be drunk if I thought that Molly and Steve could sort anything out, let alone this insane plan.

When I came out of the bathroom, I studied the picture that Zena had brought. It was pretty awful. Large, with a blobby texture, it seemed to be concentric circles, going into a mist in the middle. I peered at the back of it, where I found a sticker, inscribed with the words 'Stirring porridge in my Mother's kitchen, *circa* 1971'. Ah, it came back to me now, Zena had bought it for me to dress Mr Abraham's flat, as a sort of joke.

There wasn't a hope in hell of him liking it. I hope she'd only bought it on approval.

I went and sat on my bed and stared blankly at my open wardrobe. On days like these I saw, only too clearly, the attraction of wearing some sort of uniform, the bliss of not having to make any decision. It was cold, I felt awful, so what was needed was some comfort clothes. I pulled on my old black Joseph pants and a big fluffy, soft sweater. I wandered back into the kitchen to find Steve and Molly with pens and paper in front of them, looking as though they were planning a military coup.

Steve pushed some paper towards me 'This is your call sheet, memorise everything on it.'

'Very funny.' I glanced down and read the instructions;

Liv and Molly to be at the Bar at 19.00 (sharp).
Both to hide in Pete's office, till Steve has stolen Connie's keys.
Security code for flat is: 2424.

Leave and get taxi to my flat (£10 taxi fare enclosed).
Clear up – put flowers out – chuck rubbish – CHECK
BEDROOM.
Lock up.
Taxi back to the Bar (another £10 enclosed).
Hand keys back to me (Pete will tell me when you're
back).
MISSION ACCOMPLISHED!

Steve and Molly looked very pleased with themselves.

'Have you rung Connie in Paris yet?' I said.

'Her phone's off, but I've left a message for her to call me, and I know what time her flight is, so I'm just going to wait at the airport for her.'

'And why oh why are we meeting at the Bar? Much as I love him, Pete has the biggest mouth in London, he's going to tell everyone.'

'We did that,' said Molly with dignity, 'so that you and I wouldn't have to skulk around in a loo. All we have to do is slip out of Pete's office, then out of the bar and slip back in again.'

'Right, easy peasy. Can't think of anything that I'd rather do of an evening than break into someone's flat and clear up after an orgy,' I said. 'Have you asked Pete about all of this?'

'Yes. Well, of course I will. I have left a message for him but I shouldn't think he's out of bed yet. It is rather early you know.'

'Hmm. Well, all we can do is hope that everything goes OK.'

'It will,' said Molly, gathering her belongings together. 'But now I've got to go to work. I think those pills of Joe's have really helped, you know. I can feel my legs again, and my head is clearing. Can I borrow an umbrella? Stop worrying about everything, it'll be fine. I'll pick you up about 6.30, OK?' She bent to kiss me goodbye.

'*About* – about 6.30?' screeched Steve. 'This has to be precision timing! You have to be here at 18.20, to be on the safe side, then you have to follow the instructions.'

'Shut up, Steve,' Molly and I said in unison.

Molly left for work, complaining bitterly about the weather and the still slightly jellyfish quality to her limbs, and Steve set out to buy rubber gloves, rubbish bags and flowers. I settled down to a mountain of paperwork and a list of phone calls that I had to make concerning Mr Abraham's flat. I was methodically working my way through the list, ordering interminable amounts of beige soft furnishings. My mobile rang, and having finally located it in the laundry basket, I answered. It was John, the irate builder from Sidcup.

'I'd better give you my land number soon, or your phone bill is going to be a fortune,' I said.

'Very funny. Actually I was just going to ask you for it. How are you anyway?' He sounded nice on the phone, which I do realise means nothing. He could well have a hunchback and a broken nose, for all I know.

'Oh the usual, you know, hungover, sorting people's lives out, that sort of thing.'

He laughed, and asked me for my home number. I hesitated, and then thought, oh sod it, and gave it to him.

I noted that the next person on my list was Mark from Paintworld. I liked talking to him, he was my favourite supplier. I thanked him for the paint delivery, and we chatted about the Battersea decorative arts fair that we were both going to, next week.

'I wondered if you'd like to have a drink with me?' Mark asked.

'Umm, that would be nice,' I said, hoping that he could point me in the direction of some rich clients.

As we'd never actually met face to face, he asked me to describe myself.

'Well, it rather depends if I've been out the previous night, in which case you'll recognise me by the dark glasses and wizened look of a five-foot-six blonde witch,' I said.

He laughed. 'I'll keep a look out for you. Wave your broomstick at me – I'll be the one staggering wildly around handing out paint samples. I look a bit like Ewan McGregor. Well, just a very little bit, actually. I'll see you soon.'

I was quite cheered by my telephone encounters so far this morning and started to work on my tax return, but gave up after five minutes, shoving it in a box marked 'Far too gruesome, give to Kerrison'. Kerrison was my accountant, and he was very used to my filing methods. He had similar ones himself, which is why we got on.

I heard the buzzer go, and let Steve back in after his shopping jaunt. He staggered in under a mound of bags and a huge bunch of rather tasteless yellow spider chrysanthemums.

'She'll hate those. I would.'

'You're not her. Anyway, that's all they had. I've got all the cleaning stuff, and rubbish bags, and rubber gloves, two pairs, *and* some chocolates.' He sounded triumphant.

'Don't you think you're going a little bit over the top? I mean, have you ever met her at the airport before with flowers and chocolate?'

'They're for you to put in the flat. Have you paid any attention *at all* to my instructions?'

'Yeah, yeah. How hard can it be? Get in, clear up, get out. Simple.'

Steve sighed, rather too dramatically, I thought.

'Look, Liv, I know you don't like Connie, and I know

that I've screwed up, and I know you don't really want to do this for me, but, well, I don't want to hurt her, you know? So, please, please do it properly, won't you?' He squeezed my hand and looked imploringly at me.

'I know, don't worry, I will. But you're a cad and a scoundrel, let's leave it at that, shall we?'

'OK.'

Steve used the phone to call Connie in Paris, and then Pete, whose laughter I could hear from across the room. We were both rather hungry now, so I started to potter round the kitchen, looking in the cupboards and fridge for something for a late lunch. How I wished that I'd listened to Delia Smith about the necessity of having a well-stocked store cupboard. Even she would have been hard pushed to make lunch from a tin of squid in black ink (bought, no doubt, on holiday somewhere and well past its use-by date), some rather limp celery, and a couple of eggs. I drew out the offending smelly cheese, which Molly had not thrown away the night before, and sniffed it. Very whiffy, but probably OK. I decided to make celery and cheese soup. I was just grinding some black pepper into it, when the phone rang. It was Monty from Paris.

'What shoe size are you?'

'Five, why?'

'The most divine pair of snakeskin mules is being wrapped as we speak. I grabbed the last pair from Naomi. They're too small for her anyway.'

'How were the collections?'

'The usual, heaven or hell, depending on which magazine you work for. I've put on about a stone, I had an overdose of *chèvre* yesterday, which has added inches to my waist. Not a happy *lapin* about that, I can tell you. But don't worry about your party outfit, I've got it, and you'll love it. Think

The English Patient crossed with *Hideous Kinky*, you'll look fab, I promise. Oh, and guess who I saw canoodling last night with a very attractive Moroccan waiter at Les Bains?'

'Cherie Blair,' I said stupidly.

'My God, you have the imagination of a newt. No, no, *Connie*. Thank God she didn't see me, or I'd have been stuck with her all night.'

'What exactly do you mean by canoodling?' I asked cautiously, turning away from Steve, who was idly stirring the soup and looking at the *Times* crossword. I hoped he couldn't hear.

'I mean she won't die wondering. What do *you* mean by canoodling?'

'Probably the same as you do,' I said sadly, then said goodbye.

'Was that Monty? Has he seen Connie at all?' Steve asked eagerly.

'He didn't say. Make some toast, then we can eat.' I bustled in a head prefect sort of way round the kitchen, setting out bowls and plates. I am hopeless at this sort of thing: other people's romances are harder to deal with than my own. I certainly wasn't going to tell Steve about the wretched Connie, but it did ease my conscience a little, when I thought of Steve's appalling behaviour. I spooned the soup into the bowls and resolved not to dwell on the web of lies that we all weave in our own doomed little worlds.

Steve and I settled down to eat then spent the rest of the afternoon skulking in the drawing room, rather guiltily watching daytime TV, giggling over the appalling interior design shows that seemed to proliferate at the moment.

'You could star in one,' Steve suggested helpfully. 'I'd love to see you pontificating on TV about the beauty of chicken wire cupboard doors.'

'Yeah, we could call it "Through the Cat Flap", and I could redecorate famous people's dog kennels.'

'It'd be one way of getting rid of that dreadful frosted lime paint you've got hanging around. Or maybe getting rid of that painting Zena brought round.'

'Don't remind me.' I looked at my watch. 'Hey, isn't it time you went to the airport? You can't be late.'

'Christ, yes.' Steve jumped up and started pulling on jumpers, jackets and coats, brushing his hair in the mirror and calling out instructions to me.

'I know, I know, just hurry up and leave. You spend more time in front of that mirror than I do. Prinking, that's what it's called, you know.'

'What is?'

'Excessive time spent in front of a mirror,' I repeated.

'Well, I'm just about to prink off now. Oh God, I hope to all that's holy she doesn't miss that flight.'

'Go on now, go, walk out that door, don't turn around now . . .'

'You're not welcome any more, I know. Thanks Liv. See you at the Bar.' He kissed me goodbye and rushed out.

The flat felt strangely empty now. I should have enjoyed the solitude and peace, but I missed not having Steve and Molly around. I picked up the phone, hesitated, and then slammed it down again. I was so tempted to call Christopher, it was just the sort of situation that he adored. He would have revelled in sorting out Steve's predicament, and would have turned the whole thing into a glorious joke. We would have gossiped about it afterwards, and laughed. God, I missed the bastard. Mentally I put some starch into my resolve, and phoned Zena instead. She, of course, wasn't in. Her answering machine had so many bleeps after the tone that I knew she must have loads of messages stacked up.

Probably all from people accepting her party invitation. Oh God.

I dialled Christopher's number and, feeling like Princess Di, allowed myself the luxury of hearing his voice on the answer machine: it was a charming, very well spoken voice with a hint of honey and money in its depths. I was calling his studio, of course, I would never have called his home. That would have been impossible. I wondered what he was doing at this very moment – working so hard that he hadn't heard the phone or, more likely, recovering from a very boozy lunch with his latest conquest. I didn't ever kid myself about that, I was merely one of a long string of extramarital affairs.

I had no excuse for not knowing that he was married, it had been obvious right from the start. But I had persuaded myself that this time he'd see how happy he could be, and make that break. What a fool I'd been. I felt stupid for having been so stupid. Everybody had warned me, but I had rushed in, besotted, charmed, convinced that I could make it OK. My willpower alone could have moved mountains, but sure as hell hadn't moved his marriage. Strangely, although all my friends had warned me against him, no one had questioned why I had found him so irresistible. I suppose it was just so obvious.

Warm, talented and with the sort of charm that one thinks one is impervious to, until it is actually turned on you. I was a pushover. I hadn't put up a struggle at all, to my shame. I hadn't realised that he would complain so bitterly about his wife, but would, in fact, never leave her. Because that would be like leaving Mummy. Mummy was one of those larger than life, yet still shadowy, figures lurking in his life. She had been married five times, had been on the front cover of *Vogue* during the war (with a pink satin corset wrapped round her head, improvising for a hat) and had treated him with disdain one moment (*I should have aborted you!* screamed in his face during a restaurant meal, with one of his new stepfathers) and overwhelming, cloying affection the next (once climbing drunkenly into his bed, whilst staying with King Farouk in Egypt, when he was a boy).

He had been shunted to every private school in Europe while his mother had continued slaying the playboys. His education had been erratic, to say the least: he could quote poetry, speak five languages, was a sought-after dinner guest and yet was incapable of managing a bank account.

His wife, a Frenchwoman called Danielle, had rescued him from Mummy, given him pocket money and treated him like the indulged little boy he was. She had a great respect for his talent (he was a well-known artist) and tolerated his affairs. Very bloody French, in fact. Christopher had filled my life, and I had been only too willing to be blinded to his obvious flaws. When I had realised that he was never, ever going to leave his wife, I had done the hardest thing that I had ever done, and ended it. My friends had congratulated me, and tiptoed around me, but all the while, secretly, shamefully I had really expected him to turn up on my doorstep, bags in hand, ready to move in.

My headache was threatening to overwhelm me again, so I wandered into the bathroom to take some more pain-killers. I stood gulping down water, and saw that it was time to get ready. All I really wanted to do was crawl into bed and pull the duvet over my head, but I sighed, and half-heartedly began to get changed. When Molly arrived she came bursting through the door with a carrier bag in her hand.

'Wigs,' she announced.

'What?'

'I've borrowed wigs from the magazine, they'll be crucial to our success.'

At once I cheered up: dressing up was always a favourite thing. So we rummaged through the bag. I rather fancied a red bob one, but when I tried it on Molly said I looked like a German lesbian. I settled for a long, dark, wavy one, which I thought made me look like Elvira, Queen of the Night, Molly had a blonde curly one, which made her resemble Dolly Parton on a shopping spree, and it became strangely necessary to alter our entire make-up, to suit our new colourings. We played around with lip liner and blusher. Molly wanted to put on blue eyeshadow, but I had to draw the line at that. She also wanted to go round to frighten Joe with our new look, but as I pointed out we were already late.

We rushed out on to the street at quarter to seven, clutching all the cleaning stuff and the flowers that Steve had bought, and hailed a taxi. 'Nice hair, girls,' said the driver, giving Molly a wink. She simpered, and hissed at me, 'See, it's true, you blondes do have more fun.'

'Only if you count being leered at by a cab driver as fun,' I hissed back.

'Have you got the chocolates, or have I?' said Molly.

'You don't need 'em love, you're sweet enough already,' said the cab driver.

'I'm having my hair dyed tomorrow,' Molly whispered to me, smiling broadly in the mirror at the cab driver.

To our horror we saw Steve and Connie getting out of another taxi, just outside the Bar. Molly ducked down and yelped for our cab to drive around the block.

'Oh hell.'

'Do you think she saw us?'

'Even if she did, she wouldn't recognise us, would she?'

The taxi circled the block, by which time Steve and

Connie had disappeared, so we rushed out, into the Bar. Luckily it was packed, and Steve had seated Connie with her back to the door. I gave him a wave as we walked in, but he looked blankly at me. The wigs really did work – nobody stopped us to say hello. We rushed round the side of the bar, pushing past innocent drinkers, and went downstairs to Pete's office. The door was ajar, and as we walked in I saw Pete's eyes widen, I would like to think in admiration, but it was probably in horror.

'Good God almighty, you both look like porn stars, cheap ones at that.' He was spluttering with laughter.

'Our taxi driver didn't think so,' said Molly, smugly.

'Or maybe he did,' I added.

'For Christ's sake, sit down and stay down here, there's at least three people that you don't want to see upstairs.'

'Yeah, we know, we saw Connie and Steve walk in.'

'No – William Magpie is getting plastered in a corner, Mimi, the girl that Steve picked up the other night, is hanging around, and, well, and Christopher is there.'

My heart stopped.

Molly started gabbling, trying to reassure me, and grabbed my hand, saying, 'Look, don't worry, we won't have to see him, and you look so different, he wouldn't recognise you anyway. It'll be OK, really. Please don't get upset, we won't see him.'

'Who's he with?' I asked Pete.

'No one. He came in about half an hour ago, but by now I'd imagine that he's sitting with Steve and Connie.'

Great. I was looking like a cheap hooker, ready to clear up a nuclear disaster area, and the ex-love of my life was upstairs talking to one of my best friends, who was trying to steal his girlfriend's keys to give to me. The gossip of the century, William was there, and you could bet he would find them and start talking about Steve's and my supposed new-found love. I couldn't even begin to imagine Steve's face when he saw Mimi. Suddenly a large brandy seemed necessary. I think Pete must have seen my face, because he silently took a bottle out from beneath his desk, some glasses from a drawer and pushed them towards us.

'Cheers.'

We all toasted one another, and then jumped as the door was thrown open. A white-faced Steve threw a bunch of keys on the table.

'You know the code to get in, don't you. The big brass key is for the Chubb lock, don't forget to turn it when you leave, the silver one is for the door downstairs. And hurry, I've got to get out of here. Don't even ask how it's going upstairs, let's just say I need Valium. By the way, don't ever change your hair colour, either of you, you both look like vampires. Hurry. Oh, and Liv, don't worry, he's talking about you endlessly, but if you ever get back together with him, I'll kill you.' He rushed back upstairs.

I poured us all another drink, totally forgetting my resolve of detoxing and teetotalism. If ever a situation called for brandy, then this was it. I gulped down another, while Molly, through nerves presumably, pulled on her pair of yellow rubber gloves.

'Take those off immediately. Now you do look like a hooker, one that caters for special services,' joked Pete.

'I'm sure I asked for pink ones – these clash with my wig.'

'Come on, let's get it over with,' I said. 'Pete, would you go and make sure the coast is clear, and then we'll rush out.'

'OK, give me five minutes, then go upstairs and straight out of the door. I don't want the punters getting the wrong idea about this establishment, you know.'

Once Pete had gone upstairs, Molly, with great foresight, I thought, slipped the bottle of brandy into the carrier bag.

'Medical emergencies only. I mean, you never know . . .' she said.

We finished our drinks, and decided that on the count of three we would run upstairs and out of the door. My legs were feeling very wobbly, and I was a bundle of frayed nerves. I looked at Molly for reassurance: it helped enormously, she was shaking like an aspen.

'Ready? Right, one, two, two and a half, three!'

We made for the door and collapsed in nervous giggles as we competed for the door handle. We both got stuck in the doorway and started fighting to see who could get out first.

'Don't let anyone see you,' hissed Molly, as she finally succeeded in getting through the office door.

'Your wig's slipping, and take off those bloody gloves,' I panted, running after her up the stairs.

We ran through the crowded bar, pushing people aside in our rush to get to the front door. We burst through it and fell out on to the street, laughing hysterically. We received some puzzled looks from passers by, which just made us laugh even more. Molly was flapping her rubber gloves to flag down a taxi, and when she managed to stop one we collapsed in the back, giggling like schoolgirls. We managed to give the driver Steve's address and started to swig out of the brandy bottle, passing it between us.

'Does this count as a medical emergency?' I enquired.

'Oh yes.'

Chapter Four

We sobered up very, very quickly indeed once we were in the flat. The mess was staggering and we stared, slack jawed at the state of it.

'It looks as though a gang of teenage crack addicts have been squatting in here for months,' said Molly.

'How could it have become like this in a period of just *hours*?'

'God knows.'

'Where *shall* we start?'

'Let's just shove everything into rubbish bags, but for God's sake put the gloves back on, don't touch *anything*.'

We were whispering, even though we knew that no one could overhear us and as we started to clear up the mess, the silence was punctuated by little moans of disgust.

'Eeeow, yuk. This is revolting.'

'Not as bad as this. Ooh, gross.'

'I'm going in to tackle the bedroom, wish me luck.'

I had just found a peeled banana, which had wedged itself into a sticky goo between two cushions on the sofa, when there was a squeal from the other room.

Molly rushed out of the bedroom, holding a large sheet of paper.

'Look, look. This is positively *obscene*.' She was waving the paper at me. It was a sketch of a nude woman (obviously the very talented Mimi) doing something very pornographic with a bunch of grapes.

'Oh my God.'

We stared at the picture.

'I didn't know that was physically possible,' I said.

'I'm sure it's not. Is she a Bangkok bar girl or something?'

'Dunno. But she's not normal.'

'What shall we do with it?' asked Molly.

'Tear it up, and bin it, of course.'

'Are you sure? I'm thinking possible future blackmail material.'

I considered the idea. 'OK, let's take it with us, we can make Steve do anything for us if we keep that,' I decided.

We headed into the kitchen and started to wash up the vast amounts of glasses and ashtrays.

'Are you sure there were only two of them here? It looks like an orgy of Roman proportions has taken place, not two people off their heads,' said Molly.

'Should we change the sheets?' I asked.

'Are you kidding? I think we should probably throw them away, they must constitute a health hazard.'

I went off to look for clean bedding while Molly jammed the flowers into a vase. I was searching through Connie's airing cupboard for sheets and pillowcases when I came across a small, hard, angular object, wrapped in a plastic bag. Casually I moved it to one side, trying to find a matching pillowcase to the one I had already pulled out but the object, whatever it was, was surprisingly heavy. I opened the bag to have a look.

I screamed.

Molly came running out of the kitchen, to find me frozen with horror, pointing to the inside of the bag. It was a gun.

Well, it was an old one, I mean a *very* old one. An antique, obviously. It had a mother-of-pearl handle, with heavy foreign, swirling engraving on the silver. There was some gold on it too, and was even set with some jewels. I know nothing about antique firearms, believe me, but even I could tell that it must be valuable, very valuable. It looked very precious, and I knew that it couldn't possibly belong to Steve. Or Connie.

'Oh my God, what the hell is that?'

Neither of us had ever seen a gun before, even an antique one, let alone come upon one by accident in a friend's airing cupboard. Molly and I stared at each other in horror.

'What *are* we to do?'

'Put it back,' I said at once, 'and let's get out of here, *now.*'

'Wait, wait a moment – suppose it's part of the stuff we're meant to chuck away?'

'Are you mad? Guns weren't mentioned, were they, or did I miss that bit?'

'No, but, well, look, suppose it was part of this mad sex thing that they both did? You know, danger and sex go together, don't they?'

'You *are* mad. I have no idea what you're talking about – put it back and let's leave, right this minute.'

'No, listen, you remember that Michael Hutchence thing? You know, asphyxiation at the point of orgasm and all that? Well, maybe that's what happened here, she pulled a gun on him for heightened excitement. I think we should chuck it.'

'Chuck it, *chuck it?* You can't just throw a gun in a rubbish bag and put it out on the pavement, you know. This is London, for heaven's sake, not the Lebanon!' I was frantically hissing at her. 'Besides, it's valuable, isn't it?'

'Are there any bullets?'

'*What?*'

'Well, are there?'

'How the fuck would I know?'

To my disbelief she actually started to search in the bag that the gun was in.

'Stop it, put it down, supposing it goes off?' I was gibbering at her now.

'Livia, calm down, it won't go off.'

'*How do you know?*'

'I've watched *Antiques Roadshow* loads of times . . . I think this is a lady's pistol, probably foreign.'

'I can't believe you're talking about TV when there's a fucking *gun* in your hand,' I said furiously.

'Go and make the bed, I'll deal with this,' said Molly decisively.

I was cross with her, but I wasn't prepared to argue, I just wanted to leave and get home as quickly as possible. I snatched the sheets from the cupboard and marched into the bedroom, shoved the dirty sheets into the linen basket, and made the bed up with clean sheets. Molly came into the room, and we silently started putting the pillowcases on the pillows. We both jumped when we heard the doorbell ring.

We stared at each other, and instinctively dropped to the ground.

'The lights are on in the living room,' I whispered.

'I know. Just keep quiet, they'll go away, we *are* five floors up,' she whispered back.

It rang again.

'Suppose it's Steve?' Molly whispered wildly.

'Of course it's not him, you fool, why would it be? Just shut up.'

We crouched on the floor, holding our breath. It was so silent in the flat that I could hear the hum of the fridge in the kitchen, and the whirr and click of the boiler heating the water. The bell went again, sending us into silent, terrible paroxysms of nervous laughter. I buried my face in the clean pillowcase, praying that whoever was at the front door would give up and go away. Suddenly I had the irrational thought that it might be Christopher. I whispered it to Molly.

She shook her head at me. 'You know it's not. Stop it, you've got mascara all over that pillowcase.'

'Good.'

We stayed on the floor for what seemed like ages, then when the bell didn't go again, we gingerly stood up and threw the covers over the bed. Scurrying madly round the flat now, we looked like a speeded-up version of the Keystone Cops. We were bumping into each other, and kept colliding over the full rubbish bags that we'd left in the middle of the floor. We were desperate to leave now, and after a quick, hushed final check we decided we could go. We picked up the rubbish, turned off the lights and slipped out of the door. I keyed in the security number, turned the key, and we ran headlong down the stairs. Once out on the street, I felt a good deal better. It was cold outside, and I noticed that Molly's wig was still a little crooked. I pulled it straight, and she did the same for me. We started to giggle weakly again.

'Oh well, mission nearly accomplished. Let's get the keys back to Steve quickly. Oh God, I want my bed, I'm so tired now, aren't you?' I said to Molly.

Molly stared unblinkingly at me. I knew this look from old, and it didn't fill me with hope.

'Molly, what's the matter?' I asked warily.

She grabbed my arm. 'Liv, I've got it with me.'

'You've got what with you?'

'You know, the pistol.'

We had reached a main road now, and seeing the comforting

amber glow of a taxi light, I stuck my arm out. As the taxi stopped, I pushed Molly into the back. I was horrified.

'You'll have to give it back to Steve then, won't you? And don't think that I'm very keen on running round London with you and an antique weapon, because I'm not. Why didn't you leave it there?' We were still whispering, and it was starting to give me a sore throat.

'I can hardly walk up to him and hand it over at the table. I'm really sorry Liv, I just got a bit carried away.'

'We're not Charlie's Angels, you know,' I said crossly.

'I know,' said Molly in a bright voice. 'We'll throw it in the river. That's what they do in TV programmes when they want to get rid of something – they chuck it in the Thames. Or maybe we should sell it, it's probably worth quite a bit of money.'

'Molly, it's 8.30 in the evening, where do you suggest we sell it? Sotheby's? You'll just have to give it back to Steve. Why you took it away with you, I just can't imagine.'

'I know, I know.' Molly looked miserably out of the taxi window. 'Oh God, what a mess. Let's have a brandy.'

'No, let's not. Let's just get to the Bar, give the keys and the you-know-what back to Steve and go home and get some sleep.'

The cab arrived outside the Bar, I paid off the driver and we skulked outside for a bit, trying to peer through the windows. I could just see the back of Connie's head, but nothing else. I was dying to know if Christopher was still there, and was squinting to see if there was any sign of him as Molly gave me an impatient push towards the door. 'Let's go, come on, get it over with.'

I took a deep breath and pushed the door open. The noise and warmth of the place swept over us as we attempted to make our way downstairs, hampered by the crowds of people standing with glasses, all having a good time and in no hurry to make way for two women trying to push past them. When we eventually reached the downstairs office we pushed the door. It was locked. We looked at each other, panicking. Molly banged on the door and, to our relief, we heard it being opened.

'You two took your bloody time, what have you been doing? Did you pull a few tricks on the way?' Pete's amused voice boomed round the office.

We sat down and both started to talk at once, explaining about the mess we'd had to clear up, the doorbell ringing, the picture that we'd taken for a giggle – and the gun.

Pete sunk his head in his hands. 'God almighty, a *gun* or a pistol or whatever the hell you're calling it, and you brought it *here*? Are you both completely mad? No, don't answer that. I'm getting Steve down here, now. Stay there, don't move, either of you.'

He disappeared and we sat there like two schoolgirls waiting in the Headmaster's office to be given detention. Molly looked as though she might burst into tears at any moment. I tried to cheer her up. 'Don't worry, it's probably a fake.'

'It doesn't look like a fake.'

'We're not Bonnie and Clyde, you know, how on earth would *you* know if it was real or not? Look, just give it to Steve, and we can forget the whole thing.'

'OK.'

We sat miserably for a bit, and I looked round the office. It was the usual tat that made up all bar offices, a pile of staff coats and bags, crates of beer and mixers and a phone on top of the crowded desk that had at least three red lights flashing on it. The filing cabinet was gaping open, and I could see a tantalising glimpse of the letterhead of the company that had done the Bar's refit. I tilted my head sideways to see if I could read it, I'd have loved to know how much they'd charged Pete. I stood up to have a better look.

'What *are* you doing?' said Molly.

'Ssshh, I'm spying . . .' I tweaked the paper out of the file, not actually taking it out, just moving it so that I could see the figures. In the front of the drawer was a stack of small boxes and prescription drug bottles, all with Pete's name printed on them. I motioned Molly over, and we looked at the small pharmaceutical cornucopia stacked there.

'Oh God, poor Pete. What do you think's wrong with him?'

'Well, it's a little bit more than indigestion, isn't it?'

The bewildering amount of pills with unpronounceable names was scary. Pete certainly didn't look ill. He had always been large, and although his lifestyle, which consisted of late nights, alcohol, fags and recreational drugs, followed by large meals, had left him rotund and a bit breathless, he seemed to be his normal self. I was bewildered: if Pete was seriously ill, why hadn't he told me? I racked my brains, trying to recall if he had hinted at anything. Perhaps we hadn't been as close as usual because of the Bar, and his decision not to use me for it, but, well . . . I couldn't believe that Pete had said nothing to me. We were very old friends, we went on holiday together, spent Christmas together, that sort of thing. Mainly because I had no family, and Pete, although his parents were alive, never saw them. I mean, I even knew Pete's PIN number, that's how close we were. (Actually, I had to know it, because he always forgot it.)

We sat down again, waiting for Pete and Steve. I was uncomfortably aware that I had to go to the loo, but I didn't want to go into the Ladies, in case I bumped into Connie.

I sat wriggling in my chair, scratching under my wig which had become very itchy.

'Liv, stop it. You look as though you've got nits and you're about to wet yourself.'

'I think I am.'

We sat in silence for a bit, with me fidgeting on the chair. The wig was getting very hot now, and exceedingly uncomfortable. How people wore them all the time was a mystery. I kept thinking about Christopher, possibly still upstairs, and found myself longing just to catch a glimpse of him. Where the hell was Pete, what was keeping him? I decided I simply had to go to the loo, and told Molly.

She pulled me back into my chair, 'You can't, you know you can't, wait for Pete and Steve, they can't be much longer. Supposing you bump into Connie? Even with that wig on, she'll recognise you.'

'I don't care any more, I have to go, and I'm not weeing into a bottle or something in here.'

'Think of something dry, like a desert or something.'

'It won't make any difference, I really do have to go, I won't be a minute, I promise.'

I stood up and cautiously looked round the door. The Ladies was two doors down on the right, I could have a quick look round the door, check it out, and rush into a cubicle. I glanced up the staircase. There was no one around, and I slipped out of the door into the loos. Two girls were putting on lipstick in the mirror; they took no notice of me whatsoever. The cubicle doors were open, and I dashed into the end one. Oh, the relief.

I had just finished when there was a frighteningly loud bang from upstairs, followed by screams and the sound of breaking glass. The main lights went out, plunging me into total darkness, and the emergency lights flickered on, flooding the loo with a ghostly blue light. Then there was a loud hissing noise, and I was drenched with a fine cold spray of water. The automatic sprinklers had come on. Perfect, I was desperately trying to dodge the water, and do up my pants, when I heard a frantic knocking on the loo door and Molly shouting my name.

'It's OK, I'm here, what the hell has happened?'

One glance at Molly confirmed that she was as terrified as me. We were both shaking with fear.

'I don't know, but let's get the fuck out of here *now!*' Molly shouted.

We raced out of the door and started to run up the stairs. Was it a fire? Or, even worse, a bomb? The noise had been loud, but it hadn't sounded like an explosion, I thought. On the other hand, I wasn't an expert: what the hell did an explosion sound like?

Molly and I were holding hands as we panted up the stairs. At the top of the staircase was a solid wall of people, shouting and pushing their way out on to the street. Water was pouring on to the smoky chaos from the ceiling, drenching everyone. Molly's hand was wrenched from mine, and we were assimilated into the crowd. I could feel broken glass underfoot. It was terrifying, I couldn't see very much, but a girl was crying loudly in my ear, and a man behind me was shouting. I was frightened of falling over and being trampled on, and I had to fight to remain upright. Then the next thing I knew, we were all expelled into the cold night air.

People were milling around in a state of shock. I saw one girl, with very long dark red hair, crying and pushing through the crowd, with frantic eyes, desperate to find someone. She looked vaguely familiar, but I couldn't place her. I fell over Molly, who was sitting on the pavement, nursing her foot.

It looked swollen and she was hunched over, rocking to and fro.

'Oh my God, Molly, are you OK?'

I knelt down beside her and looked at her foot. She was moving it, so I guessed that nothing was broken, but she obviously needed medical help.

'Where is everybody? Have you seen anyone?' I asked her.

'Steve and Pete are over there,' she said through gritted teeth, obviously in pain. She motioned with her head. 'I told Pete that we'd got out, he was trying to go downstairs to get us.' A man with blood streaming down his face walked past us. I could hear sirens approaching and knew that the ambulances would be here soon. I ran over to try and find Steve and Pete, also frantically looking for Christopher. In the end Steve and I walked slap into each other. His face was pale and his eyes were huge, and he grabbed me with both arms.

'Liv, thank God you're OK.'

'Yeah, I'm fine.'

I found I was crying; Steve and I held on to each other, shaking. He had glass in his hair, and I began flicking it off. He had a small cut on his cheek and some blood on his hands, but otherwise we both seemed fine.

'What about Connie and Pete, and Christopher?' I said anxiously.

'Connie's OK, she's hurt her leg, she's sitting round the corner, Pete's fine, and Christopher left about half an hour ago. Look, I'd better get Connie home, are you OK?'

'Yeah, but Molly's hurt. I'd better get back to her, here are your keys.' I passed him his keys, and we hugged goodbye, promising to call in the morning.

'Steve, wait. About Pete, is he really OK?'

Steve looked strangely at me, and shrugged.

I went back to Molly, who was standing up with her arms round Pete; both were leaning against the wall.

'Pete, what happened, what was it?'

'God knows. Probably the Casa, they never could stand a bit of competition. I must go, I don't think anyone is seriously hurt, but can you take Molly home? The police will need to see me, there's loads to do, I just can't believe it . . . Let's talk in the morning . . .' his voice trailed away. He leaned forward to give me a goodbye kiss, and I could feel that he was soaking wet, and very cold.

'Pete, get some dry clothes on, you'll freeze out here.'

'Yeah, OK.' He whispered in Molly's ear. She nodded, and he looked relieved.

Molly and I dragged our sopping wet, bedraggled wigs off and with her leaning on me, we made our way to an ambulance. She was complaining bitterly about her foot, which made me relieved, as I knew then that it couldn't be serious.

'How did you do it?' I asked.

'Some fat bastard stomped on me, trying to get out the door first,' she grumbled. Her bag was slung across her body, and it was banging into her as she limped. A kindly paramedic told Molly to sit down, and said that he would see to her in a moment. He slung a red blanket over her, and we both shivered underneath it, sitting on the pavement.

'I feel like a *Big Issue* seller.'

'Well, we both look like one,' I said.

The scene was awful. Loads of people had poured out of other bars and restaurants, and the police were hurriedly trying to clear the area. Firemen had arrived and were going into the Bar, walkie-talkies were chattering everywhere, and people were asking everyone they saw what had happened.

'Fucking IRA . . .'

'Gas explosion . . .'

'Cooking fire . . .'

'Somebody set the alarm off by accident . . .'

'Electrical fault, dodgy wiring . . .'

'A warning was phoned in . . .'

'The owner's gay, isn't he? Well . . .'

'I saw a woman leave a bag inside . . .'

'Fucking Irish . . .'

'Fucking Muslims, you mean.'

The police were taking everyone's names. Suddenly I thought of the gun. What had happened to it? I asked Molly.

'Still in my bag,' she said miserably. So that was what Pete had whispered to her: he was asking if she had left it in his office. I could understand that he didn't want to have to explain that away, but now we were left with the problem. Molly scrabbled in her bag, and for one terrible moment I thought she was going to get it out, but in fact what she produced was a hairbrush which she passed to me.

'Trust me, you need it.'

I dragged the brush through my tangled hair, then handed it back to her. If I looked as dreadful as she did, we could well be arrested soon by the fashion police. We were shivering under the blanket now, and feeling very sorry for ourselves. The paramedic came over to us, and squatted down by Molly.

'Let's have a look at that foot, love.'

Molly's ankle was badly swollen, and she winced as he touched it. He prodded it as gently as he could.

'It's a bad sprain. I'll bandage it now, but keep your foot up for a couple of days, use ice to reduce the swelling, and take some painkillers when you get home. There's no need to go to hospital, they'll be overcrowded now, but I want you to go straight home. Keep warm. Give your names to the police before you go.' Once Molly's foot was bandaged, we staggered to our feet, and saw that the crowds had thinned a little. God knows how we were going to get home: the road was closed, and Molly could barely walk. A policeman walked towards us, with a notebook open. Molly tightened her grip on my arm.

'Can I have your names and addresses please, and can you tell me where you were when the incident happened.'

'On the loo,' I chipped in.

He smiled, briefly. We gave him our details and were directed to a car that was parked alongside an ambulance. It had been detailed to drive people home, and Molly and I climbed gratefully in.

'I think you'd better stay the night with me, don't you?' I said. Molly nodded. The police were waving the car to leave, and as we started off, we heard a screaming from the pavement. The woman I'd seen before, with the long red hair, was crying and pointing at us, waving her arms wildly, and I saw a policeman restrain her. As I turned back to look, I still felt I'd seen her somewhere before. The car moved further away and I couldn't see her any more.

'Did you see her?' I asked Molly.

'See who?' she said sleepily.

'Never mind. We'll be home soon.'

Getting Molly up the path and the few steps that led to my flat was no picnic. I propped her against the front door as I fumbled for my keys. I saw Mrs Grieg looking curiously out of her window, and I gave her a little wave of acknowledgement. I'd go over and see her tomorrow, it would thrill her to the marrow to know that we'd been in an 'incident'. As I was twisting the key in the front door I heard my name being called. It was Joe.

'I saw you getting out of the car. My God, what's happened?'

Briefly I told him, and he turned towards Molly and picked her up. She smiled sweetly at him and murmured 'My hero', as Joe carried her into the kitchen and sat her down on a chair. He filled the kettle and started to make tea. I sank down at the table with Molly, exhausted and soaking wet. I grabbed a towel and gave one to Molly, telling her to put on my dressing gown. Then I decided to take a very quick hot shower, before doing anything else. I was just about to head towards the bathroom when I saw Molly making swivelling movements with her eyes, towards her bag.

'Oh, right. I'll umm, I'll put your stuff in my bedroom,' I said rather weakly. I picked up her bag, took it into my room and stuffed it under the bed. Then I took it out. Wasn't that the first place that anyone would look? But then, why would anyone look? I took the plastic bag that had the pistol in it and put it at the bottom of my wardrobe, under a pile of shoes. I was getting paranoid, I decided, and the only drugs I did nowadays was popping the odd cod liver oil capsule now and then. I heard Joe and Molly call me from the kitchen. 'Liv, quick, it's on the news.'

I rushed into the kitchen and heard the modulated tone of a Radio 4 newsreader announce that an explosion had taken place earlier this evening in Soho. There had been no fatalities, but several people were being treated in hospital for cuts and burns. The police were on the scene and were appealing for witnesses who might have seen anything unusual. The newsreader went on to talk about the latest financial crisis so I leaned forwards to turn it off, and sipped the hot tea that Joe had made. Molly was filling Joe in on what had happened, not mentioning the pistol, I was pleased to notice, so I escaped to the bathroom.

After my shower, I wrapped myself in a huge towelling

gown (pinched, I'm slightly ashamed to admit, from a very posh hotel in Paris). I was drawn by a tantalising smell coming from the kitchen. Joe, bless him, was cooking supper: he'd gone back to his place and had returned, laden with food. Being a healthy, clean-living, boy next door (Molly and I often referred to him as the BND) he was grilling, not frying the bacon, and poaching, not frying the eggs. We demanded butter on our toast though, and though he muttered about cholesterol under his breath, he did begrudgingly spread it on the hot toast for us.

We fell on the food, both starving. Perhaps that's what being in shock does for you, makes you eat like a horse. I'd soon be the size of one as well, I thought as I slathered some strawberry jam on another piece of slightly burnt toast. I reached out an arm to answer the ringing phone. It was Zena checking to see if we were OK, she'd heard the news and was worried about us. Had we been there? Was everyone OK? I reassured her, and as I replaced the phone, it rang again. It was Christopher.

'Hello my darling, I'm so glad you're home, I've been so worried about you. Have you heard about the explosion? Thank God you weren't there.'

My heart was doing very strange things inside my body. It had leapt at the first sound of his voice, then strangely sank again. I was searching for the right tone to take with him. I was thrilled to hear from him, at least he'd called me, but I was very wary. Obviously, neither Steve nor Pete had told him we had been there, so I couldn't either, but I did want him to know that we'd been in danger. I mean, who doesn't want to worry an ex now and again? I muttered something about having popped in for a quick drink with Molly, and that she had hurt her ankle.

'But you're OK? Thank God. We must have missed each

other by minutes. I saw Connie and Steve in there, are they OK too?'

'Umm, yes, I think so.'

I had to control the wobble in my voice. Dangerously close to tears, I really wanted to lay my head on his shoulder and tell him everything that had happened. I turned away from Joe and Molly's curious eyes.

'Darling, listen, I could come round, now. It would take me half an hour to get there, let me come to you. Danielle is visiting her family in Lyons, so I could stay the night, it would be so lovely. I miss you so much . . .'

Bastard.

'No, absolutely not. I'm not alone anyway,' then I added in an ultra-polite, hostessy voice, 'but thank you so much for calling, goodbye.' I hung up.

'Bloody married men,' I joked, pouring more tea into my mug. Joe and Molly looked sympathetically at me. When the phone rang again, I asked Molly to get it while I made up a bed for her in my so-called office.

I had to move piles of magazines out of the way and a boxed sample of glass mosaic tiles (they were lovely, they looked like boiled sweets) before I could open up the sofa bed. I had just thrown a duvet over the bed and switched on a lamp, when I heard Molly calling from the kitchen. She was holding the phone out for me.

'It's Monty, he's calling from Paris. The jungle grapevine has got to him, and he's concerned that we might have ended up in hospital, wearing, heaven forbid, knickers from that patron saint of underwear, St Michael's.'

I spoke to Monty for a few minutes, reassuring him that we were OK, but I didn't go into any of the gory details about the flight of mercy to Steve's or of what we had found there. He told me he was off for a late supper at La Coupole and that he'd see me the day after tomorrow. We wished each other love, and hung up.

Joe was washing up.

'I do like to see a man with his arms in my sink,' I said to Molly.

'I'd rather sink into his arms,' she joked.

I was yawning my head off now, and Joe offered to carry Molly to the bathroom, then into bed.

'Don't even think of saying anything funny,' I said. 'It's the best offer you've had all evening, I'd accept it if I were you.'

When Joe had gone home, and Molly and I were calling out goodnights to each other, I thought fleetingly of the gun hidden in my wardrobe, but sleep overwhelmed me and I drifted off. The last thing I heard was Molly, speaking from her bed in the study. 'How many days do you think I can get off work? I am in exquisite agony, you know, with this ankle. Joe might have to carry me everywhere . . .'

Chapter Five

The phone rang at some ungodly hour during the night, but I turned over, ignoring it, and went back to a deep dreamless sleep. In the morning, after having kitted Molly out and given her a phone that she was now squawking instructions into, I tried to concentrate on my own work. I had to do a presentation for a new client, and complete Mr Abraham's flat. Using my office was out of the question. Molly was firmly ensconced there, using the computer to send e-mails to her secretary, and the phone to elicit sympathy from all and sundry – so I decided to get some fresh air, and was walking to the end of the road, to get the papers and some milk, when I thought of Mrs Grieg and decided to pop in to see her.

Mrs Grieg had a divine flat, and it was always a pleasure to go and visit. She had a love affair with roses, and they romped everywhere in her flat, on the curtains, carpets, walls and cushions, with real and fake ones bunched in vases on every surface. She usually made tea in tiny, paper-thin, bone china cups and saucers and provided odd little sweet pastries to go with it. She let me in, leaning on a walking stick, and we went into her living room. Whereas other people's houses had chairs grouped around a fireplace or a TV set, she had hers all facing into the bow window.

'Well dear, what a palaver, sit down, sit down, 'ow's your poor friend? That leg looked nasty, I could see by the way you 'ad to carry 'er, I thought to meself, well, she'll be stayin' over there for a while, I'll be bound.'

I smiled to myself, we didn't need neighbourhood watch when we had Mrs Grieg. She missed nothing, nothing at all, that went on in this street. She must have been well over seventy-five, and was as sharp as a needle. She had been an artist's model, and had several portraits of herself dotted around her flat. Occasionally she sold one or two off, if times were hard. She had a particularly ravishing one by Laura Knight, painted when Mrs Grieg was about seven years old. It showed a golden-haired girl, looking down at a book on her lap. It had that gentle, misty, English impressionism about it, and I was always drawn to it. It seemed impossible, looking at Mrs Grieg now, that she had ever been that sweet, innocent child. She saw me gazing at it and remarked. 'I know you like that. Me too, always one of me favourites.'

We sat drinking tea, and I told her of the previous night's events. She was a gratifying audience, thrilled to hear the details.

'Just like the Blitz. Brings out the best in some people, sorts the fools out anyway. The police won't do anything, waste of time, they are,' she said knowingly. 'Course, they say they'll try, but they won't. Bloody useless, couldn't find a needle in a bleedin' 'aystack. I 'ope your friend's insured. Place like that must be worth a fortune.'

I assured her that he was, and we sipped tea, looking out of her window. She wound her shawl a little more closely around her shoulders.

'Least it's not bleedin' rainin' today. Chilly, though.'

I knew this was my cue to leave. Whenever she started to chat about the weather, she'd had enough company for one day. I asked if there was anything I could get her from the shops.

'No thanks, love, I like to trot down on me own. It gets me out.' I waved her goodbye; she was a gallant old girl, and I always left, cheered by her. Most people might have assumed the cheering went the other way round, but it didn't.

I bought the papers and a bunch of startlingly red tulips and was sauntering home, reading the front page, when my mobile phone started to ring. It was John, the bloody builder again from Sidcup.

'Hello, are you always this grumpy on the phone?' he said.

I was slightly nettled by this. I'd always thought that I was charming on the phone.

'I can assure you that I'm only rude to people I don't know . . . Usually I have an unimpeachable phone voice . . .' I said.

'Well, you can be rude to me after you know me, then. That is if I ever manage to leave the site. I thought we might meet up one evening for a drink?' He sounded rather flirtatious.

'Did you indeed?' I said tartly.

I was surprised. I mean, this man had practically just accused me of bad manners, and now he was asking me out for a drink. Then I realised that he must have stored my number, and felt ridiculously flattered.

'So, what do you think? I warn you now, I also have your home number so I can pester you there, too.'

'I'll think about it,' I said. Meaning, of course, no. Having not yet rid myself completely of Christopher, I wasn't at all ready to go and meet any other men. I wasn't sure if I ever would be.

'Well, I'll leave you to think about it then. By the way, what colour hair do you have?'

'It all depends on the mood of my hairdresser,' I said.

'Oh good, I always think that women with their natural hair colour show no imagination whatsoever.'

We laughed, and hung up.

I saw in the papers that the 'distinguished and respected journalist William Magpie was rushed to hospital after the explosion last night. He has been kept in for the night, and is being treated for cuts and bruises'. Hmm, I thought cynically, we were certain to hear of his brave efforts of last night in his column, for days and days to come.

Molly had a list of people who had called while I had been out. She handed it to me, saying, 'It's rather gratifying to know that so many people care, isn't it? Just think, there'd be loads of people at our funeral after all.' (On very low days we'd torture ourselves by the thought of a meagre and sparsely attended funeral, promising each other that whoever went first would bully other people to come, paying them if necessary.)

I had to help Molly into the bathroom, where she decided that she simply had to find a way to have a bath, without getting her bandaged foot wet. 'If you're thinking of using this as a ploy to get Joe to come and lift your naked body out of steaming, scented water, forget it,' I laughed. 'He's at work, there's only me. So I'd settle for a strip wash, if I were you.'

'Damn. OK.'

'Besides, aren't you saving yourself for Guy the Gorilla?'

'Mmm. I left a message for him in New York, telling him I'd been hurt, but he hasn't called yet.'

I banished the unworthy thought that I was going to be

stuck with a bill for a lot of international phone calls. 'Has Steve called yet?'

'No, he and Connie are probably billing and cooing at each other, don't you think?'

'Yeah, that or fighting like cat and dog. We need to talk to him though, don't we,' I said rather pointedly.

'Well, let's give him till this afternoon, and if he hasn't rung by then, we'll call him. God, I hope we didn't miss anything incriminating at the flat. I really want to know whose pistol it is, don't you? Do you think he'll know why Pete's taking all that medicine?'

'Maybe, they're pretty close. As to the pistol thing, I'm not sure that I want to know. I just want to get it out of here, that's all.'

'OK, OK, stop banging on about it.'

'Very unfunny . . .'

I left Molly to her one-legged ablutions and went to call back the people on the list she'd given me.

I was stealing my nerve to call my new client, that Julian, of all people, had recommended to me. She had apparently gone into a restaurant that we had done in London, liked it, and had called JJM. Julian, to his credit, had passed on my name and number. When I'd found out who it was, I nearly screamed with excitement. It was Nicola Bentley, probably the most famous rock wife in history. She was currently splashed over every tabloid page, with the announcement that she and her rock star husband, Sam, had separated.

She wanted her London home completely revamped, to get rid of all of his Gothic rock'n'roll memorabilia. I wasn't sure I had a hope in hell of landing the job, but I was going to give it my best shot. I really needed the work, and hoped that she might then want me to do her other homes (of which there were many).

Apprehensively I dialled her number, and held on for what seemed like ages till someone finally answered. She probably had fleets of staff running around for her while she was lounging around having a manicure or something. What *do* rock stars' wives do all day? I was about to find out.

'Hello . . . Nicola Bentley's residence, who is calling?'

I gave my name and waited.

Eventually Nicola came to the phone, apologising for the delay, saying that she had been doing her power yoga. (Well, now we know, don't we?)

I gabbled nervously, 'God, how energetic of you, I can barely stand up first thing in the morning, let alone do yoga.'

She laughed. 'Well, I've got to do something, I've done nothing but stuff myself with carbohydrates since Sam left . . . and I can't face going out. Have you had time to think about my house? I'd really like to make some changes around here.'

She was surprisingly easy to talk to, and we were soon chattering away. Although she was obviously miserable about Sam Bentley, she was serious about having her house done (much to my relief).

'Do you have any colours or styles that you absolutely hate? Then I'll know what to avoid,' I asked.

When the intercom buzzed I had the phone to my ear, listening to Nicola tell me about her ideas for the bedroom makeover. I opened the door. It was young Roger. I knew he'd come to collect the paint for Mr Abraham's flat, so I motioned him back outside, pointing to the cupboard, I watched him stagger to the van under the weight of the paint and plonk it in the back. He drove off down the road, giving a little beep on the hooter. Nicola was making me laugh with her instructions for what she didn't want in her room.

'No black satin sheets, no skulls, no leather, no leopardskin print covers, no bloody gold discs stuck on the wall, and above all, absolutely no bloody joss sticks . . .'

'Don't worry, I promise that. Look, talking to you has given me some ideas for you, give me a couple of days and I'll come over to discuss it. I really think you'll like what I have in mind.'

'No pastels either, I don't want to go from one extreme to the other. I hate flowers and frills.'

'Me too, sounds like one of your ex-husband's albums, doesn't it? Flowers and frills live from New York,' I joked, almost pinching myself that I had the nerve to tease Nicola Bentley.

We laughed together, then arranged a meeting for later in the week. I hung up. It was a total lie, of course, I hadn't had the time to think about anything for her. She sounded really nice, though, and I wanted to do my best for her. That, and the fact that my bank balance could certainly do with a top up.

I started to flip through books and magazines in my office, looking for inspiration. If I were an ex rock star's wife, what would I like to have, I mused. Maybe a calming, soothing environment. Something using natural materials – stone, wood, linen. I'd sharpen the look with some steel, and maybe some glass. Yeah, that was it, with a hint of Japanese Zen to it.

I started to create a presentation board for her, ripping out pictures from magazines. A lot of plants, too, maybe a tree and a water feature inside the house. This was the best part of the job, really, interpreting the client's taste into reality. Nicola was exceedingly rich, so money wasn't too much of a problem.

Molly limped into the room, using an umbrella as a walking stick.

'Ooh, great, this is just like Blue Peter, can I help?'

We spent a very satisfying hour ripping up magazines and pasting them on to a board, then when we finished, we propped the board against the far wall, and sat back to appreciate our work.

'What's she *really* like?' Molly asked.

'I dunno, do I? I've only talked to her on the phone.' But we'd all seen her photo in *Review!* magazine. She'd certainly looked the part, dressed in skin tight leather from head to toe, and wearing a pink cowboy hat.

'Boulders . . .'

'What?' said Molly.

'I need a few strategically placed, large, pale boulders. Trust me, it'll pull the whole look together.'

'If you say so.'

I stuck a pair of bamboo chopsticks to the board, to give it the right flavour, and reached for the ringing phone. It was Guy, calling for Molly. I left her to it and went into the kitchen.

I was making some tea when I heard her calling excitedly to me, 'Livia, he's back, he got his messages when he got home, and he wants to come round and see me, so, I, well, I asked him to dinner.'

'Tonight? Won't he be jet lagged?'

'Yes tonight, sorry, is that OK?'

I groaned. 'I'm gonna kill you, so if that's OK, yeah, fine.' The phone rang again. It was Steve.

'Is everything OK?' I asked.

'Well, sort of. Connie's leg is still sore, and she found an empty bottle of vodka in the bathroom, so she thinks that I've had a bit of a session of solitary boozing, which hasn't gone down at all well, but apart from that, yeah.'

'I do hope there is no hint of accusation in your voice

about us missing an empty bottle in your bathroom, when quite frankly, we had more than enough to deal with,' I said tartly.

'No, no, of course not.'

'Good. Have you heard from Pete?'

'Yes. He called just now, I was going to go down to the Bar to see if I can help.'

'Will you be allowed in?'

'Dunno, really, but I feel I should show willing.'

'Listen, we have to talk to you, it's about something we found in your flat . . .' I explained about the pistol, and there was a horrified silence.

'Well, is it yours?'

'Are you mad? Of course it's not mine. Or Connie's, either.'

'Are you sure?'

He practically exploded on the other end of the phone.

'Of course I'm fucking sure!'

There was a pause. I could almost hear his frenzied thinking.

'Oh God,' he said very slowly.

'What, what? Tell me, for Chrissake.'

'Well, you know Mimi . . .'

'Not intimately, no.'

'Listen! Well, I've just remembered that she asked me if I would look after something for her. And then, well, when I saw her at the Bar, I thought she was hanging around, you know, wanting to see me again, but I guess she wanted to collect it.'

'Nice class of pick-ups you indulge in, isn't it. The girl with the gun. Great.'

'Oh shit. Well, I'll have to find her and give it back, won't I? Where did you put it?'

'Well, for some deranged reason, known only to herself, Molly took it with her.'

'Well, where is it now?'

'In my wardrobe.'

Molly was hissing at me and trying to grab the phone.

'Hang on a moment, Steve, Charlie's Angel here wants a word with you.' She took the phone from me.

'Look, Steve, come over tonight and pick it up. Guy's coming for dinner, and you promised you'd come anyway, so you've got to, and if you don't, we have the material to blackmail you with. And don't forget to flirt with me.'

I started to gather up my keys and purse. At the rate we were going, we'd soon have half of London for dinner; I had to get to the supermarket. I left Molly making arrangements with Steve; waving to her, I walked towards the front door. Sticking through my letterbox was a hand-delivered cream envelope, with my name scrawled on the front. I opened it curiously. It was from Mr Abraham.

My Dear Miss Hunter,

Please find below the names of the guests I would like to invite to my housewarming party. The flat is going splendidly, I went in to see how things were progressing this morning, and was very pleasantly surprised indeed. I'm looking forward to the day that I move in. I found the head builder there, Douglas MacPherson a very knowledgeable chap, would it be infra dig to invite him as well? I shall leave it to your discretion.

As ever,

S. Abraham

P.S. It was dreadful about the explosion in central London, last night, wasn't it? I do so hope that you were not caught up in it in any way.

There were five names on the list (well, that was going to be a wild party) and one of the names was William Magpie. I was astounded: how on earth did Mr Abraham know him? I couldn't possibly imagine. The other four were women, all living, I noted, at rather grand addresses. I stuffed the note into my jacket pocket, and headed for the shops.

I strolled aimlessly around the supermarket, wondering, not for the first time, how it was that I always got the trolley with defective steering, and trying to think of something to buy for dinner. Molly wanted to impress Guy with some home cooking, and if she had her way I'd cook nothing but roast chicken (with all the trimmings and bread sauce and crunchy roast potatoes). I also knew that she'd be counting on my fabulous chocolate mousse (I'm not boasting here, that's what we actually called it – go on, do your fabulous chocolate mousse, or, I know, I'll do my fabulous chocolate mousse for pudding tonight). The only secret about it is using absolutely the highest cocoa solids that you can find in a chocolate bar. That, and loads of rum.

I cast a desperate look inside my purse, determined *not* to use a credit card, and wondered if I could feasibly palm off a cheap frozen chicken as an organic, corn-fed one. Probably not. My mobile went off in my pocket.

'Are you hanging about in the ready-cooked-meals-for-one section, looking for Mr Right?' Molly asked.

'I've had Mr Right, Mr Wrong and Mr Right Now, thank you very much. No, I'm staring mindlessly at some parsnips at the moment.'

'Well, I just phoned to say that Steve wants to bring Connie and to remind you that she's vegetarian.'

'She would be, wouldn't she,' I said gloomily. 'I thought he was meant to come by himself, so that he could flirt with you.'

'I know, but he's promised to throw me longing glances across the table. He's also going to pick up the you-know-what and give it back to Mimi.'

'Hmm. What do you want me to cook, then?'

'What about roast chick chick and . . .'

'I knew it, you are *so* predictable. Besides, what about Connie?'

'Oh, let's give her a few potatoes to remind her of her Irish roots.'

We laughed rather nastily, it has to be said, at that.

'Liv, buy loads of wine, I'll give you some money when you get back. Oh, and Doug called, he said his wife has gone into labour, so he's left the boys there prepping, getting ready to paint.'

'OK, see you later.'

Doug and his wife, Maggie, had been eagerly expecting their first child. Doug would be an excellent dad, I thought, strong and kind. They were about the only couple that I knew of who were genuinely happy. I walked round the supermarket, piling things up in my trolley. I threw in a bag of dried apricots, and opened them, popping one in my mouth and chewing it. I had never wanted children, but there had been one time, at the height of my lust with Christopher, when I had felt the broodiness descend. He soon disabused me of any romantic ideas I'd had, he'd already got several illegitimate children scattered throughout France. Danielle, of course, was angelic to them and bought them wildly extravagant presents, but didn't actually have them to stay. I sighed; maybe I should have had one. It was too late now though; I couldn't imagine ever wanting anyone else's child other than Christopher's, and that was definitely over. At least, that's what I kept telling myself.

When I arrived home, my arms stretched to breaking

point with heavy shopping, I found Molly in a state of nervous exhilaration. She had set the table with candles, flowers and the good glasses and cutlery, and was hopping into the bathroom with some clothes over her arms.

'Hi, I've been through your wardrobe and I'm just going to try all these on. Tell me what looks best, OK?'

'They'll all be too big, you're much thinner than me,' I grumbled, shoving the wine in the fridge, 'and don't spend all day in there. You might not be able to cook, but I know that you can peel vegetables.'

I put a saucepan of water on the stove, placed a bowl over it and started to break the chocolate into it, ready to melt, realising rather guiltily that I was putting just as much chocolate in my mouth as into the bowl. Molly came limping into the room, wearing my black Jasper Conran dress. She tried to execute a twirl, but failed dismally, nearly falling over.

'Be careful, for God's sake, you don't want to hurt your other leg.'

'What do you think?' She held her arms out, looking for approval.

'What look are we trying to achieve here? Sexy? Or just plain available?'

'Both.'

'Well, it works, but try on the chocolate brown English Eccentric thing, that's always worked for me. You need a biggish necklace with it. Then if you spill any mousse down your front, it won't show.'

Molly is renowned for being clumsy when she is trying to impress. She had once been trying to charm a man at dinner in a very posh restaurant when she got her finger stuck in a bottle of wine. She tried to extract it unobtrusively, by rubbing butter over her finger, but it didn't work. She had to be led into the kitchens where it had to be smashed off her hand.

She came back into the kitchen. 'Do you think I'm trying too hard? Maybe I should just wear jeans and a top. A tight top, you know, something strappy. Oh God, why isn't Monty here,' she wailed.

'Phone him in Paris. I'm sure that if you explained your predicament he'd stop interviewing Karl Lagerfeld and hotfoot it back here.'

'Oh, stop it, I'm getting nervous. Let's have a drink.'

'No, it's far too early. You know what'll happen, you'll get tight, and then it'll be a disaster before Guy even arrives. And we've got the hell of Connie to deal with, so don't even think about it. OK?'

I started to whiz up breadcrumbs for the bread sauce, and the stuffing, and chop herbs and zest a lemon at the same time. I liked cooking, but not when press-ganged into it, and Molly was obviously not going to be any help at all, she was far too wired. I was studding an onion with cloves ready to drop it into some simmering milk for the bread sauce, when I counted the number of places around the table. She had set the table for six, not five. I called out to her, asking who the other place was for.

'The BND, he called when you were out. I felt I should invite him, he's been so sweet . . .'

I looked at the chicken, trying to estimate if it was large enough: Joe's appetite was legendary. Oh well, I'd chuck in a few more potatoes. I'd just got everything prepared when Molly wandered in, leaning on the umbrella, looking sensational.

'Anything I can do?' she asked innocently. She was wearing a pair of my old jeans (that were far too small for me) and an antique bodice that I'd bought in a Paris flea market and had never actually worn. She was also reeking of my perfume.

'No, but you can wash up afterwards.'

She gave me a broad smile. 'Of course I will, that is, of course, if I can stand at the sink with this terrible pain that I'm very stoically not complaining about.'

I gave her a dirty look. 'Pain or not, you will be washing up, Cinders.'

Molly settled herself on to the sofa in the drawing room, with her make-up bag, her foot up on a stool, a glass of wine to hand, and started to apply eyeliner.

'Go easy, you don't want to frighten him off, and if he works with models all day long, he's bound to appreciate the natural look.'

'The natural look takes twice as much make-up as anything else,' grumbled Molly, digging around in her bag. 'Liv, I can't find my tweezers, can I borrow some? If I don't pluck a few eyebrow hairs I'll look like a werewolf.'

I went into the bathroom to get ready myself. I had almost forgotten that dizzy feeling of anticipation, getting ready for a potential new man. I still felt emotionally frozen inside; I might have got to the stage where logically I knew that Christopher and I were finished, but I certainly had no stirrings to find myself another partner, the mere thought of it made me feel faint with boredom. All that getting to know someone, getting used to their ways, laughing at their jokes and putting up with their appalling bedroom behaviour while training them to more acceptable levels of sexual conduct seemed far too much like hard work. Perhaps gardening was the answer. I could quite see that growing peonies was infinitely more interesting than cultivating a man.

I lay for far too long in the hot bath, and staggered out of it looking like a cooked lobster. I wrapped a towel around me and went into my bedroom to try to find something to wear. It looked like a jumble sale: clothes were everywhere, Molly had pulled nearly everything out of my wardrobe, and my belongings lay half on the floor, and half falling off the bed. I pawed through them, looking for something cool. At last I found a very simple, long, pale grey, stretchy jersey dress. It touched in all the right places, and covered everything else up. I put on a heavy silver necklace with it, slipped on my velvet, hand-embroidered Indian slippers, and tried to tone down my glowing-red face with some make-up. I was beginning to smell the chicken that was roasting in the oven with lots of lemon, garlic and basil and it was making my mouth water. I realised that I hadn't eaten anything of nutritional value at all, today. I'd had some toast, pastries with Mrs Grieg, and some chocolate. Oh well, I'd scoff lots of veggies tonight (either roasted in olive oil, or swimming in butter) I thought, popping a multi-vitamin pill in my mouth.

I started to replace my clothes, hanging them back in the wardrobe. God, there were things here I hadn't seen for years. I held out a slinky long scarlet dress, trying to remember the last time I'd worn it. I couldn't even remember the last time I'd been able to get in it. I threw it by the door, making a mental note: *take to charity shop in the morning*. The pile increased – a silver tank top, a pair of floral leggings (why?), a tartan jacket (it might well have been Vivienne Westwood, but it made me look like an extra from *I'll Take the High Road*). The last thing to hit the pile was a very short leather skirt, bought to wear on a weekend away to Paris with Christopher. I suddenly didn't want to see it any more. I stuffed the discarded clothes into a rubbish bag, and went to peer into the oven, to see how the chicken was getting on.

Either my eyes were playing up, or I'd unknowingly taken hallucinogenic drugs, but there were now seven, not six, places set around the table. Oh God, who else had Molly invited?

I went into the drawing room and accused Molly of opening the telephone directory, sticking a pin in it, and inviting a total stranger to dinner.

'No, I haven't, but it's a really good idea. Go on, I dare you, it'd be a real laugh.'

'Have you been drinking?'

'No, well, half a glass of wine, but I have taken a few painkillers. My foot really hurts, you know.' She had the same tone in her voice that she had used when getting off games at school. No wonder Miss bloody Yardley, our sadistic games teacher, had never believed her.

'Have you eaten anything today?'

'No, but I've drunk lots of fluids. That's what they tell you to do in hospital, isn't it? Well, they do on *ER* anyway.'

I took her glass away from her, walked into the kitchen with it, and called out over my shoulder, 'I'm making you a snack, you know how you get, you're *not* having another glass of wine till you've eaten something. And lay off the painkillers – the last thing we want is an accidental overdose.'

I came back with some cheese and biscuits on a plate for her.

'Who else is coming for dinner? You still haven't told me.'

'Oh, Pete called, and he sounded a bit down, so I thought . . .'

'You thought we might as well open a restaurant, did you?'

I went to peel more potatoes, and hurriedly made a salad, as well. Molly had definitely managed to surround herself with enough people to impress Guy. I hoped that he was worth the effort.

'Moll, have you thought how we're going to slip the pistol to Steve tonight, in front of Connie?'

'Yes, I've arranged it with Steve. You're going to leave it on your bed, and he's going to pop it into his coat when he goes to the loo or something.'

'OK.'

'And how are we going to explain to Connie about your foot, when we weren't officially at the Bar yesterday?'

'We'll say that we popped in for a quick drink, on our way back from somewhere.'

'You seem to have thought all of this out remarkably well.'

'Yes, I must say I'm quite impressed with myself really. I think I may have what it takes to work for MI5, or do I mean MI6?'

Molly was arranging herself becomingly on the sofa, bandaged foot prominently to the fore. We poured ourselves a glass of wine each, and talked about the explosion, or whatever it had been.

'What do you think caused it?' she asked.

'I have no idea. Thank God no one was badly hurt.'

Molly looked reproachfully at me. 'I didn't exactly come away unscathed, you know. I might phone up for post-traumatic counselling.'

'You know what I mean — we could have been killed.'

'Do you think we should visit William Magpie in hospital?'

'Good God no! He'll be out by now, surely. He was only being treated for cuts and burns, it said so in the papers.'

'Let's watch the news, there might be something on there about it.'

I switched on the TV, just in time for the Channel 4 news. While we were watching, I told Molly about Mr Abrahams's request to have William at his party. She was as curious as I had been. Neither of us could possibly imagine how they knew each other, they were such worlds apart. We speculated on the four women that he had asked me to invite.

'Ex-girlfriends, probably.'

'God, they must be old, do you think they've all remained unmarried, pining away for him, all these years?'

'Ssshh, they're talking about the explosion.'

We sat in front of the TV, watching an earnest police officer stutteringly appeal for witnesses. He was standing in front of the Bar, which had been boarded up and had bits hanging off it, and there was still broken glass everywhere. Then the camera pulled back, and we saw what he was holding in his hands: two very bedraggled wigs, one long and dark, one blonde and curly. I focused in to hear what he was saying '*and we would especially like to talk to anyone who saw two women, aged between thirty and forty who were wearing these wigs. If either of the two women are watching this themselves, please contact the police so that we can eliminate you from our enquiries*'.

'Thirty or forty, bloody cheek!' shouted Molly.

I gave her a stony glare. '*Now* what do we do?'

'Sue the bastards for libel, or is it slander? I never know the difference.'

'Molly, I'm serious, what do we do? We'll have to call them, you know. We could be in serious trouble if we don't.'

'We could pretend that we hadn't seen it,' said Molly hopefully.

'You're joking. Aren't you?'

'I don't know. I mean, what are we going to say when they ask why we were wearing them?'

'It's not against the law to wear a sodding wig, is it? We'll just say that we were having a bad hair day, and that you'd borrowed them from work, and we wore them for a giggle.'

'Hmm, OK then, I suppose.'

I stood up to make the phone call. Molly suddenly screamed 'Stop!' at me. I looked at her enquiringly.

'Not now for Chrissake, they'll come round, and supposing they search the place. There's a bloody pistol in your bedroom, in case you've forgotten. Don't you need a licence for one?'

'Not an antique one, surely?'

We stared blankly at one another.

'But if I don't call now, won't we look really suspicious?'

'Not if we haven't seen it. Turn the TV off now, we'll call them in the morning after Steve has taken it back, OK?'

We poured some more wine, and I went to baste the chicken. I also went into the bedroom, wrapped the gun in a Waitrose carrier bag, and left it in the centre of my bed. I examined it closely before I wrapped it, it really did look old. It must be worth a fortune. It was certainly making me very nervous and I wanted it out of my flat as soon as possible.

Back in the drawing room, Molly had managed to get herself off the sofa, and was hobbling around lighting candles, muttering to herself, 'Thirty or forty, I'll bloody give them thirty or forty. I'm going to have collagen put in tomorrow, we do *not* look bloody forty . . .'

'You speak for yourself, I think it's a nice age, actually. Is that why you're lighting all the candles, because it's a more flattering light?'

'Shut up. I can't handle getting older.'

'Of course you can, and there's nothing you can do about it anyway. You might as well accept it with a smile and serenity.'

'Oh, stop it. If the next thing you say is about growing old gracefully I shall have to slap you.'

We laughed at each other and I looked at her. She did look forty, but what was wrong with that? There were a few lines, a little give around the neck, but those words of Gallic wisdom rang in my ears 'I like my women, like I like my salads, *un peu fatigué*'.

I left Molly making unnecessary minor adjustments to her face and to the lighting and went to put the potatoes into the oven. I am justly famed for my roast potatoes, and will share the secret of them with you. Actually, there is no secret at all, just parboil them for seven minutes, drain them, and hurl them around the colander quite roughly, so that they break up a bit and go fluffy. Then put them immediately into very, very, hot oil. Goose fat is the best. I know that we don't all have a bowl of goose fat hanging around in the fridge, so use olive oil, then sprinkle them with sea salt. Delicious, I promise.

I was squeezing a lemon on to some French mustard to make a salad dressing when the intercom went. Someone was early. I could hear Molly squawking with excitement in the drawing room, so I wiped my hands to answer the door. It wasn't the gorilla, though, it was Pete. He came through the door, clutching two bottles of champagne and a huge bunch of flowers, gave me a bear hug and immediately opened one of the bottles.

'Thanks for letting me come, I don't think I could have faced an evening by myself. The Bar looks terrible. Where's the invalid? Has she been running you ragged?'

I told him where Molly was, he called out an obscene greeting to her, and took her in a glass of champagne. He was back in the kitchen within seconds, closing the door.

'Liv, I came early, 'cos I need to talk to you. Sit down a minute, will you.'

His serious tone alarmed me. Lighting a cigarette and holding a glass of champagne, I sat down next to him.

'I need to ask you a favour. I need you to come to Brighton with me tomorrow.'

'Why?'

'I know that you saw all the drugs I'm taking. Oh God, I'm sorry, Liv. There's really no easy way to say this.' He paused. 'I'm ill, I have to tell my parents, I can't go by myself.'

The sense of his words didn't register for a moment, and when they did his calm, matter-of-fact voice made the content of what he was saying even more disturbing. I stammered out a few platitudes, not knowing what to say. I did know that the worst thing I could do was to be emotional and he obviously didn't want that so I asked him what was wrong with him. I suppose I already knew.

'Yeah. The modern plague of our times.' He went on to describe the hell he had been living through for the past year, the endless tests, the drugs, and then the realisation that he would have to live like this, hoping and praying that a time would come when he could be cured. I saw that I had finished my drink without knowing. I was staring at him.

'How do you manage?' I asked, in awe.

'One just does. The hardest thing is telling people, I can see them change in front of my eyes. They start, God forbid, to feel overwhelmingly sorry for me. They start to pity me, they start to make allowances for me. So, I'm warning you now, don't you bloody dare, don't you *dare* change towards me.'

His voice was low and urgent.

I felt as though I was moving underwater, everything

seemed to be in slow motion. My breath was fast, and my limbs felt numb, my body wanted to shut down, but my mind was whirling. I was gasping for some fresh air.

'There's something else, Liv, too. It's my heart . . . I really need a transplant, but well, that seems to be out of the question. I don't know how long I've got, so I try to make every day count, you know?' He was looking intently at me.

I nodded, numbly. Not trusting myself to speak. Oh God, I can't breathe.

'You're having a panic attack. Relax, breathe slowly.'

Pete stood behind me massaging my shoulders. I felt a complete fool, what a useless idiot I was. I tried to pull myself together. Abruptly I stood up and started to walk around the room, I felt better once I was moving. I asked him who else he had told.

'Just a few people. Steve knows.'

'Connie?'

'Good God, no, I may be ill but I'm not insane.'

It felt good to laugh; the tension had been unbearable. I found myself looking with admiration at him. Just what he hadn't wanted me to do, I realised. But it was impossible not to. How could you not behave differently, how could you behave normally? What was normal?

We made arrangements to meet at Victoria station in the morning. He had booked a restaurant for lunch in Brighton, and wanted me there when he told his parents.

The kitchen door pushed open and Molly hobbled in carrying her empty glass.

'What are you two talking about in here? You both look very strange. I've been calling for another glass for ages, you know. You seem to have forgotten that I'm ill and require constant attention,' she said in a mock *grande dame* way.

I couldn't look at Pete.

'You need a slave, not a nurse. Sit down for Chrissake before you fall down.'

Pete poured us all another glass, and I faffed around with the food preparation.

I heard Molly telling Pete excitedly all about Guy the Gorilla, and Pete promised Molly that he wouldn't make a pass at him. I made a huge effort, and tried to join in the general conversation, which revolved, not unsurprisingly around the Bar. As they chattered on, I found that I was close to tears, of admiration mainly, for Pete. How did he do it? *How?* And how was I going to cope as well as he was? Then I heard the welcome sound of the intercom buzzing.

Chapter Six

Joe was the next person to arrive. Followed closely by Steve and Connie. I had knocked back quite a few glasses of champagne by this time, and had made a mental promise to myself that I would do my damnedest to match Pete's good behaviour. I think the champagne helped.

We were all in the drawing room, gossiping away like crazy about the blast in the Bar. Pete told them his theory about the Casa trying to blow away the competition.

'I don't think they'd do that, honestly,' Connie said earnestly. Her lack of humour was practically Teutonic. Molly and I rolled our eyes at each other, but Steve looked on her fondly, as an indulgent parent might at the delinquent behaviour of a hyperactive toddler. She was easy enough on the eye, but very taxing indeed on the brain. She was wearing one of those nylon suits that had hundreds of zips and bits of velcro on them; no doubt very cool, but intrinsically hideous. I excused myself and went into the kitchen to turn the oven down, took the chicken out to rest, and poured myself another glass while I was alone. God, I hoped I wasn't turning into a secret drinker. I banished the thought while knocking it back. The buzzer went again: it must be the gorilla.

I ushered him in and had the immense satisfaction of

seeing Molly looking extremely flustered. She half tried to stand up then, obviously remembering her bad foot, sank down again. And true to form she managed to spill her drink. I suppressed a smile, and went to find a cloth to mop her up with.

When I returned I thought Guy seemed slightly daunted by the group of people, but was holding his own pretty well. He was telling Connie about the beggars he'd seen in Central Park, and how enterprising they'd seemed in comparison to their laid-back British counterparts.

'I saw a beggar in Oxford Street, he had a little puppy with him, it was so sad it made me cry . . .' said Connie.

'Oxford Street has that effect on us all,' I muttered.

Pete was gurgling with laughter. Molly was fiddling with her hair, and fluttering her eyes at Guy. It didn't seem to be having much effect, in fact he seemed rather drawn to Connie. I thought it was time that we ate, so shooed people into the kitchen. Molly demanded that Joe and Guy help her to walk, and she leaned heavily on Guy, showing off the cleavage that the bodice had given her. He didn't seem to notice.

The table looked lovely with Pete's flowers on it. All the candles were lit, and they cast a warm glow, making us look like a group of people at a Renaissance banquet. Molly had kept Joe and Guy on either side of her, and I noticed that Connie was very quick to settle in on the other side of Guy, motioning Steve to sit on her other empty side. Oh dear, there was a bit of competition going on for the gorilla. Molly would not be pleased.

I carved the chicken and passed it around the table. Connie looked up and said, 'So much meat is eaten in Western Europe, isn't it? Did you notice there is fantastic vegetarian food in New York now, I can't bear to think of all those little animals giving their lives for us.'

'Does it make you cry?' said Molly sarcastically, helping herself to a leg of chicken.

Pete and I started talking at the same time, and Steve launched into a spirited attack on modern art. We all wolfed down the meal, while Connie had most of the salad and asked me if there was any meat in the stuffing.

'No,' said Molly, before I could even open my mouth to answer her. 'Do have some, it's delicious, it's just got lemon, apple and pine nuts in it.'

'And bacon,' I added softly.

Pete spluttered into his glass and Joe was coughing wildly. I went to collect some more wine, and took the empty bottles off the table. Connie asked if I had any uncarbonated mineral water.

'Umm, no. Do you want some orange juice?'

'No thanks, it's got so much sugar in it, you know. You really should be drinking the water without bubbles in, it gives you terrible cellulite. I drink several litres a day, it's so good for you.'

'Water on the brain,' Pete said, laughing his head off and opening another bottle of white. He filled his glass.

I started to spoon the fabulous chocolate mousse into glasses. There would be about a teaspoon each, as there were so many of us. Connie, of course, refused it, saying, 'Even though I went to the gym every day when I was away, I mustn't let myself go. The food in Paris was so rich, I'm sure I've put on weight.' Then she was off, boring for Europe on the subject of the new equipment at her gym, and her new workout routine. Even Guy was stifling a yawn; I could tell by the way he was clenching his jaw.

'Did you eat out much then, Connie, in Paris?' I asked

innocently. 'Try any of those Moroccan places? They're very popular now, aren't they?'

'Oh yes, they're fab, I went to one that was amazing, it had the sweetest interior. You should go there, Liv, it might give you some fresh ideas.'

I gritted my teeth. The woman was so bloody irritating, she had all the sensitivity of a charging rhino. I wondered how she'd react if I asked her about smooching with one of the Moroccan waiters at the sweet little restaurant. When I stood up, and started to clear the table, Steve jumped up to help, and mouthed 'sorry' at me. I made coffee, and let the conversation flow around me. People were settling back into their chairs, sipping brandy, lighting cigarettes and pouring coffee. Suddenly I wished that I could magic them all away, so that I could go to bed. I wanted to be alone to think about Pete, and what I could do for him, if anything.

Molly had turned towards Guy, and was talking softly in his ear. Pete and Steve were having one of their endless, long-running mock arguments about why the Casa was still the busiest club in Soho, and Joe was listening to Connie drone on about exercise and aerobic heartbeats.

'. . . the whole *point* of the Casa is that there's a waiting list to join. If there wasn't one, they'd say there was, just to make it look good . . .'

'. . . No, I take vitamin B12 directly after breakfast, and *before* I go for a run, it helps the digestion a lot, you should try it . . .'

'. . . *Nobody* pays any membership fees, even *I've* got a bloody picture hanging in the bar, so I didn't have to pay to join . . .'

'. . . and the rowing machine really works for me, but only *after* the treadmill, then of course I do my weight training . . .'

'. . . If I'd wanted a bleeding gallery I'd've bloody opened one, wouldn't I? I don't *want* a stuffed bloody shark on my wall, do I?'

'. . . My ankle really, really hurt, you know, the medics said I'd been *so* brave, it was awful. I'm sure that if I had a bit of help I could go home tonight . . .'

'. . . it's not stuffed, you daft sod, it's pickled . . .'

'. . . I've improved my swimming distance, too, my stamina has increased dramatically, but I still need to work on it . . .'

'. . . great, so you could drive me home, I only need a bit of help up the stairs, I think the bandage could come off tomorrow . . .'

'. . . stuffed or pickled I don't want it leering down at me from the wall, I've had enough punters who look like that anyway, without the aid of formaldehyde, thank you very much . . .'

Tiredness swept over me. Those lines by Byron came into my mind '*I stood among them, but not of them, in a shroud of thoughts which were not their thoughts.*' All I could do was admire Pete's fortitude, and try to learn from his example.

I watched Steve leave to go to the bathroom, then made some excuse and followed him outside. I motioned him into my bedroom and pointed to the pistol wrapped in its carrier bag.

'Don't forget to take it with you, I don't want the bloody thing here any more, it gives me the creeps.'

'OK, OK. I've got to find Mimi, though, to give it back to her, haven't I?'

'Luckily, that for once is not my problem.'

He looked at me and said, 'Pete has told you, hasn't he?'

'Yes. Is it that obvious?'

'No, but I think I was the same when he told me.'

I had a quick stab of pain at the thought that Pete had

told Steve before telling me; I tried to dismiss it as stupid and unworthy.

Steve was looking round the room, searching for his coat. He stooped to the floor and pulled out a sheet of paper that had been under the bed. It was the obscene sketch he'd done of Mimi, which Molly and I had pinched from his flat.

'What is this doing here?' he demanded.

'Molly and I thought we could use it for blackmail purposes. Did she *really* do that? Or is it a figment of your warped and diseased imagination?' I said staring at the picture. Suddenly my memory was jogged. 'Oh God, I know where I've seen her now. It's the woman outside the Bar, with the long dark red hair. She was waving at us when Molly and I were leaving. How did she know us?'

'Dunno. Maybe she saw you coming out of my flat. And yes, she really *did* do that.'

We were studying the picture when my bedroom door was flung open, and Connie marched in.

'What are you two doing in here?' she asked, wrinkling her eyes up to show that she was smiling. 'I want to go home now, so I've come for my jacket.' Her gaze wandered to the drawing on my bed. It had crossed my mind to sit on the picture, as soon as she'd walked into the room, but I would have got charcoal all over my dress. Let Steve deal with it, I thought, rather malevolently.

'Ooh God, what on earth is that?'

'I would have thought that was fairly obvious,' I muttered. 'It is, after all, anatomically correct.'

'Yes,' agreed Steve enthusiastically. 'Livia was showing me what she'd found in Mr Abraham's flat. What a dirty old man he must be, huh? Now, let's get you home, shall we?'

I turned slowly and stared at him in disbelief.

'It's disgusting, and you brought it home with you! Why?' exclaimed Connie.

'I'm starting a collection of hard pornography for my bathroom,' I said acidly, still glaring at Steve. 'I was just asking Steve how he thought it should be framed.'

Steve hustled Connie into her jacket, studiously avoiding my eyes. I turned into the hallway and found Molly leaning against the wall with both of her arms around Guy, trying to persuade him to go home with her. She was on to a losing wicket, I could tell: he was protesting that he had a shoot to go to very early the following day, that he'd arranged to drop Connie and Steve home as they didn't live too far from him, and that he was knackered from his flight.

She gave in gracefully enough, once he'd promised to call her tomorrow and arrange to take her out to dinner, as he wanted to discuss the next layout he was going to do for her magazine.

We eventually waved goodbye to the three of them and went back to the kitchen, where Joe and Pete were laughing, sitting round the debris of the meal, elbows on the table, an open bottle of wine in front of them.

'Bloody men,' Molly grumbled, sitting down and swinging her bad leg up on to an empty chair. 'How *could* he be attracted to that humourless cow? She's truly dreadful, isn't she?'

Pete poured her a glass of wine, saying, 'I'd forget him love, if I were you, he's got ice in his veins.'

Joe looked bewildered. 'I thought she was OK. I mean, she doesn't talk like you two do, but she's, well she's . . .'

'Got big tits, blonde hair and is stupid.' Molly finished his sentence for him, and we all burst out laughing.

We stayed at the table till the wine was finished and then Pete got up to go home saying, 'Thanks for the meal, Liv, see you tomorrow at ten.' He kissed us all, including Joe, goodbye. Joe looked a little surprised, and also a little flattered.

'Never been kissed by a bloke before,' he said once Pete had left.

'What, not even in those communal baths after a big game?' I teased.

He looked suitably shocked. 'Good God, no. Nothing like that goes on, you know.'

'Shame.'

'He's a nice bloke, isn't he?'

I sighed. 'Yes, he's a very nice bloke indeed.' I got to my feet. 'I'm going to bed, I'm so tired. You can let yourself out, can't you, Joe? Night, Moll, see you in the morning, and don't worry about Guy, you can get him if you want him.' I yawned and made my way to bed. I had a lot to think about, I was dreading tomorrow. I'd never met Pete's parents, and could only imagine the pain that his news was going to cause. I waved goodnight to Joe and Molly, closed the bedroom door and threw myself into bed.

I was exhausted, far too tired to do the nightly routine of make-up removing and teeth cleaning (which I'm usually so obsessive about that sometimes I feel like Lady Macbeth and her hand washing). I lay in bed hearing movements from the kitchen, then the front door close. I turned over: and saw the pistol was still lying there in the plastic shopping bag. Bugger, and I'd nearly gone to sleep on the bloody thing. Gingerly I picked it up and shoved it as far as I could under the bed. I must get it back to Steve, let him deal with the damn thing, was the last thought I had, before I fell asleep.

The following morning I was up very early, far too early, in my opinion, knocking out invitations for Mr Abraham on my computer, trying not to wake Molly with the tapping of my fingers on the keyboard. When the printer started, however, she sat bolt upright in bed.

'What the hell are you doing?'

'Printing out the invites to the party of the century. It's going to be wild, wild, wild.'

'What?'

'You know, Mr Abraham's little bash. I'm inviting Zena, she can charm him. And we can knock up a few nibbles. I'm setting the date for very soon, I just want to get it over with.'

Molly groaned. 'I had the most appalling night's sleep. I dreamt that a monkey was running away from me, and I had to chase it through skyscrapers.'

I snorted with laughter. 'That's ringing with symbolism, isn't it?'

'What do you mean?'

'Oh, come on, a monkey? Try a gorilla instead. Skyscrapers? Where has Guy just come back from? Honestly, Molly it's textbook stuff, isn't it? Stop chasing him, you might catch him.'

She threw a pillow at me.

'My ankle isn't any better, you know, I'm going to have to take another sick day from work.' She swung her legs out of bed, wearing a Katharine Hamnett T-shirt, with the slogan SAY NO TO MISSILES in faded letters printed on the front.

'My God, how old is that?' I asked. 'I'm not surprised Guy didn't end up in your bed if you wear such attractive nightwear.'

'Oh shut up, you're just cranky because you're up too early. Why are you up, anyway?'

I explained about having to go to meet Pete and wanting to get the invitations out of the way, and then I quickly headed off to the bathroom, shouting over my shoulder, 'Look, go back to sleep, but call Steve later and tell him to come over and pick the you-know-what up, he didn't take it last night. I've got Monty coming over tonight, so let him in, won't you, I'll bring supper back with me but I've got to get ready now because I want to pop into Mr Abraham's flat before I meet Pete.'

'Why are you meeting Pete?' she yelled.

I hesitated. It was pointless not telling her, I reflected. But it wasn't my secret. 'I have to go and meet his parents in Brighton. He's having lunch with them and just wants another person there, that's all,' I shouted back, trying to make myself heard over the sound of the running water.

I dressed and made phone calls at the same time. I spoke to Doug, who was still at the hospital with Maggie, who'd been in labour now for hours, but there was no news. I asked him to give her my love, and then I phoned young Roger. He sounded very self-important and assured me that everything was fine, and I had no need to worry, everything would be ready. I hoped to God he was right. I licked some stamps and put them on the envelopes that held the invitations to Mr Abraham's housewarming. I was just making my way out of the door, when the phone rang. It was Nicola Bentley.

'Livia, can you come over tomorrow? I'd really like to make a start on changing this mausoleum into a home. It's getting too depressing, sitting round here. And *he's* splashed all over the front pages of the tabloids this morning, arm in arm with some smiling disco bunny with a silicone chest and whitened teeth. She looks about twelve, I can't stand it.' Her voice was wobbly, close to tears.

I made sympathetic noises. It must be like Jerry Hall, looking at pictures of Mick with yet another bimbo.

'Nicola, I'll come over tomorrow morning. Try not to be too upset, OK? We'll make you a wonderful new home . . .' I felt a bit cheeky, trying to give words of comfort to Nicola Bentley, but she seemed cheered by it, and thanked me.

I put my head round the door to the office to say goodbye to Molly.

'That was Nicola, she wants me to go over there tomorrow. If you feel up to it, could you finish off that presentation board? You know the look I'm after.'

'Whoo! Fancy being called by Nicola Bentley . . . Get you! Yeah, OK. Do I get paid for being your assistant?'

'No, but you get dinner.'

'I'm not here, am I? Guy said he'd call, and take me out.'

'I wouldn't hold my breath, if I were you,' I said, poking my tongue out at her.

I decided not to go to Mr Abraham's, as I didn't want to be late meeting Pete. I walked down the road and pushed the invitations into the postbox, reflecting again on the impossibility of Mr Abraham knowing William Magpie. Mrs Grieg was beckoning to me, but I couldn't stop, so I gave her a wave and continued on my way.

I arrived at Victoria half an hour early. I always do. I'm so worried about being late that I invariably arrive in time to catch the train or plane before the one I'm scheduled to travel on.

I scanned the headlines of the newspapers lined up at WH Smith's. Three of them carried pictures of Nicola's ex-husband (looking, I was pleased to see, like every ageing rock star does, dressed in too tight leather trousers, wristbands, far too many necklaces and sporting dark glasses) hurrying through an airport dragging a scantily clad girl with him. I picked a paper up, and saw that there was a small column about the bomb at the Bar. They were taking the tack that it was a right-wing protest against homosexuality. Oh great, I bet Pete's parents were reading this over their breakfast coffee by now. I realised that we still had to call the police about the wigs. I called Molly from my mobile.

'Livia Hunter's assistant, how may I help you?'

'Molly, it's me, you fool. We've got to phone the police, can you do it?'

'Oh God, do we have to? I think it'll all blow over, won't it?'

'Of course it won't blow over, it was a bloody bomb for Chrissake. We have to call them,' I hissed into the phone.

'OK, OK, I will, but shouldn't the you-know-what be dealt with first?'

I cursed, causing two businessmen to look at me with alarm.

'Yes, yes, phone Steve and tell him he has to come and get it *now.* Don't take no for an answer, OK?'

'OK.'

I wandered over to Tie Rack and idly flicked through a rail of fake pashminas. I tried on a few hats, and then wandered out again and bought myself a croissant. The number of shops in the station was staggering, I mean, who the hell goes there? Why would any sane person go shopping in a train station? I just couldn't see any busy commuter thinking to themselves 'Ooh, yes, I'll miss the 17.15 to East Grinstead, so I can go and check out the latest line of linen shirts in Next instead.'

I stood at the ticket windows waiting for Pete, munching my croissant, dropping crumbs on my chest and smudging my lipstick. I was getting nervous about what the day would hold, and when I'm nervous, I eat. I was just wondering if I had time to go and buy myself a bar of chocolate when I saw Pete walking towards me. I looked at him, and marvelled that he could look so normal and so confident. Oozing briskness and energy, he was carrying a plastic bag and a case; he waved the carrier bag at me, crying, 'And she shall have bubbles wherever she goes!'

We hugged each other in a wordless greeting, and queued up to buy our tickets.

'Pete, I don't think I've ever seen you without a bottle of champagne. Do you have a secret cache?'

'I never travel without it.'

When we reached the ticket window, Pete asked for one single and one return to Brighton.

'Are you staying there?'

'I think I'll have to.'

I looked enquiringly at him.

'The Bar'll be closed for a while yet, and I need some fresh air. I can't stand to be in London at the moment.'

'I'm not surprised after what's happened. Will you stay with your parents?'

'God, no. I have a flat there.'

This was news to me.

'Do you? You've never mentioned it.'

'Well, I don't want you lot turning up for dirty weekends, do I?' he grinned.

I wondered what other secrets he'd kept from me.

We walked towards platform 17, where the Brighton train was waiting, and once we'd settled ourselves in, Pete started to wax lyrical about the past splendours of the coast train.

'It used to be fabulous, with a proper buffet that you could smoke in, and with great characters,' specially the last train back. We all used to sit clutching our gins, telling jokes and having a laugh. Huh, look at it now. Connex, I ask you! Not even comfortable seats, twice as expensive, three times more unreliable and a toilet too small to have sex in. Ridiculous. Well, that's privatisation.'

The train was pulling out, and heading towards the coast. Pete took out two paper cups and opened the champagne. A slight holiday feeling had entered both of us, even though we were heading towards a grim appointment, and I asked him what his parents were like.

'Loaded. Unhappy. My father's a bit of a bully, he thinks he married beneath him. My mother's got too much time on her hands. I don't see much of them. They live on a sort of white man's private estate near Preston Park. It has hideous large houses with leaded windows, full of crap reproduction paintings and swimming pools that no one uses. The gardener comes twice a week to manicure the hedges, my mother probably fantasises about seducing him. My father plays golf or struts around on a yacht that he keeps at the Marina, where he wears deck shoes and shorts that are too long for him. They don't like me much.'

'Dear God. And you only brought the one bottle with you? I'll need more than this to get through it. How do you think they'll react?'

'To what? The gay bit or the HIV bit, or the dodgy heart bit?'

'Oh God, Pete. They really don't know about anything?'

'Nah, could never be arsed to tell them. I mean, it's fairly bloody obvious that I'm gay, isn't it? And when I became ill, I couldn't see the point.'

'So why now?'

'It's like tying up loose ends, I guess. It feels right.'

We sipped our drinks, looking out at the speeding scenery through the grimy windows of the train. The houses along the side of the tracks always held a fascination for me, those private little glimpses of other people's lives seen through a window can reveal so much. A line of washing flapping in a back garden makes a huge impact of colour on a drab suburban lawn. Pink shirts, red skirts, and yellow towels waving in the wind. A beacon of colour on a grey day. We had passed Haywards Heath by now, and the fields of Sussex rolled away to the horizon.

'Sussex always makes me think of *Cold Comfort Farm*, does it you?' I asked Pete.

'Something nasty in the woodshed, you mean?' he laughed.

'Umm, or the Downs, wreathed in mist like a snarling beast . . .'

'Just like my father.'

'Please don't, I'm nervous enough already, I can't think why you want me along.'

'I need the moral support. I was thinking of telling them that you were my girlfriend, but I'm sick of all the lies. I just want to tell them so that, well, so that when the time comes they're prepared for it, you know? So that it won't be too much of a shock to them. If it would be at all.'

'Do they know about the bomb?'

'Yeah, I called and told them about it.'

A pretty young boy was walking through the swaying train carriages, looking for somewhere to sit. I watched Pete appraise him, looking him up and down. Pete saw me watching him, and laughed.

'I know just what you're thinking, My God, he could be dying and he's *still* looking at boys! Well, it doesn't stop, you know. In fact, I think it probably gets worse.'

The train was pulling into Brighton station now, and people were queuing up at the doors, waiting for the train to stop. As soon as you left the station and headed downhill, you had a framed view of the sea. Admittedly it was grey and choppy, but it did lift the spirits.

We walked arm in arm down the hill, towards the seafront, passing sex shops and junk shops full of tat. Who was it that said that Brighton 'looked like a town helping police with their enquiries'? I couldn't remember. It was very windy, and we fairly sailed down the hill, blown by the wind.

Pete pulled me into a warm pub with a lot of padded red velvet and dark beams, and I sat down while he went to order drinks. Now that we were here, I felt strangely at ease. If Pete's parents didn't recognise that they had a very special person as a son, well, that was their problem. My duty lay with my friend. I watched him carry back the drinks. His hair was windswept, and I had a sudden urge to brush it for him.

'Where have you booked lunch?'

'The only place my parents go to. I thought that if there was any possibility of them throwing a scene, it would curb them, knowing that the waiters all know them there.'

He pushed my vodka towards me. I picked it up and we silently toasted one another. His slightly satanic eyes were so full of life, so knowing, so wickedly glinting, that I couldn't bear the thought of them being dulled by illness and pain. He saw the look on my face and said, gently, 'Stop it. You promised you wouldn't do this.'

'OK, OK. Just tell me, how ill are you? Really?'

He paused, and looked down at his drink.

'Try and look on it like I've got diabetes, or something. I'm going to be on medication for the rest of my life, anyway, it's my heart they're more worried about. Will you tell Molly and everyone for me? I can't bear to keep repeating myself.' He smiled gently. 'I can deal with it if you can, all right?'

'Right, now come on, let's go and look at the sea, before

116

we meet your parents.' I grabbed my bag and we headed for the door.

It was bright and breezy outside, and the seagulls were wheeling overhead. We went down to the beach and threw some stones into the sea.

'Why do you think people do that?' I said.

'Do what?'

'Throw stones in the sea. I mean, it's totally pointless, isn't it?'

'What isn't?' he said with mock world-weariness.

We left the pebbly beach and walked back into the narrow lanes towards the restaurant. We gazed in the windows of all the jewellery shops and I picked out what I'd buy if I ever won the Lottery.

'My God, Liv, for an interior designer with a great deal of style, you have incredibly vulgar taste in jewels.'

'I can assure you, there is absolutely nothing vulgar about a £35,000 diamond, specially if it was on my finger.'

'Hmm I'm not convinced. I see you more as an emerald lady.'

'Oh, do you? Well, in that case, how about this one?' I pointed to a huge square Cartier cut emerald, on a thin band of platinum. It was an art deco ring, and it looked fabulous. Pete had to drag me away from the window.

'Come on, you piece of white trash, let's go, we're going to be late.'

We hurried through the Lanes and soon came to Gills. The minute we walked inside I knew that I'd hate it. Over-dressed, over made-up women and middle-aged men in suits were sitting at the remarkably uncomfortable looking tables. It smelt faintly of slightly rancid fish oil and was staffed by fake Italians. The décor was appalling, with a really bad mural of tarty Edwardian floosies on one wall. I had an awful feeling that I was going to giggle, and thought I'd better go to the Ladies and compose myself, I was sure that I could do with brushing my hair and applying some warpaint, too.

I was shown the way by an overenthusiastic waiter, and as I climbed the stairs and had a good look around me, I knew that the food was going to be awful too. Everything would come swamped in sickly sauces, disguising the poor quality of the food. When I joined Pete at the table, one glance at the menu confirmed my suspicions. Pete had ordered a large vodka for me, and we sat sipping our drinks, jumping every time the restaurant door opened.

'I'd stick to the oysters, if I were you,' Pete said.

'No thanks, I'm going to have Dover sole and a green salad. Where are they? If they don't get here soon, I shall be tipsy. For God's sake, don't pour me any wine, will you? I've had half a bottle of champagne for breakfast and two vodkas with no food, I don't want to disgrace myself.'

I nibbled on an olive, and spat it out. It was horrible, full of brine. I opened a pack of grissini, and nibbled on them instead.

We were both getting edgy now, and had lit cigarettes (much to the disapproval of two businessmen sitting the other side of the room, who started waving their hands in front of their faces, and making loud comments about air pollution).

'Makes me want to smoke more.'

'Me too.' I knew that Pete shouldn't be smoking at all, but I also knew how pointless pointing it out would be.

We puffed furiously away, filling the minute glass ashtray. I was getting decidedly jumpy now, and, as usual when I was gibbering with nerves, my stomach gave me away by rumbling loudly.

'God, Liv, it sounds as though you've swallowed an outboard motor.'

'I know, I need some food. Let's order some bread, so that I can pick at something. Are your parents always this late?'

'Probably having trouble parking the Rolls.'

'You're joking.'

'Afraid not. They give the term *nouveau riche* a bad name. Wait till you meet them.'

I was dreading it. The waiter sashayed across the room placing a basket of bread on the table with a flourish and casting a rather long, lingering look at Pete.

'I've pulled!'

'Stop it, right now, I mean it, and pass me that bread.'

Hungrily I tore off rather too much bread. It was not very fresh, and had that ungiving, scratchy quality that made it hard to swallow but I was starving. I was just stuffing it into my mouth when Pete suddenly stood up, and greeted a couple that had just walked in.

'Livia, may I introduce my parents, Suzanne and Michael Aston. Mum, Dad, this is my friend Livia Hunter.'

I held my hand out, trying desperately hard to swallow the bread. It had turned into an unyielding lump in my mouth, and try as I might, I simply could not persuade it to go down my throat. His parents were looking strangely at me. I realised that my face was going red with the effort of trying to swallow and not have a choking fit at the same time. I picked up my glass, in a vain attempt to dislodge the semi masticated dough with some liquid. Neat vodka flooded my mouth, and I started to choke in earnest.

Gasping for breath, I stood up in my panic, knocking the brimming ashtray on to the floor, and all over Suzanne's suit. Pete banged me on the back, which did nothing at all, and I was reduced to the inglorious act of finding a napkin and spitting out a mouthful of grey bread. His mother, who looked like a blonde Joan Collins, was obviously revolted, and his father looked as though he was about to have a heart attack. I was wiping saliva and crumbs from my face, thinking, great start, things can only get better. Can't they?

Chapter Seven

There was a flurry of waiters around the table. Suzanne and Michael Aston were obviously very important customers. The waiters solicitously waved napkins and removed glasses, and immediately arrived with a bottle of 'their' wine. Spluttering, I asked for a glass of water, and tried to regain my composure.

We had been seated at a strange horseshoe-shaped table at the end of the dining room, so all the other customers could get a good look at the freak who had nearly choked to death. I had Pete to my left, and Michael the other side of me, whilst Suzanne sat opposite her husband and next to her son. She was wearing what I took to be a genuine, pale pink, Chanel suit. She was very attractive, in a brittle sort of way, with steely blue eyes. Her husband was wearing far too much cologne, but at least it drowned out the rancid fish smell. He, too, had glacier-like blue eyes. I wondered if they indulged in staring each other out at home, and I resolved to stick to water throughout the meal. We all tried to make small talk, and choose from the menu. Michael and Suzanne barely glanced at it; they must know it off by heart, I thought. Both ordered lobster, and sat back, waiting for Pete to start telling them why they were here. Suzanne asked me what I did for a living.

'I'm an interior designer,' I explained, sipping water.

'One of the best,' said Pete, proudly.

I saw Suzanne catch Michael's eye, an eyebrow slightly raised and an expectant look on her face. There was a slight thaw in the atmosphere. Michael started to tell Pete about the repairs he was making to his yacht, and Suzanne unbent enough to confide in me that she didn't sail much herself, it played too much havoc with her hair.

'Me too,' I said rather absent-mindedly.

'Oh, do you sail?' asked Michael.

'Well, no, not really, it's just that if I did, I'm sure I'd feel the same way about my hair, as well, umm, that and seasickness of course,' I tailed off miserably.

Suzanne cast a professional eye over my hair. This was a woman who probably lived in a hair salon and beauty parlour: she could tell at three paces that I coloured my hair myself, and trimmed it with nail scissors in front of the bathroom mirror.

'No such thing as seasickness. You must come out with us – bring her along, Pete. We'll soon find your sea legs for you.' Michael gave the laugh of a man who secretly knows that he has said nothing remotely funny.

'Pete never fancied life on the briny, did you?' he said rather belligerently to Pete.

'Messed my hair up too much,' muttered Pete.

'Now then, darling,' interrupted Suzanne. 'Tell us why you and Livia have come down.'

The waiters descended again, making a big fuss of Suzanne, who simpered unbecomingly at them. They waved alarmingly huge phallic pepperpots over our food and generally made a nuisance of themselves. One of the waiters lingered a little too long for Michael's liking.

'That boy's a bloody poof,' he said.

'Which one?' asked Pete, innocently.

I kicked him under the table. This was not a good start to the proceedings. I mean, I could see why he didn't get on with his parents, but antagonising them deliberately was not the way forward, I felt.

'Now darling, some of them are very artistic, and I'm sure Livia meets many in her line of work,' Suzanne said.

'Artistic, my foot! Waste of space, the lot of them. They'd be laughed out of the Yacht Club, let me tell you.'

Michael was attacking his lobster with relish, though it looked a bit rubbery to me. He picked up a red claw and cracked it with unnecessary violence.

'Delicious lobster, darling,' said Suzanne rather mechanically. Fleetingly it crossed my mind that she could be on tranquillisers.

I glanced at Pete to see how he was taking this attack on homosexuality. He seemed numb, and was gazing down at his plate. Michael was warming to his subject now, and a ceaseless tirade against 'poofs' and 'shirtlifters' was streaming from his mouth. I was appalled, I had to stop this, but I wasn't sure how. I grabbed Pete's hand under the table, gave it an encouraging squeeze, then cleared my throat and said tentatively, 'Umm, well, you see, one of the reasons that we're down here is that, well, why don't you tell your parents, Pete?' I turned towards him with encouraging eyes. I was still holding his hand under the table, and he gripped it convulsively.

Suddenly my phone trilled in my handbag. I retrieved it and excused myself from the table, and walked outside with it. What a relief. Literally saved by the bell. It was very good timing, whoever it was. I felt that Pete should really tackle them on his own now, then I could rejoin the table and help smooth things out in a moment or two. It was Doug on the phone telling me that Maggie was going to have an emergency Caesarean, and that he couldn't leave the hospital.

'God, no, of course not. Is she OK?'

'Aye, she's a good lass, but she's scared. We both want this to be over, now.'

'Of course, Doug, thanks for calling, I'm thinking of you both.'

I said goodbye, and turned to look through the restaurant window. To my utter surprise Suzanne was smiling and Michael was waving his napkin in the air. Well, the news had gone down better than I'd hoped. I walked back into the restaurant, and nearly collided with a waiter who was bringing champagne over to the table.

'Well, well, this calls for a celebration, doesn't it? I'm so glad to hear the news, it's super. Very good, very good indeed,' Michael said, looking pleased with himself and rubbing his hands together. I looked towards Pete for help. What the hell was going on?

'Darling, I really am so glad, you've no idea . . .' Suzanne was actually wiping a tear away with a red-taloned, heavily ringed hand. She leaned forward to kiss me, and sat back in her seat, beaming.

The waiter was pouring champagne, offering congratulations. Pete picked my hand up and kissed it, saying 'Yeah, I'm very lucky, she said yes, and so of course we came down to tell you of our engagement.'

At once I had another coughing fit. My mind was reeling – how the hell was I going to get out of this? Obviously, now it had come to it, Pete just couldn't face telling them, and had said what they had wanted to hear, but, oh God, what a mess. If I'd been a brave woman, I would have stopped this little charade right there and then. But I'm not, and I didn't. So, I drank my champagne (sod the water) and smilingly joined in the toast, while pinching Pete so hard on the leg that he winced.

'Well, darling, let's see the ring,' said Suzanne, turning her own diamond solitaire round on her finger.

'Yes, let's see the ring, Pete,' I said brightly.

'You women, you don't give a man a chance, do you?' said Michael jovially, smiling at his son. 'I've got a much better idea – let's go and buy one, now.'

'Yes, do let's,' Pete said very weakly.

So we all trooped off to the Lanes, where only an hour ago I had been lusting after an emerald. I was tempted to make a beeline for it, to teach Pete a lesson, but I didn't have the heart. So, I made cooing noises over little antique garnet rings, and feigned interest in one of them.

'Nonsense, my dear,' boomed Michael. 'You're going to be an Aston, soon, you know, should have something fitting. What do you say Suzy?' Suzy looked as though her legs wouldn't carry her much further and she tottered into the next jeweller's and sat down on a chair. She motioned me over to her, and whispered in my ear, 'I can't tell you how relieved we are. We were beginning to think he would *never* settle down, it worried us both dreadfully, it didn't look good. You choose a good ring, Michael will pay, I shall insist.'

'What's that?' Michael demanded.

'I was saying to Livia that the ring is our treat, isn't it, darling?' She held his eyes with a flinty stare.

'Of course, of course, only too delighted. Now then, what's your fancy? Sapphires, rubies or diamonds?'

'She likes emeralds,' said Pete smugly.

We left the jeweller's shop in a haze of champagne, with me sporting the huge emerald ring I had seen earlier. Everything was starting to seem very surreal and I spoke very little.

There was a taxi rank on the corner of a road, by a large, rambling department store, and it was there that we said our goodbyes to Mr and Mrs Aston. I seem to remember agreeing to meet them in Brighton again, soon, and we watched them recede into the distance.

I was too stunned to talk, but kept glancing down at my hand. I don't think that I even thanked them for the ring, what was I going to do? I turned to Pete and said, 'I think this is the weirdest day of my life, what *are* we going to do?'

Pete looked grey with tiredness. The glint had gone from his eyes, and he looked ill.

'I don't know. I should apologise to you, but I'm too tired, I need to lie down.'

'Where is your flat?'

'In Brunswick Square, it's not far from here, but I'm going to get a taxi. Don't come back with me, please. I'm sorry I fucked things up. I need to be by myself for a while, I'll call you, OK?'

I kissed him goodbye, and watched the taxi turn the corner. Well, I reasoned to myself, I've got a very snazzy ring. I stared down at it, at the pale sunlight glancing off the facets. It was a flawless dark green, perfect. I knew that I couldn't keep it, but it didn't stop me enjoying it while I had it. I started to think about really mundane things, like insurance, I mean this thing was worth a fortune, supposing I lost it, or it was stolen? I walked back up the hill towards the station, aware that I had over £20,000 hanging off my left hand. That made me so nervous, that in the end I had to walk with my hand in my pocket. How on earth did Liz Taylor walk round with that diamond on? Oh yes, she had bodyguards.

Brighton station had a wonderful flower stall in it, and I bought an armful of mimosa to take home. I still felt in a bit of a daze, and sank into my train seat with considerable relief. At least I had an hour in which I didn't have to think about anything. I could suddenly see the attraction of commuting: there you were, stuck in a train, unable to do a thing. Then I realised that, with the invention of mobiles and laptops, you could be reached even there. With that thought, true to form, my phone went.

'So what colour is your hair today?' The mystery builder had a very flirty voice, I decided. But I just wasn't in the mood for it. I started to tell him about the very strange day I'd had.

'That sounds terrible, I am so sorry to hear about your friend, Pete. You must be very worried about him . . . Is there anything I can do?'

'No, not really. But thank you, anyway.' There was rather an awkward silence, and we both started to say goodbye at the same time.

I flexed my hand so that I could look at my ring again. Already I was calling it my ring, not the ring. I had to be careful, I didn't want to get too attached to it.

The train journey went by in what seemed like moments, and when I reached Victoria, I stepped out feeling a bit disorientated and made my way back to my flat, calling Molly as I went.

'Molly? Hi, it's Liv, how are things?'

'Hmm, well, OK, I suppose.'

'What do you mean?'

'I think you'd better come home, and I'll tell you when I see you. Let's just say it's been a hell of a day.'

'What's happened? Tell me now, I can't bear the suspense.'

'Well, let's just say, we have a guest.'

'Who?'

'Umm, I really think you should be here, let's leave it till you come home, shall we?'

I thought for a moment that it might be Christopher.

'No, bloody tell me now. I mean it, Molly, who is it?'

'Well, you're not going to like it much. But it's, well, it's Mimi.'

'The Bangkok bar girl that carries guns around?'

'That's the one.'

'What the fuck is she doing in my flat? Get her out of there, fast.'

'What do you think I've been trying to do all day? It's difficult, she doesn't seem to speak much English, and she cries a lot.'

'What do you mean?'

'I mean exactly what I say. She hardly speaks English, she's Russian and there's a lot of boo-hooing going on.'

'Where's Steve?'

'He's gone to the Casa.'

'What the fuck for?' I said viciously.

'Look, come home and we can talk properly. How was your day, what went on in Brighton?'

'Hah, you wouldn't believe it.' I didn't believe it myself, so I very much doubted that anybody else would.

I hung up, and clutching the mimosa, fled to the sanctuary of a black cab. I toyed with the idea of going straight to the Casa and bearding Steve, but decided against it. I wanted to get gangster girl out of my flat, first. I paid the taxi off at the top of the street and picked up some food for Monty. He'd said he'd had enough fancy food in Paris, so I was going to cook him bangers and mash. The butcher sold me some coarse cumberland sausages that he made himself, and I hefted up a large bag of potatoes from the greengrocer's. I walked down my road, and because my arms were too full to wave at the ever present Mrs Grieg, I just nodded at her. She waved frantically at me, but I just nodded again, motioning to the amount of shopping I was carrying. I promised myself I'd pop in to see her tomorrow.

I let myself into the flat, calling out to Molly. She answered from the kitchen, so I went in there, dumping things down on the table. She was sitting, with her bandaged foot up on a chair finishing off a phone conversation. She looked very pissed off.

She slammed the phone down and said, 'Bastard.'

'Who?'

'Guy. He's wheedled out of taking me to dinner, and I was going to wear your Jasper Conran dress and everything.'

'Molly, where the hell is Mimi? I think that's our priority, not a bloody photographer, who's broken a dinner date with you.'

'She's in the bath.'

'Why? What the hell is she doing in my bath?' I felt very territorial, and didn't like the idea of a complete stranger soaking in my bath.

'Calm down. Jesus H. Christ what is that rock on your finger?'

'OK, OK you tell me what's happened here, then I'll tell you how I got engaged.'

She did a double take. 'Engaged, *engaged*, who to?'

'To whom. And I'll tell you later, just tell me what's been going on here, OK?'

Apparently she had phoned Steve and demanded that he come over straight away to pick up the you-know-what. He had been very reluctant, but in the end he had agreed and had promised to come over at about 11.30. Then she phoned Guy ('big mistake' I interrupted) to see where he was taking her this evening. She hadn't been able to get hold of him, so she'd left a message. She'd finished off the presentation board for Nicola, and then Steve had arrived, with Mimi. He had found her hanging around outside his flat, and he'd brought her with him.

'That doesn't explain why he hasn't taken her back with him, does it?' I said nastily.

'Umm, well, she doesn't really have anywhere to go, and the pistol is hers, it's a family heirloom, apparently. She had an awful lot of trouble getting it through Customs . . . it was her grandmother's. She's frantic to get it back and I didn't know where you'd hidden it,' she finished lamely.

'I am not turning my flat into a bed and breakfast for Russian refugees, let's just give it to her, shall we?' I said, furious.

Just then the kitchen door opened and Mimi walked in, with one of my towels draped around her dripping wet body and long hair trailing down her back. She was absolutely stunning. She looked like she had been crying all day, and even that didn't detract from her beauty. She walked towards me, leaving wet footprints on the floor.

'You to be Leevia? Yes?' she said, rather hesitantly.

'That'll be me,' I said, not knowing really how to react to her. I mean, it's quite hard to be rude to a strange girl, who has just used your bathroom, and is dripping water everywhere. I suddenly found, to my horror, that I was becoming a bit British Nannylike with her.

'I really think you should get dressed, you'll get cold. Would you like some tea?'

I heard Molly stifle a giggle. To my surprise, Mimi sank to her knees, and threw both of her arms round my legs, nearly knocking me off balance.

'You so kind, I not know how to thank. My babushka she geeve me her pistol, ees my 'ow you say? My good luck

130

charm! I must 'ave eet. I sell eet to make photographs! I am to become model! Steven, he say you kind, now I know! But, I must 'ave somewhere safe to keep it, unteel I get house. The immigration must not find it on me . . .'

I dragged her to a standing position. 'Please, go and get dressed, we will talk later, and, um, decide what we are going to do with you. But the pistol. I really don't want it here. We'll have to find somewhere safe for it.' Steve could damn well look after it, I thought. She trailed from the room, throwing a mournful glance at me over her shoulder.

I turned towards Molly. 'How long has she been here? What have you said to her? More to the point, how the hell are we going to get rid of her?'

'All I know is that you and I are "kind" and Steve told her we would look after her. That's about it, really. Maybe we could ask Monty to help her? You know, to become a model?'

'Bloody typical, isn't it? I'll keel Steve, when I get my hands on him. She is *not* staying here. That I do know. Get Steve on his mobile, the little sod, and tell him to get over here and fetch her. As soon as Monty gets here, we'll see what he thinks of her.'

'OK, but now you have to tell me about that ring. Is it real? Can I try it on? Come on, tell.'

I recounted the day's horrors as I made tea. Molly sat open mouthed. 'Oh my God,' she said very slowly, then, 'Oh, poor Pete. This is terrible . . . Do you mean they won't give him a heart transplant because of his HIV? Why won't his parents help him? Are they really awful? Oh Liv, I know you said that he wants us to behave as usual, but I don't think I can . . .'

I handed Molly some kitchen towel, and she wiped the

tears from her face. I knew how she felt, but promised myself I wasn't going to let the side down by joining in.

Then she added, 'Why didn't he ask me? I'd marry him like a shot.'

'You're obviously not suitable marriage material,' I said, trying to lighten the atmosphere. 'Now please call Steve, I have to sit down and have a small nervous breakdown.'

Just as Molly reached for the phone, the intercom buzzed. Mimi came running into the kitchen and threw herself under the table, crying 'Is not immigration? They make me go back! Help me, help me, to help me, pleese to help.' She was wearing, I noticed, an Agent Provocateur matching bra and pants in apricot satin. And nothing else. She might well have nowhere to stay, but she had unreasonably expensive underwear. The British Nanny came to the rescue again.

'Stop that noise, of course it's not them,' I said with far more confidence than I felt. 'Go and get properly dressed, and please stop making that noise.' I stood up and went over to the intercom.

'Hello?'

'Hi, Liv, it's Joe.'

I buzzed him up, making Mimi go into the bathroom to dress. Molly had her head buried in her hands, laughing and crying at the same time.

'What's so bloody funny?'

'Nothing, nothing at all. It's just getting like a Brian Rix farce round here.'

'You can always go home, you know,' I said acidly.

'I wouldn't miss it for the world.'

Molly and I were squabbling like an old married couple. I think we both found it quite comforting, somehow.

Joe breezed in. 'I was just going to the gym, and Mrs Grieg was waving at me, so I went over to see her, and she asked me to . . .' He tailed off, staring slack jawed past my shoulder. Mimi was sauntering out of the bathroom, still only in her underwear. She gave him a smouldering stare, and went into my office, closing the door.

'Who is that?' he asked, dumbstruck.

'Remember vegetable girl?' I said.

'No!'

'Oh, yes.'

'What is she doing here?'

'Don't ask. I mean, really don't ask, because I'm damned if I know.'

He was still staring at the closed office door. If he'd been Clark Kent, I'm sure he would have used his X-ray vision to pierce through the wood.

'Joe, hello, anyone there?' I patted him gently on the arm.

'Oh, right. Anyway she wants you to go and see her.'

'Who does?'

'Mrs Grieg. Will she be staying here long?'

'Who?'

'The vegetable girl.'

'No, no, no. And please put your tongue away. Go and have a healthy workout or something, followed by a long cold shower, OK?'

He left, with the look of a hungry man who has just ordered a steak and had it whipped away from him.

I put my coat back on, and went to tell Molly that I was going over to see Mrs Grieg.

'I shan't be long. Keep trying Steve on his mobile, and peel some potatoes.'

'You're so bossy, no wonder they made you a prefect at school.'

(Molly had never got over the fact that I had been made

a prefect and she hadn't. I had taken great delight in booking
her for running in the corridors.)

Mrs Grieg answered the door looking grave. She was
holding a newspaper, and fixed me with a hard look.

'I've been reading the papers, and watching the news.
Them two women they want to interview, 'oo were wearin'
wigs. It was you two, wasn't it?'

Oh God. It felt like Judgment Day. I took a deep breath
and agreed that, yes it was.

'Why 'ave'nt you stepped forward then? What've you got
to hide?'

I sat down, and looked at her. I thought that I'd better
explain everything, so I told her exactly what had happened.
The last thing I wanted was one of my neighbours
denouncing me as an international terrorist. To my huge
surprise, she started hooting with laughter. She was rocking
backwards and forwards in her rose-splattered chair, cackling
with delight.

'Cor, it beats the telly, it really does. I knew you wouldn't
have done something stupid, not a nice girl like you.'

I was immensely cheered: no one had called me a girl for
years.

'And the Russian tart, she's over there with you now, is
she? You sort it out with the police, love. Sooner the better.
Get rid of that nasty gun first, mind.'

I reflected, rather sourly, that I'd been trying to do that
for some time.

To my surprise, she then said, 'Bring it over 'ere love, I'll
look after it for you. Go on, no one'll think of lookin' over
'ere. I'm just some old woman what's past it, to all of them.
I'll show 'em!'

I tried my best to dissuade her, but she wasn't having it,
so reluctantly I agreed. I suppose she did have a point. It

was probably the safest place to keep Mimi's good luck charm, but why the hell couldn't she find her own safe place, why did we have to do it for her?

My flat was a scene of domesticity when I returned, with Molly drinking tea, her leg still up on a chair, and Mimi, wearing an exceedingly tight little black number and killer stilettos, peeling potatoes. It made an incongruous picture. I asked Molly if she'd got hold of Steve.

'I've left a series of increasingly rude messages on his mobile, but he hasn't called back, yet.'

Mimi stopped peeling potatoes at the mention of Steve's name.

'He must come, no?'

'I think he's come rather a lot, if the amount of condoms we cleared away is any indication,' I muttered.

Molly snorted with laughter. 'Don't remind me, please.'

Mimi continued her self-imposed task of peeling potatoes.

'That girl has a thing about vegetables,' I whispered to Molly. 'How many is she doing? We haven't got the Russian Army coming for dinner, have we?'

'She just wants to help,' Molly whispered back. 'Anyway, just be thankful we don't have any cucumbers in the house.'

'I don't want her to help, I want her to go.'

Mimi turned, at the sound of her name.

'I cook for you, no? Mimi very good cook, all men love my bortsch.'

'I just bet they do,' I said. 'Look, Mimi, we will have to sort something out, you know, you really can't stay here. As soon as I've got hold of Steve. You must go.'

Her eyes filled with tears, and her face crumpled. I have to say I was quite impressed: this girl could turn the waterworks on and off at a moment's notice. What was really annoying was that she didn't go red and blotchy, either. Her nose didn't run, and her eyes didn't go pink and piggy. All in all she looked just as beautiful, crying as she did not. I wondered if it was particular to her, or something deep within the Russian psyche that made suffering seem so attractive to look at. Anyway, beautiful or not, she had to go.

She left the kitchen, holding a tea towel to her face and managing to convey deep grief, and a hint that really, it was all my fault.

'Now look what you've done,' Molly said.

'Don't even go there,' I warned her. 'I am not turning this flat into a refugee camp. I'm going to phone Connie if I can't get hold of Steve on his mobile, and tell her that a friend of Steve's has turned up here. And that I'm sending her over in a cab, to wait for him at their place.'

'You wouldn't.'

'Oh yes, I would.'

Molly was quite right, though, I probably wouldn't. I sighed. I wish that I had more iron in my soul, but in my experience, if you haven't, you just haven't, and there's not much you can do about it. I suppose you could try taking iron pills, or eating more spinach. Or is it watercress?

I went on to tell Molly about Mrs Grieg's extraordinary offer.

'Great idea, take it over there immediately, and then we can phone the police and confess.'

'Confess to what, for God's sake? We were only wearing wigs, we didn't plant the bomb, you know.'

The police had rather been on my mind, too. I decided that if we called them now, at least it would be one less problem to think about. Reluctantly I went into the bedroom and found the pistol, wrapped in a carrier bag, underneath my bed. I called out to Molly that I was taking it over to Mrs Grieg, and that we'd call the police as soon

136

as I returned. At the mention of the word 'police', Mimi was off again.

'No, no I beg, I cook, I clean, but, no police. Mimi good girl, no police, OK?'

'No, not OK,' I said, trying to disentangle myself from her grasp. 'Molly will explain. Police not for you, for me.'

She looked very bewildered, as well she might. So, I called out to Molly again, 'For goodness' sake, explain to her that we're not calling the police for her, will you? She seems to think that she's going to be dragged off to some gulag, or something.'

I set off for Mrs Grieg's, nonchalantly swinging the gun in its Waitrose bag. She took it in with a definite air of the resistance fighter. I wondered if we were ever going to get it back. She clasped it to her bosom, and said, 'You leave it with me, duckie. Now you haven't touched it, have you?'

'Why?'

'Prints, of course.'

'What?'

'Fingerprints. Don't know nothing, do you?'

'Well, we were wearing rubber gloves, at the time, I seem to remember.'

'Just as well. Go on, be off with you. I'll look after it till you can find the Russian tart a home.'

I really wondered where Mrs Grieg got her vocabulary from. Re-runs of *The Sweeney*?

When I returned to the flat, I made the dreaded call to the police. They didn't seem very interested, to be honest, but said they would send a detective over to see us, and would we be in for the rest of the evening?

'Oh, yes. We're not going anywhere,' I said.

Molly became very excited. 'Did they say we couldn't leave town?'

'Don't be so bloody silly, of course not. They just want to talk to us. Anyway, don't forget, we haven't actually done anything – so you can stop carrying on as if we'd robbed a bank. Relax, all we did was to go for a drink there, wearing wigs, OK?'

'OK, OK, keep your hair on.'

'That is not remotely funny. Where's vegetable girl?'

'In the bathroom, either crying or having multiple orgasms, I'm not sure, the sounds are very similar.'

'Oh God, do you think I should go and see if she's OK?'

'I wouldn't if I were you. She'll come out soon, she wants to cook dinner for us.'

The intercom sounded again. That should flush her out, I thought. I went to answer the door, and collided with Mimi, who'd shot out of the bathroom, reeking, I noticed, of my perfume. She clutched me, pleading, 'Is Steven, yes, he come for me, no?'

'Yes. I mean no, I mean I don't know, till I answer it, do I?'

It was Monty, carrying several bags bearing Parisian names.

I introduced Mimi to him, and she tried out the smouldering stare again. It cut no ice with Monty. I gave him a quick rundown on her, and asked if he could help her to become a model.

He stepped back to assess her. 'Very last year's look, darling, try a smile. Unless you've got yellow teeth, of course, but that can be fixed. Can you walk?'

Mimi looked very puzzled.

'Walk, please? Of course I no walk, I not a *paysan* I have own car, Mercedes, but is in Moscow.'

'No, no. I mean *walk*.' Monty gave a passable imitation of a model sashaying down a catwalk. Mimi threw her head back, put one hand languidly on her hip, and sauntered down the hallway, pausing at the end and doing a twirl.

Monty started to look excited. 'You know, Russian is just so *in* at the moment. I could call an agency, I suppose . . .'

Molly and I both sensed a way out of this mess, and turned to Monty hopefully. Mimi was tense with excitement, gazing intently at him.

He turned to me. 'I do always meet the most extraordinary people at your flat. Let me use the phone, I need to call Thunder at Typhoon.'

I was puzzled for a moment, but I quickly realised that he was talking about one of the leading model agencies.

He was soon jabbering away to Thunder (model bookers always give themselves the most ridiculous names, I suppose it stops them suffering from huge inferiority complexes) and had soon arranged a meeting between Mimi and Thunder for the following day. Monty and Mimi were looking delighted with each other, and started chattering away in broken English about catwalks, designers and the best way of flying to New York.

Molly and I were a bit put out, to put it mildly. Molly hissed at me, 'Open the bags up, or she'll snaffle the lot for herself. I didn't realise that we were harbouring the next Kate Moss, did you?'

'No I bloody didn't. Don't you think that her modelling career might be cut short once they find out that she's probably a Russian refugee?'

'No, it'll just add to the mystique, won't it.'

'Damn.'

Molly and I left Monty and Mimi gabbling in the kitchen, and went off to my bedroom to look at the party outfit Monty had bought back from Paris for me. It was divine. A tunic top and wide trousers in pale green silk chiffon with heavy fringing. It had exquisite embroidery of flowers and leaves over the top. The snakeskin mules that he'd snatched from the hands of Naomi were very high, and I was practising walking in them, when the phone went. I teetered over to it. 'Hello?' It was Steve, finally.

'Livia, don't shout at me, I've been trying to find somewhere for her to go to . . . and I bumped into some old mates . . .'

'Are you drunk?' I said suspiciously.

'No. Well, not that you'd notice. Liv, I'm coming over now, OK?'

'Well, I wouldn't if I were you. You were so long in getting back to us, we've given it to someone else to look after.'

Steve groaned.

'And,' I added, 'the police are coming round to talk to us about the wig thing, and Monty is here and is about to make vegetable girl famous.'

'What?'

I explained about Mrs Grieg, and about Thunder.

'Oh shit. Look, don't let Mrs Grieg do anything with it, will you?'

'Like what? Kill the cat? Don't be silly. I really think you're enjoying this, aren't you,' I said accusingly.

'Well, you have to admit, it's quite exciting, isn't it?'

There was a peal of laughter from the kitchen, followed by a rattle of cutlery. Mimi was obviously cooking something. I said goodbye to Steve and Molly and I went to investigate. Mimi had just placed a steaming bowl of potatoes and cabbage on the table and was spooning a rich dark brown savoury mess onto plates. The sausages had been cooked in onions and garlic, with a lot of red wine. It all smelt delicious. I decided to postpone my resentment of Mimi annexing my flat till after I'd eaten. We'd all just taken our first mouthful of food, when the intercom buzzed. I went to answer it. It was the police.

Chapter Eight

Detective Constable Neal Williams was remarkably understanding about the wigs. He did, however, read us the riot act about wasting police time, and not coming forward immediately to eliminate our names from the investigation. Mimi (who'd immediately turned the old smouldering routine on him) seemed a bit disappointed that he wasn't about to interrogate any of us. The fact that he was a policeman seemed to make her a little nervous all the same, and she disappeared into the drawing room, clutching a copy of *Vogue*.

Monty made a lot of fuss over the detective, and saw him out of the flat. Molly and I exchanged meaningful glances.

'Absolutely typical, isn't it?'

'Do you think there are only gay men left in London?'

'No point in asking me, is there? I'm engaged to one.'

I waved my hand at her, and we both looked down at my ring. It glinted most satisfyingly in the light. Monty came back into the room.

'Well, what a gratifying evening. A star is born, and *he* was absolutely charming. Really, Livia, I leave to go to Paris for a few days, and all hell breaks loose. What *have* you been up to?'

'I'll leave Molly to explain everything, I've got to go and see Mrs Grieg so Mimi can have her good luck charm back.'

I put my coat on. It was cold, and I could see frost beginning to form on patches of the road. I looked up at Mrs Grieg's window: it was completely dark, there didn't seem to be any lights on. I stood under the lamp-post, to look at my watch. It was quite late, but she usually stayed up longer than this. I didn't feel comfortable waking her up, and I stood undecided, bathed in the yellow glow of the lamp. It reminded me of the last time that I'd been in Venice, and how the lamps there cast a very flattering violet light. London was a harsh yellow, and Venice a subtle mauve – that made sense, I suppose.

I went back to the flat, to be greeted with screams of laughter. Monty was mopping his eyes with a large silk handkerchief.

'My God, you two really have been through it, haven't you? I haven't laughed so much since Elizabeth Emanuel's last collection. Let's see the ring, then.'

He was suitably impressed.

'It'll look fantastic with your party outfit, won't it?'

'As fantastic as it is, and I really thank you for the clothes, my party outfit, or indeed the party, isn't really uppermost in my mind at the moment,' I said rather despondently.

'Nonsense. Get those heels on, I want to make sure you don't fall over in them. I'll come round early to do your hair, OK? You'll knock them dead. You're just tired, go to bed. Molly and I'll clear up.'

'What about veggie girl?'

'Who? Oh, yes, I see. Well, I'm taking her to meet Thunder first thing, so I suppose she could stay the night with me.'

'Really? Oh God, that would be great.' I suddenly felt hugely relieved.

'But, Monty, how can she be employed by Typhoon? I mean, I bet she hasn't got visas or anything,' said Molly.

'Darling, I always forget what an innocent you really are. Typhoon will sort all that out. It's what they do. I mean, they fairly swoop on young girls in the Serengeti, who don't even have a birth certificate, let alone a visa. Believe me, they'll sort the paperwork out.'

I gave a huge, jaw-cracking yawn.

'Keeping you up, sweetie?' said Monty acidly.

'No, no, sorry. It's been rather a long day . . .'

'I know, I'm only teasing. Let me take Mimi back with me. As you know, I only keep eggs and bread in my fridge, so she'll be quite safe from the demon vegetables. We'll have to think of a name for her, though, Mimi is just too, well too girly. How about Aubergine?'

'Monty, you can't. You might as well call her Carrot, it's not fair,' I protested, though very mildly, I admit.

'Hmm, we'll see, I think Aubergine has a certain *je ne sais quoi* about it. And Liv? Don't worry about Pete, I'm sure he'll be fine. Get him to stop smoking and drinking, and with the right drug combination, he'll be OK.'

We kissed goodbye and went to find Mimi, who was curled up on a sofa, fast asleep. Monty dragged her to her feet, explaining on the way out of the door that she was going to be staying with him. She kissed Molly and me goodbye, begging us to keep her good luck charm safe, and we both heaved a sigh of relief.

'Where's the pistol?' asked Molly.

'Mrs Grieg's asleep, it'll have to wait for the morning. I didn't have the heart to wake her up.'

'Liv, go to bed, you look shattered.'

'OK. I'm not even thinking straight, I'm so tired.'

As I got into bed, I looked down at the emerald on my finger and wondered if Pete was asleep in his flat in Brighton. If I wasn't so exhausted and it wasn't so late, I'd call him. But that, too, would have to wait for the morning. As I was drifting off to sleep, I heard Molly chattering away on the phone and wondered if she was ever going to go home. Perhaps we were destined to spend the rest of our lives in an adults' boarding school. Oh, well, I thought philosophically, at least it keeps me from dwelling on the rat Christopher.

The following morning I was awoken by Molly bringing me a cup of tea in bed.

'My God, this is a surprise,' I said.

'Yeah, well, the bloody phone's been ringing all morning. Pete, Nicola Bentley, Steve and Mr Abraham have all called. I thought I'd better let you lie in for a bit. Do you want some toast or anything?'

'No, I just want another two hours' sleep.' I pulled the duvet over my head, and Molly yanked it down again. She also, rather brutally I thought, pulled the curtains open.

'Molly, stop it. You know I'm horrible in the morning, go away. I'll get up in a minute.'

The phone started to ring again, and Molly limped away to answer it, then called back to me: 'It's Zena, she wants to make sure you arrive early tonight, and what are you going to wear, and have you got business cards?'

'Tell her I'll call her back. Now go away.'

I sipped my tea, listening to Molly potter around the flat. Her foot seemed to be much better now. I decided that I really didn't mind her staying here at all, though she'd have to stop being so bloody perky in the mornings.

Reluctantly I dragged myself out of bed. The usual morning depression settled on me, so I decided to ease myself into the day with a long, hot bath. I took the radio in with me and listened to Jenni Murray segue seamlessly from making jam to ovarian cancer. After half an hour or so, I was soothed enough to tackle the phone calls, so I settled into the office with my second mug of tea, and picked up the phone. I called Pete first: there was no reply from his mobile, so I left a message. Who was going to be next? Zena, I thought. She, of course, was engaged, and even though the anonymous voice told me that the caller knew I was waiting, she didn't get back to me. I tried Steve next. He sounded dreadful.

'What's the matter with you?' I asked.

'Russian flu.'

'Is that a euphemism for something?' I asked cautiously.

'No, I really feel awful . . . I think I must have eaten something funny.'

'And drunk an awful lot of vodka?' I said unsympathetically.

'Bison Grass. I feel like I'm going to die. Also, Connie's not talking to me.'

'Quite a relief, in my books.'

'Stop it. Anyway, I'll come over about one to pick it up, OK? I promise I'll look after it till she's settled somewhere. It's not fair to leave it with Mrs Grieg, is it?'

'No . . .'

'Do you know that Mimi's planning to sell it, to support herself and start a modelling career? I think it's worth a lot of money.'

'Well, I won't be here, I'm seeing a client. But I'll go and get it, and leave it with Molly. Has she told you that Mimi is going to be the next Slav Supermodel?'

'Yeah, I sort of remember something about it when she called last night. How's Pete?'

I filled him on yesterday's débâcle. We gossiped for a little while longer, and Steve angled for an invitation to Zena's party tonight.

'I thought you felt so awful, you were about to die?'

'Oh, go on. What time should I get there? I need somewhere to hide from Connie at the moment.'

I told him and we hung up. I then spoke to Mr Abraham, who wanted to know if I had time to go shopping with him for some new clothes, for his housewarming party. Was everybody going party mad? It certainly felt like it: I could hear Molly rootling through my wardrobe, looking for something to wear tonight. Perhaps she could go shopping with Mr Abraham? He sounded rather pleased with the idea, but wanted to know if she was experienced.

'She has been my assistant for many years,' I lied through my teeth. 'And prior to that, she was fashion editor on the *Jewish Chronicle*.' That clinched it: he agreed to be picked up by her at three.

I broke the news to Molly that she was now a personal shopper to Mr Abraham, and warned her not to take him to Harrods.

'Where shall I take him, then?' she wailed.

'Oh, walk him down Jermyn Street. That should do it, and for heaven's sake, control his urge to buy beige.'

I called Doug on his mobile, and found him incandescent with joy.

'A wee baby girl, she's an angel, seven and a half pounds!'

'How's Maggie?'

'Very tired, and very happy.'

'Take as long as you need, Doug, everything's going well,

and I'll pop in on Roger on my way back from my meeting this morning. Give them both a kiss from me, won't you?'

Molly was making sick noises: she did this traditionally at any sign or mention of the newborn. I think she'd been doing it for so long that it had become a reflex.

It was quite a cold morning, and I was dressing for my big, nerve-wrenching first meeting with Nicola Bentley, A-list babe and mega-watt rock wife. What to wear? I put on layers of woollens, in various clashing shades of red. I've found that colours do improve my morale, and although the majority of my wardrobe is black, I do occasionally try to add some colour. 'Is this OK?' I asked Molly, giving her a twirl.

'Well, if you're going to have champagne with a rock star's wife, I think it's very suitable.' Molly poked her tongue out at me, and then smiled.

She knew how important this meeting was to me. I'd checked my bank balance this morning and was horrified, I simply *had* to get this job. But I knew that if I started to look (or sound) desperate I wouldn't. Hence the bright colours, and a great show of far more confidence than I felt.

I grabbed the presentation board that Molly and I had compiled for Nicola, along with some samples of flooring, and a sheaf of papers with quotes on, and propped them by the front door, ready to take out with me. I had to pass the picture that Zena had dumped on us every time I walked into the hallway. God knows what I was going to do with it, it was really hideous. I grabbed my coat, and ran over to Mrs Grieg's. To my surprise, she wasn't sitting at her window, but I rang the doorbell anyway. There was no reply, she must have gone shopping. I'd have to catch her later, after I'd come back from seeing Nicola and Mr Abraham's flat. I went back home, and picked up the stuff for Nicola. Molly had to give me a hand with it, as we'd managed to compile rather a formidable amount of files and boards for her. We struggled down to the road with them, and hailed a cab.

'Don't let Mr Abraham buy anything with even a remote shade of brown to it, OK?' I said to her.

'Yeah, all right. Good luck with Nicola. Be back early, we'll have to spend ages tarting up in the bathroom, getting ready for tonight, and you know Monty's coming over early to transform us from the Ugly Sisters.'

'You *shall* go to the ball, Cinders. Don't worry, I'll be back on time. Keep an eye on Mrs Grieg's window, won't you? She must be out buying up roses, or something. Bye.'

The taxi dropped me outside Nicola's house. There was a handful of reporters hanging around outside, no doubt hoping to get an exclusive shot of the grieving, dumped wife. I pushed my way through them, and spoke into the security camera and microphone mounted in the wall. The large gates swung open, and I crunched my way up the gravel to the massive, oak, nail-studded front door. I was feeling rather nervous, and took deep breaths to try and calm myself. I was anxious about being here. I mean, it's not every day I walk into a rock star's home. The garden that surrounded the house looked very forlorn on this early spring morning; just a few daffodil shoots out, and a tiny clump of snowdrops under a tree. I caught a whiff of bonfire smoke; it was a smell that instantly took me back to autumn days spent with my mother, in her rambling garden in Cornwall. There was a broken, framed glass award, that had obviously been hurled from a window, lying on the gravel. As I stepped over it, I saw the words *'one million copies sold in the UK of Satanic Girl'*. I remembered whirling around madly to that lovely little number, when I was about fifteen, in a local dance club. And at fifteen, I had thought that the leather-clad lead singer was a sex god. Unfortunately, the sex god hadn't changed with the passing years, and had become something of an embarrassment. At least, an embarrassment to his wife. However, there still seemed to be an endless supply of überbabes, who were willing to jump into the arms (and, presumably, the bed) of an ageing sex god.

A butler opened the front door to me, just as I had raised my hand to the massive iron door knocker (shaped, I'm sad to tell you, as a contorted naked woman). He had on a formal suit and a leather tie, but was sporting a rather greasy long ponytail. Very rock 'n' roll.

He escorted me into the library, where Nicola was on the phone, crouching in front of a sulky log fire. The tabloid papers were spread out on the floor in front of her. I looked around the room, studying the books. Suddenly it dawned on me that they weren't real books at all. They all were bound in the same claret red leather, and on closer inspection, all had titles like *Chained To Me* and *Bonds of Lust*. I had to strongly resist the urge to pull one out and open it.

'Livia, hello. Thank you for coming at such short notice.' Nicola stood up, replacing the phone. She had followed my eyes, and gave a flat, humourless chuckle. 'Awful, aren't they? They'll have to go. He thought they were funny; they give me the creeps'.

She had on a shapeless black jumper. She was hugging herself, and had the flat, blank eyes of a woman in pain. She asked me if the reporters were still outside. I nodded.

'God, what can I do? The bloody vultures just won't go away, I can't face them, I just can't. All of this – ' she said her arms sweeping the room – 'reminds me of that bastard, you've got to help me.' Her voice was rising, and although she was clearly fighting to control herself, I could tell that tears were not too far away. My heart sank. I'd had clients like this before: they thought that they'd employed you to change the kitchen, and what they really wanted was for you to change their lives. I sighed inwardly, then felt mean. I did like her, but I wasn't sure I was equipped to deal with this.

I put down my bags and board, and walked purposely towards what I imagined to be a drinks cabinet (it was one of those huge reproduction globes) that opened up to reveal every spirit known to mankind. I made us both a stiff Bloody Mary, and as I handed it to her I said, 'Look, Nicola, they're not going to go away till they get something. I suggest that we drink these, we go upstairs, slap some make-up on you, put you in something stunning and go and give the vultures a photograph and a quote. You know, something dignified and yet upbeat, something like *I'm too busy to talk at the moment, I'm planning some renovation inside my house, and then I'm flying to Italy to start work on my book.* OK? Trust me, they'll go away then, and you'll be left in peace.'

She looked at me uncertainly. 'That's not a bad idea. Will you come out with me, though? I can't face them by myself.'

I hesitated. This was a bit more than interior decoration. But she looked so miserable that I couldn't say no.

'OK, come on, let's go and make you look like you've just come back from Paris with a brand new lover,' I joked.

'Huh, I look like I've been lying on the couch for a week crying and eating chocolate.'

'Well, we've got our work cut out for us, haven't we?' I teased her, draining my drink and following her out of the room.

I felt very presumptuous ordering around Nicola Bentley, but she really was a slightly pathetic sight. She was obviously in a great deal of pain, and wanted a friendly ear to pour her troubles into. And I just happened to be here.

We crossed the hallway, which was full of framed gold

records hanging on the walls, and photographs of Nicola and the ex, in various stadiums around the world with other famous rock stars. The faces peered down at us as we climbed the stairs; we passed Mick Jagger, Elton John and Alice Cooper on the landing, and headed off to the master bedroom.

Nicola started to repair her face at her dressing table (which was fashioned to look like an Egyptian tomb, in black lacquer and mirror) and I pulled out some clothes from her smoked mirrored wardrobe. Most of the clothes were very rock chick, but I did find an Armani trouser suit, and a cream cashmere jumper (that I made her wear back to front, as it was so low cut) which I thought would fit the bill. Nicola was applying layers of mascara, when she said, 'It's not a bad idea, you know, writing a book. The things I could tell you . . . You have no idea.'

'I can imagine,' I said drily.

'No, really. I've always kept a diary, you see, it gave me something to do when we were on tour . . . Maybe I could write it up, that would show everyone, wouldn't it?'

I made affirmative noises, whilst all the time I had to keep pinching myself. It was so bizarre. Here I was sitting in Nicola Bentley's bedroom, choosing clothes for her. It seemed so unreal, and yet I had lost all nervousness with her, she seemed so normal – not like a rock star's wife at all. But then, what would I know? I hardly hang out with Jerry and Meg and Patsy on a regular basis, do I? Perhaps the very rich aren't so different from us, after all.

'What do you think of this colour lipstick?' Nicola asked uncertainly.

'Maybe a bit too dark.' I rummaged through my handbag. 'Here, try this one.'

I stopped her from pinning a large diamond pin featuring

a leaping tiger on to the lapel of her trouser suit, and briefed her on what she was to say. I promised her that I would give her five minutes with the reporters, and then come and rescue her. She looked apprehensive. 'Those bastards'll twist anything I say to them, you know.'

'I know. That's why you're not going to answer any questions, just say about the house, about writing the book, give them a smiley photo and walk back in, OK?'

'Yeah, OK.'

We walked down the stairs together, and after she'd taken a few deep breaths I pushed her out of the front door. I followed behind her, and as the gates swung open, the clicking of the cameras started.

'Nicola, Nicola, look this way, love.'

'What about the paternity suit, then?'

'Any chance of a reconciliation?'

'Nicky, how do you feel about the age gap between your husband and his new girlfriend?'

'Nicola, any chance of you taking your jacket off, love?'

'When did you last speak to him?'

Nicola kept her composure, smiled for the cameras, and spouted the words that we'd rehearsed. I gave her a couple of minutes, and then walked forwards and muttered in her ear, 'Well done, that's enough, let's go.'

'What's the book going to be called, then?'

'Who's publishing it?'

'Who's writing it?'

We turned to walk away. Nicola put a shaky arm through mine, and leaned her head on my shoulder. One of the reporters shouted, 'Who's your friend, Nicola?' She turned towards him and shouted, 'Just a friend, for God's sake, now piss off, all of you.'

The gates closed behind us, and we walked towards the door.

'I shouldn't have said that, should I?' she said.

'I'm sure it'll be OK,' I said doubtfully. The butler was holding the door open for us, and Nicola slammed it shut once we were inside.

'God, I hate them, but you were right, thanks, Liv. They've got what they wanted, haven't they? They'll go now, surely.'

I hoped she was right.

We went back into the library and I started to explain to her the concept I'd had for her house. She became quite animated, and asked how long it would all take. I hedged my answer: so many things have to be taken into consideration, and working to a deadline when you are doing structural work can be very hard. I explained that a lot of time would be taken up with surveys and planning permissions, and that this would be out of my control. I hesitated, then tentatively said, 'Do you really think you might like me to do it? Because if you do, I can start planning everything . . .'

'Yeah. Yes, I'd love you to do it. All the other people I've seen have treated me like a freak . . . You're the only person that I've been able to talk to properly.'

I was delighted (and relieved) and stammered out my thanks. I asked her if she intended to remain on site, as there would be huge upheavals, and probably no hot water or heating for days on end. She smiled. 'No, I think I'm going to be somewhere warm, writing my book.'

'You're really going to do it? Great,' I said. I hoped I sounded convincing. I didn't think that Nicola had written anything but her signature on a credit card slip for years.

'Oh, yes, I'm going to do it,' she said grimly. 'You don't think I can, do you? But I will, I'm going to tell it exactly like it was. I knew that diary would come in bloody handy one day.'

I blushed, and stammered, 'It's not that I think you can't do it, it's just, well, you might not feel up to it, might you? I mean if you and he do get back together . . .'

'Never. It's over, finished, finito. He's welcome to his under-age bimbos. Let them prop up his ego, and clear up his disgusting mess . . . I've had it.'

She looked very determined. Then her eyes filled with tears, which she angrily brushed away. I thought of all the women (including myself) who had been left in this position. You sink or swim. You get stronger and learn to laugh again, or you become bitter and sad. I looked again at her, and saw the strong set of her jaw, and the steel in her eyes. She'll make it through OK, I thought. On an impulse, I asked her what she was doing tonight.

'Absolutely bloody nothing. None of my friends want to see me, they've all dumped me, too.'

I explained about Zena's party, and impulsively asked her if she'd like to come. She looked astonished and, to my surprise, genuinely touched.

'I'd love to. And I tell you what,' she added with a smile, 'we'll go in style. I'll pick you all up in the Cadillac.'

'Monty and Molly will be dead chuffed. Are you sure you want to come, though?'

'God, yes. I don't think I could stand another night here alone in this mausoleum.'

'What about the butler? Does he live in?' I knew I was being nosy, but I couldn't help it.

'Hmm, well, he lives with his wife in the flat over the garage. I don't like either of them. They'd sell any story to the papers, but I pay them too well.'

I looked at my watch: I'd have to leave soon, if I wanted

to stop at Mr Abraham's flat on the way home. I explained to Nicola that I had another client to see, and that I'd see her tonight. She gave me an affectionate kiss goodbye, and we parted at her front door.

'What's the butler's name?' I asked.

'Rick.'

'Well, why don't you get Rick to dismantle this?' I motioned to the naked iron lady writhing on the front door. 'Get a dolphin, or something. Anything, in fact, other than this monstrosity.'

She grinned at me. 'Good idea, it's horrible, isn't it? Dave Lee Roth gave it to us one Christmas. Consider it gone.'

The gates swung open again for me. I was relieved to see that the reporters had gone and felt very pleased with myself that it had gone well (considering what a potential disaster it could have been).

I walked down the road and pulled my mobile out to check my messages. To my horror there was one from Suzanne Aston, inviting me to Brighton for the weekend. Molly had called, too, saying that Mrs Grieg still wasn't home, and that Steve was pacing the flat waiting for her. Pete had left a brief message, sounding a bit sheepish, saying that he hoped to feel well enough to go to Zena's party tonight. There was also a message from John, leaving his number. On impulse, I called him back.

'Hello, this makes a pleasant change, you calling me . . . I thought I'd call to see how you were, I've been worried about you . . . I know that sounds strange, as we don't even know each other . . .'

I thanked him, and decided that he had a very nice voice. We talked for a few minutes and then I hung up, after telling him I would give serious consideration to his offer of a drink. I pulled my coat around me and put my gloves on; it was getting very cold, but the sky was blue, and a pale sun was shining on this extremely grand part of London.

Most of the houses were set behind very high walls, but you could catch a glimpse of latticed windows or white façades as you passed by. I decided to walk through the park to Mr Abraham's.

Regent's Park was emptier than I'd seen it for a long time. I skirted around the outer path, and headed towards Chester Terrace, my breath forming icy clouds in front of my face as I walked. A few buds were out on the trees, but the grass looked hard and muddy. Diehard joggers and dedicated dog walkers were the only people to be seen.

I crossed the busy road and bought myself a cup of take-away tea before heading to Mr Abraham's flat. I'd tell the boys there about Doug's baby, and we'd send flowers and a card. I banged on the door, swearing under my breath that I'd been so stupid as to leave the keys behind. I could hear the cheerful sound of pop music coming from the flat, and the boys calling to each other to answer the door. Young Roger was eventually dispatched for the job, and the door swung open.

Very proudly he escorted me around. Everything had arrived, and was standing around in huge boxes ready to be unpacked. The electricians and plumbers had gone, and the boys were making good, ready to start painting.

'I thought you'd started the paint job?' I said.

'Only the undercoat. Don't worry – we're on top of it all. It'll be ready,' he said.

'It's got to be, we're having a housewarming in here next week. You all know about Doug? Good, well, he's going to be off for quite a bit longer, so it's all up to you, Roger. As it's Friday, I suppose you're all off early? Yeah, I thought so.

I want you all here early on Monday, the paint's got to be finished by Tuesday, the party's on Wednesday, OK?'

There were murmurs of agreement. I checked off all the furniture, and went into every room. It all looked fine, I was just a bit worried because Doug wasn't there. The large cans of paint Roger had collected from me were stacked up against the wall, ready to use.

'I want this lot up on the walls, on Monday, OK? Anything that needs another coat, you've got Tuesday, but no longer.'

'OK, OK. Blimey, we have painted before, you know.'

'Yeah, you're all regular Michelangelos, aren't you?' I smiled and waved them goodbye, and Roger plucked up the courage to wish me a good weekend.

I walked to the tube station and caught the train to Warwick Avenue. It was a relief to get into the warm, I felt absolutely frozen, and when the tube arrived I sat down, rubbing my hands together for warmth. I ventured back out into the cold at the other end, waved at Bert, the flower seller, and went straight to Mrs Grieg's. She wasn't at her window seat, and there was no reply again when I knocked on her door. I walked back to the flower stall and asked Bert if he'd seen her today.

He looked thoughtful. 'Can't say that I have, love. But it's a bit parky, isn't it? She's probably tucked up in bed.'

I didn't think so. I was worried. She loved her window seat, and she certainly wouldn't have gone to bed this early, no matter how cold it was. I went round to Joe's, and I told him that I was concerned about her.

'What do you want to do? Call the police or ambulance, or something?'

'No, no, not the police. I don't know, really, maybe social services? Do you think we could get in there?'

'You mean break in?'

'Yes. I mean, Joe, she's always there. Something's not right.'

He looked at my anxious face, and agreed. He took a ladder from the basement and we ran across the road. I held the bottom of the ladder, steadying it as Joe climbed up.

'Can you see anything?' I called up to him.

'No. She's not in this room, that's for sure. Hang on, I'm going to see if this window will open.'

He was wriggling and banging gently on the sash. I heard him pushing the window open, and then Joe eased himself head first into her room. Within seconds he'd run down the stairs and opened the front door to me.

The first thing I noticed was how cold it was inside. Apprehensively I pushed open the doors, one by one, calling her name. I think I was expecting to see Mrs Grieg's body slumped on the floor. We ran from room to room, but there was no sign of her. Her bed was undisturbed, the kettle was cold, and the real roses in the vases were shedding petals everywhere. Some post was lying on the floor in the hallway, with a pint of milk standing sentry.

I bit my lip with worry. Where the hell was she? I sent Joe over to my flat to fetch Steve and Molly, while I poked round looking for clues to where she might have gone, as well as looking for the gun. Again I went into her bedroom, and slowly opened her wardrobe. That's where I'd put the pistol; maybe she had, too. I noticed that her rather shabby fur coat was missing and felt slightly relieved. Hopefully it meant that she hadn't been abducted. I heard Steve and Joe downstairs.

'I'm up here,' I called.

They pounded up the stairs, and we all searched the flat again. Steve and I looked at each other in dismay: what the hell were we going to do?

'OK, let's take a room each, and look everywhere, the

bloody thing must be here somewhere. Her coat's gone, so has her handbag,' I announced.

'Shouldn't we call the police?' asked Joe.

'No,' Steve and I said in unison.

'Look, for all we know she's gone to visit a friend, or something. We just need to find the – well – the you-know-what, OK?' I said, panic making my voice sound reedy.

Joe went to the drawing room, Steve went to the kitchen and I stayed in the bedroom, looking in every drawer and cupboard. I dropped to my knees, to look under the bed. Again, that's where I'd once put it. The floor was dusty and there were signs that a box, or maybe a suitcase, had been dragged from under the bed. Nothing there. We searched the flat again but found nothing. God, what were we going to tell Mimi? We looked at one another in dismay, and slowly walked outside.

'Where's Molly?' I asked.

'She was in the bath, I couldn't make her hear me,' Joe said. 'Where do you think Mrs G has got to?'

'I really don't know. I don't even know if she's got any relatives, do you? Maybe we're being overly worried, maybe she's just gone away for a few days.'

'I think we should call someone.' Joe sounded worried. I was too, but I really didn't want the police involved.

'OK, well, why don't we call the police if she's not back by tomorrow?'

Joe agreed. I thanked him profusely for his help, and he blushed with pleasure.

'Hey, what's the BND for, if not to scale walls?'

'How do you know we call you the BND?' I said.

'Molly told me. She's also invited me to Zena's party tonight. Is that OK with you?'

'Why not,' I laughed. 'The more the merrier. I warn

you now, though, it's going to be hell. I'm meant to be plying my wares, in more ways than one, so don't expect it to be a laugh. It's going to be full of horrible media types and new money. You have to go round telling people how wonderful I am, OK?'

'It's a deal.'

Chapter Nine

Molly was singing blithely in the bathroom, enveloped in clouds of steam, plucking her eyebrows. She seemed rather put out that she'd missed the brouhaha at Mrs Grieg's.

'Joe and Steve did bang on the door, but I was dealing with the bushy bunny look that I seem to be developing at the moment. Ouch, that hurt!' she said, tweezing another hair.

'Stop now, or you'll look permanently surprised,' I advised.

'What, like Denise Van Outen, you mean? You'd better get in the bath, I've left you loads of hot water. Where can Mrs Grieg have gone?'

'I have no idea. I don't like it, though. We'll call social services tomorrow if she's not back. But wherever she's gone she's taken the pistol with her . . . God alone knows what we're going to say to Mimi . . .' I felt horribly responsible.

'Good. At least that's out of our lives,' Molly said cheerily.

'That's a bit brutal, isn't it? She was going to sell it, you know, to support herself.'

'Well, let's just hope she'll be a successful model . . . What time is Monty coming over?'

'Soon, I hope. Oh, and we're being chauffeured to Zena's in a terribly vulgar, large, American car.'

'Whayhey! Things are looking up! Whose?'

I told her all about Nicola.

'Good grief. We are going up in the world, aren't we. Oh God, I don't think I'm ready to meet Nicola Bentley . . . do we have to avoid mentioning her straying husband? He's just a bit of a joke now, isn't he?'

'Hmm, well, probably not to her. I feel very sorry for her. She loved the plans for her house, she wants it done as soon as possible.' I was so grateful for this, I felt like kissing her shoes. Nicola would have no idea how much the contract meant to me.

'That's brilliant! Was it wise though, inviting her? I mean she's probably used to very wild rock 'n' roll stuff, isn't she?'

'Well, it'll be a change for her, won't it? Now get out of the bathroom, I've got to get washed and dressed before Monty waves his magic wand over us.'

I turned on the taps to run a bath, and went into the bedroom to lay out my party clothes. I brushed my hand against the soft fabric and admired the emerald against it. It did look stunning. I hadn't taken the ring off since I'd got it. I'd slept with it on, washed with it on. I was terrified of losing it.

I went back into the bathroom, and sank gratefully into the steaming water. So much had been going on that I hadn't had much time to dwell on the horrors that lay ahead tonight. I knew that anybody else having a party thrown for them by Zena, with the express intent of getting work and/or a new boyfriend, would be better prepared than me. I had no business cards, I'd cancelled my hair appointment (and the roots were beginning to show, in a very chip shop girl way) and I hadn't even spoken to Zena today.

I gave myself a mental 'could do better' comment on my report, and concentrated on what the hell I was going to say to these perfect strangers that Zena had conjured up for me.

I have never perfected the art of business small talk, dreading seeming too pushy. Very often, when asked what it is I do for a living, wild, unbidden occupations spring to my tongue. 'Oh, I'm a police informer' or, 'I look after the reptiles at London Zoo' are two of the more memorably idiotic things that I've said. I resolved to improve myself, starting tonight.

Molly and I were getting dressed in our party clothes when Monty arrived. He, of course, looked fabulous in a Versace suit, and a black silk shirt with long cuffs that flopped over his hands. He had curled his moustache with wax, and had perched a pair of unframed glasses on his nose. A heavy, silver linked bracelet jangled at his wrist.

'Well, dears, let me tell you: Mimi – or should I now say, Babaganoush (it's an aubergine paste, rather appropriate, I thought) – is, as we speak, winging her way to Milan for a crash course in catwalking. She is going to be *sensational*. And I, of course, am taking the credit. Thunder is probably going to buy me a Rolex, which I shall immediately sell, as they are *so* hideous, and then I shall take us all out to dinner at the Ivy. Am I not brilliant?'

'Brilliant, indeed.'

'Now who wants what done first?'

Molly and I sat in the drawing room having our faces painted, and hair backcombed, pulled, tweaked and sprayed by Monty.

'Livia, you have acrylic hair, I swear, do you *ever* condition it?' Monty complained.

'Well, do you know, I do, but it really doesn't seem to make any difference. Ow, that hurt.'

'Beauty comes at a price,' he said sternly, turning his attentions to Molly. He twisted her long, dark hair into a tower on the top of her head, and began teasing out strands, curling them around his finger so that they fell in tendrils around her face. The intercom buzzed and I went to the door. It was Joe.

'Good God!' he said.

'I do hope that is admiration, and not horror, in your voice,' I said.

'Oh, definitely admiration. You look amazing – you all do. I feel distinctly underdressed, should I go and change?' Joe was wearing a white shirt, with a dark jacket.

'Into what? A football strip?' asked Monty.

'No, I do have a suit, but it's, well . . .'

'Don't tell me, let me guess, you bought it from Next three years ago,' said Monty.

'How on earth did you know?'

'One just does, dear. No, I think apart from the danger of you being mistaken for a waiter, you'll do.'

Joe looked immensely relieved. Monty had finished with the two of us, and we twirled in front of the mirror, admiring our reflections.

'Oh God, I'm starting to feel nervous,' I said.

'Me too, I know I'm going to spill something,' moaned Molly.

'Then you can pay for the dry cleaning,' I teased.

'Nonsense.' Monty interrupted. 'Have a drink to calm your nerves. You look fantastic, and don't you forget it. Go and open a bottle of wine, you need the practice, walking in those heels,' he added, giving me an affectionate slap on the behind. He was right, I really did need the practice. The snakeskin mules looked fabulous, but they were dangerously high, and hideously uncomfortable.

We all sat in the drawing room, sipping wine and looking exceedingly glamorous. Molly, in her heightened state of agitation had already managed to ladder her tights, and was changing them in the bathroom, when the buzzer went.

Monty answered the door, calling out to me, 'Someone called Rick?'

'Who? Oh, yes, it's Nicola's butler, he must be driving us. Could you tell him that we're not quite ready yet, and invite Nicola in for a bit?'

'Oh God, you don't mean Nicola Bentley, do you?' said Joe in alarm.

'Relax, she doesn't bite. She's coming with us,' I said.

Nicola walked into the flat, and we all stared open mouthed at her. She was wearing the most repulsive dress I had ever seen in my life. It looked like a *Come Dancing* frock that had been attacked by glue-sniffing punks. It was of Day-Glo cerise net that had been ripped and was now held back together with diamanté safety pins. It plunged to the waist, was slit to the upper thigh and had silver dust sprinkled everywhere. She had on fishnet stockings, and pink and white high-heeled cowboy boots. I could not bring myself to look at Monty, or anyone else, for that matter. Hurriedly I introduced everybody, and made a lot of fuss, pouring her a glass of wine.

'Do something, quick,' I whispered in Monty's ear. 'It's what you do for a living, for God's sake. Help her!'

Monty rolled his eyes at me, and sank dramatically down into a chair. 'In the name of the holy, dead father of fashion, Gianni Versace, I don't think that I can.'

Nicola was chatting to Joe, who was completely tongue-tied. Molly came back from changing her tights, and screamed. Nicola looked startled. I introduced them, and gave Molly a warning glance. I knew that we were in terrible danger of getting the giggles, and busied myself at the other end of the drawing room. Monty stood up, and walked over to Nicola.

'Moschino?' he said, touching her dress, almost recoiling from the feel of it.

'Yes,' said Nicola, uncertainly. 'I wish I hadn't worn it now. It was one of Stan's favourites, but I feel a tad overdressed, looking at all of you. I haven't been out by myself for so long, I didn't really know what to wear . . . Perhaps I shouldn't go . . .' She looked miserably down at herself.

Monty took a deep breath. 'Rubbish. I can sort you out in no time. What size shoe are you? Five or six? OK, not a problem. By the way, is that his real name, Stan? How divine. Follow me, Livia! We shall need you.' He swept her into my bedroom.

I trailed behind them, agog. Monty was brilliant, he never offended people, and here he was, giving a spontaneous make-over to one of the most well known rock wives in the country. In my bedroom. God knows what he was planning to dress her in. Molly was wearing my Jasper Conran dress, and there was very little left in my wardrobe that was remotely party-like.

'Right,' he said, throwing open the wardrobe. 'Where's that long black silk slip I gave you last Christmas? OK, then I need a pair of sheer black tights, we'll deal with shoes later. Oh, and that Chinese kimono I've seen you waft around in?' I scrabbled around in my underwear drawer, trying to find a pair of tights that weren't laddered. Monty had bustled Nicola out of her dress, saying, 'You know, darling, I think it would be too cruel to even give this to Oxfam, let's keep it as a souvenir of past times, shall we? Oh, Livia, we need a bra, or a body, black, of course. Don't worry, I've seen everybody naked. You've got a great figure, let's pop those tights on, shall we? There, once I've done your hair, and Livia has run an iron over that kimono, you'll look perfect. I think we should lose a tiny bit of the jewellery, too.'

In no time at all, he had transformed her. In the drawing room Monty fixed her hair and I ironed the kimono. He made Nicola stand up, then arranged the kimono so that it slipped off her shoulders. He had drawn her hair away from her face, and waxed it smooth to her head. He'd toned down her make-up, and replaced the bright pink lipstick with a soft red. She looked sensational. He pushed her in front of the mirror, saying '*What* an improvement, don't you think?'

We all gabbled our approval. Nicola stared at herself for a long time in the mirror, silently. We held our breath. Then she turned to Monty, with tears in her eyes. 'It doesn't even look like me, I mean, I don't recognise myself. Thank you. Thank you, so much.'

We were all a bit wet eyed now, and even Monty had to clear his throat. 'Not at all, darling, my pleasure. Now, come on, let's go. Livia, you can't be late for your own party.'

We traipsed down to the street, and there, on the kerb, was the biggest pink Cadillac I had ever seen in my life. It had rocket-tail fins, white leather upholstery and smoked windows.

'Bloody hell!' exclaimed Joe. 'I wish the boys at the rugby club could see me now.'

'We could always drive round there,' said Nicola helpfully.

Joe, Molly and Monty piled into the back of the car; Nicola and I sat in the front, next to Rick. Who was, I saw, still wearing the same leather tie. Perhaps Monty could give him a make-over, too. We were all giggling like school-children on a field trip. I glanced up at Mrs Grieg's blank windows. How she would have enjoyed seeing this, I thought.

'Where to?' asked Rick.

I gave him Zena's address in Cheyne Walk. I felt gloriously comfortable in the car, and didn't feel like getting out at all. 'Perhaps we should all go the Casa for a quick drink first?' I suggested. The plan was approved, I think because we all secretly wanted to be driven around London for a bit, in this outrageous car. Nicola opened a vast glove compartment and withdrew a mirror, a razor blade, a gold straw and a wrap. And she proceeded to chop out five huge lines of coke for us all. She snorted her line in one expert sniff and handed the mirror to me. I was placed in a bit of a dilemma.

About ten years ago I had discovered that cocaine had been invented by God, specifically with me in mind. I had used it and abused it, with no dire consequences. That is, none that I could see. It had, of course, burnt a large hole in my bank account (but luckily, not through my nose) and I thought that I was having a great time on it. Sure, I'd had a few sleepless nights, missed a few meetings, lost a few friends, talked utter drivel at three in the morning, slept with a few unsuitable men, but, hey, who doesn't?

Quite a few people, actually. Finally I realised (I know, I know I'm a very slow learner) that when I wasn't taking coke, I wasn't having a good time. Without it, everything seemed flat, dull and very, very boring. Something had gone horribly wrong. What had been the one drug that I had loved (and I don't use that term lightly) had suddenly gone sour on me. So, I had given it up. I hadn't touched it since New Year's Eve well over a year ago, now.

I stared at the sparkly white line in front of me. Then I picked up the straw, held it to my nose, and snorted it, hard. I mean, I'm not perfect, and I was in a Cadillac, going to a party, after all. An instant white rush hit the back of my head, and that sparkle of delight shivered in my brain. I must just go with the flow, I told myself. This is a special evening, I shall just do it tonight, that's all. I won't buy any, I shall just take what is offered to me. It would be churlish, or even downright rude, to refuse, wouldn't it? All of this, of course, went through my head in about a nanosecond.

I turned and leaned towards the back seat, handing the mirror to Molly. She was looking at me in amazement (she'd been the recipient of many a late night phone call from me: did she know that although it was five in the morning, I was spraying my fridge red, and would she like me to come round and do hers, too?) and then, catching my eye, she muttered, 'Oh, well, one can't hurt, can it?' She snorted her line and passed it to Monty. He hardly stopped talking as he did his, and then passed it to Joe.

I could see that Joe was caught in one of those peer pressure moments that are all of our own making. I mean, I don't know about you, but I've never, ever, had any of my friends urging me to take drugs. Or even so much as sniggering, if I've said no. I guess we all just think that they *might*. I wanted to reassure Joe that whatever he wanted to do was OK with all of us, in fact, we wouldn't notice whether he took it or not. I faced towards the front of the car again, to give Joe a bit of privacy and heard him say, 'Oh, not, umm, not for me, thanks awfully.' He sounded very embarrassed.

'Quite right too, Joe. Who knows where it could end? One minute you're having a line of coke, the next thing you know, you've missed training and you're shooting up heroin, begging on the streets of Glasgow.' Monty had an affectionate tone in his voice, as he teased him.

Joe burst out laughing, and hit Monty playfully, calling him 'a daft bugger'.

'Steady, Joe, Monty could interpret that as a pick-up line, you know,' warned Molly.

'Hardly. It takes *much* more than that for me,' drawled Monty.

'Yeah, even I know that I'm not your type,' said Joe.

The streets were packed, and the huge car had to crawl the narrow roads of Soho. We were all delighted to see that people were craning their necks, trying to see who was in this extraordinary car, but as I glanced at Nicola I realised she must be used to all this attention. When we reached the Casa we all poured through the revolving doors and Monty and I signed everyone in. The bar was crowded, but Molly and I spied a small table near the piano. We made a beeline for it, leaving Joe and Monty to go for drinks. We sat down, and Nicola said, 'It's so odd, not being recognised, I think I like it.'

'Oh, they recognise you all right, everybody here is just too damn cool to show it,' I told her.

I looked around the place, all the usual suspects were here. Ben was frantically busy behind the bar, his long white apron blurring with the speed of his movements. I saw Sarah waving to me, and rushed over to greet her. I was very pleased to see her, she was a good friend, but her high-powered job meant we didn't get to spend enough time together.

'Is that who I think it is?' she whispered.

'Mmm, long story. I'm doing her house for her. Great, isn't it?'

'Fantastic. Can I come to the party with you lot? Bloody Angie's here, and you know what she's like.'

I did indeed. A minor PR bitch, who dogged our footsteps. We hardly knew her, but she always seemed to be hanging around.

A few TV presenters were being loud at the bar, and a famous author was pretending to hide behind dark glasses. Monty and Joe came to the table with a tray of vodka and cranberry drinks. Joe was impressed: this was his first time at the Casa, and he was positively drooling at the talent here.

Molly, Nicola, Sarah and I went to powder our noses (literally) in the Ladies, which provides chest-high tiled ledges in every loo, that are terribly convenient to sniff coke from. (One evening, Kath, the manager, was in a vicious mood and sprayed all the ledges with spraymount. You could hear the squeals of dismay from upstairs, as all the women found that their precious white powder had stuck irretrievably to the ledges.) Two women were brushing their hair in front of the mirror. One of them was Angie. She was one of those rich, svelte, brunettes who just dabbles at their job and seems to resent any woman who has to work for a living. We nodded hello, and she said, 'Livia, how nice to see you. You're looking very glam tonight, off somewhere nice?'

'Thanks. Yes, we've only stopped for a quick drink, we're going to a party.'

'Oh? Anyone I know? They must have forgotten to invite me.'

'Umm, well it's at Zena's.'

'Zena! But she and I are awfully close, I'll just give her a quick call, there must be a mistake, surely? I mean, she must have mislaid my number or something.' She leaned forward and put her hand on my arm, lowering her voice and saying, 'I do think it's frightfully brave of you, going to a party on your own. I heard that you and Christopher broke up, and he's gone back to his wife. Well, inevitable wasn't it, really? It takes quite a lot to hold on to a man like Christopher. Champagne, one could say, instead of *vin ordinaire*.'

'Not at all,' I said, flashing my emerald at her. 'I've just got engaged.' What a cow. I watched her eyes widen, as she looked at my ring. Nicola emerged from a loo, discreetly wiping her nose.

'There's a really terrible smell down here, Livia, I think it's jealousy. Come on, we've a party to go to.'

Molly burst from her loo with a ball of tissue clamped to her nose, and said furiously, 'Champagne gives me nothing but an instant freeze-dried headache, a bit like listening to you. And don't bother calling Zena, you're not invited. So there.'

We swept upstairs, giggling. Nicola said, with surprise, 'I *am* enjoying myself. This is fun, isn't it?'

We collected Monty and Joe, and in that garbled, coke-fuelled way, told them about our encounter in the Ladies.

'Molly, did you *really* say, "so there"?' asked Monty.

'Yes.'

'Very grown up and sophisticated, darling.'

We piled back into the car, Rick pulled the monster away from the kerb, and we started off towards the river. It was amazing what just two lines of cocaine can do, I wasn't even feeling slightly nervous now, just filled with a pleasant anticipation and an inflated idea of how funny and charming I could be.

Zena has to have one of the most beautiful houses in London. It's on the bend of the river and has a Trafalgar balcony and an exquisite garden. The rooms are lined in silver-leaf backed glass which creates a wonderful shimmer. The floors are a beautiful old elm parquet and there are Syrie Maugham type long cream sofas dotted in the double reception rooms. It is a perfect party house.

When we drew up outside, I could see that even for Zena, she'd pushed the boat out. Two doormen stood at the gateway, armed with a guest list each and walkie-talkies. The path to the front door was lined with flaming torches, and white fairy lights climbed the trees.

Zena greeted us at the door saying, 'You all look fabulous, and you're nice and early, too. Come in and have a drink, Livia, there's a woman I want you to meet.' She embraced us and we were treated to a waft of her perfume (I can never find out what it is, she probably has it made for her, and it smells gorgeous, a mixture of jasmine, honey, leather and roses with a hint of something sharp and green). Zena pulled me gently into another room, and stood back to admire my outfit.

'But darling, you look wonderful, Monty *is* a star, isn't he? Are those shoes impossible to walk in? Don't answer that, I know they must be. Now then, I had some cards made up for you, *tell* me, if you hate them, won't you? It's just that they are *so* important, especially for the Japanese.'

She handed me a card.

Olivia Hunter
0441 223112
Interior Design And
Transformation

By Appointment Only

I was astonished, and stammered out my thanks, then added, 'Japanese? What do you mean, Zena? We're not going to Japan, are we?' (In my addled state, anything seemed possible.)

She gave a husky chuckle, 'No, of *course* we're not, but they do so love cards, you know. Now have a drink.' She waved her hand and almost by magic a boy carrying a tray of what looked like lethal vodka martinis appeared at my elbow. 'And follow me, we have some serious introductions to do.'

Zena led me into the main room, which was thronged with people, chattering their heads off. I followed meekly in her wake. She was wearing a long cream bugle-beaded dress, that had been made in the thirties. It glistened against the shimmering walls, and I trailed along wondering how she managed to look so consistently beautiful. I was in awe of the effort that she'd made for me, it was amazingly kind and generous of her. But then, she was amazingly kind and generous.

She halted in front of a small woman with short dark hair, and introduced us. The woman's name was Frankie, and she was a TV producer who made programmes mainly for the Japanese.

'They think we're funny,' she explained, shaking my hand, 'and eccentric. Which of course, in comparison to the Japanese, we are.'

Zena had wandered away, whispering to me, 'I'll come and get you in five minutes, darling. Tell her about the TV thing.'

I had no idea what Zena was referring to. What TV thing? I started to get worried – had two lines of coke given me amnesia? There *was* no TV thing. Gradually it dawned on me that Steve and I had joked about the awful interior design programmes on TV, and I had jokingly told Zena about 'Through the Cat Flap'. She couldn't possibly mean that. Could she? She must do, I decided.

I gave a somewhat truncated version to Frankie. To my utter surprise, she took what I was saying to her seriously.

'You know, that's a very good idea. The Japanese are convinced that the English are mad about their pets. We could get a few well known faces on, you could do a kennel one week, a stable the next. Hmm, let me work on it. Do you have a card?'

Zena glided up to us. 'Darlings, I hate to break you up, but Lord Abbingdon wants to meet you, and he has to catch a plane soon.' I let myself be wafted away by Zena. I hissed at her, 'Who is Lord Abbingdon, and why does he want to meet me?'

'Oh darling, you know Freddy, he was here when we all played that silly card game in the summer, and he sulked when he didn't win, remember? Anyway, he's just got divorced, and he wants to entice his new girlfriend down to his *ghastly* country pile, and I've told him that he simply must change his bedroom. It's such a passion killer, and he doesn't have a *clue.*'

We passed a group of friends that Monty and Molly had been assimilated into, but Zena would not let me stop.

'You can have a break *after* you've spoken to Freddy, darling.'

She placed a hand on the velvet jacket of a rather dissipated looking middle-aged man.

'Freddy, you remember Livia, I'm sure. She's *perfect* for your bedroom.'

'I'm sure she is,' he said, smiling down at me.

I was starting to enjoy myself. Perhaps parties were easier than I remembered. I asked him about his house, and we were off. I heard all about the drain problem, the dry rot, the wet rot, the lead roof, and the flying buttresses. The master bedroom hadn't been decorated since the 1950s, and it sounded truly vile. I spouted a lot of nonsense about 'architectural rhythm' and 'integrity of values'. Freddy looked rather impressed.

'Do you have a pen? I must write down your telephone number,' he said. I handed him a card, with a flourish.

'Perhaps, you could come down for a few days, look round the place, give me some ideas?'

'Perhaps I could.'

'Zena tells me that you told Viscount Linley exactly what to do with his problem wing?'

I didn't bat an eyelid. 'Yes, indeed.'

Zena walked up to us, and after promising Freddy that she would return me to him, we waltzed off.

'Who next?' I said gaily, giving Zena's arm an affectionate squeeze.

'Well, there's quite a few on the work front, darling. And one or two on the romance side, as well.'

'Forget the romance bit. Didn't you know? I'm engaged.' I waved the emerald under her nose.

'So I'd heard. Pete has just arrived. Tell me, do you get to keep that *divine* emerald?' I looked at her, trying to judge if she knew about Pete's illness. It was hard to tell with Zena, so I decided to play it down.

'Shouldn't think so. He is a sweetie though, isn't he?'

'Yes. He is. One of life's treats. It's so sad, though. Don't get too involved, Livia, will you?'

I realised that this was a woman who had never been too involved with anyone, in her life. For all her beauty, and wealth, and kindness, Zena had never been entangled in a human way, with anybody. It would be impossible for her to understand my feelings for Pete: that he was a good friend, and that I loved him. I didn't think Zena really loved anybody. She was fond of people, and she managed her friends with affection and generosity, but not love.

We were approaching a formidable group of oddly dressed

men and women. They all wore heavy glasses and were dressed in uncompromising black Japanese clothes.

'Now, these sweet people are all from that wonderful journal *Paste*,' said Zena, feeding me to the wolves.

I gave what I hoped was an inaudible groan. *Paste* was a style bible, it came out quarterly, and sold for about £50 a copy. It was on students' reading lists, and was the most pretentious crap you've ever read. It mistook stippling for a social statement, and it had articles, written by academics, on the significance of plasterwork.

They were staring unsmilingly at me. I took a deep breath, and started to talk. 'In today's wintry, economic climate, I think that cutting edge realism is the key to any design function . . .' They started to nod, and I knew I had them. The editor of *Paste* asked for my card, and handed me his. It was made of acetate, with his name and e-mail address etched into it. It was like trying to read braille.

I was then led off to meet an American psychologist called Aric. I had absolutely no idea why, but I assumed that he was either a potential client, or Zena had lined him up as one of my romance interests. The roar of well over a hundred people shouting was now so great, and the vodka martinis so liberal, that it was hard to hear what he was saying. We mouthed inanities at each other, and swapped cards.

The waiters were handing round hot titbits of food. Baby new potatoes with daubs of sour cream and caviare were being devoured by the crowd. Even looking at them made me feel slightly nauseous.

Molly, Nicola and Sarah swooped down on me, grabbed me by the wrist and pulled me towards the stairs.

'Bathroom, now,' hissed Molly.

I led the way upstairs, passing the overflow of people who were now perched on the wide elegant staircase with glasses in their hand. One woman was stroking the hair of the man sitting in front of her, and he was saying, '*Gestalt* or Jungian? Now that is a question.'

We ploughed in to a bathroom, threw ourselves inside and locked the door. Nicola immediately set about chopping out more coke, while Molly took the opportunity to repair her make-up.

'You've been busy,' she said, putting on lipstick.

'I've swapped cards with the best of them,' I said, proudly.

Sarah was gazing at Nicola, till I swiftly kicked her on the ankle.

'Ouch . . . sorry, I'm just not used to doing recreational drugs with a star,' she said. We giggled. Nicola, I was relieved to see, was taking it all in her stride.

Oh, well, I thought, sniffing, I might as well be hung for a sheep as a lamb.

Nicola was sitting on the edge of a huge marble bathtub. It was in the centre of the room, and had lion claw feet; an authentic green stain of limescale dripped down from where the large brass taps were.

'Is that what you'd call old money?' she said, pointing to the stain.

'Yes, if you mean that the *nouveau riche* would have immediately re-enamelled the bath,' I replied.

'I've never minded being called that. It's the *riche* bit that's important, anyway.'

We all cackled with laughter. 'So, Nicola, are you enjoying yourself?' asked Molly.

'It's kind of strange, you know? I mean, nobody knows who I am, they just keep asking what I do. People don't usually ask me that. They know I don't do anything, I've spent my adult life being Mrs Rock Star.'

'What have you been saying to them?' I was curious.

Maybe she too made up peculiar occupations, in times of stress.

'Oh, I've told them I'm writing a book. That shuts them up.'

There was a banging on the door, and I heard Pete's voice saying, 'Is my betrothed in there? I think she is, in which case I demand that this door be opened immediately so that I can ravish her.'

I opened the door, and Pete and Steve fell into the bathroom. I introduced Nicola to them. They tried to behave as though meeting such a famous celebrity in a bathroom happened to them every day of the week.

Steve started to chop some coke. I thought about telling him that we'd just had some, but the thought passed very quickly. That's another problem with the damn stuff, it makes you so greedy. Everybody was soon gabbling away.

'Come on, let's go back to the fray, we can't start our own private bathroom party, it looks rude,' I said.

'Yes, you're right. And you've got to put in a good word for me with Zena, OK?' said Steve.

'What about Connie?' I said nastily. 'Or Mimi, or Babaganoush, or whatever the hell she's called now.'

Steve laughed. 'Connie's at home, creating new textile designs.'

'Yeah, gingham is very hard to do, isn't it? Measuring out all those little squares can be very taxing,' I said, unlocking the door and leading the way downstairs.

The party had swelled to huge proportions and Zena was controlling it all. She looked perfectly at ease, and was obviously enjoying herself. She collared me again, and I had another round of introductions. Soon business cards were oozing from my bag.

I saw that Sarah was being chatted up by a very thin, shiny-faced lesbian. 'Why do they all think I'm gay?' she asked me.

'Maybe they know something you don't,' I teased her.

'Well, I could have it done to me, but I couldn't possibly do anything back. Why aren't there any straight men around any more?'

'The perennial cry of the thirty-something woman,' said Molly, dropping a kiss on Sarah's cheek.

Personally, I've never felt that there's a lack of suitable men. And even if there were, so what? Finding a man to walk through life with is hardly a quest, more like shopping in a supermarket. Not a challenge for most intelligent women.

Zena wafted by, trailing a wake of adoring men. One was holding her glass, one was holding an ashtray, and yet another had her lighter. Zena turned round and, catching our eye, gave us a slow, lascivious wink.

I had cocaine running around my brain now, as the song said. I rushed about the room, talking to absolutely everybody, handing out cards to all and sundry. I didn't stay long enough with anyone to have a proper conversation, and was reduced to catching snippets here and there.

'Darling, I'd simply *love* to have dinner next week, but I'm not *too* sure where I'm going to be, call me . . .'

'People always quote London's tube maps as the most user friendly design there is, *but* . . .'

'No, no, I think that analysis still has a valid place in . . .'

'She does look great, doesn't she, yes, just something I picked up in Paris, you know . . . yes, I promise, *snatched* away from Naomi . . .'

'Rugby is a very underestimated game, you know, now take the popularity of football . . .'

Nicola suggested that we continue the party at her place. I looked around the room and, to my surprise, saw that the crowds had thinned out and the waiters were starting to clear up. It must be quite late, Zena was nowhere to be seen. My guess was that she'd gone to bed. She's famous for doing that at her own parties, secure in the knowledge that she has staff, I guess.

We staggered rather wildly on to the street. Nicola's car was waiting, with Rick asleep at the wheel. She rapped her knuckles on the car window, and we all piled in. Sarah begged to be dropped home, as she had to work the following day. (See what I mean about high-powered jobs?)

'Home, James and don't spare the horses!' we all shouted.

Chapter Ten

The journey home was wild. I remember sitting on Pete's lap, with Molly draped over Joe and Monty. Steve and Nicola were in the front of the car, swapping tales of excess. Rick, who must have seen this sort of behaviour countless times, drove impassively. The electronic gates swung open to admit us, and we were all soon ensconced in what had been Stan's playroom.

The playroom was a basement that ran the length of the house. It had a snooker table, a jukebox, several state-of-the-art video games, a piano and a well stocked bar. Pony skins were dotted over the vast floor, and black leather sofas were ranged against the walls. Nicola opened a safe (hidden behind a Peter Blake picture of the Beatles) and withdrew what she called 'the last of Stan's Colombian'.

Pete and I sat on a sofa, watching Steve make drinks behind the bar. Molly and Monty played pinball, whilst Nicola was, inevitably, chopping out more coke.

The night went downhill from then on.

The things that I do remember stand out like snapshots in a very dysfunctional family album.

Nicola teaching Molly and me how to dance, rock chick style. (This seemed to mean standing quite still, with your hands on your thighs, licking your lips and pouting.)

Joe trying to teach Monty how to play billiards.

Pete and I declaring undying affection for each other.

Monty saying to a vase of flowers, 'Oh, you *sweet* little things.'

Molly and Steve having a furious argument about, of all people, Virginia Woolf.

Steve explaining (again) to Joe exactly what Mimi had done with the vegetables.

Me phoning Christopher to tell him he was a bastard at four in the morning.

Nicola removing all of the gold and platinum discs from the wall and breaking them.

Molly and Steve doing a tango, on top of the billiard table.

Monty and I rearranging the furniture, and measuring up the room, to see if we could fit a swimming pool in there.

Molly convincing Joe that he really did want to learn how to play paper, scissors, rock with her. (The loser had to chop the next lines of coke for us all.)

All of us trying to remember exactly where we were (and then relating in very boring detail) when John Lennon got shot, Elvis died, Marvin Gaye was killed, etc.

Steve telling Nicola that 'it wasn't good for people to sleep alone', while gently stroking her hair.

Nicola holding my hand and telling me that I was 'the best interior designer in the whole of the western hemisphere, possibly the world'.

Steve running out of fruit, and making tomato daiquiris.

Raiding the cold, huge, silent kitchen for more ice, and all of us screaming like children playing murder in the dark.

A huge discussion about how murder in the dark was actually played.

Trying to play murder in the dark.

Molly getting her foot stuck in the U bend of the loo –

'I was standing on the loo seat, to get a better look at the light fitting, and I slipped.' Why, Molly? 'I don't know.'

Ceremoniously taking the last line of coke.

Losing one of my snakeskin mules.

Being driven home at 8.30 in the morning by Rick.

I was frantically searching my bathroom cabinet for a sleeping pill, having gone into that clenched-jaw, slightly paranoid, exhausted state. The sort of walking dead condition that a night of ridiculous behaviour induces. In my experience (and trust me, here) the best thing to do is something normal, something that will soothe and calm you without taxing you too much. So, I made soup. I made the life-affirming, life-saving soup that you are crying out for after abusing your nervous system to the point of collapse.

Should you ever find yourself in a similar position, this is the recipe. You will need two potatoes, two carrots, two or three sticks of celery, one or two leeks or an onion. As much garlic as you can be bothered to deal with, but at least three cloves. A tin of borlotti, or cannellini beans, something green, like Savoy cabbage, spring greens or courgettes, a handful of parsley and some parmesan cheese. Heat three tablespoons of olive oil in a large pan, peel, and chop all the vegetables quite small, and stir into the hot oil, making sure that everything is coated. Throw in a bay leaf and a lot of black pepper and salt. Stir mindlessly for a few minutes (you don't actually have to do this, but it really is very soothing, and I advise it). Make about two pints of stock, either vegetable or chicken (from a stock cube). Let the vegetables sweat in the oil. While this is happening you can either stare sullenly at the sink for ten minutes or have one last cigarette (assuming that you've got one left). Then add the stock, and a squeeze of tomato purée, and – brace yourself for this, because you won't want to – add a good slug of alcohol to the soup. Red wine, vermouth, or sherry. Honestly, I know it's the last thing you want to smell at the moment, but trust is involved again here, just do it. You've just got time to remove your make-up, clean your teeth, brush your hair and put your comfort nightclothes on. The soup should now be ready, after having simmered for twenty minutes or so. Throw a handful of chopped parsley on the top, grate some parmesan over it and eat with a wedge of bread covered in butter.

I took this feast into the drawing room and curled up on a chair, balancing the tray on my lap. I'd put an afghan blanket (made by my mother, and known in my household as 'the sickie blankie', as it was used to cover everyone when they were unwell) round my shoulders, and I stared out of the window at a cold, wet street. Mrs Grieg's blank windows gazed reproachfully at me. I spooned the soup greedily into my mouth, and tried to work out what I was going to do about Mrs Grieg. I had just about enough common sense left in my brain to realise that I shouldn't do anything until I'd had some sleep. So, after looking in on Molly, who was muttering in her sleep, stretched, fully clothed across the bed, I swallowed a sleeping pill, unplugged the phone and sank gratefully into bed.

It seemed only moments later that I was being shaken awake by Molly. It was, in fact, six in the evening.

'Livia, wake up. I can't find the aspirin.' Molly was holding her head, whimpering with pain.

'Bathroom,' I muttered, turning over and settling down again.

'No, no, you have to wake up. Look, there's a recorded letter for you that I had to take delivery of, the bloody postman would not go away, and I had to sign for it. He looked at me like I was mad, or something.'

I opened one eye and squinted at her. She was still wearing my Jasper Conran dress, her tights were laddered, her hair looked as though birds had nested in it overnight, and her make-up had slid halfway down her face.

'Not surprised. You look mad. Leave me alone.'

'But this could be urgent, and there's about twenty messages on the answer machine. Do get up, I feel extremely unwell. Where did you say the aspirin was?'

'Oh God, I feel like I've only had five minutes' sleep. Can't it wait?'

'No it bloody can't. Why can I smell garlic?'

'Soup. Last night. This morning, rather. Oh God, I feel like shit. I remember this feeling, that's why I gave up coke. My nose feels like it's going to drop off.'

'You're lucky. My whole head feels as though it's going to drop off.'

'Yeah, well, my body feels like it's going to drop off.'

'That's nothing, my body *has* dropped off.'

I knew that trying to regain sleep was impossible. Once Molly and I started to compete to see who had got the worst hangover, I realised I might as well just get up. I staggered out of bed. It was freezing, so I put on my huge towelling dressing gown and fired up the central heating. I poured us both large glasses of water and found the aspirin. Even swallowing them was difficult: I thought I was going to gag. Tea seemed an obvious solution, but the energy required to put the kettle on was too much for either of us. We sank our heads in our hands and stared at each other.

'I feel like a rancid old cod,' said Molly.

'I look like one.'

We sat in silence for a while. The letter sat on the table in front of us. I dragged it towards me. I was never keen to open recorded delivery letters, they were usually from the taxman, but this one was handwritten. I turned it over: there was an illegible address on the back. I put it back on the table, it was just too much effort. Molly and I jumped when the intercom buzzed.

'You'll have to get it,' said Molly. 'Because I think I've lost the use of my legs. My foot, the bad one, hurts even more now.'

'That's because you had it wedged down a loo last night.'

'Don't be silly. Why would I do that?'

'We did ask you, but it was something to do with looking at a light fitting. I didn't understand it then, and I sure as hell don't now.'

The buzzer sounded again, and I shuffled over to answer it. It was Joe. He walked into the kitchen and stared at us.

'My God, what have you two done to yourselves? You both looked amazing last night, how can one night have wreaked so much havoc?'

'Shut up,' we both said. I added, 'Make yourself useful and put the kettle on.'

'Did I try to kiss you last night?' asked Molly.

'Yep.'

'Oh God, I'm sorry.'

'I'm getting used to it now, I quite enjoyed it, actually.'

Joe made tea, and we sat slumped around the table, sipping it. Joe looked exceedingly hearty, and I suspected that he'd been swimming, or something else disgustingly healthy.

'Last night was great, wasn't it?' he said, brightly.

We stared at him.

'Well, it was. I thought so, anyway. I've never been to places like those before, it was great. I couldn't do it every week, of course . . . my liver wouldn't stand it, but it was fantastic. I mean, I can say that I've been inside Nicola

Bentley's house . . . and Zena's, and the Casa, it was brilliant—'

I interrupted him. 'Joe, are you sure you didn't take any coke?'

'No, I mean yes I'm sure I didn't. Why?'

'Because you're burbling on now as if you had. Shut up, there's a dear. Do something that's going to make us feel better, if that's possible. Though actually it may be too late, I feel like I'm going to die.'

'Me too,' said Molly, practically lying across the table.

'Anyway, Joe, much as we always love to see you, why are you here?'

'To talk to you about Mrs Grieg. What are we going to do about her? She's not at home, and I've asked around. Nobody has seen her for days, now.'

Molly groaned. 'My head hurts too much to think about it, I'm going in the shower. If I'm not out in ten minutes, I've drowned myself. Please tell my parents I love them.'

I watched her limp from the room with a great deal of sympathy. I felt exactly the same. Listlessly I picked up the letter, trying to think about who to call about Mrs Grieg. It was a Saturday evening, social services probably weren't even there, let alone answering phone calls. I made Joe make some more tea, then I opened the letter.

Dear Livia,
By the time you get this, I'll be gone. The pistol, as I expect you know, proved to be quite valuable. I've sold it and am going to live out my life somewhere warm, where I can grow my roses. England's too bleeding cold. Ask that nice young man next door to get into my flat, I want you to have the Laura Knight picture.

You always liked it. The bad news is, it's a fake. Cheer up, love. Things always turn out all right in the end.
Yours sinsereley,
R. Grieg.
P.S. You're a nice girl, don't whatever you do get back with that smarmy married bastard. He's a wrong one, no mistake.

There was a sheet of paper enclosed with the letter, which simply stated that Mrs Grieg gave me authority to take her picture.

If I had been in a Charles Dickens novel, I would have fallen down backwards, and sat on the garden path with amazement. My God! And here we'd all been worrying our socks off about her. The charming elderly woman living opposite us had turned into an international antiques thief. I could hardly believe it. I passed the letter over to Joe and went to bang on the bathroom door to tell Molly. She emerged dripping wet, swathed in towels. She snatched the letter from Joe, to read it for herself.

'My God. This is incredible, what can we do?'

We were all shocked. It seemed impossible to believe. But I didn't think that there was much we could do, really. I mean, we could hardly go to the police, could we? I said as much.

'Christ, what are we going to tell Mimi?' I exclaimed suddenly. I felt terrible enough already, without this on my conscience too.

I picked up the phone to call Steve, but there was no reply, so I left a message for him, and tried his mobile. It was switched off. I then tried Pete. He answered, sounding very groggy. I explained what had happened.

'Good God. Well, here's a pretty kettle of fish, I must say. How are you feeling?'

'Appalling, and you?'

'The same. Let me have a bath, and I'll come over. I'll stop by Steve and Connie's and see where they are, OK?'

'Yeah. Bring some orange juice over, would you?'

'OK, see you later. Who'd have thought it, huh?'

'Indeed.'

'Pete, how are you feeling really?'

'I told you, appalling. But after last night I'm not surprised. I must say I don't expect my doctor to be very pleased with me.'

I hung up, and stared at the letter again. It really was incredible. If I didn't have the proof in front of my own eyes, I don't think I would have believed it. I decided to have another bath. A long hot soak was just what I needed to restore myself to something near human. As I ran the bath I heard Molly trying to persuade Joe to go and get a takeaway curry.

'Let me cook you a stir fry, it's so much more healthy.'

'Bollocks to healthy, I want grease disguised as a chicken tikka masala. Go on, Joe, I can't walk properly, or I'd go. Liv made her soup, and I've finished that. Go on, please.'

As I lay in the hot bath, I heard the front door close and Joe run down the stairs. Molly must have got her way. I hoped he remembered the poppadoms. I lay in the bath for ages, hoping that the hot water would ease my aches and pains. I had a large bruise on my calf, but no recollection of how I'd got it. It must be an MDI (Mysterious Drunken Injury). I dragged myself out of the bath and got dressed in my warmest jumper and jeans. I was still cold, I could quite see why Mrs Grieg wanted to live somewhere warm. Molly had lit the fire in the drawing room, and we sat huddled in front of it, speculating on Mrs Grieg.

Pete arrived two minutes before Joe came back with the curry. We spread the boxes out on the floor in front of the fire and swigged orange juice, piling curry on to our plates.

I propped some cushions behind my back, and ate greedily. There was just the sound of the logs crackling and people eating. After a while, Pete sighed, 'Ah, that's better. Anybody want that last onion bhaji?'

'Go ahead, it's got your name on it,' I said.

Molly gave a huge burp.

'Very ladylike,' observed Joe.

We were all in a state of collapse, sprawled over the floor. I didn't have the energy to clear up, so we just kept moving the plates out of the way.

'Do you think I should phone Steve again?' I asked.

'Yeah, I can't think where he can be,' said Pete; 'there was no light on, and I rang his bell for ages.'

'I take it that he did go home?' I said. 'I mean, he didn't end up staying with Nicola, did he?'

'I have no idea. Who remembers him in the car?' asked Pete.

We all shook our heads.

'I'm going to call Monty, he'll know,' I said.

Monty sounded dreadful.

'I have only *just* surfaced, I simply can't do this sort of thing any more. I'm *far* too old. What are you all doing?'

'Eating curry and talking about Mrs Grieg.'

'Why?'

I filled him in on what had happened. He was suitably dumbstruck.

'Good for her. Look Liv, much as I'd love to stay and

gossip, I have got to go back to bed and get some beauty sleep. Call me with any further developments.'

'Wait, where's Steve, is he with you?'

'Are you mad? Of course he's not.'

'Oh God, well, we've lost him too, then.'

Monty gave a very unsympathetic laugh, and hung up.

My next phone call was to Zena to thank her profusely for the party. She gave her husky laugh, and told me that it was a pleasure, and that I should follow up all the introductions that she'd made for me at the party. I promised that I would.

I tried to call Nicola, but there was no reply.

'Perhaps she and Steve are entwined in each other's arms, and are being far too passionate to answer the phone,' suggested Molly.

'I can't really see it,' said Pete.

'Oh can't you? That boy would chance his arm with anyone, wouldn't he. Little sod, I mean, look at the mess he got himself into with Mimi. I'll kill him if he upsets Nicola, and what about Connie? Where the bloody hell is she? Why isn't she answering the phone?' I said indignantly.

'Maybe she was so furious with Steve for arriving home at nine in the morning that she's killed him,' Molly speculated.

'Assuming he *did* go home,' I said.

I tried Nicola's number again. I let it ring and ring and finally a man's voice answered. 'Hello, Nicola Bentley's residence, how may I help you?' I assumed that it was Rick.

'Hi, it's Olivia Hunter here. May I speak to Nicola?'

'I'm afraid that isn't possible. She's left strict instructions that she is not to be disturbed.'

'Umm, I see. The thing is, well, is she alone, do you know?'

'I'm afraid I couldn't possibly comment on that.'

'No, I see. Well, could you ask her to call me, please?'

'Certainly. Thank you for calling.'

I put the phone down.

'Well, I don't know if he's there or not. Let's try his mobile again.' I dialled his number, but his answering service was on. I left a message, asking him to call me. I felt wave after wave of tiredness engulf me, I'd almost forgotten how tired a coke binge made you feel. Tired and somehow slightly grubby. I gave a jaw-breaking yawn. Pretty soon everybody was doing the same.

'My God, we've only been up four hours,' I exclaimed, 'but I'm ready for bed again.'

'I know how you feel. Let's watch a mindless video and not think about Mimi, or Steve, or Mrs Grieg till tomorrow. How about that?' said Molly.

'It's sure got my vote,' said Pete, adding, 'Come over here Liv, I'll give you a foot massage and we can watch a film together. Afterwards we can have a row and put up some shelves.'

'What are you talking about?'

'You know, getting you ready for married life, with me. That's what Victoria Wood says married couples do — put up shelves and row.'

'Well, I can put my own shelves up, thank you very much.'

I lay on the sofa with my feet in Pete's lap. My feet really did hurt, it was all that standing I did yesterday in those snakeskin mules. I'd still only found one. God knows what had happened to the other. We all had a good-natured squabble about which video to watch. Pete and I wanted to see *High Society*, Molly wanted to see *Bladerunner* and Joe wanted *Apocalypse Now.*

'Bad luck, two to one, Liv and I win. Losers make tea,

I'd like a biscuit with mine, off you go.' Pete sounded amused. I lay back and groaned with pleasure as he massaged my feet.

'Liv?' he asked tentatively.

'Umm, oh don't stop, that's bliss . . . what?'

'Well, I know we haven't talked about it, but I want to thank you for going along with my parents. I know I shouldn't have said that we were engaged, but, well . . .'

'Ssh, it's OK, I know.'

'Mmm, but well, what I was going to say was, you haven't forgotten that you're coming to Brighton next weekend, have you?'

I groaned, loudly.

'Pete, let's not talk about this now, shall we? I'm too frazzled. Remind me never, ever to take that white poison again, OK?'

'OK.'

Molly and Joe came back in with the tea, and we had a peaceful hour and a half in front of Grace Kelly and Frank Sinatra. I replayed the song and dance number between Frank and Bing Crosby singing 'What a Swell Party' three times, we all sang along to it, and somehow it made me feel a whole lot better. It felt like being amongst family. Maybe, I thought, being without Christopher isn't so bad after all.

I fell asleep in front of the TV, and was vaguely aware of Joe and Pete leaving. I dragged myself into the bedroom, and instantly fell asleep.

The following morning was hell. Molly had gone to the shop to pick up the Sunday papers and to buy milk and eggs. She came back into the flat and dramatically threw two of the tabloids on to my bed.

'Look!'

I looked down. On the front pages of both were blurred pictures of Nicola, holding my arm and leaning her head on my shoulder. The headline was NICOLA IN LESBIAN TANGLE. The other headline was HEARTBREAK OF NICOLA BENTLEY, SHE TURNS TO A WOMAN FOR COMFORT. I shot up in bed and scanned the papers. The pictures had obviously been taken at her gates, when she had gone out to face the reporters, and I had had to rescue her.

'Nice picture of you,' said Molly with a giggle in her voice.

'I really, really hope you're not being serious. Oh God, what a nightmare. Poor Nicola, do you think she's seen them yet?'

'Don't know. I think you'd better call her, don't you?'

As I reached for the phone, it rang. It was Pete.

'Oh my God, why didn't you tell me you were gay? You know you could have come out to me, of all people, I would have understood . . .' He was spluttering with laughter.

'Shut up. It's not funny, I was just trying to call Nicola, oh shit! I've just thought, what about your parents? They're not going to like it, are they?'

'I wouldn't worry about that. They only get the *Telegraph*, and that's delivered. I don't think they'll see it. Besides, you're not named, and it's a blurred photograph, isn't it?'

'Hmm, well, I don't like it. What about Nicola? I bet she's furious.'

'Give her a call. By the way, have you heard from Steve yet?'

'No, not a word, and you?'

'No, but I've had Connie squawking at me. He didn't go home, so where the hell is he?'

'So Connie's on the warpath is she? Well, I can't say I blame her. Maybe he's run off with Mrs Grieg.'

'Yeah, right. Well call me, OK? I'm off to sort the Bar out, we reopen soon. You'll come, won't you?'

'Of course.'

We said goodbye. The phone rang again, immediately, and it was Monty.

'Well, well, well. I'm going to have to buy you a monocle and a pair of jodhpurs aren't I? I know that lipstick lesbians are the vogue, but I see you more as the butch type, you know, dungarees and no make-up, think what a fortune you'll save in not having your legs waxed.'

'You can shut up, too, I've just had Pete on the phone. God, who else has seen it?'

'Most of London, I would assume. Come on, it's funny, darling, we all know what rubbish it is. Relax, no one takes what they print seriously.'

'That's not the point, is it? Oh bloody, bloody hell. I never thought I'd be on the front page of a sleaze tabloid!'

'Fame comes to us all eventually, but sometimes not in the way we expect it. Would you have preferred the front cover of *Gay Times*?'

'I'm saying goodbye now, and I want you to know that I've never liked you, and I hope that your Armani shirts shrink in the wash.'

Monty laughed and hung up.

The phone rang again, and it was Nicola. To my relief she found the whole thing hilarious, it had even prompted Stan into calling her.

'Mind you, he's probably hoping that it's true, you know what men are like, he'd just want to watch.'

'I was really worried that you'd be upset.'

'The rubbish that they've printed about me over the years . . . I'm used to it. Look, don't let it bother you, OK? And Liv, I'm writing to you, I'm authorising you to start work on my house. I'm going away, so you'll have responsibility for it, if that's all right. I'd like it done as soon as possible.'

'Where are you going?'

'I'm taking your advice, I'm going to sit in the sun somewhere and write my book.'

'Well done, and good luck with it. What's it going to be
called?'

'Well, I thought about "My Life with a Complete
Wanker" but I don't think they'd publish it. Maybe "Diary
of a Trophy Wife", but I'll work on it and let you know.'

We spoke some more about the house, finalising plans,
then I asked her, rather delicately, if she'd seen Steve. She
laughed, 'Rick found him, last night. He'd fallen asleep
behind a sofa, but he woke up, wandering around the house,
trying to get out. He set all the burglar alarms off. He's now
fast asleep again in a spare room.'

'Do me a favour, shake him till he wakes up, and make
him call Connie. Stand over him, though, he'll wriggle like
an eel to try and get out of it, OK?'

'Yeah, sure. I've given up the marching powder, after the
other night. How about you?'

'I had anyway, but yes, me too. I felt *so* bad, did you?'

'God yes! Steve made breakfast for me, and then we slept
again.'

'We?'

She laughed, and hung up.

Molly and I speculated about Steve and Nicola over a
plate of very rubbery scrambled eggs. Then she decided that
she was going back to her own flat this afternoon, and set
about packing up.

'Don't think that you can slip my Jasper Conran dress into
your bag, because I shall be watching you like a hawk,' I
said, knowing her predilection for appropriating my things.
We have had an ongoing argument for fifteen years about
the true ownership of a silk shawl.

We trailed round the flat, clearing up the debris of last night's curry, and throwing Molly's belongings into bags. Exhausted, we had to sit down again for a cup of tea.

'I hate this, it's like the last day of term at school,' said Molly, with a mournful look.

'No, it's not. We loved the last day of term, remember? We couldn't wait to get home. Come on, you know you want to get home. Besides if you don't get back to work soon, you won't have a job to go back to.'

'Yeah, I know, but still . . . it's not the same.'

'Look, we'll see each other on Wednesday. You're arriving early with Zena for Mr Abraham's party, OK? And—'

The intercom buzzer sounded loudly in the flat.

It was Joe. He had arrived to drive Molly home. We kissed farewell, and I waved them off. The flat felt terribly empty.

I did all those Sunday things that you do if you are on your own. The washing machine started whirring, I cleaned the oven (well, to be honest I attacked it with a hammer and chisel), I washed the windows and the kitchen floor. I then sat down to read the papers (broadsheet, not tabloid) and learned about the newest restaurant, the hippest bar, the hottest company to invest in, what to go and see at the theatre and what not.

I tried hard not to miss Christopher, and all the times that we had spent lazy Sundays together. Loneliness threatened to overwhelm me and I wandered into the bathroom and started to clean the tiles (I knew I was in trouble then). I decided that the best thing I could do was to change the colour, this awful frosted lime had to go. I started, in a very half-hearted sort of way, to stick on the glass mosaic tiles that I'd received as samples over the tiles that were already there. I got dreadfully bored, and deserted the job. I went back into the kitchen.

Molly had been gone for about two hours and I was falling apart. I stared at Mrs Grieg's letter again: she wouldn't fall apart after a couple of hours without company, so neither would I.

I lasted approximately five minutes before I caved in and phoned every friend that I hadn't spoken to recently. I spoke to Kath, Ben, my mad aunt in Taunton, and Pete.

Virtuously I squeezed some oranges and a grapefruit into a glass and drank it. I swallowed two multivitamin pills, a cod-liver oil capsule, two St John's Wort tablets, and some arnica homeopathic remedy and went to bed. As Scarlett said 'Tomorrow is another day'.

Chapter Eleven

On Monday morning I was frantic. I didn't even have time to worry about Pete or feel depressed about waking up, I had too much to do. I had to confirm all of the work that needed to be done at Nicola's, arrange the housewarming party at Mr Abraham's, reply to all the messages that I hadn't dealt with over the weekend. And, to my surprise, quote for a redecoration job at Lord Abbingdon's (or, please do call me Freddy). And I was due to meet Mark from Paintworld. I was just about to tackle my life when the intercom buzzed. It was Connie. She stormed into the flat, obviously in a foul mood.

'Livia, where the bloody hell is my boyfriend?' she demanded.

'Really Connie, I don't know. I mean, we all went to Zena's party, and umm, well, then we went to Nicola's but I haven't seen, or heard from him.'

'How on earth do *you* know Nicola Bentley? Hmm, I saw the Sunday papers, you know.' She looked sideways at me: 'He *always* calls you,' she added grudgingly.

'Honestly, I haven't spoken to him.' (Well, that was true, at least.)

'I've just about had enough of this. It's all very well for

people like you to think that Steve is being funny, but let me tell you, he's not.'

'What do you mean, people like me?'

'Well, you know, people that don't matter . . .'

'What? What the fuck do you mean, I don't matter?' I was livid.

'Well you're not serious about anything, are you? Nothing seems to mean that much to you, you probably wouldn't care if Steve went missing . . .'

I was absolutely furious, and felt myself building up to shout at her.

'Right, Connie, you hold it right there. For a start, I am very fond of Steve and it would matter greatly to me if something happened to him. Which it hasn't. Secondly, you know very well what he's like. He drinks too much, he can't say no to anything and often goes to a party and doesn't come home for two days. And thirdly, you're not perfect yourself, are you? I do know about your smooching with a waiter in Paris. I think you'd better go now. If Steve does call me, I shall ask him to get in touch with you. Goodbye.'

Connie glared at me and then stomped off down the stairs. I sat in the kitchen and lit a cigarette. I hated having what my grandmother would have described as 'words' with people. True, I have never liked Connie, but I did see her point of view. I would hate to be Steve's girlfriend, never knowing where he was, or who he was with. But to tell me that she didn't think that I cared about anything really annoyed me; I thought half my problems were that I cared too much.

All of this had started because I'd tried to help Steve out, and now I had his ranting girlfriend on my hands! I had been very tempted to tell Connie that Steve had spent the night at Nicola's, but I just couldn't. Protecting Steve and covering for him had become second nature. But I was damned if I was going to do it again after this. He'd have to look after himself from now on.

I grabbed my coat, and headed off towards Battersea. It was a cold, wet London day. The pavements seemed harder than usual, and the sky was pressing down to meet the earth, full of ominous dark clouds.

The fair was huge, and packed with people, most of them antique dealers and traders. There were always a lot of Americans there, and some interior designers too. Most of the stands were awful, crammed with hugely expensive furniture and monumentally dull pictures, but I was very interested in a set of mirrors in frames on one stand that was exhibiting antique metal. They had fairly severe lines, offset by metal wreaths. I wondered if Freddy would approve, I could see the swirling metal offset by sexy prune-coloured silk walls. I grabbed some details from the stand's manager and went off in search of Mark. So many people were crushed together that I'd developed a headache and realised I was also very cold. At last I spotted the Paintworld's stand, and pushed my way towards it. Sure enough, there was a man handing out samples, looking very stressed.

'Mark?' I asked him.

'Yes,' his face suddenly broke out into a smile, 'and you must be Livia, you don't look like a witch at all!'

I laughed. 'You should have seen me yesterday.'

We chatted for a while, and he suggested that we go and find a pub for lunch. We squirmed out, and, bracing ourselves against the cold air, walked towards a large Victorian pile that promised 'Home Cooked Food'.

'Hmm, home cooked by a robot in a factory, deep frozen and then reconstituted in a microwave,' said Mark suspiciously. 'We're probably better off sticking to sandwiches, don't you think?'

I agreed, and he ordered smoked salmon sandwiches and a bottle of white wine. I had to tell him that I was drinking water, at which he laughed and admitted that he was too; he cancelled the wine. A good-looking Australian barman, who was obviously dreaming of the outback, said he'd bring our food over to us.

We sat as close to the fire as we could, and Mark asked me what I was doing at the moment. I explained about going solo, and the various jobs that I'd got on.

'What did you really think about the metallic paint I sent you?'

'Well, I did my bathroom in it, and it makes me look so ill that I have to avoid looking at myself in the mirror. I can't believe it's a big seller.'

'Well, it was an experiment for us. Awful as it is, we'd got stuck with being thought of as the company that produced all those Aga-saga paints, you know, limewashed walls and Tuscan terracotta, so we thought it was time to revamp our image. Can't say that I like it too much myself. I was quite surprised that you ordered some more . . .'

The barman plonked our plates of sandwiches in front of us, managing to knock over the bottle of water. It cascaded on to my lap, and I jumped up, dabbing myself ineffectually with a paper napkin. The water had gone all over the files that Mark had been carrying, and he was separating the papers, trying to dry them out. My skirt (dry clean only) was now sopping wet so I excused myself and went to the Ladies to try to repair the damage. I was reduced to taking the skirt off and holding it in front of the hand dryer; every time the door opened, women were treated to the spectacle of me in some tights with a hole in them, and a pair of rather too small knickers. My skirt was now a bit wrinkly, but at least it was dry, so I slipped it back on and rejoined Mark.

'God, sorry about that, are you OK?'

'Yeah, what about all your papers?'

'Oh, they'll dry all right. So tell me, why are you on water?'

I explained briefly (omitting the gorier details) about my weekend.

'Goodness, and I thought I'd had a pretty wild time. I just went out with my best friend from art college, he'd had a private view last week, and he's actually managed to sell some paintings. So we decided to celebrate. I drank Scotch, which was a big mistake. I'm not used to it, I don't even like it, and I'm certainly paying for it now.'

Mark was easy to talk to. We chattered away like old friends. It had started to rain heavily outside, making the prospect of leaving the pub uninviting. We agreed that it was a shame neither of us was drinking as there was nothing we'd like better than to settle in front of the fire with a bottle of wine, and while away the afternoon.

'Look, I know you're very busy at the moment, but, well, I was wondering if I could persuade you to come out to dinner with me? We might both have recovered from our hangovers, by then.'

'You mean, dinner, like a dinner date?' I said cautiously, 'Or a business dinner?'

'Which one would you say yes to?'

'Oh God, I don't know. I mean, yes I'd like to, either of them, it's just that I'm very busy at the moment, and life is a little complicated.'

Mark looked amused. 'Well, I shall look forward to hearing about it over dinner. How about Wednesday?'

'No, it's Mr Abraham's do, talking of which . . . I simply have to go, Doug is still away, and I really want to stop by the flat and make sure that it's all OK.'

I glanced out of the window: freezing rain was pelting down. It felt very cosy by the fire, but somehow I still felt cold.

'Are you OK?' asked Mark suddenly.

'Why?'

'You look a bit flushed. Maybe we should move away from the fire.'

'Are you kidding? I'm freezing.'

Mark put a hand out to feel my forehead. 'You've got a temperature, I think you should go home. Come on, I'm going to get a taxi for you. I would drive you myself, but I'll never get out of the exhibitors' car park.'

I let Mark wrap my coat around me. He insisted I stand inside the pub till he got a taxi for me and he was gone for so long that I sank into a dreamlike state waiting for him. I really did feel rotten. Could it still be a vodka and coke comedown? Or was I really ill? I couldn't tell. All I knew was that I wanted my bed, now. At last Mark popped his head round the door of the pub, saying, 'Sorry it took so long, it's pouring with rain, come on let's get you home.'

It was quite pleasant being fussed over and I made no complaint as he settled me in the back of the taxi. I gave my address to the driver, and to my surprise Mark got in with me and closed the door.

'You don't have to come back with me, you know, I shall be quite all right.'

He looked with astonishment at me.

'You're shivering. I'm just going to make sure you get home OK, and then I'll come straight back. Have you got orange juice and aspirin at home?'

I assured him that aspirin was the one thing he could count on me always having at home. I really did feel dreadful. My head ached, my throat was sore and I could not stop shivering. I leaned back in the taxi and closed my eyes. It hurt to swallow, and my ears were ringing.

Very soon we were pulling up outside my flat. Mark asked the taxi to wait, then took my keys out of my hands and opened the front door. He pushed me inside, saying, 'Get into bed, I'm going to make you some tea, and where do you keep the aspirin?'

'Bathroom.'

I clambered into my flannel nightie, and hurriedly leapt into bed. I certainly didn't want Mark seeing me in my comfort nightie. He knocked discreetly on the door and came in with a tray of tea, painkillers and a glass of orange juice.

I stammered my thanks, and he smiled. Nice eyes, I thought to myself.

'It's a gorgeous flat, may I ask where you got the picture that's propped up in your hall?'

'Oh, the ghastly porridge thing? It's a bit of a joke, really . . .'

He interrupted: 'I'm glad you think it's ghastly too. It's by my best friend, the one that I was out celebrating with.'

'No! How extraordinary, it's all to do with Zena, and me telling her that Mr Abraham was living in a bowl of porridge.'

Mark looked bewildered. 'Drink this,' he said firmly, holding out the orange juice. 'Take your pills and go to sleep. I'll call you in the morning. I must dash, the cab's waiting, and I need to get back to the stand. Are you sure you'll be OK? Is there anyone I can call for you?'

He left the flat and as I heard his footsteps disappear I sank back into my pillows, and started to feel very sorry for myself indeed. Two large wet tears rolled down my face. I felt awful, I'd got loads of work to do, and there was nobody to look after me. Steve had gone AWOL, so had Mrs Grieg, and I'd still got to sort out Mr Abraham's party. And of course, there was Pete. I could hardly bear to think about him, it made me feel frantic with worry. I tried to cry out loud, to see if it would help. It didn't, it just made my throat sore, so I sniffled and sipped my tea. I wanted to be coddled and taken care of, but it looked like I was going to have to do it myself. So what's new? I thought.

I drifted off to sleep, and had a fitful couple of hours of horrible dreams involving hot spiders that wanted to devour me. I woke up, gasping and drenched in sweat and staggered out of bed to stand under a hot shower for five minutes. I caught sight of myself in the bathroom mirror, and nearly screamed. I looked like a hamster. A hamster with two patches of uneven rouge on its fat little cheeks. My eyes were glazed and my glands were so swollen that it looked as if I were hiding some particularly tasty bits of food there. I was flushed, and my whole body ached. I was definitely ill. This was not a coke and drink induced sickness, this was a fully fledged bout of flu.

I put on a clean nightshirt and collapsed back into bed before picking up the phone. Who was I going to call? Molly had only just left here, but I really did need some help. Perhaps I could ask her to go over to Mr Abraham's flat for me? I punched in her number at work. Her assistant answered, telling me that Molly had gone to Norwich to see the printers and was expected back on Wednesday morning. Oh great! I tried Steve's mobile, with very little hope of success. I croaked a message into it, and hung up. I felt it wasn't fair to call Pete, he'd got so much to do himself with the reopening of the Bar, besides which, I didn't want to pass on to him whatever it was that I'd got. Anyway, it was just a bad cold or the flu, and in comparison to his troubles I realised that I was being pathetic. Zena? No, she was far too busy being one of the beautiful people. Monty? I whimpered with relief, and pushed the numbers in. His recorded voice told me I could reach him in Milan, or to leave a message and he would return all calls on Wednesday evening. Damn. I tried Sarah at work, but was told that she was in a meeting. Joe! The BND, of course, that's what BNDs were for. I listened to his phone ring and ring: he was probably kicking a ball somewhere, or swimming, or something else equally useless. Bloody hell. I took more painkillers and drank some water. I decided that everything would have to wait, I was ill and there was nothing I could do about it. I retreated back under the covers and closed my eyes.

The ringing of the phone pierced my slumber. Groggily I answered it, croaking, 'Hello?'

'My God, Liv, you sound awful, are you OK?'

It was Steve.

'No, I feel dreadful. Where are you?'

'I've just got home. Connie told me that she'd been round to see you, sorry, I know it's all my fault. Is there anything I can do for you?'

'Yes, no, I don't know. I feel terrible, I think I've got flu.'

'I'll come round, I'll be about half an hour. Is there anything you need?'

'Yes, a new body, this one's had it.' I nearly sobbed with relief: there was someone out there after all. I don't want you to get the wrong idea here, I'm not generally such a complete wimp, but I really felt *awful*. When I'm not well, there really is only one person I want – my mother. When she was alive she'd bring calm, comfort and delight into a sickroom, along with cigarette smoke, a good book and a jug of homemade lemonade.

I dozed off again. The intercom woke me this time and it took me ages to answer the door. Steve came running up the stairs carrying a large canvas bag and a bunch of daffodils.

'Christ! You look like you've swallowed a tennis ball, go back to bed.' I didn't need telling again. I flopped back into bed and listened to Steve pottering round the kitchen. He came into the bedroom carrying a bowl of soup, and some water. I sat up and tried to eat some soup, but couldn't manage it. That worried me: I have to be near death's door to refuse food. I pushed it away, and watched Steve jam the flowers into a jug. He wandered around the room, tidying up.

'You'll make someone a lovely wife one day,' I whispered.

'Hmm, well, I have to be honest and tell you I'm not just here out of the goodness of my heart. Connie's kicked me out.'

'I'm not surprised.'

'Save your voice, it must hurt.' He looked enquiringly at me and I nodded. He sat on the edge of the bed, and filled me in on the details. He had genuinely fallen asleep at Nicola's and had woken up, not knowing where he was. He'd triggered the burglar alarms, and Nicola had appeared at the top of the stairs, very worried. Rick had burst in from next door, and Steve had had to admit that he'd been trying to get out. He'd cooked Nicola breakfast and as she'd seemed very upset, he'd comforted her.

I snorted in a derogatory fashion.

'No, not like that. I mean we did go to bed together, but we just cuddled. Anyway, then she saw the papers, and we had a laugh about that, then I came home. She's really nice, isn't she? Not at all how I imagined her to be. Connie has been shouting at me all day, and I just decided that I'd had enough. I mean, I just don't think I'm cut out to live with anyone. So is it OK if I stay a few days?'

I nodded.

'Do you want the sickie blankie?'

I nodded again.

Steve tucked the blanket around me and I pressed my face into it, and breathed in. If I tried very hard I could conjure up the past scent of my mother. It consisted of Madame Rochas, wood smoke, apples, cloves, face powder, yeast and simmered stews. I drifted off to sleep, believing that I was secure in her kitchen in Cornwall where she was lighting her twenty-fifth cigarette of the day, pouring gin and tonics, and leaning against the Aga, humming along to Nellie Lucher, whilst telling me that I was her 'lovey dovey cat's eyes'. I went to sleep, smiling.

Later that night I woke up, and had to stagger to the bathroom. Steve was in the drawing room; he made me sit down on the sofa while he changed the sheets on my bed. I still had a raging temperature, was aching all over and my throat was red raw, but at least I had stopped looking like a hamster.

The clean sheets were lovely to slip into, and I whispered to Steve that I needed some paper and a pen. I wrote a list of things that I needed him to do.

1. Check on Mr Abraham's flat and make sure everything is OK for Wednesday.
2. What are we going to tell Mimi?
3. Book caterers for party – I'm far too ill to stuff a mushroom.
4. Send flowers to Zena, thanking her for party. Also remind her to go to Mr Abraham's party.

5. Ditto Molly.
6. Phone Doug and find out health of new family.
7. Phone young Roger and put the fear of God into him.
8. Talk to Joe about Mrs Grieg's flat & get picture for me.
9. Chase up quotes for Nicola.
10. Phone Frankie, Freddy et al, and say I am ill.
11. If Mark calls, thank him for looking after me.
12. How long are you staying?
13. Remember to put the loo seat down.
14. Do I still have to be nice to Connie?

I made a mental note to myself as well to call John. I don't really know why, I just wanted to hear his voice. Steve read the list and smiled. 'Look, just relax, it'll all be OK. Who's Mark? No, don't answer, I'll find out. Stop worrying, just get some rest. Mimi won't be back from Milan for ages, we'll work something out. Take some more pills, oh, and William Magpie has just called. He recognised you from the Sunday papers, so be warned, he probably wants to run a story on it, and he says he wouldn't miss Wednesday for the world. And, well, if it's OK with you, I'll stay till I sort myself out, but I really think it's over between Connie and me.'

'Hooray,' I whispered, then groaned and sank back into bed. Bloody William Magpie. But there was also something else worrying me, something that Mark had said . . . I couldn't quite remember what it was. I could barely remember my name at the moment. I thanked Steve, asked for more orange juice and fell asleep again.

I had a really horrible night. I couldn't sleep and every hour seemed like a day. My eyes hurt too much even to read, and

I was reduced to listening to the World Service all night. The signal changed to Radio 4 and I'd just got into *Farming Today* when I finally dropped off. I was dreaming that Christopher had broken into my flat and was trying to light a fire in the drawing room, but all the wood was damp and filling the place with smoke. I started to cough, and it woke me up. Morning light seeped through the curtain. To my terror I heard Christopher's voice: oh God, perhaps he *had* broken in, and maybe the flat *was* on fire. I sniffed for smoke, trying to decide what I would take with me (other than the emerald, which I was wearing, of course). Then I heard Steve's voice, saying, with surprising authority, 'She's not at all well Christopher, and I know that she doesn't want to see you, I really think that you should leave. Goodbye.'

There was the noise of stumbling in the hall, and then I heard the front door close. Steve popped his head round the door.

'I thought that would wake you up. Don't worry, he's gone now. He was drunk, I think he'd had a night out and decided to call on you. You'll be very pleased to know that he looked like a raddled chimpanzee with a hangover, not fanciable at all. Try to go back to sleep, it's only 8 o'clock.'

I waited for my heart to do its usual flip-flop at the sound of Christopher's voice, but there was nothing. Perhaps I was too ill to care, or maybe I really had got over him. The thought of Christopher looking like a raddled chimp made me smile, he *did* have rather a low hairline.

I snuggled back down and let sleep drift over me once more. Steve was chattering away on the phone, and every now and then he came in to give me an update.

'Zena says that she hasn't forgotten tomorrow night, and to take along the porridge picture, as she wants to give it to Mr Abraham as a housewarming present.'

'Monty's rung from Milan, he sends his love and says that Mimi, or rather Babaganoush is doing remarkably well.'

'Young Roger says not to worry and that everything has been done.'

'Someone called Mark has just called and wants to know what your favourite flowers are, I said roses – I thought they'd remind us of Mrs Grieg.'

'Pete rang, he sends his love, he also wants to remind you about going to his parents. I really think you should drink some water or something.'

'The quotes for Nicola's house will be here by the end of the week, do you want some more orange juice?'

'Molly rang from Norwich, she says it's like Stepford Wife country, she thinks they're all interbred, and can't wait to come home. Could you eat an egg?'

'An American called Eric or Aric called and said, "it was real nice meeting you the other night" and do you want an appointment?'

'Sarah called, can she borrow your new shoes, she's got to go for a very smart dinner, and she knows that you take the same size as her.' (She'd be lucky, I could still only find the one.)

'Freddy says can you go for a weekend to look over his house? I wouldn't go if I were you, he oozes lechery just down the phone.'

'A complete asshole from *Paste* called Noir rang, he wants to know if you can write an article on metallic finishes for next month. What about baked beans on toast?'

This went on all day, and I just lay in bed, letting it drift over me. I managed to have a bath, and then sat for half an hour in the drawing room, as I was worried about getting bedsores. I still ached, and my throat was very painful and in the end tiredness defeated me and I crawled back to my warm nest. Steve was running about the flat with a list in one hand, and the phone in the other. It was strange watching somebody else run your life for you. It made me tired just looking at him, no bloody wonder I was ill if this was how I usually carried on. I fell asleep to the sound of Steve speculating on the whereabouts of Mrs Grieg.

I managed to get out of bed by early evening and spent a couple of hours staring mindlessly at the TV with Steve. I asked him about Connie: if it really was all over between them.

'Well, you know, I think it is. I know I'm a complete bastard . . .'

'All men say that,' I interjected. 'They think it lets them off the hook for behaving appallingly. They think that if they've warned you in advance, you can't then turn round and accuse them of being a shit.'

'As I was saying, I *know* I'm a bastard, but honestly I don't want to be. It's a huge relief, really. She and I were not meant to live together. It's just going to be a huge pain trying to sort everything out, financially, I mean. Oh well, I can always sell my body on the street, can't I?'

'I wouldn't try it, if I were you. You could be standing there for a very, very long time.'

'Thanks.'

'My pleasure.'

Steve made me a Lemsip, and I sat clutching the hot mug. It was disgusting, too sweet and with a nasty chemical aftertaste. I'd rather have had hot water and lemon juice with honey in it.

'Do you think you'll be well enough to go to Mr Abraham's tomorrow?'

'I've got to be. I can't not go, much as I'd like to. It's all part of the job really, isn't it? I shall dose myself up to the eyeballs, and stay for as little time as possible. There's only going to be a handful of people there, anyway.'

'Don't forget William Magpie.'

'Oh God, as if I needed reminding. I still can't imagine why he's been invited, can you?'

'Absolutely no idea at all. Perhaps Mr Abraham wants to get into the gossip columns.'

'Very unlikely. I bet I will though, after Sunday's outing in the tabloids.'

'Yeah, I bet William is licking his lips about that.'

'Me too. Perhaps I should wear jeans and a T-shirt with a strident feminist slogan on it.'

'I thought lesbians were all very chic now.'

'They are,' I said gloomily. 'I can't tell if I've met one or not any more. They always used to look like they belonged to a vegan collective in Islington, now they wear MAC make-up and dress in Armani. It's very confusing.'

I finished my hot drink, and started to go back to bed, after making Steve promise to wake me early. I was just going into the bedroom when the intercom buzzed. Steve answered it and said, 'It's Mark, do you want to see him?'

'God, no! I look dreadful, tell him I'm asleep.' I scuttled into the bedroom.

I heard voices in the hall, and then the front door closed. Steve came into the bedroom clutching a huge bunch of white roses. He handed me a card which said '*Get well soon. When you're better we'll have a proper lunch, consider it a date, nothing to do with business. Love, Mark.*'

Steve looked at me. 'Well, well. It seems you have an admirer. I'd go easy on him, you'd eat him for breakfast.'

'Yeah, like you'd know,' I taunted.

'Go to sleep, you're ill. And I don't have to remind you that you're engaged, do I?'

'Goodnight.'

'Night, Liv, you'll feel better in the morning.'

I lay in bed wondering about Mark. I mean, he was a nice enough man. But then, I don't know about you, but nice has never really appealed to me. As Becky Sharp says in *Vanity Fair*: I'd rather love a rake than a milksop.' Well, that got my vote all right. Still, I thought, I've never actually *tried* a milksop . . . maybe it was time to give it a whirl.

Chapter Twelve

The following morning, as I lay in bed, I tentatively moved my arms and legs to test how much they ached. Not too bad. But I felt very washed out, and it was tempting to pretend to myself that I was more ill than I was, just to have another day in bed. I could hear Steve moving around the flat, and soon he came into my bedroom with a cup of tea.

'How's the invalid today?' he asked.

I groaned, and turned over again. I heard him leave the room and close the door behind him. He knows how vile I can be first thing in the morning, and was clearly anxious to avoid any flak.

I drank my tea, and decided that I really did have to get up and get dressed. I had a bath and looked at my grey face in the mirror. Then I slapped on every beauty treatment I could find, and hoped they would make a difference, though somehow I doubted it. Short of a week in a health spa I couldn't see that anything was going to have much of an effect. My skin had that dull, lifeless look that being ill gives you, my hair was dank and dull and I had got suitcases, not bags, under my eyes. I'd read somewhere that if you put a fork in the freezer and then pressed the cold handle under your eyes it made them better. Well, anything was worth a try. I had just taken the fork from the freezer, and was standing in front of the mirror in the bathroom, with the door open, when Steve walked by.

'What in the name of God are you doing?'

'Trying to gouge my eyes out with a blunt fork, of course.'

'Oh, well, that's OK then.'

He sauntered past me, muttering, 'Women. Can't live with them, can't live without . . .'

Later I sat slumped on my bed, trying to decide what to wear. My plan was to go over to Mr Abraham's, arrange the flat, fiddle with some flowers, check the caterers, and make a few calls. I'd take my mobile with me and do it all from there, so that I'd be ready for the party. There was no point in coming home, as I knew from experience that there would be a hundred and one last-minute jobs to do. I decided on wearing my fake Gaultier pinstripe trouser suit (a present from Monty, via Hong Kong. 'It's perfect, just don't get it wet') and a pink cashmere jumper that I hoped would add colour to my lifeless appearance. I slapped on a lot of make-up, and then had to take most of it off, as it made me look like a clown. I'd have to settle for the pale and interesting look.

Steve forced me to eat breakfast, well, a banana and some orange juice, before I left. I took the keys to Mr Abraham's flat and made Steve promise that he would arrive early.

'Well, I'm not doing anything at all today, I could come with you now, if you like.'

'That would be great. Are you ready?'

'Yes, let me just do my hair.'

I sat down and started to read the paper. I knew how long 'doing' his hair could take. Steve had to wax it, brush it, decide it was wrong, stick his head under the shower and start all over again. You could make hollandaise sauce in the time it takes him to do his hair. I decided to call Molly as I waited; she was on her way back from Norwich.

'How are you feeling? Steve said you were ill.'

'I am, but I'm a bit better now, thanks. What's that awful noise?'

'Children, I'm in a packed train full of a school outing going to London for the day.'

I giggled. 'I bet you're giving them dirty looks. Try making friends with the little darlings.'

'No thanks, they're all monsters, one of the little buggers tried to pinch a cigarette off me! They're only ten!'

'It's never too young to start having fun,' I said sternly. 'Anyway, how were the printers?'

'Pretty bloody. Norwich is awful, though the cathedral close was pretty. Do you want me to come tonight?'

'Of course. You *are* Mr Abraham's official dresser, and my assistant, after all. Don't let me get stuck with William Magpie, OK?'

'OK. Is Joe coming?'

'No, why?'

'I just wondered, that's all.'

'Just because the gorilla is proving elusive, for God's sake don't fall for the BND.'

'He's sweet.'

'That's as may be. Nevertheless, don't do it! See you tonight, bye.'

Steve emerged from the bathroom with dripping wet hair.

'I knew it!' I said triumphantly, 'I knew you'd have to wash it and start again.'

'Can I borrow your hairdryer?'

'Yes, and the electric curlers are in the bedroom.'

'Shut up, I'll only be a minute.'

I started to do the crossword, and got stuck on 'Russia

and I were hungry!' (6), ending with 'T'. I was chewing the end of the pen when Steve finally appeared. He leaned over my shoulder, looking at the clue.

'So, we eat. So, "ve et!" Soviet, get it?'

'Very clever, who thinks these up? Right, are you ready? Come on then, let's go.'

My legs were a bit wobbly and I was definitely feeling light headed as we left the flat. It was still cold outside, and Steve insisted we get a taxi. As he said he'd pay, I agreed. We were carrying the porridge picture between us. I gave a mental wave towards Mrs Grieg, hoping she was somewhere warm by now.

I must admit, I was thrilled about having her Laura Knight (fake or not, it was gorgeous). I had always loved it, and I could see exactly where it should hang in my flat. I wondered about the legality of her bequest, but then I suppose an international thief didn't normally deal with solicitors.

We got a cab to Mr Abraham's. I unlocked the door. For one moment I thought that I was hallucinating. I closed my eyes and opened them again, convinced I couldn't be seeing things properly.

The entire flat was green. Bright, metallic, frosted lime green. Steve clutched my arm. We were both completely silent. I ran from room to room, hoping against hope that something, anything, had been painted the requisite beige. But no. Room after room was the same bright green. Steve had his mouth open, and his hands clamped to either side of his face. He looked like a cartoon character depicting horrified amazement. I sank down into a beige sofa that still had its plastic cover on.

Everywhere I looked, walls, woodwork, doors, ceilings – even the bloody radiators – were frosted lime green.

Mark's words came back to me: 'I was surprised that you

221

had ordered more' . . . I remembered Joe taking a paint delivery for me, I remembered young Roger picking it up, I remembered seeing all the cans from Paintworld stacked in the corner, ready to be opened. Oh God! And I hadn't checked them, not once. I wondered for a minute about fleeing the country, then tried to calculate how long it would take to paint it the right colour. If I called everyone I knew, and we started now, how long would it take to dry – it would need at least two coats. I gave up. It was impossible.

'Dear God! It looks like Garry Glitter might live here,' I said.

'Yes, and look what he turned out to be.'

Incapable of moving, we sat aghast on the plastic-covered sofa, gazing around rather wildly.

'What *am* I going to do?'

I knew I had just asked a purely rhetorical question. There was nothing I could do. It was a glorious cock-up. I started to laugh. Steve joined in, and soon tears were rolling down my face, and Steve was doubled over.

'It looks like an Eastern bloc dance hall.'

'What shall we call it? Krakow 70s disco green?'

'That is an insult to Krakow. Oh my God, is there nothing we can do?'

'Short of repainting, no.'

We'd calmed down a bit by now and I was pondering my fate. It really was all my fault, Doug was away, and young Roger had simply not known otherwise. He'd even left me a note, wishing me well and hoping to work again with me soon.

Steve was striding round the flat, tearing off the packaging from newly delivered pieces of furniture, and coming up with bizarre solutions.

'How about if we cover all the wall space with pictures?

I could get all of yours, then I could go to my studio and get all of mine, then I could hang them, and then . . . Well, and then . . .'

'Stop it, I'm thinking.'

My mind was whirring furiously. There really was nothing I could do, today. I could cancel the party, but I didn't have people's phone numbers. I could just phone Mr Abraham now and make a clean confession, or I could try and do something about it. What was going to make a metallic lime green flat look better? Other than pretending that this was the colour we'd chosen all along, and I knew that, even for me, famous bluffer that I am, this would be an impossibility.

'Chrome!' I suddenly exclaimed.

'What?'

'Chrome. We have to go and buy hundreds of chrome things, you know, ashtrays, beakers, vases, candlesticks, lots of chrome tat, it will pull it together, trust me, I'm an interior designer. It has to be chrome, though, not silver, OK?'

Steve looked doubtful. 'Are you sure?'

'No, but it's worth a try. Come on, let's go.'

There followed an exhausting couple of hours. We agreed to split up, and I tried to give Steve a wad of money from the cash machine. It didn't happen – I was overdrawn. We looked despairingly at each other; I knew that Steve didn't have any money either.

'Shit shit *shit*! What am I going to do?' I felt like crying.

'Who do we know with some dosh?' Steve said.

'Sarah!' we screamed at each other.

I called Sarah and explained the emergency. She was angelic about it, and sent a courier with an envelope full of cash twenty minutes later. The nice thing about having an old friend in a posh job is that you don't have to be too grateful. I practically snatched the money from the courier. Then Steve and I went shopping.

He hit the big stores – Habitat, Heals and Liberty's – while I ran round the smaller shops, madly buying anything and everything that had a chrome finish to it. We met back at the flat several hours later hardly able to walk with the weight of the carrier bags we had draped over our arms. We unloaded our booty, and compared notes.

'I am particularly proud of this lamp, it's got a sort of art deco feel to it, hasn't it?' Steve said, pointing to a singularly unlovely object.

'That's nothing – I got a chrome chess set!'

'Does he play chess?'

'I have no idea, but it's chrome, and that's all that matters at the moment.'

We spread the tat around the flat. I knew that so long as we had enough of it, it would work. And trust me, there *was* enough of it. Kitchen and bathroom objects had been the easiest, and those two rooms didn't look too bad.

There was a ring at the door, and I jumped guiltily, praying it wasn't Mr Abraham. It was the caterers, with the florist bringing up the rear.

'What a super flat.'

Steve and I exchanged glances, not trusting each other to speak. The caterers drifted into the kitchen and began to make smoked salmon pâté and chill the champagne. I had ordered only white flowers from the florist anyway, so luckily they looked all right. Soon, huge drooping arrangements were placed strategically around the flat. I was hoping that candlelight would help to soften everything down, and started to light the numerous candles I'd bought, all, of course, in chrome holders.

'What on earth are you going to say to Mr Abraham?'

'Well, I don't know, I've been thinking about that all day. At first I thought I'd say something about trying out a different finish on the walls, and that it hadn't worked, and it would all have to be repainted. Then I thought about fainting, or throwing some sort of fit in the hope of creating a diversion . . .'

Steve snorted.

'Or – damp! Damp has come through the walls, and made it this very peculiar colour because it combined with the paint, and the chemical effect was such that . . .'

There was more snorting from Steve.

'Or, I guess I could just say sorry and offer to repaint tomorrow.'

'I'd go with that version, if I were you.'

'I know. Oh God, what a mess.'

The doorbell went again, and I braced myself for Mr Abraham. I opened the door, and almost sobbed with relief: Zena, Molly and Sarah had faithfully arrived early.

I pulled them inside and started a garbled explanation. Zena stared at the walls in silence for a moment and then headed over to the table where glasses of champagne had been poured for the early arrivals. She picked one up, drained it and then picked up another. Sarah was also too shell shocked to say anything, but followed Zena's example and picked up a flute of champagne.

'Don't worry, darling,' Zena eventually reassured me, 'leave him to me. I'm sure he won't kick up about it, and if he does, we'll just tell him that it's *too* perfect and he mustn't change a thing.'

Molly was looking thoughtful. She started to say something to me, but my attention was distracted by the doorbell going again. It was Mr Abraham. I took a deep breath. He walked in, looked around and beamed, 'Well, it all looks splendid, doesn't it?'

I introduced Zena, and immediately she started to charm him. It wasn't hard, and he was soon, metaphorically, at her feet.

I looked at Molly for reassurance: she had tears of silent laughter running down her face.

'He's colour blind,' she mouthed at me.

'No!'

I looked at him chatting away to Zena and Sarah, smiling the proud smile of a man who'd got his dream flat. He was wearing a new suit, obviously the one he'd bought on his shopping spree with Molly. It was dark grey, and he wore it with a blue shirt and a pink and blue striped tie.

Molly grabbed me by the arm and we went into the kitchen.

'Honestly, Liv, it's true. When I went shopping with him I noticed that he didn't really know what beige was, so I kept quiet, and when I guided him towards blue, for instance, he didn't seem to notice anything at all! It's remarkable, isn't it?'

Faint with relief, I grabbed a glass of champagne and drank it.

'What do we do if somebody mentions it?' I hissed at her.

'We'll have to head them off at the pass,' she hissed back.

The next guests to arrive were two well upholstered, immaculately dressed elderly women. They had obviously been friends of Mr Abraham's mother, and they seemed quite content to make the rounds of the flat, commenting more on what had been there, than what actually was now. I made Steve escort them, giving him strict instructions to keep their glasses permanently topped up.

'This used to be a lovely room.'

'Not that it isn't now.'

'Oh no, but it used to be lovely, didn't it?'

Mr Abraham, rather surprisingly, winked at me when we overheard this exchange.

The next guest was a plump middle-aged woman wearing a fur coat. She purred at Mr Abraham, who blushed slightly and withdrew with her to the hallway, giving her a guided tour.

The two elderly women seemed scandalised.

'The nerve of her, walking in like that.'

'She'll nab him now, sure as eggs is eggs.'

'And his mother not cold in her grave!'

I was intrigued. Was this the woman from his past, who ate all of the asparagus?

The doorbell went again. William Magpie sauntered into the flat, a trifle unsteady on his pins, and said in a very loud voice, 'So the charming Olivia does it again! Well done, my dear, a vast improvement on my late mother's home, and where is my brother?'

'Your what?'

'My brother, Sol Abraham. We haven't spoken for years, but when I got your charming invitation, I thought to myself, well, let bygones be bygones. So, here I am! Now then, I simply must ask you, Olivia, what truth in the rumour about you and Nicola Bentley?'

'None whatsoever,' I said rather faintly.

I was much more interested in how Mr Abraham would react to seeing William in his flat. I couldn't imagine two more different people, and then to discover that they were brothers! It seemed extraordinary. The two elderly women were having a ball now. They were fanning themselves and looking flustered.

'My God! What would she have said? Him as well as her! The nerve, the sheer nerve!'

'Don't distress yourself, Queenie, have another drink. Remember your blood pressure.'

'Do you want to leave?'

'Leave! Are you mad?!'

They were hanging on every word. And, I have to admit, so was I. Mr Abraham came back into the room with the fur-coated woman on his arm and stopped at the sight of William. The two men looked at each other in silence for a while and then suddenly embraced.

'Solly!'

'Bill!'

They held each other for quite a while. Then William spotted the woman in the fur coat.

'My God! Sylvia!'

It was her turn for a kiss and a hug. Mr Abraham looked like the cat who'd swallowed the cream. He tapped his champagne glass and said, 'Can I have your attention, everybody. First of all I should like to welcome you all to my new home, especially my brother, Bill. Then I would like you all to offer me your congratulations, as this charming lady here – ' he gave a courtly little bow to Sylvia – 'has just consented to be my wife.'

William Magpie bellowed his congratulations, and we all crowded round the happy couple.

'Get your coat, Queenie, we're going.'

The two elderly women walked indignantly to the front door, but nobody seemed to care. Mr Abraham was opening more champagne, and filling glasses. Zena kissed him on the cheek, and Molly spilt her drink over the carpet in her excitement. Sarah was smiling, and mouthed at me 'Thank God!'

Steve and I looked at each other in amazement. I was bewildered at the turn of events: the flat which was a disaster had turned into a triumph, and now there was a reunited family, and a wedding in the offing.

Zena whispered in my ear, 'Do you think it's time to go, darling, I think we're a little *de trop* here, now, don't you?'

I agreed.

We all said our farewells, William lingering a little too long for my liking in saying goodbye to me. We left, agog with the evening's outcome, decided to go to the reopening of the Bar, and managed to flag down a taxi. That was one of the best things about going out with Zena, she always succeeded, even in the pouring rain, in hailing a taxi. She just stood by the road, and a black cab would glide up to her. We were chattering madly as we climbed in the cab.

'Well, what an evening! I thought at first I was going to have to leave the country in a fast car!'

'Don't tell me – the amount of chrome I managed to get for you today has to go in *The Guinness Book of Records*.'

'Colour blind! What luck!'

'He's a darling, *most* unlike his brother, a nasty little man if ever there was one.'

'And who was *she*?'

'I reckon she's one of William's exes and that's why the two of them stopped talking.'

'Do you think we'll all be invited to the wedding?'

'Oh, I *do* hope so, darling.'

'God, imagine what William's column is going to be full of now! We'll never hear the end of it.'

'Wait till we tell Pete . . .'

'Wait till we tell Monty!'

'Steve, what *is* that in your bag? You haven't, have you?'

Steve admitted, very shamefully that yes, he had whipped a chrome candlestick.

'Whatever for?'

'A memento.'

'You're mad . . .'

'Barking, definitely.'

The cab stopped outside the Bar. On entering I was glad to see that the place was full. Pete was behind the bar, opening the inevitable bottle of champagne.

We kissed him hello, and told him of the day we'd had. I was concerned to see that Pete looked exhausted, and was trying hard to be his normal self. I could see that it was a struggle and had to remind myself not to fuss over him.

'My God! Get those drinks down your throats immediately. What a hoot!'

There were a lot of friends in the place, so we table-hopped for a while. I was talking to Sarah, who was moaning about her job, when Molly whispered, 'Liv, Christopher has just come in.'

I turned to look, and came abruptly face to face with him. There was an awkward silence, broken by him saying, 'Livia, I must talk to you. But not here. Come for a drink, please.'

Steve was glaring at him, and I saw that Molly had taken up a protective stance by my side. I deliberated.

Christopher touched my hand, and said, 'Please, just one drink.'

I handed my glass to Molly, saying, 'I'll be fifteen minutes, max.'

I followed him out of the door, and walked in silence by his side. Instinctively, we trod the path to the Casa, and walked in to find a table. I sat down and waited to hear what he had to say. I remembered Steve's comment about a raddled chimp, and how it had cheered me up, but now, nose to nose with Christopher, the old feelings had started to return. He placed a drink in front of me, and I rather nervously played with it. He cleared his throat, and I glanced up at him. I saw his low hairline, weak chin, and the deceit in his eyes.

'That's better. Oh, Liv, I have missed you so much, darling. I had to see you.'

'Umm, I gather you came round the other morning . . .'

'Yes, sorry it was so early. What's Steve doing there?'

'It's a long story. What do you want, Christopher?'

'You.'

'What exactly do you mean?'

'I want you. I can't go on like this, I love you Olivia. I miss your friendship, your foul moods in the mornings, your toes, your laughter, your hand in mine, your kiss goodnight, your tone-deaf singing, your green eyes, your breath whispering in my ear, your heartbeat next to mine, your hands on my back, your—'

'Shut up.'

'Please, darling, listen to me. I love you, don't you understand that? I can't live like this any more. I can't work, I can't do anything but think about you.'

I sipped my drink, studying him. Mrs Grieg had been right. He was a wrong 'un.

'What about Danielle? Where does she come into all of this?'

'I'll leave her.'

'I don't want you to.'

'Darling, please, please Liv, give me another chance. Let's go away together, let me show you what it could be like.'

'No thanks. You'd be in bed with the waitress within two days. I don't know how Danielle has stood it, all these years.

231

You're a bore, Christopher, an unfaithful man is a bore. I don't think I even like you any more. Go home. Go home to Danielle, and leave me alone.'

I stood up, ready to leave. His hand shot out and grabbed my wrist, hard.

'Stop it, you're hurting me.'

'And what do you think you're doing to me! I hurt all of the time . . .'

'Oh grow up. You think that you're being intense and interesting, but you're not. It's just tedious. And, in case you've forgotten, I've heard it all before.'

His grip tightened on my arm. 'I've said please, I've asked you nicely, and now I'm going to make you listen. Sit down – once you know how much I love you, you'll understand.'

I wrenched my arm away from him.

'You're right about one thing: I do understand. I understand that you are a married man, and it was my fault that I ever got involved with you in the first place. But now it's over. Go home to your long-suffering wife.'

Ben appeared at my side, 'Is everything OK over here?'

I looked at him gratefully. 'Yes, thanks. I'm just leaving.'

'I don't think it's you who should be going. I think the gentleman was just leaving,' Ben said, looking pointedly at Christopher.

I dreaded a scene. It all rather depended on how much Christopher had had to drink. He was famous for causing a fuss, I'd lost count of the times I had been in bars and restaurants with him, praying for the ground to open up and swallow me. I hoped this wasn't going to be one of them.

Christopher stood up, knocking his chair over. He picked up his drink and for one awful moment I thought he was going to throw it at me. He looked like a baby having a tantrum: a nasty man had come and taken his toy away. Then he slammed his glass back down on the table and stormed out.

Ben returned to his place behind the bar, giving my shoulder a reassuring squeeze on his way. I lit a cigarette with rather shaky hands. As luck would have it, I saw Angie in the corner of the room, smirking at me. I ignored her and sipped my drink. On reflection I was rather proud of my behaviour. I had told him to go, and I had meant it. So I hoped. It seemed to me that I was one of those people who find it very hard to stop loving someone, even when they don't even really like them any more. I sipped my drink and tried to decide what to do. I didn't want to go back to the Bar. Christopher would have gone straight back there.

Ben brought me over another drink, and as I thanked him I saw that Angie was bearing down on me. Great, just what I needed.

'Livia, I saw you in the papers on Sunday. I was surprised! I didn't know that you were that way.'

'What way?'

'You know, gay . . .' She trilled with laughter.

I couldn't be bothered to answer her.

'Anyway, I saw Christopher leave just now, it's simply no good pleading with him, you know. If it's over, you just have to let it go. Perhaps you should go and find Nicola Bentley?'

'Angie?'

'Yes?'

'Fuck off.'

'Well, really.' She flounced away.

I went to the Ladies, pulled out my phone and rang Molly. She answered immediately.

'Liv? Are you OK?'

'Yeah, so-so. I'm at the Casa. Look, Moll, I think I'm

going to go straight home, I don't feel like seeing anybody, really. Is Christopher there?'

'No, he's not. Don't go. I'll come over there, we all will.'

'No, no don't, please. I'm perfectly OK, but I am really tired. I have been ill, you know. I just want to go to bed. Tell Steve not to make a noise when he comes in, and give Pete a kiss for me, OK?'

'Hang on a moment, Zena's saying something.' There was muffled talk in the background, and Molly came back on the phone.

'Zena says not to worry about anything, and do you want a lift?'

'Thank her, but no. I'll call you in the morning. Bye. Oh, and thank Sarah for me, will you? Tell her I'll repay her as soon as I can.'

I stared at the noticeboard, wondering if I could add something nasty to it about Angie. I decided against it, congratulated myself on not being childish, and headed back upstairs to finish my drink. Then I sat down and gave myself time to figure out how I really felt about Christopher. The truth was, I didn't know. All I seemed to know for certain was that I wanted to go home. I realised that all I'd eaten today was a banana, with several glasses of champagne and now a couple of vodkas. Home and food, that's what I needed. I stood up and made my way to the door, waving goodbye to Ben.

I'd just got on to the pavement outside the Casa, and was looking for a taxi, when I heard my name being called. Mark was running from the other side of the road towards me.

'Livia, how are you? Feeling any better?'

I looked steadily at him. Perhaps this was the port in the storm that I'd been looking for. Yeah, he'd do. Well, he'd do for tonight, anyway.

'Where do you live?' I asked him.

'Belsize Park. Why?'

'Because you're going to take me home and I'm going to thank you for the lovely, lovely roses that you sent me.'

He looked terribly surprised, but not, I hasten to add, too displeased. I was drunk enough not to care what I was saying, and not quite drunk enough not to know what I was doing.

We found a taxi, and I insisted on stopping to buy champagne which, disgracefully, I opened in the taxi and swigged straight from the bottle. I made Mark drink some as well, then I stumbled out of the cab and propped myself up at his front door. Rather nervously, Mark opened the door and I followed him in, swinging the half-empty bottle by the neck. He had the look of a man who'd grabbed a tiger by the tail and didn't know what to do with it.

His flat was pretty much how I expected it to be: single man, neat, tidy, and tasteful in the extreme. Mark found glasses and poured more champagne, and even as I was drinking it I was thinking to myself, 'Stop it right now, go and eat something and go home, alone, and go to bed.' But I didn't.

I stood up, took my jacket off and threw it across the room. I slipped my shoes off and walked rather unsteadily towards Mark. I put my hand out towards him and said, 'Now, why don't you show me where your bedroom is?'

Chapter Thirteen

I walked through Belsize Park shivering. There was a weak sun but it was very cold and I bitterly regretted not having a coat with me. I punched in Molly's number and said '*Africa*'. It was our own private code: it meant, I've done something stupid, drop everything, I need to talk. (This had originated with one of Molly's particularly adventurous sexual encounters. They had both agreed to try a little S& M, and Africa was the code word they'd agreed to use for when they wanted to stop. Molly found herself blindfolded and trussed up like a chicken, and unable to remember it. She'd been crying out 'Australia' and 'America' till she finally hit on the right continent, much to her relief.)

'Oh God, where are you?'

'In Belsize Park.'

'Well, I'm at work, I can meet you in half an hour some-where, where do you want to go?'

I thought for a bit. I wanted to go somewhere calm, and cosy.

'The Mock Turtle.'

'OK. Are you all right?' Molly sounded anxious.

'Oh yes, if you count feeling an absolute idiot all right . . .'

The Mock Turtle was a tea room that we occasionally frequented. It had oak tables, squat brown china teapots and a lemon drizzle cake to die for. It was the sort of place that nothing bad could ever happen in. I walked there briskly, trying to warm myself up, keeping a picture of a plate of hot cinnamon toast in my mind to spur me on. People all around me were wrapped up against the cold, but I needed the fresh air, and persevered against the icy wind.

I finally reached the tea room, my ears were stinging from the cold air outside, and I gratefully sat down at a small round table. The relief of being in the warm was bliss. I ordered the cinnamon toast and tea, and waited for Molly. Soon I saw her from the window, running down the street trying to keep her coat together with one hand and holding her phone to her ear with the other. She burst through the door, sat down beside me and turned her phone off.

'Well?'

'Oh, Molly, I've made a *huge* mistake.'

'Tell, tell. Where *were* you last night? Steve's been going crazy, he thinks you've run off with Christopher . . .'

'No! Oh, I'll call him in a moment . . . Oh God, it was awful . . .'

'Let's start from the very beginning.'

'A very good place to start. OK.'

I paused while the waitress brought the tea and toast, Molly ordered a teacake and we sipped and munched for a while.

'Well, after a short, sharp exchange of views with Christopher at the Casa, it suddenly hit me that I was a bit drunk, I mean, not falling down or anything, but aware that I was in need of food and bed . . .'

'Obviously not your own, more's the pity, by the look of you.'

'Thanks. Anyway, I'd just told Angie to fuck off and—'

'No! you didn't! Oh, well done.'

'Anyway, I'd just got outside and was looking for a taxi, and I ran into Mark.'

'Who?'

'The man from Paintworld, who keeps sending that awful metallic stuff. I met him at Battersea the other day, and he took me home in a cab because I wasn't feeling very well. It turns out that his friend painted that terrible porridge picture that Zena bought for Mr Abraham. He seemed really nice, and he asked me out to dinner, then he sent roses, and when I saw him last night outside the Casa . . .'

'You went home with him, and now you regret it?'

'It's much, much worse than that. Listen, I thought he was nice, you know? Like, *nice*, not kinky or anything. In fact, when we first got to his flat, I did all the running, really. I wanted to shake off Christopher and I thought some mindless passionate sex would do the trick.'

'So what happened?'

'Oh God, well, I was drinking heavily and I dragged him into his bedroom, and then . . .'

'What? For God's sake, Liv, what happened?'

'Well, we were pretty much naked and on the bed, when he suddenly stopped and asked me if I was 'up for it'. I thought he meant poppers, or something. So I sort of said yes, and he said he'd be back in a minute.'

'I don't think I like the sound of this.'

'Well, he was gone for ages, so I finished the champagne and realised that I was very drunk indeed. The door opened, and he walked in dressed from head to foot in black, spiky rubber.'

'No!'

'Ssh, keep your voice down. When I say head to foot, I mean he had on a hood, with a zip where the mouth should be, a tube coming out of it, rubber straps across his chest, a sort of spiked thing round his dick, and he was pierced. I mean he was pierced *everywhere*, oh and he was shaved.' I was leaning forward whispering all of this.

'What do you mean he was shaved?' Molly whispered.

'Shaved balls, no pubic hair. Oh, and he was wearing thigh-length rubber boots. With *heels*.'

'No wonder he was gone ages, it must take hours to get into all of that stuff.'

'Yeah, well, anyway he was carrying something.'

'What?' Molly was whispering with horrified curiosity.

'Something for me.'

'Oh God, what was it, tell me quickly.'

'A black rubber catsuit that had strategically cut out holes in it.'

'No!'

'Oh yes.'

'Then what?'

'Well, all I can tell you is that it takes talcum powder and a lot of determination to get into it, specially when you're so drunk you keep falling over.'

'You didn't!'

'I did. But worse is yet to—'

'Please don't say come.'

Molly was stifling her laughter by holding a paper napkin to her mouth, she poured us some more tea, and leaned forward eager to hear more.

'Well, the worst thing is that I fell asleep . . .'

'You *can't* have done.'

'Well, I did. I mean we sort of did it, and the . . .'

'I really hope you had safe sex.'

'With all that rubber? Are you kidding? Anyway, as I was saying, I think we made some pathetic attempt at it, and then I just fell asleep. I woke up this morning and he was stroking my hair, and gazing at me . . .'

'Oh yuck.'

'I know, there's nothing worse, is there? A pair of puppy dog eyes looking at you with slavish devotion, it only means one thing.'

'Yeah, he's going to call you the next day.'

We both burst out laughing.

'The most embarrassing thing was, though, that this morning I couldn't get out of the bloody catsuit by myself. I had to ask him to *help* me, for Chrissake.'

Molly was helpless with laughter by now. She clutched my hand, and said, 'Oh, Livia, you really are—' then stopped suddenly and clutched my hand harder, looking at it.

'Liv! The ring, where's your ring?'

I glanced down sharply at my hand. My fingers were bare. Oh my God, where was it? I ran through last night's hideous experience, trying to remember . . .

I closed my eyes, and I could see, quite clearly, the ring balanced on the ledge of Mark's washbasin. I'd had to take it off when I was struggling out of the catsuit, the black rubber arms were so tight.

'Shit shit *shit*. I know exactly where it is. In his bloody bathroom.'

'Well, at least we know where it is, and that it's safe.'

I looked appealingly at her, 'Moll, I *can't* go back there.'

'Well, I can't go can I?'

'Why not?'

'Oh excuse me, Mr Rubber Pervert, you don't know me, but I believe my best friend left her engagement ring in your bathroom this morning, may I have it back please?'

'Oh, go on. Please . . . Well, at least come with me?'

'Oh, OK then, but when? I mean, he's probably at work now, isn't he?'

She was probably right. I wasn't even sure I could remember the address; that meant I'd have to phone him at work, and arrange to go over there later. Damn. Molly had to go back to work, and I got a cab home. She kissed me goodbye, and told me not to beat myself up. I promised to call her later and then phoned Steve to tell him I was OK, and that I'd see him in a minute.

I leaned back in the taxi and closed my eyes. It was all very well for Molly to tell me not to beat myself up about it, and I certainly didn't suffer from that most wasted emotion, guilt, but I did feel pretty awful, all tacky and grubby. I sighed. I probably felt hungover too, but when didn't I recently? I opened my eyes and looked at the cold grey London streets. Tired of London, tired of life? Well, maybe I was. Perhaps I just needed a holiday, I thought. The taxi was in the usual midday gridlock; it would have been quicker to take the tube, but I was so cold.

I let myself into the flat, and Steve immediately called out 'Dirty stopout!' I gave him a friendly slap, and ran myself a bath. Hot scented water has miraculous restorative properties, and I felt ten times better by the time I got out.

I told Steve of last night's adventures, over hot chocolate in the kitchen.

'God, and you think I'm bad. It's so unfair. What was it like wearing a rubber catsuit?'

'Nowhere near as sexy as you obviously think,' I said acidly. 'Uncomfortable and clammy, and exceedingly difficult to get in and out of.'

'When you say he was pierced everywhere . . .'

'Yes, I do mean everywhere. Enough! I really don't want

to think about it any more.' I'd started to feel queasy. What *had* I been thinking of?

'And just imagine, I opened the door to him, he certainly doesn't *look* weird, does he?'

'That was the whole point, it was such a surprise. Anyway, I think you should come with us tonight to get my ring back.'

Steve started to protest, but I quelled him with a glare, saying, 'Do I really have to point out to you all the things that I have done for you, over the years. What about the time that you woke up on a train in Lewes and you thought that it was in Scotland, and I had to—'

'OK, OK, I take your point. Come into the other room, I've got a surprise for you.'

I got wearily to my feet, I wasn't in the mood for surprises. Steve took me by the hand and opened the drawing-room door. Hanging, exactly where I'd imagined it would go, was Mrs Grieg's picture.

'Joe and I got it this morning. What do you think?'

'It's gorgeous. It's certainly the classiest thing I've got. Damn good fake, isn't it?'

Its misty glow shone from the wall. It was beautiful, and I knew that every time I looked at it I would wonder about Mrs Grieg. I hoped she was happy growing her roses somewhere as beautiful as her picture.

I asked Steve if there had been any messages.

'Yes. Kerrison rang, will you call him as soon as possible.' My heart sank: it's never good news if your accountant wants to speak to you urgently.

'Anyone else?'

'A man called John, and Nicola. She'd like to see you before she goes.'

'OK, I'm going to lock myself in the office and make some calls. Have you heard from Connie?'

'No, and quite frankly I don't want to either.'

'Hmm.'

'What does that mean?'

'It means the lady doth protest too much, I think.'

'We'll see.'

I closed the door to my office, then opened it again. 'Have you thought what we're going to say to Mimi yet?'

'No . . . That reminds me, Monty called. Apparently she's doing really well and she might even get some magazine work.'

'That would be a relief, wouldn't it? I mean, they pay squillions, don't they?' I said hopefully. Maybe she wouldn't mind so much about losing her heirloom if she was coining it in.

I sat down and started to do some work. I called Nicola, and after discussing the plans for her house, she told me that she'd booked a flight for two days' time, and could she buy us all dinner?

'Honestly, Nicola, that's really nice of you, but—'

'Look, you and your friends have been so nice to me, I'd really like to thank you all. How about tomorrow night? I'll book the Ivy.'

That stunned me. Anyone who can get a table for a Friday at the Ivy was very impressive indeed. I thanked her and promised to round everyone up.

I called Pete, who was delighted to go. He reminded me: '. . . and the following morning we're off to Brighton, for a weekend of hell. So I don't want you worming out of it, OK?'

I agreed, and then he asked what had happened to me last

night. I gave him a shortened version, and he roared with laughter.

'Well, that'll make a nice topic of conversation over the roast beef on Sunday, won't it? Why don't you nick the rubber catsuit when you go back to get the ring? I can see you wearing it down to the Yacht Club – very nautical.'

He was still laughing when I put the phone down.

I left a message for Monty, and then steeled myself to speak to Kerrison. I delayed this chore by making myself a cup of tea and gazing mindlessly out of the window for a while. Eventually I dialled his number.

Talking to him certainly wiped the smile off my face. I was in debt, I owed the taxman, the bank, *and* Kerrison. The bank wasn't very happy about extending my overdraft (well, neither was I, but I had to eat, as I pointed out to them). I was going to have to get some money from somewhere. Mr Abraham had paid me, but the money had just got swallowed up in the general debt. Nicola's job was going to be large, but I wasn't sure about asking for front money. Ironically, the fact that we'd become friends made me much more circumspect than I'd usually be about it.

I thought about Freddy. Even if I did do some work for him, I was pretty sure I'd spend most of my time being chased around his Jacobean four-poster. Suddenly, working for myself didn't seem quite such a good idea any more. I wasn't sure if I could go on financially and I wasn't even sure that I wanted to.

Tarting up other people's homes wasn't much of a job, was it? Maybe I should try to get myself a partner, someone to share the worry with? I sighed, and stared out of the window once more. It was raining, again. When I'm dictator of the world, I thought to myself, the first thing that I do will be to tow Britain somewhere warm. Not tropical, or where nobody would get anything done, somewhere just off the south of France would be lovely. I sighed again then picked up the phone, and spoke to Molly.

'You sound fed up,' she said.

'I am. Apparently, I'm in debt. Plus it's raining, I've got rubber burns all over my body, I still hate my ex, married lover, and I've got to go to Brighton to Pete's parents for the weekend . . . Oh but I do have some good news.'

'Excellent. You were starting to depress me. What's the good bit?'

'Dinner at the Ivy, tomorrow, on Nicola.'

'Fantastic! That's really nice of her. Is . . .'

'Joe coming? Oh God, Molly, stop it. I suppose so, I'll ask him.'

'You're just cranky because you're tired. Go and sleep for an hour or so, I'll come and pick you up. Have you spoken to rubber man?'

'Not yet, he was my next call.'

'Good luck.'

I put the phone down and stared round the office. It had doubled as Molly's bedroom, and was now Steve's. It was a mess, with papers and journals in piles on the floor and stacked on every shelf. I'd have to have a huge clearout, one day. Maybe I should do it now, get some rubbish bags . . . I sighed again. I was just putting off phoning Mark.

Steeling myself, I picked up the phone and heard myself ask for him. He came on the line quickly, sounding a bit breathless.

'Livia! How nice to hear from you,' he gushed disconcertingly. 'I was just about to call you. How are you feeling?'

Surprised, grubby, tacky, sore and definitely not keen on seeing you ever again.

245

'Umm, well, I'm OK. The thing is, Mark, I left a ring in your flat, and I need to pick it up. Are you in this evening?'

'Definitely. Honestly Livia, I really, really enjoyed last night. Why don't you come over about seven, I'll cook dinner and . . .' he trailed off suggestively.

Yuck! No thanks, mate.

'Umm, well, the thing is, I've arranged to go out with some friends, so, if it's OK with you, I'll stop by with them on our way out, just to pick up my ring.'

He gave what he clearly thought was an alluring, low laugh.

I practically shuddered as I put the phone down. How *could* I have mistaken such a slimeball for a nice man? I went into my bedroom and chucked his roses into the bin.

I lay down on my bed, and tried hard not to feel too disheartened. Perhaps it was the after-effects of being ill, or dwelling on Mark, but it seemed to me that my life at the moment was a bit murky. I was definitely drinking too much. I'd forgiven myself for the coke binge the other week, and had promised myself not to go back to it, but it was more than that.

It seemed impossible to have a relationship with a man any more. I wasn't sure if I even wanted one. What was the point? Even sex wasn't that simple. What was the problem with modern relationships? Was I ever going to find a man who wasn't married, strange or gay? Gradually I fell asleep, wondering if it was possible to give up sex completely and take up knitting or gardening instead. Maybe, but probably not.

I heard the buzzer go, and then I heard Molly and Steve talking in the hallway. I looked at my alarm clock, and was surprised to see it was six in the evening. I'd slept for ages. I got out of bed and went to the bathroom, calling out hello. I threw cold water over my face and brushed my hair, then dressed in black pants and a black jumper, pulled some boots on and went through to the kitchen. Molly and Steve were rocking with laughter, sitting side by side at the table.

'What's so funny?' I demanded.

'The price of latex has just shot up on the Stock Exchange,' joked Molly.

'Stop it, you two. We've got to go over to rubber man in a moment. You've both got to come in with me, I can't possibly face him on my own.'

I wasn't nervous about seeing him again, more horribly embarrassed, but I certainly wasn't going to go alone.

'OK, shall we go out to dinner afterwards?' Steve asked.

'No, I can't. After my talk with Kerrison, I'll be eating baked beans for the rest of my life.'

'Is it that bad?'

'Let's just say that it's not that good, shall we.'

'Is it economy drive time?' Molly asked, gloomily.

'Yes. I'm afraid so. I'll cook you both supper, though, how about it?'

'Great, I'll buy the wine.'

I shuddered at the thought of it, and made a mental promise to stick to water.

In the taxi to Mark's, I told Molly and Steve that we had to pretend we were going on somewhere, and we'd keep the taxi running. I jumped out when we got to his flat, dragging my two very unwilling friends with me.

'Suppose he answers the door in all his gear?' Molly whispered.

'Don't be silly, of course he won't. He wouldn't, would he?' I whispered back.

Steve was looking a bit nervous by the time Mark opened the door and asked us all to come inside. I introduced Molly to him, explained that we'd got a taxi waiting, and could I just have my ring, please?

He looked disappointed, and asked us in anyway, while he went to get it. We all stood in an uncomfortable silence in his hallway, and listened to him moving around his flat. The previous night's activities flashed through my mind, and I wanted to curl up and die.

'There's a funny smell in here,' Molly said.

'Burning rubber,' Steve whispered back.

I hushed them, and we avoided looking at one another, waiting for Mark to reappear. I had an urgent need to go to the loo, but was determined not to use his bathroom.

Steve was sniggering, so I pinched him. We were scuffling around in the hallway when Mark came back with my ring in the palm of his hand.

'It looks real. Is it?' he asked, handing it to me.

'Umm, yes it is. It's my engagement ring, actually.'

He looked unbelievingly at me. 'So, where are you all off to then?' he said, after a rather long pause.

'The theatre.'

'A restaurant.'

'The theatre, followed by dinner,' I said firmly. 'OK, then, thanks, Mark. Bye.'

'Livia, do come back later, won't you?'

I gave my best imitation Zena vague smile and pushed Molly and Steve out of the flat muttering 'Not bloody likely' as the front door closed behind us.

As we ran to the taxi I pushed the ring firmly back on my finger. I was never going to take it off again.

Back at the flat, having first run hurriedly to the bathroom I started to cook supper. Pompously I declined a glass of wine and poured myself a huge glass of water.

'You might as well drink wine, if you're going to insist on drinking London tap water,' said Molly.

'Shut up. It's my liver and I'll do what I want with it.'

Steve walked into the kitchen and said hopefully, 'Liver, are we having liver for dinner? ooh, yummy.'

'Livia's liver, not offal, which is disgusting, not yummy at all.'

'Why on earth are you talking about your liver?'

'Because my liver feels in the need of a complete rest. Don't you ever feel grubby inside? All I've been doing recently is drinking too much, and it's making me feel decidedly liverish. If it wasn't for the state of my bank balance, I'd go on holiday. I'm really fed up with London at the moment. Don't you ever feel like that?'

'Frequently, and then something happens, and I can't imagine living anywhere else in the world.'

'But Steve, what about the traffic, and the cold, and the dirt. What about the bloody bomb at the Bar, for God's sake?'

'Those things happen everywhere, you know,' Molly objected. 'But I wouldn't say no to a little bit of sun. Why *don't* we go on holiday?

'Oh yes, I can see it now. My bank manager will be falling over himself to lend me money to go on a bloody holiday, won't he?'

I tore up some spinach, and started to slice garlic ready for the spaghetti. I gave Steve the cheese grater and a hunk of parmesan, and handed Molly the lemons to squeeze.

'I just want to go somewhere that's sunny, where there's no cold wind blowing, in every sense of the word. Somewhere people smile instead of bashing into you in the streets looking grumpy and miserable. I want to see olive trees and vines growing and . . .'

'And stunning Italian men who don't care if you've got a big bum,' Molly said wistfully.

'And you can buy a decent bottle of wine for under three quid,' Steve added in a dreamlike voice.

I was warming to my theme now.

'Yes, and there are fields of lavender, and men don't dress up in rubber, and there are no taxi queues, and tomatoes taste of tomatoes and are still warm from the sun. There are no colour-blind elderly men who want their mother's flat ripped to pieces, in fact, there are no interior designers. Because everyone lives in cool, whitewashed villas . . .'

'And you can hear the sea from your bed, and there is watermelon for breakfast, and slightly shabby rattan furniture on a balcony, with jasmine climbing up the walls.' Molly had joined in.

'And a fabulous little taverna just up the road that cooks divine mussels, and the owner's daughter looks just like Zena, but not quite so vague, and she gives me free drinks when her papa isn't looking because she likes me so much . . .'

'Goats, there have to be goats, just so that we can hear the bells round their necks tinkling in the distance.'

'Can we have an orchard, I really need an orchard nearby, I've always wanted to sit in an apple tree and sketch.'

'What about the wasps?'

'There won't be any. And there'll be terracotta tiles in the kitchen, that have to be swept every morning, and delicious coffee that we can drink out of oversized cups.'

'And olives. They'll be the most delicious olives in the world . . .'

'Will there be a swimming pool?'

'Hmm, I'm not sure, the sea is so close, I don't think so . . .'

'And the local village will have a fiesta every week, and

carry a statue of the Virgin into the sea, wine will flow in the streets, and the priest will get pissed, but no one will mind . . .'

'And I can waft about in white linen, looking extremely arty and clever and carry a notebook with me, and everyone will think that I'm a famous author.'

'I'm a bit worried about the fiesta thing, will there be fireworks? I'm not keen on fireworks.'

'Oh God, I *love* fireworks.'

We finished dinner and washed up, still dreaming out this fantasy, then wandered into the drawing room and switched on the TV.

A poker-faced middle-aged man in a suit said, 'One of the legendary rock stars of this country, Sam Bentley, has been found dead in his hotel room in New York. The police are treating the death as suspicious.' There followed a montage of hastily thrown together clips of Sam in his heyday, singing 'Satanic Girl' at Wembley Stadium to a very unimpressed Prince of Wales.

'Oh my God . . . Poor Nicola,' I gasped. I couldn't believe it. None of us could, and for a few minutes we just sat there, watching him gyrate around the stage.

'What can we do?' Molly said.

'I wonder what really happened?' asked Steve.

'God knows,' I said. 'But I've just had the rather unworthy thought that it's a bit *Spinal Tap*, isn't it?'

'Livia!'

'I know, but it is. I mean, rock star dies in hotel room, was he murdered, was it an overdose, was it some sex game, or did he explode while plugging in his guitar?' Believe me here, I'm not at all proud of this, but it *did* cross my mind. But I was really sad for Nicola, and wondered if I should call her.

'Liv, I really think you should call her, you know,' Steve said.

Molly agreed with him.

'She's hardly going to be answering her phone, is she?' I objected.

'Well, leave a message at least. I really think you should,' Molly urged.

I knew she was right, so reluctantly I dialled her number.

Her answering machine clicked on. 'Hello Nicola, it's Liv here. We've all just seen the news . . . I am so sorry. Please call if there's anything we can do, won't you? God, I hate people who say that . . . But, just call, OK? It would be lovely to hear from you. We're all thinking about you.' I hung up.

We all sat around speculating on the awful death of Sam Bentley, and I wondered what Nicola was doing, and just how upset she was. I also, rather gloomily, thought that it might affect my job with her. I could well imagine how thrilled my bank manager would be about *that*. I was in the kitchen making some tea when the phone rang. To my great surprise it was Nicola. She sounded very upset indeed and incredibly touched that I had bothered to call, it seemed that all her other so-called friends were more interested in Sam than her, and hadn't called her at all.

'Oh Livia, it's awful here . . . Reporters are arriving by the carload, bloody Rick has gone off somewhere, I'm all alone. The phone is ringing off its hook, the vultures have got hold of the number, so I have to screen all the calls. I don't know what to do.'

'Would you like me to come over?' I hesitantly offered.

There was a pause, then she tearfully suggested that instead of me going over there, perhaps she could come over to me and maybe stay for a few days. I was stunned: I hardly knew the woman, and it gave me a sudden insight as to how few friends she must really have, if she wanted to come here.

'Yes, yes of course you can. Molly and Steve are here — but how will you get past all the reporters?'

We decided that Steve should go and pick her up in a taxi, and she told me to get Steve to call her on her mobile when he was outside the house.

Steve and Molly were delighted to help, and secretly rather thrilled to be part of such a drama. Steve spent an inordinate amount of time prinking in front of the mirror, arranging his hair till Molly and I pointed out to him that it was very dark, no one was interested in him, and it was his job to remain anonymous and simply help Nicola out of her house. He left, looking like the man in the Milk Tray advert.

Chapter Fourteen

Molly and I continued our speculations about the death of Sam Bentley while we were waiting for Steve to return with Nicola.

'Can you imagine what the funeral's going to be like?' asked Molly.

'Stop it. You're picturing yourself in black, meeting David Bowie, aren't you?'

'Well, aren't you?'

'No, I'm thinking more along the lines of, why the hell does Nicola want to come here?'

'She strikes me as a woman who completely sank herself into her husband's so-called career, and hasn't got any friends other than your basic Eurotrash.' Molly tried to look wise as she uttered this, but I could tell she was thrilled I had a genuine rock widow coming to stay.

'Umm, maybe. I wonder if she'll still write her book?'

'I wouldn't think she'd have to, would you? I mean, he must've been worth a fortune.' I tried not to work out how much she must be worth, as I was aware that it was an unworthy thought, but it *did* cross my mind. I thought of my own perilous finances, and added, 'God, I know this is horrible of me, but I hope she still wants her house done. I desperately do need the job.'

'What do you think *really* happened in the hotel?'

'I should think we'll soon find out, don't you?'

The phone went, and I left the room to answer it. It was William Magpie.

'Livia, my dear, so very tragic isn't it, about Sam Bentley. How's poor Nicola taking it?'

'I wouldn't know, William. I'm sure she's very upset, though.'

'Now, Livia, you know as well as I do that the nation's press is at her door. Being an old friend of yours, I would like to think that if you could see your way to giving me an introduction . . . I'm sure she'd like to talk to someone sympathetic, you know, give her side of the story, what it was really like living with Sam.'

'That's where you come in, is it, William?'

The old goat would try anything, I thought. You had to admire his perseverance.

'Well, I would of course make it worth your while. We'd call it an introduction fee – cash, of course, no need for those nasty accountants to know about it. I'm sure that I can count on your good sense, Olivia.'

'If I see her, I'll certainly tell her that you called, William. How's your brother? And his charming new fiancée, Sylvia?'

'Oh they're fine,' he said blandly, determined to get back to the subject in hand. 'In fact, I was so delighted with the work you'd done on my late mother's flat, I was going to ask you to, umm, do some work on my own flat, well, the umm, the bathroom could do with a bit of sprucing up.'

I shuddered at the thought of William Magpie's bathroom. I also knew it was a complete fabrication, he just wanted to worm his way round here.

'I'd be delighted to quote for some work for you, William,

let's make an appointment for next week, shall we? I'll pop round, and have a look . . .'

'No, I mean, it would be much more convenient if I came to you . . .'

'But your bathroom is not in my flat, is it?' I said sweetly, calling his bluff.

Eventually he gave in, and when I'd promised once more that I'd tell Nicola (if I saw her) that he'd called, he rang off.

The phone immediately rang again. It was Monty.

'My God, all hell tends to break out around you, doesn't it?'

'I know. Do you think someone's cursed me with that Chinese thing, you know, "may you live in interesting times"?'

'Could be. For heaven's sake do tell Nicola that I'll get her some funeral clothes. You *know* what Paula Yates looked like, God rest her soul, we can't have that. I suppose this means the Ivy's off?'

'Monty! The poor woman's husband's just died and you're thinking about sticky toffee pudding!'

'Very clever of you, darling. How did you guess?'

'I do know you. Anyway, she's on her way over here.'

'No! Why?'

'That's what we're wondering, too. I really don't think she's got any friends. It seems she wants to stay for a few days.'

'You'd be better off opening a bed and breakfast place. I can see you as a landlady, curlers and a pinny, telling people that they have to vacate their rooms before eleven.'

'Thanks, you do say the nicest things.'

'You know I'm only teasing. Please do give her my love, won't you, and tell her that I'm thinking about her.'

'Yes, of course I will. Look, I'd better go and try and find some clean sheets and things, speak soon.'

Molly and I fluttered round the flat trying to find enough bedlinen, and tidying up. I made some tea and we settled down to wait. I was trying to guess how upset Nicola was going to be. It was hard to tell, I mean I hardly knew her, but it was flattering, I suppose, that she thought that I was a good enough friend to have called me when she was in trouble. But it did worry me that she didn't have any closer friends.

I tried to remember if she'd ever spoken of any family. I didn't think she had. But then again none of my friends had any close family. Molly had a sister who lived in Ireland, and she didn't see much of her. Steve had a sister too, whom he disliked and avoided at all costs, though he was quite close to his mother, but she had retired to Dorset. Monty and I were both only children, and none of our parents were alive.

Maybe that's why we were all such close friends: we'd substituted each other for our real families. My friends meant more to me than my father. When he died I hadn't known about it for years. My parents had divorced and I had lost contact with him. It was different with my mother. I had adored her, and when she died I was devastated and had relied heavily on my friends for comfort.

The phone rang again, and it was Joe. I put Molly on to him, and as she excitedly told him about Nicola, it suddenly struck me that we had turned the sweet BND into a camp, raving gossip. When she had finished, I asked her if she really wanted to stay the night.

'Well, I do, but I won't. I mean I can see that you're a little crowded. It's just that I get a bit lonely . . .'

I thought, not for the first time, that the way we all lived in London was ridiculous. Molly and I probably spoke at least three times a day on the phone, she often stayed with me, but as soon as there was the merest sniff of a new man around, we both dropped everything to be with him. Then when, inevitably, it didn't work out, we threw ourselves back into our friendship. There had to be a better way of sustaining relationships than this. It was the same with Pete and Steve, too: if a romantic interest came along, we divided like spilt mercury. Then, like mercury, we all came back together again.

'I'll just stay to say hello to Nicola, do you think that's OK?'

'Yes, of course. I'm sure she'd like to see you. They've been gone ages, haven't they? I hope everything's all right.'

'Why don't we phone Steve on his mobile?' she said impatiently.

'Let's give them ten minutes. Nicola's probably still packing, or fighting off the gentlemen of the press.'

'I *hate* waiting for people, don't you?'

The phone rang again.

'Liv darling – '

Oh God, Christopher. I very gently put the phone down. I didn't have the energy required to talk to him.

'All we need now is for Mark to call,' said Molly.

'Don't! I've tried to push that firmly from my mind.'

'Are you really, really finished with Christopher?'

'Yes. Most emphatically yes.'

I told Molly about the raddled chimpanzee description and she giggled. 'Well, he does have something sort of simian about him, doesn't he?'

We heard Steve unlocking the door, and he and Nicola walked in looking shaken. Molly and I made a fuss of Nicola, and we bustled around, hugging her, and making drinks for us all. (I stuck to tea, but I was not in the majority.)

Nicola sank down into the sofa with a sigh of relief.

'God, what a day. Stan's manager called and told me this afternoon, and the next minute, all the press were outside. How do they know things so quickly? And they just keep calling me. That's another thing as well, we're ex-directory, and have our number changed every three months, but they still found it, and my mobile number too! It's unreal.' She ran her hands through her hair and rubbed her brow.

Steve was pacing the room, occasionally peeking out of the window, careful not to let the curtains part too much.

'I don't *think* we were followed, but I'm not too sure.'

'Thanks for putting me up, I didn't know where else to go . . .' Nicola's voice was breaking, and we could see her fighting to hold back the tears.

I made sympathetic noises, and Molly impulsively jumped up and put her arm around Nicola's shoulders. Steve was still curtain-twitching and making pointing motions out of the window to me. I went to stand beside him, and looked out of the window. Two men had just got out of a car, and another car was pulling up. Reporters.

'Damn!'

The doorbell went, and we all looked at each other.

'What shall we do?'

'Maybe you should go out there, Liv, and say she's not here. Otherwise they'll never leave.'

'Me? No way, look what happened last time.'

Nicola was wildly apologetic. 'I'm so, *so* sorry to land you all with this.'

'Don't be silly, we're fine, it's you we're concerned about. I just don't know how to get them off your back . . .'

'I know!' Molly shouted, 'I'll be a decoy. I'll borrow Nicola's coat, wear a hat and sunglasses and lead them on a wild goose chase . . . What do you think?'

We looked doubtfully at her. She didn't look at all like Nicola, but they were both dark haired and about the same height.

'Maybe it's worth a try,' Steve said slowly. 'We could get Joe to have his car ready, then you and I could slip into it and make a quick getaway.'

'OK, let's do it.'

I phoned Joe and explained the situation. He sounded thrilled to be part of the action.

'It's a shame we haven't got a back door, or a way out through the garden, isn't it?' Molly said.

' Duh! No, you idiot, the whole point of it is to let the press *see* you, isn't it?'

'Oh, yes. I'd forgotten that . . .'

'Are you sure you're the best person for this mission,' I said acidly.

'Of course I am! I'm a master of disguise, it's a shame we haven't still got the wigs.'

'Wigs?' asked Nicola.

'It's a long story,' I explained. 'You need more lipstick on. What about a scarf?'

'I like it, a bit of the Jackie O look,' Molly said, studying her appearance in the mirror.

To my relief, Nicola was giggling rather weakly.

'I think you should wear my boots, too.'

'Great, I've always wanted a pair of thigh boots. God, they're a bugger to put on, aren't they?'

Steve was ready to give the pre-arranged call to Joe. The plan was that Joe would then pull his car right up to the front door with his back doors unlocked, Molly and Steve would jump in, and he'd roar off.

Molly had on Nicola's leather coat and boots, a huge pair of dark glasses, and a silk headscarf tied around her head. At a brief glance, she could be mistaken for her. The intercom had stopped buzzing, and I had a quick look outside from behind the safety of the curtains. I counted eleven reporters, mostly on mobiles, lounging around a car.

'I think now would be a good time. Go on – good luck, phone us from the mobile, and don't let Joe drive too fast. OK?'

'Right.'

Somehow it all worked with military precision.

I watched Molly and Steve hurl themselves in the back of Joe's car – Molly even had her hand in front of her face, with a sort of 'no press, no cameras' action to it. The reporters lunged at them as soon as the front door was open, and I could see flashes coming from the cameras. Then they poured into their own cars and gave chase. It had worked. I was pretty sure it wouldn't hold up for very long, but it did give us some breathing space. I turned to Nicola, to see how she was bearing up.

'Did the press follow them?' she asked.

I nodded.

'Thank God. I just couldn't face them. Thanks, Livia, I really owe you one.'

'That's what friends are for, don't worry about it. Can I get you anything? Have you eaten at all today?'

'No, I didn't feel hungry. Maybe I should have something.'

I walked her through to the kitchen, and sat her down at the table.

'How about a cheese omelette and some salad?'

'Thank you, that would be nice.' Her voice was wobbling again, and I handed her some kitchen towel.

'I'd have a damn good cry, if I were you. You could go into the bathroom if you want some privacy, or just sit and howl where you are, it's up to you. It must have been a terrible shock.'

Nicola burst into tears, and sobbed for a moment. I sat beside her, and stroked her hair. Gradually she stopped and blew her nose.

'Thanks.'

'You're welcome. Have another drink and sit there while I whip up some food for you.'

'OK.'

I started to grate the cheese, giving it a surreptitious sniff as I did so. The last thing I needed was to give Nicola lysteria, and I knew for a fact that it had been in the fridge for a very long time. I prayed that it was OK and started to crack some eggs into a bowl.

'The thing is, that I just feel angry with Stan. What an idiot. I forgave him, and forgave him for so long that it became second nature. Somehow, it seemed all the groupies and all the hangers-on were normal, you know? The drugs and the sex went hand in hand with the lifestyle, and I became immune to it, I just became dead. I even found two of them in my bed once, two naked girls that is, waiting for Stan. He thought I might like to watch. And do you know, I wasn't even shocked, I just closed the door and left them to it. I was numb, I suppose.

'I started to take more and more drugs. I once wrote "Happy birthday" to myself in one line of coke, and took it. It was always there. I partied for years, on uppers, downers, the lot. It wasn't until I became ill that it slowly dawned on me that I had to stop. I got clean, then so did Stan. That was about the only happy time that I remember. Well, to be honest, it was the only thing I do remember.

'People say drugs are crap, but they miss out the bit about how good they can make you feel, I mean, if they didn't make you feel good, you wouldn't take them, would you? It was hard, stopping. Then, well, then he got a bit odd, he became dependent on me. It was horrible, and then, well, then I found out about his . . .'

She started to cry again, crumpling the kitchen towel and holding it against her mouth. She sniffed, and blew her nose and continued her story. I was moving very slowly, mindlessly grinding black pepper into the frothy egg mixture. I guessed that she needed to talk and if I interrupted, it would stop her.

'He just followed me around all the time. It was pathetic . . . I hated it. He couldn't think of anything to do. All he knew was sex and drugs, that's when the porn and the prostitutes took over. I did everything I could to make sure that nobody found out, but, deep down, I didn't care really. I was ashamed at first, and then I just didn't care. I mean, other musicians find something else to do, why couldn't he?'

I put the omelette and salad in front of her, placing some bread and butter within reach.

Nicola wolfed down the omelette, and started to butter some bread and eat the salad. I went to the fridge and got out some olives and houmous: she ate that too.

'. . . he had offers to do movies, but he wasn't interested. The collection of porn took over the whole house. I was burning it the day you came over. He was so stupid! He'd make videos of himself, doing it with all these groupies. Then he'd expect me to understand! He would beg me to join in . . . he even offered to film me.'

Her eyes were roving the table for something else to eat so I went and peered hopefully into the fridge. There was nothing suitable, other than a pot of plain Greek yoghurt, so I spooned some into a bowl, sliced a banana over it;

drizzling some honey on top I pushed it towards Nicola who spooned it greedily into her mouth.

'. . . and I don't even care that he's dead. I began to hate him, I was glad I'd got rid of him. Every time I saw his picture with some little bimbo, I'd think to myself "poor cow". It's a relief, really. That's why I'm crying, I feel so guilty that I don't feel anything. I'm glad the sick bastard's dead. Does that make me a terrible person?'

'Absolutely not.' I found some biscuits in the cupboard and put them in front of her.

'But I'm worried,' she said between mouthfuls. 'Suppose they found him in the hotel room with some incriminating stuff . . . I know it'll all come out, and it makes me so ashamed. What can I do? I've tried to burn all his sick porn and photos, but the fool is bound to have kept some somewhere. I don't even know how he died . . . But I can't, I can't let them know all of this. I just can't!'

I opened the freezer and took out a half-full tub of caramel ice cream. I stuck two teaspoons into it, and we sat dipping the spoons into the mixture and licking it off.

'I don't mean that he's some icon whose memory must never be defiled, I mean, he is, *was*, only a bloody pop star, but I can't take the shame. People will look at me – and it'll be the only thing they ever, ever think of. I once met Priscilla Presley, you know, and that's all I could think of, her husband had been found on the loo, stuffed full of cheeseburgers and downers. It's *not* going to happen to me, I shan't let it . . .'

She paused, then said, with some surprise, 'I've never told anyone about this.'

'Well, it's OK, I shan't tell anyone, either.' Then I added, 'Nicola, what about the book you were going to write? Wasn't that to be full of all of this? Or weren't you going to put that in it?'

'I don't know, I was angry. I might have done, but I would have done it *my* way . . .'

We looked briefly at each other, then she gave a yawn, stretching her arms above her head.

'I thought I'd have to take a sleeping pill tonight, but I'm so sleepy. Can I get to a bed somewhere?'

'Of course. Come on, we've put you in the office. It's a bit of a tip, I'm afraid, Steve has been using it . . .'

'Please Liv, don't apologise, you've no idea how happy I am to be here. I'd gladly sleep on your kitchen floor!'

I said goodnight to her, and told her that we'd work something out in the morning. She was practically asleep before I'd even closed the door.

Back in the kitchen I cleared away the debris of her comfort eating, then called Steve on his mobile to find out how the wild goose chase was going. He sounded breathless, and in high spirits.

'Liv, it's great, I think we've lost them. Joe's a fantastic driver, we've been scooting round London, but Molly's getting a bit too into the part for my liking, a thwarted actress, if ever there was. Hang on, she wants to talk to you.'

I could hear traffic in the background, then Molly came on the line.

'How's Nicola?'

'She's asleep. Where are you now?'

'God knows. I don't recognise anything. Joe's going to take me home, and then he and Steve are coming back. We've had great fun.'

'Just make sure that you've lost them.'

'Yeah, we have. It's like being in a movie, you know the high speed chase sequence.'

'Well, for God's sake don't get a speeding ticket. Take it easy.'

'Yes, Mum.'

'OK, OK, tell Steve and Joe to be careful. I think I'm going to go to bed now, too. I'm going to unplug the phone, so tell Steve not to forget that he's sleeping on the sofa tonight. I don't want him climbing in with Nicola.'

'Is she really all right?'

'Mmm, I think so. We'll talk in the morning, and don't wear those boots to work.'

'Spoilsport.'

I hung up and went into the bathroom. The colour reminded me of Mark. I'd have to repaint it soon.

I was wiping make-up from my face with some cotton wool, idly trying to get inspiration for a new bathroom colour, when I heard my mobile go off somewhere in the flat. I ran from room to room trying to locate the bloody thing. At last I tracked it down in the drawing room, shoved behind a cushion.

'Hello?'

I heard the roar of people in the background, and knew it must be Pete.

'Livia, I've just heard about Sam, or should we say Stan? How's Nicola taking it?'

'Well, she's OK, she's asleep at the moment.'

'I thought she'd be with you. It's a bit like the Priory at yours, isn't it?'

'Yeah, but without the druggies. How are you?'

'I'm OK. Is Steve with you?'

I explained about the press chase, and Pete laughed. It left him breathless.

'Pete, are you OK?' I knew he wasn't, but I didn't know what to do for him.

'Yeah . . . had a bit of a scare last night, but I'm fine now. Please don't fuss, I really don't want to talk about it.'

'OK.' I hated this. I bit my lip. I'd just have to go along with his wishes. There was silence, then Pete asked how it had gone with Mark.

'Well, I got the ring back. I keep answering the phone with great trepidation, though, in case it's him,' I answered in the light tone of voice that he demanded.

'I suppose we're not going to the Ivy tomorrow?'

'Not you as well! Do you boys think of nothing but your stomachs?'

'Yes, but it's usually a little lower down the anatomy.'

'Don't I know it . . .'

'Oh, a friend of yours came in tonight.' Pete sounded amused.

'Who?'

'Angie.'

'What did she say?'

'She didn't get a chance. I pointed to the sign that says "No Dogs" and refused to serve the bitch. She's banned.'

I laughed, but was a little uneasy. I didn't want to start a war with her. Pete's sense of loyalty was sometimes a bit misplaced, I'd noticed. We said goodnight, and I went into my bedroom.

As I got into bed I caught sight of my chequebook, sticking out of my bag. I shoved it further in, so that I couldn't see it. Out of sight, out of mind. I really didn't want a sleepless night worrying over money. I knew from past experience what that would be like, my mind would start like a hamster running in a wheel: what could I do? What could I economise on? Should I go crawling back to JJM? (Assuming they'd have me.) I mean, money matters are horrible anyway, but at three in the morning they take on monster proportions. I felt guilty that I didn't even have a pension, or a PEP, or whatever the hell they were called.

I turned the emerald ring on my finger: I could always sell it. But was it really mine? I didn't know. That reminded me of the upcoming weekend in Brighton, which started a whole other train of thought . . . Pete, what was going to happen there? I had a horrible lurch of fear as I tried to imagine life without him. And how long were we going to have to keep up the charade that we were engaged? His parents would have to know some time, wouldn't they? I mean, we weren't actually going to have to get married, were we?

I'd done it once, when I was twenty-two, it had lasted five years, and we hated each other at the end. He'd hated me so much, actually, that he'd had to move to Australia. Occasionally I had news about him from a mutual friend. Apparently he'd opened a chain of restaurants and was doing very well, but he didn't accept wedding parties at any of his outlets. I lay in bed, my eyes wide open, and sure enough, a hamster on a treadmill in my head.

Chapter Fifteen

'We can't go to the Ivy, but the Ivy can certainly come to us,' Nicola announced, sitting in the kitchen over coffee, late the next morning. She was wearing a slashed red T-shirt with MY BODY IS A NIGHTCLUB splashed over it in black ink, and a pair of leather jeans. She looked ready for business, and she'd had her mobile phone clamped to her ear from the moment she'd got up.

I wished I had some of her energy; a sleepless, worried night left me feeling groggy, and fuzzy around the edges.

'Really?' I said. 'The Ivy doesn't do takeaway, surely?'

'They will for me,' she said, grimly. 'There'll be seven of us, right? Anyone a veggie?'

'Umm, no. But, really you don't have to, I can easily cook something.' (Something that costs ten pence each, I nearly added, already seeing myself trawling the supermarket looking for the red reduced label on food that was past its sell-by date.)

'Nonsense, we'll eat about 8.30, I think, does that sound OK?'

'Yeah, sure.'

'Right, I have a lot to do, so I'm going to lock myself in your office, if that's OK. You tell everyone to be here at eight, I've got something I want to tell you all later. I thought about it last night, but I need to make loads of calls. Do you think you or Steve could get the newspapers for me?'

'Umm, yes, as soon as I'm dressed, I'll go out. I think Steve is still asleep. I didn't hear him come in last night, did you?'

'I wouldn't have heard an earthquake last night, I slept so well. You don't look so hot though, what's the matter?'

I was embarrassed. I mean, a sleepless night worrying over money, compared to the problems that Nicola was about to face, paled into insignificance.

I muttered something about 'cash flow' problems. Nicola looked sceptically at me.

Then on impulse I told her about Pete. I found that I was close to tears. She looked shocked, and put her arm around me sympathetically. I went on to say that the hardest thing to deal with was he didn't want to talk about it, or have anybody fuss over him.

'I can understand that – but it must be hard for you, you love him so much.'

I nodded. She gave me another hug and then, once I'd assured her that I really was OK, she went into my office, closing the door firmly behind her.

I was impressed: she was bursting with energy, and confidence. There wasn't a trace of the woman who'd sobbed at this very table last night. I wished I had her strength of character.

Steve came shuffling into the kitchen, and made himself some coffee. He sat opposite me, running his hands through his hair, and yawning.

'Where is she?'

'Giving lawyers, accountants, record executives and the Ivy hell over the phone, I think.'

I switched my phone back on, and listened to some

messages. William again, Mark (to my horror) and a very distraught Molly.

'Molly was OK last night, wasn't she?' I asked.

'Yes, fine, she really enjoyed herself. We dropped her off, and she said she was going straight to bed, something about a huge staff meeting at work this morning. Why?'

'I don't know, she sounds awful, she left a message to call her at home this morning, I'm calling her now.'

She answered immediately.

'Liv?'

'Yes, it's me. What's up?'

'Oh Liv, I've been fired!'

'Oh Moll, why?' (I knew that once Molly had been fired for arriving at work consistently late. She pointed out, in her defence, that she always left early.)

'Oh, it was horrible, I've been made redundant.' She was sniffling, and I could hear her trying not to cry.

'Where are you now?'

'At home.'

'Shall I come over?'

'Yes, please.'

'OK, give me an hour, I'm not dressed yet . . .' I really felt very untogether today, but then I reckoned that I'd had about three hours' sleep, in total.

'I'm sorry, I know I'm being a wuss. How's Nicola?'

'Fighting fit. I'll see you soon.'

I told Steve where I was going, and went to have a shower and get dressed. I asked him to keep an eye on Nicola, and to call everyone to tell them to come over for the Ivy takeaway, tonight.

'Give Moll my love, she'll be OK,' he said as I was on my way out of the door. 'Tell her to start painting, we'll have a joint show.'

In my new mood of economic reform, I walked to the tube station. With a start of guilt I phoned John, as I realised that I hadn't returned his call, I had just been too busy, what with the flu and Mr Abraham's party. His answering service was on, and an anonymous voice told me to leave a message. I felt a bit deprived, as I had wanted to hear his voice. God, I hoped I wasn't turning into some sort of cyber addict. Did mobiles count as cyber things? I wasn't sure, but I left a rather garbled message anyway.

The flower stand, manned by Bert, was the only patch of colour in the cold grey street. I stopped and bought Molly a bunch of tulips, and as he wrapped them for me, he asked after Mrs Grieg.

'Yes, well, I have heard from her, actually. She's, umm, moved. She's gone abroad.'

'Bleedin' hell! Wouldn't have put her down as a deserter. Shame, too. She was the best buyer of my roses by a long shot, I can tell you.' He sighed. 'Oh well, good luck to her, say hello from me, won't you?'

I thought it highly unlikely that I would ever see Mrs Grieg again, but I nodded anyway and moved off down the filthy tiled steps to the even dirtier tube platform. Gusts of cold wind were blowing the rubbish around in swirls, and the plaintive strains of a lone busker could be heard echoing along the tiled corridors. It sounded horribly like 'The Streets of London'.

When the tube finally arrived it was peopled by the usual nutters. One elderly woman had a nervous tic, and it looked as though she was perpetually laughing at some unheard lewd joke, her eye twitching into a wink every five seconds. A middle-aged man sitting opposite me kept clearing his throat, very loudly, at irritatingly regular intervals. God, the tube was depressing, I thought. This was what I was condemned to. Why hadn't I made more of an effort at school? I could have been in regular, highly paid employment, but I'd been far too keen on bunking off for days on end, smoking dope with my mates, and getting my mother to do my homework for me.

My mother had loved drawing maps, and had once done one of Europe, missing out Germany (which she disapproved of greatly) altogether, squishing Belgium, Prague and Poland next to each other. Miss Harding, my geography teacher, had called me up in front of the class, holding out my map for all to see. She'd asked me to point out Germany, I'd spent ages poring over it, before I realised that it just wasn't there. Then I thought it was a trick question, you know, like maybe Germany wasn't in Europe at all, perhaps after the war it had been banished to the Middle East or something. It never occurred to me that my mother had simply chopped it out of Europe. She'd roared with laughter when I got home to tell her about it.

I had to change tubes twice before I got to Highbury and Islington. The wind outside was freezing when I emerged from the comparatively warm underground. I saw that the Cock, the pub by the station, hadn't changed its gold-lettered banner, which ran around the front of the building, 'We do not discriminate against race, sex, colour or creed . . .' and it still served the best breakfast in London, too.

I remembered a job as a photographic stylist that I'd had once, with Molly art directing, in this area. The studio was just around the corner, and we'd spent three months in there creating a Christmas catalogue in the middle of June. I'd had a hell of a time getting hold of a real Christmas tree, and Molly had just kept shouting 'I need a touch of red in the left hand corner' every time she'd been invited to look through the camera. We'd had a lot of laughs, and used to

273

go to the Cock for a fry-up once a week, on the way to the studio, as a treat.

I turned into Canonbury Square, and rang Molly's bell. She buzzed me in, and I took the alarmingly creaking antique lift to the fourth floor. She had the door open, waiting for me, and I walked straight into her small, but beautifully proportioned flat, with its graceful curves and high ceilings. Molly's taste was quirky in the extreme, and amongst the books lining the living room tins of baked beans and spaghetti hoops that had Barbie on the labels could be found, along with wonderful kitsch objects that she'd picked up from her work. I handed her the tulips, and she thanked me.

'Come on then, what happened?'

'Oh Liv, I'm so pissed off. I should have seen it coming, you know? We've been taken over by some French holding company, and we all had to go and shake hands with them, but that was ages ago . . . I thought everything was OK. I mean I had to go to Norwich and shake the printers up a bit, but, well, we've used them for years. Then I got this bloody memo, asking me to go to this big meeting this morning, and I thought that it was going to be a bit more Gallic handshaking. But, well, I walked in, and there was just a row of extremely frosty French faces, and the bloody personnel manager, and you know how off-putting that can be.'

I nodded encouragingly and handed her a tissue. She wiped the tissue under her eyes and continued.

'Then they handed me this bloody letter, all about costing and efficiency and that my job was no longer applicable to the future of the magazine. And then they had the bloody cheek to ask me to clear my desk immediately and go home!'

She pointed to a rather battered looking cardboard box in the corner of her room. It had files and photos piled up in it, and balanced on top was a cactus and a pink-sequinned Barbie doll that I'd last seen sitting on the top of Molly's computer at work.

'But that's not the worst of it!' she wailed. 'I haven't told you what I was wearing.'

'You didn't wear Nicola's boots, did you? I *told* you not to.'

'I know, but I thought I'd give the girls a giggle at work, you know? I thought we'd all have a laugh about me turning into a rock chick, and instead . . . I got bloody sacked!'

'Oh Molly, I am sorry. But look, did you get any redundancy money?'

'Yeah, about enough to keep me in fags for a month.'

'There are other jobs,' I said firmly.

'You know, Liv,' she said seriously, 'there aren't. I'm too old . . .'

'Christ, Molly, you're forty-one, that's not old!'

'It is in this business. I'm being realistic, not pessimistic. I'm just telling the truth. It's *so* competitive, everybody wants someone who's young and hungry, and cutting edge, whatever the fuck that means. I mean, if I go for an interview, I'm sitting in a room full of girls, not women. *Girls*. They have none of our sisterly feelings, I can assure you. They've all got electronic organisers, and Apple laptops, and £150 hair cuts. And they all wear sterling silver rings, and have bloody platinum friendship bangles. I can't compete with that, I don't even want to try!'

I passed her some more tissues, and she cried in earnest.

'I don't know what I'm going to do, Liv, honestly I don't . . . I've got no savings, do you know I haven't even got a pension, and I'll be retiring soon . . .' she was sobbing, now.

'Me too, I was thinking that last night. But you're not

retiring, you're not old, and you *will* get another job. You are talented and experienced, and it's their loss. OK?'

'If you say so,' she said rather grumpily, wiping her eyes.

'I do. Come on, you're just feeling sorry for yourself at the moment, and there's nothing wrong with that. But it's not a permanent state of affairs, is it? You know I'm right.' I looked at her: she seemed to be improving. 'Come on, let's go and see a really bad film, and eat some chocolate. But not too much, or you'll spoil your dinner.'

I told her about Nicola ordering takeaway from the Ivy. I also told her that Nicola had something she wanted to say to us all, and Molly cheered up slightly. 'Perhaps she wants us to organise the funeral, you know? Like party planners, hey, we could go into business, Death with Style could be our slogan . . .'

'Yeah, or how about Hearses'r'us?'

'Or, Dying a Gogo?'

We were giggling now.

'Coffins for Ravers are our speciality,' I intoned.

'Wakes *can* be a party: tears guaranteed, or your money back.'

'Funerals of Fun.'

I started to look through the paper for a listing of movies. We needed something awful to watch. A couple of hours sitting in the dark watching a bad film and eating chocolate always raises the spirits.

'And another thing, they took my mobile! It came with the job, you know.'

'That's awful, but you know, Moll, you did hate it, and you rarely answered it.'

'I know, but at least I had one! I'm now mobileless!'

'I'll buy you a children's fake one, now come on let's go.'

We walked arm in arm around the windy square, cutting

down to Upper Street, and I stopped at a newsagent's to buy some Cadbury's Fruit and Nut for me, Galaxy for Molly.

'Oh my God!' I heard Molly exclaim, and turned to look at her. She was pointing to the row of newspapers: on three of the tabloids there were blurred pictures of Molly dressed as Nicola. The headlines were all along the lines of *Nicola Flees in her Hour of Grief* and *The Lady Vanishes*. We bought a couple of papers and scanned them as we walked towards the cinema.

'*Nicola Bentley stopped for a short while at the home of her woman friend, top interior designer Olive Hunter last night, before vanishing to an unknown destination.*'

'Olive, *Olive*! It makes me sound like something from *On the Buses*!'

I couldn't believe I was in the bloody papers again.

'Yeah, but I like the "top" designer bit.'

'*The New York police are not disclosing any circumstances about the manner in which Sam Bentley died. They are, however treating the incident as suspicious and wish to interview two girls who were seen leaving his hotel room.*'

'I think "girls" is a nice touch, don't you?'

'Oh, look, they've got a pull–out–and–keep section of Stan's career. God, I'd forgotten that he'd been around for so long. Oh, and the record company are reissuing "Satanic Girl" as a commemorative single. I didn't think they made singles any more, did you?'

'Shit! Nicola's going to love this bit ... *Sam and Nicola were one of rock music's devoted couples, rarely out of each other's sight, till the temporary separation, some say, caused by the new sexual proclivities of Nicola.* Bloody hell! Can they get away with that?'

'Great, I'm now going to get hate mail about splitting up rock's most devoted couple. If only they knew!'

'Knew what?'

'Oh, you know, all his screwing around,' I said weakly.

Molly narrowed her eyes at me. 'You know something, don't you?'

'No, not really.'

'You do! I know you, you've got that evasive tone in your voice. Come on, tell me.'

'Look, it's just some stuff that Nicola told me about Sam, Stan, whatever we're calling him. OK? Sex stuff. You know, pretty personal. I can't tell you, honestly.'

'Hmm, we'll see. I'll ask you the next time you have a vodka martini, you'll tell me everything then.'

She was depressingly right. I have a huge mouth after a few drinks. I'd never have made a good spy, I mean, they wouldn't have to torture me, just give me a drink and I'd tell everyone everything. And really, what's the point of having a secret unless you can share it?

We walked into the foyer of the cinema, and were enveloped in that warm, stuffy popcorn smell. I don't like popcorn much, I always think I'm going to choke on it, but the smell evokes cinemas instantly for me.

We settled down in the soft red seats, and waited for the lights to dim. We had twenty minute of trailers, which I quite like, as they make me believe that I've actually seen the films, even the ones with submarines or monsters in, that I have absolutely no intention of ever going to. I passed Molly her chocolate, and we broke into our bars just as the film started. It was one of those British supposedly romantic comedies. It engaged me enough for an hour and a half, but I knew that I would forget it the moment I left the cinema.

Molly and I walked back to her flat. There was an ominous pile of unopened brown envelopes on her table; we looked at them and decided to put them all together in a big envelope, labelled 'To pay'. It doesn't help really, but it does give you the impression that you are being organised. Molly decided to dress up, if she was having a posh takeaway, and I waited for her while she titivated in her bedroom.

I was in a financial fix myself, and I knew how horrible it was to suddenly lose your job. I thought about what Molly had said. Perhaps she was right, if she felt too old for her business, maybe she was. It was becoming a more and more ruthless world out there, one that seemed not to value experience or maturity, but hungered after youth. Molly had always painted, but hadn't done any for ages. I looked around the room: she'd got a few of her paintings on the wall, they were quite old now, but I remembered them well. She had a loose, flowing style and a great sense of colour. Maybe she should take it up again.

Molly emerged from her bedroom in a very tight little black dress, and killer heels.

'Is that dress wise? Will you be able to eat in it?' I asked her.

'Oh yes, it's very, very stretchy.' She pulled on it, to show me how far it stretched. It seemed to be made entirely of elastic.

'I suppose we have to get the tube?'

'No, sod it. We'll split the taxi fare, the tube's just too depressing.'

We jumped into a cab, and my phone went. It was Pete.

'Where are you?'

'Just going home, I'm in a taxi with Molly.'

'Great, can you pick me up?'

'OK, see you in a minute.'

We made a small detour to pick Pete up, and he staggered out of his flat, laden down with a crate of champagne. I jumped out to help him but he pushed me aside. I could see that I was going to be accused of 'fussing'. He climbed into the cab and gave us both a huge kiss on the cheeks.

'Do you really *never* travel without it?' I forced myself, again, to talk normally, but I was shocked at his breathlessness.

'Nah. What have you two troublemakers been up to? I do hope you haven't been leading my girlfriend astray,' he said to Molly. She told him about my mercy mission to cheer her up.

He laughed. 'Don't worry, you can always come and make cocktails for me.'

'No, thanks. I've no wish to be the oldest barmaid in town.'

'You wouldn't be, dear, I have the honour of that title.'

Pete waved our money away as he paid the taxi. I opened the door to my flat, and was immediately hit by the smell. Lemons and pine and wax – my God, it was clean! That's what it smelt of, cleanliness. Steve walked out of the drawing room, looking very smug.

'I have been on my hands and knees all day! And no, before any of you say anything, it was not some sexual marathon. I have cleansed the entire flat! Including, may I add, your rather revolting bedroom. Liv, the things I found under your bed . . .'

'Do tell,' Pete said, sitting down abruptly on the nearest chair, trying to catch his breath. Like well trained dogs, we studiously ignored him.

'No, don't. Why have you suddenly got a Lady Macbeth complex?'

'I felt like it really. I mean Nicola's been locked in the office all day, apart from the occasional cup of coffee, so I thought I'd better do something. And I have to say, I really enjoyed it.'

'It looks great, thanks.' I kissed him on the cheek. 'I'm going to get changed, where's Nicola?'

'She's getting changed too. Shall we all have a drink?'

Everybody moved into the drawing room, and I went into my bedroom. Steve really had cleaned, it was amazing, he'd even done the windows. I hastily pulled on my long Nicole Farhi dress and my favourite necklace (an antique Venetian glass string of swirly, cloudy beads that had been my mother's), touched up my make-up and squirted myself with Mitsouko. That would have to do. I mean, we were only having dinner in my kitchen after all. It's not like we're actually *going* to the Ivy.

The drawing room too was gleaming. Steve had lit a fire, and the candles, and drawn the curtains against the cold night sky. Pete had poured champagne and he and Molly were admiring the picture that Mrs Grieg had given me. Nicola came into the room and kissed everyone hello, looking great, but a little nervous. She fiddled with her watch and said, 'If they don't arrive in five minutes, they'll be late . . .' With that the intercom buzzed and Steve went to answer it. Five men, carrying what seemed like a hundred boxes, went into the kitchen and closed the door firmly behind them. The intercom went again, and this time I answered it. Monty and Joe had arrived at the same time.

'People are going to start talking, you know, if you persist in arriving everywhere with me,' Monty said to Joe.

Monty and Joe made a big fuss of Nicola. Monty had brought her some beautiful white freesias. She looked very touched, and thanked him. We had more champagne, and Monty lifted his glass and said, 'I think we should drink to our hostess, Nicola.'

We raised our glasses to her, and she blushed, and said, 'No, really, it's me who should be drinking to you lot, I don't know what I would have done . . . especially without you, Liv. Honestly, you have no idea . . . Anyway that's enough of that. I've got something to ask you all. I was going to wait till after dinner, but I may as well ask now.'

We were all intrigued, I could tell. Perhaps Molly was right, maybe she *was* going to ask us all to go with her to the funeral, or arrange it.

She cleared her throat, and said, 'I told Livia that I was going to go away to write a book. Well, it was her idea really. But the more I thought about it, the more I thought how lonely I would be. I'd already booked the villa that I was going to stay in for three or four months, it's in a tiny village called Assos on a very small Greek island. It is quite beautiful, it's on the edge of the sea . . .'

'The *very* edge?' Monty whispered to me, pinching a Noël Coward line.

'. . . and, well, I'd like you all to come with me for as long as you can, as my guests. I mean, I'm not saying this very well, but what I mean is, I'm loaded. I can afford it, so, look, all I'm asking you is that you'll all try and come out, and stay for as long as you like. OK?'

We were silent. I could see that everyone was rapidly doing financial calculations in their heads, desperately trying to work out if we could afford to go.

'God, Nicola . . .'

'Wow, thanks, that would be brilliant.'

'Nicola, what a sweetheart you are.'

'Fantastic.'

It seemed unlikely that we *could* all go, but it was such a treat to even be asked.

The door to the drawing room opened and a stunning waiter said, 'Ladies and gentlemen, dinner is served.'

We trooped down the hallway, carrying our glasses into the kitchen and chattering like a flock of starlings. It was strange going to a dinner party in my own flat when I hadn't done any of the planning or cooking. When I walked into the kitchen, I gave a gasp of amazement. It looked beautiful. The table had a white linen cloth over it, and was set with heavy silver cutlery, crystal glasses, candles and flowers. There was music in the background and champagne in our glasses. The waiters started to serve the food. Molly was so excited that she had spilt her drink twice, once over herself, and once over the table.

We toyed with caviare with our champagne, then moved on to some serious food. Lobster-filled ravioli, followed by meltingly tender scallops with mind-blowingly gorgeous white wine. We then had a pause, and were treated to a red wine: when Pete caught sight of the label, made him cross himself. It accompanied a beef dish so delicious that I had to stop myself from licking my plate. Then Monty had his wish, and soon there were seven of the Ivy's infamous sticky toffee puddings in front of us, with a glass of liquid nectar in the form of a dessert wine. Coffee, brandies and chocolate truffles followed.

When we'd finished the waiters magically cleared the table, leaving the brandy glasses, coffee and flowers, and packed up in a space of minutes and left the room. Nicola and I went to the door with them and she asked, 'Now, none of you boys know who I am, do you?'

'No, Madame.'

'Good.' She stuffed a £50 note in each of their pockets, and they disappeared into the night, taking the dirty washing up, and rubbish, with them.

Everyone applauded her as she came back into the room. She was grinning.

'Well, if you've got it, flaunt it, that's what I say.'

Her eyes were shining, and she looked happy.

'I know that you all don't want to hear this,' she said, playing with her coffee cup, 'but honestly, I can't thank you enough. You're all great . . .'

'Funny, we think that as well,' Pete said, laughing.

We all cheered her, and Molly got up to give her a hug, knocking over the cream jug. There was another cheer at that.

The phone rang, and I leaned over to answer it. It was Christopher.

'Livia, please talk to me.'

'Christopher, fuck off and leave me alone.'

The cheers this time were deafening. We raised our glasses and toasted each other. This is one of those golden moments, I thought to myself. I should like to capture it, and encase it in amber. Everyone was happy, but it was more than that. A feeling of contentment, I suppose. Then the bleeps from Pete's watch went off, reminding him to take his medication, and I was brought back to reality with a bump.

Chapter Sixteen

I set off to Victoria station in the morning, leaving Nicola hunched over the papers in the kitchen, muttering 'bastards' as she read the lies that had been printed about her this time. She was still waiting for the New York police to inform her about the way Stan had died, and was constantly on the phone to lawyers and managers, barking orders and making decisions. She seemed very much in control, writing lists of things to do as well as wearing out her mobile phone.

There wasn't a trace of the Ivy left in the kitchen. I wished that they came every week.

William Magpie had left five increasingly urgent messages for me, asking for interviews, photographs, and a taped 'at home' with me. Needless to say, I hadn't called him back.

Pete was wearing dark glasses when we met at the station and, for him, was rather subdued. I asked if he was OK (secretly hoping that he'd say no, and we could go home). He just nodded, and we walked towards the train. I hoped that this weekend we could clear up the lies that Pete had told his parents, even though it would mean giving the emerald ring back.

The train pulled away from London, and an exceedingly spotty teenager pushed a trolley down the swaying aisles, asking if anyone wanted tea or coffee. I bought a tea for myself, and a coffee for Pete, and while I was struggling to open one of those infuriating little packets of reconstituted milk, I said, 'Look, Pete, what are we going to do about this? I mean, how are we going to tell your parents? We can't let them go on thinking that we—'

'Why can't we?'

I paused to consider the question. It's drummed into everybody that the truth is a *good* thing, and that the truth must *always* be told, even when it hurts. Were we just going to hurt his parents if we told them the reality, that their son, who was gay, had a life-threatening illness, a heart condition and had told them that he was engaged to me, not because he was scared of them, but because he wanted to protect them? I didn't know. I knew that I couldn't possibly have done it to my mother, but she and I had had a very different relationship to that of Pete and his parents. We had adored each other, and besides, it was absolutely pointless lying to my mother, she always knew instantly.

The train jolted, and scaldingly hot tea spilt partly on to my hand, and partly sloshed over the rather grubby Formica table. Pete mopped it up with the miraculously unabsorbent napkin supplied by Connex to hold your paper tea or coffee cup with. There was nowhere to put the sodden napkin so it remained in a sticky wet ball on the table. I sighed, I didn't know what to say to Pete. They were his parents, not mine. As much as I loved him, it had to be his decision. Maybe what he really wanted from me was what Americans called 'unconditional acceptance'. I suspected that I wasn't going to be very good at that.

'Look, Pete. It's up to you. Whatever you want to do, I'll go along with it.'

He gave me a wicked grin, then leaned over and squeezed my hand.

'I was really hoping you'd say that. Look Liv, I know that for the record you'd like to go down as saying that you're not happy about it, and you'd rather tell them the truth. Well, in an ideal world so would I. But, it's not going to happen. This will be hard for you to comprehend because you were loved, and you, in turn, loved your mother, but my parents, well, they don't even *like* me, let alone love me. They never have. They made my life hell when I was young, and I left home as soon as I could. For quite a long while we didn't communicate at all.

'Then, well . . . then I grew up a bit, and I saw them for what they really are. They are two narrow-minded, bigoted, wealthy, unhappy people who shouldn't have married each other and certainly shouldn't have had a child. I can look at them now, and feel pity, a certain sort of sadness that I can't share anything with them. But I'm old enough not to want to hurt them. Let's just leave them alone in their world of ignorance.

'I made a mistake, I thought that I should tell them, it became an obsession with me, and that's why I asked you to come with me last time. Then, when we got there and I saw them, I knew, I just *knew* that I couldn't. I'm sorry. I suddenly wanted to show them that whatever they had done to me I could still have something that they hadn't got – a happy relationship. There's still enough of me that hasn't grown up to want to make them pay for all the wrongs that they did to me.'

'Do you mean they hurt you?'

He looked away from me, and stared out of the window.

'It was a very long time ago.'

I stared out of the window too. Oh God, this was worse than I had anticipated. I tried to gauge whether he wanted to talk about it, or not. My blood boiled at the mere mention of child abuse, and I was meant to be spending a weekend with the couple involved? I glanced at Pete. His jaw was tense, and he was still staring fixedly out of the window. I groped awkwardly for the right words to say.

'Pete, I don't think I'll ever understand why you want to do this. But, I'm here and if you have decided that this is the way you want to play it, well, I'm with you, kid.'

Pete looked at me, and smiled. 'Thanks.'

There was silence between us, but it was a comfortable sort of silence. We English have never been very good at spilling our hearts and secrets out on the table for all to see, but then, I've never felt that this was necessarily a bad thing. I mean, we're not on *Oprah*, are we?

The train slowed down and stopped at Brighton. Arm in arm we walked down the platform, my overnight bag banging against my leg.

'So let me get this right, we're playing the happily engaged couple and sod the both of them, is that correct?'

'Yeah, more or less.'

I took a deep breath, because I had to ask, even though I knew he wouldn't want to answer, 'Are you going to tell them you're ill?'

'I think it's beginning to show. Not that they'd notice. But no, I'm not. It's my heart more than anything. I get scared sometimes, but I just have to believe that I'll get better, or that I'll finally get cured and get a transplant. So, we're just the happy couple, OK?'

'Christ!' I stopped abruptly. 'Does that mean we've got to sleep together? Because I warn you now . . .'

'You know you want to, you know that you've been secretly lusting after me for years – this could be your big chance to turn me straight,' Pete laughed.

'Forget it, honey. You've got more chance of getting hit by a flying pig!'

I debated about buying his mother some flowers from the stand in the station, then decided against it. Outside the station we joined the queue for taxis. Seagulls were wheeling above our heads, and the sky was a cloudy grey. I shivered slightly, whether from the cold or the dread of meeting Suzanne and Michael again, I wasn't sure.

'So, what's the plan then?' I asked.

'Taxi to my flat, then I thought a wander around Brighton. Then over to Rosemary and Fred West's for dinner. Tomorrow will undoubtedly be the Yacht Club or something equally gruesome, then you and I can scamper off on a train as early as possible.'

'*Please* don't call them the Wests. It's not funny! I'm scared enough already.' Pete's usual irreverence sometimes fell wide of the mark with me.

We had reached the top' of the queue now, and climbed into a blue and white taxi. Several pictures of the Virgin Mary were plastered over the windscreen, and rosary beads and a crucifix dangled from the driving mirror. Quite frankly, with his driving, we needed all the help we could call upon. He drove off at breakneck speed, and I felt as though the G force alone would have kept me sitting upright in the back seat. He ran us along the seafront, racing up to every red light and then stamping on the brakes. It was with great relief that I eventually climbed out of the taxi. Pete paid him, and we watched him career up the square, tyres squealing.

'My God, are all the taxi drivers like that here?' I asked.

'They're all pretty mad. I think it's the sea air, it seems to affect people.'

We were in a beautiful cream Regency square. There was a hilly green in the centre, with black railings around it. The sea was at the end. I could just about hear the waves scrunch on the gravel above the noise of the seafront traffic. Pete unlocked the front door, and we were in a huge black and white tiled hallway. Together we crammed into a lift which was very reminiscent of Molly's and juddered up to the top floor. His flat looked out over the choppy sea and rooftops. I was drawn immediately to the windows. The view was wonderful.

'I'd never get any work done if I lived here. I'd be staring out all the time.'

'I know. It's compelling, isn't it.'

He came to stand next to me, and we gazed out over the waves for a while. The wind buffeted against the windows, a hypnotic, lulling sound. I tore myself away and looked around the rest of the flat. It was enchanting. It had all the original features: marble fireplace, inside shutters, beautiful old doors and plaster cornices, and Pete had put very little in it. A few comfortable chairs with dark yellow throws draped over them, and a dark drum table that had two bentwood chairs pulled up to it.

I walked through the rest of the flat – a small, immaculately clean white bathroom, a similar kitchen and a bedroom containing the largest bed I had ever seen. All the walls were painted a pale honey and even on this cold blustery day, it gave the impression of sunshine.

'How often do you come down here?' I asked.

'Whenever London gets too much, which, I find, it has increasingly. It's soothing, isn't it?'

'I'm glad I'm not the only one who feels like that about London. It must be lovely having a bolthole somewhere.'

'Yeah, and Brighton's fun, you know? It was always called Little London by the sea, but I think that does it a grave disservice.'

'Mmm, *and* it's the gay Mecca, isn't it?' I teased.

'That's part of the attraction, I guess. But really, the main reason I like it is that it's just not London, and it doesn't have that awful melancholy about it, even in winter, that most English seaside towns have.'

'Oh God, I know what you mean, those awful shuttered rock shops, and roundabouts boarded up, and a large population of elderly people hopelessly trying to find somewhere to sit out of the wind.' I remembered only too clearly dreadful seaside holidays as a child and the depressed feeling that overcame me in such places.

'And restaurants that have a sign on the front door saying "Open at Easter", and sullen, bored teenagers hanging around the off-licence trying to persuade someone to go in and buy them some cider.'

Pete then suggested that we have a wander through the town, and I looked at him doubtfully. It seemed that every time I saw him, he looked worse. He was pale and breathless and sat down at every opportunity. But he waggled his finger at me when he saw me looking concerned, and I laughed.

We set off along the seafront, battling against the wind. There were a surprising number of people around, and as we neared the West Pier, it became quite crowded. The archways beneath the seafront had mostly been converted into artists' studios, bars, clubs and restaurants, which even on this windy day were doing a brisk trade. There were the usual tat shops too, selling dodgy sunglasses and hideous silver jewellery. We climbed a slope that led from the seafront promenade up to the main road; crossing it, we were nearly mown down by another manic taxi driver. We trawled the second-hand bookshops that proliferated in the town, and I triumphantly came up with a battered paperback of an Angela Thirkell book that I hadn't read.

'I think my idea of heaven would be a place where Angela – or rather *Miss* – Thirkell comes out with a new book every month.'

'What's it about?' Pete asked.

'Absolutely nothing, that's the bliss of them. You can usually guarantee a wedding or two, but even that's not central – Oh my God, look at that!' I pointed across the street, where a man dressed as a nun was fire-eating and juggling with knives.

'That's Brighton for you, and look, nobody's watching. We're just so blasé down here.'

We stopped at Browns, for some hot chocolate. Pete had a brandy with his. The bar was jammed full of people and I was in no hurry to get to Suzanne and Michael's. For all my bravado, I was *not* looking forward to this evening.

'Pete, do we have to stay the night with them? Couldn't we go back to your flat?'

'Not really, they don't know that I've got it, you see. So we'd have to say we were staying in a hotel, and then they'd be offended.'

'OK, OK. I was just trying to get out of it. *Why* don't they know you've got a flat, I mean, how can they *not* know? They live in the same town. You're often down here, don't you bump into them.'

'No, never. We don't exactly hang out in the same places, sweetie. I really can't see my parents getting on down at Revenge.'

'What's that?'

'The Brighton equivalent of Heaven, you know, the gay club. Lots of naked men with whistles around their neck getting sweaty at three in the morning and the overwhelming smell of amyl nitrate on the dance floor.'

'OK, but how come they don't know about the flat?' I said, doggedly.

He sighed, and drained his brandy.

'My grandmother bought it for me just before she died, when I was seventeen. I think she knew what it was like at home, and she wanted to provide somewhere for me to feel safe in. So, you see, they've never known about it.'

'Oh.'

We walked home, via the most outrageously camp pub I'd ever been to, tucked away in the top corner of another Regency square. Pete seemed well known in there; he greeted a few regulars, and the man behind the bar who was wearing a pink shirt, orange tie, a silver brooch and just a touch too much mascara.

'How's that poncey London place of yours doing, Pete?' he asked.

'Better than this dump. At least I haven't got fairies on the ceiling,' Pete bantered back. I looked up, and sure enough, the ceiling was covered in Botticelli-style fairies. It seemed rather jolly to me.

Back in Pete's flat we picked up our bags, to head towards hell. Pete called for a taxi, and all too soon we were sitting in the back of a cab again. This time the driver was chatty, and insisted on discussing the football results with us, even though it should have been patently clear we had no idea what he was talking about.

The cab turned into what Pete had called the white man's ghetto, a large private estate a mile or so from the centre of Brighton. The houses were all set in manicured lawns, and had names like Glendower and The Hollies.

'What, no Dunroamin?' I giggled nervously.

'No, but there is The Laurels.'

'No!'

'Oh yes indeedy . . .'

We climbed out of the taxi and picked our way across the lawn, using the carefully embedded stepping stones. The house loomed out of the dusk, with bogus leaded windows and an intimidatingly large oak-studded front door. There was a weak light in a wrought iron fitting above the door, and as we stepped into its sallow glow, the front door swung open. Suzanne was standing with a glass in her hand, and a fixed smile on her face.

'Hello, you'd better come in. You're rather early, aren't you?' She waved us into the hallway, kissing the air two inches above my left cheek. I thought with a sudden, sharp longing of my own mother who was always hopping up and down with excitement, pacing the courtyard, waiting for me and any friends. There would be hugging and kissing, and a huge palpable feeling of warmth and love. Nothing like this chilling reception.

The hallway was panelled in that very expensive oak that looks like imitation wood. More wrought iron light fittings were dotted along the corridor, which had several doors leading off from it.

'I'm sure you'll want to change before you do anything else, so I'll show you to your room. We are, of course, very *modern* parents.'

I caught Pete's eye, and we trailed upstairs behind Suzanne. She was wearing a long black woollen dress that rather disconcertingly had spangled animals embroidered on it. She flung open the door to a bedroom saying, 'I suppose you'd better come down when you're ready. Drinks in the sitting room . . .' and wafted away again.

I sat down heavily on the bed and looked around me. It would have been easy to imagine that we were in an over-priced motel bedroom. It was spotlessly clean and completely impersonal. Pete and I stared at one another. Wordlessly he took out a bottle of vodka from his bag and passed it to me. I took a hefty swig and passed it back.

'Tell me, is it me, or is this house freezing?' I asked.

'Oh yes, in more ways than one. It's the house, it always was. I remember shivering in bed. I think they're both vampires and don't feel the cold.'

I rubbed my emerald ring across the bedspread, and stared down at it. Well, the vampires weren't getting this back, I decided. The frostiness of the house crept through me: I was chilled to the bone. Pete was quiet, and we padded around the bedroom, changing for dinner.

'We must snap out of this mood quickly, or the wicked witch will have won,' I said eventually.

'You're quite right, let's have another vodka and go and be loud downstairs. What *are* you doing?' I was wriggling into my dress.

'Giving myself a cleavage.'

'Why?'

'I don't know, really. It cheers me up I suppose.'

'OK then, ready? Don't forget, all for one and one . . .'

'For all! After *you*, Aramis.'

We swept down the stairs and into the sitting room. A vast, chilly room with club-like leather furniture spread around it. Wrought iron appeared to be the leitmotif of the house: all the light fittings, candlesticks and fire irons were made from heavily twisted black metal. There were various triffids propped up in the corner, planted in wrought iron pots, and the glass coffee table was supported by yet more of it. Michael stood behind a small glass and metal bar, pouring drinks, and Suzanne was draped in an armchair picking at some needlework.

Michael came forward jovially and we politely kissed

cheeks. He slapped Pete on the back (rather too hard, to go by Pete's wince of pain) and stood in front of us rubbing his hands.

'Well,' he boomed, 'what are we all having? Care to join Suzanne in a G and T?'

'I'd much rather a vodka, if you have any, I find gin very depressing. It's the smell, a bit like dentists' waiting rooms, I've always thought.' I closed my mouth quickly, aware that I was nervous, and when I'm nervous I either eat, or I ramble endlessly on. Sometimes both together.

I went over to admire Suzanne's needlework. It was one of those hideous tapestry cushion covers that are so dear to the heart of the aesthetically challenged. This was a particularly nasty example of the genre, a picture of a hawk carrying some small fluffy creature aloft in its talons.

I pretended to be impressed, then wandered over to look out of the leaded windows. It was very dark outside, but I could make out the outlines of a swimming pool, and a pool house.

'It must be wonderful having a pool in your garden, do you use it a lot?' I said, more for something to say really, than out of genuine curiosity.

Michael spluttered, and Suzanne shot him an icy glance of hatred.

'I try to swim every day. Michael is making that extraordinary noise because he considers the pool an extravagance. Whereas I consider it a necessity.' Suzanne smoothed her hands over her non-existent hips with a gloating look of satisfaction.

Michael started to bore for England about the comparative running costs of keeping a yacht at the Marina and maintaining a pool.

The evening took on a deathless life of its own, with every

minute lasting an hour. We had a curiously tasteless meal, where I tried my best to get slightly drunk, but to no avail. All that resulted was a nasty headache. Michael taunted his son and his wife with tales of their incompetence and stupidity, Suzanne ignored him. Pete, I was relieved to see was rather enjoying himself. Perhaps facing his own personal paper tigers, he parried his father's jeers and taunts with a cheerful indifference.

After dinner we slid around on the leather furniture and discussed weddings. Suzanne became misty eyed remembering her own, and Michael was anxious to know if we'd set a date.

Pete and I looked at each other, and I said that perhaps the summer would be nice.

'As long as it doesn't clash with Cowes.'

Michael locked horns with Pete again about his lack of business acumen, and then Suzanne decided it was my turn for a mild grilling.

'Have you been in the design game a long time?' she asked, in a bored voice.

'Yes, umm, well I've just set up by myself, so it's a very exciting time . . .' I rambled on, making small talk, all the time marvelling at the complete lack of animation on Suzanne's face.

'Pete is such a fool about money, I do so hope you'll be a good influence on him . . .' Her voice trailed off, and she glanced without interest at her son.

I gave a rictus smile and resolved to keep my mouth firmly shut. I thought I'd try to cultivate Zena's vagueness and hoped that she would leave me alone. It must have worked, as she was soon discussing their next holiday with Michael (St Kitts).

I stifled a fake yawn, and caught Pete's eye. I stood up,

excused myself, made my goodnights, and escaped upstairs. Pete soon followed.

We threw ourselves on to the bed. 'That was the *worst* evening of my life!' I groaned dramatically. 'My head is killing me, have you got any painkillers?'

'*You've* got a headache, what do you think I've got?'

I didn't even know why it had been so awful, but it had. They hadn't been especially horrid, but there had been no laughter, no proper conversation and it was clear to me that they disliked Pete very much indeed.

Pete rummaged through his bag, and pulled out some pill bottles. He shook a few tablets into his hand, and held it out to me.

'I'd take a blue one for the head, and red one to make you sleep.'

'Christ! It's like going out with a drug dealer!'

'And you should know, sweetie. Remember Nick the Greek?'

'Oh, don't remind me.' That was a whole episode of my life I'd far rather have wiped from my memory banks.

'Come on, take your pills and pop into bed, we've got the delights of the Yacht Club in the morning.'

I chucked the pills down my neck and looked affectionately at Pete. He was taking his clothes off, and folding both his and mine up. (I am naturally untidy in a bedroom, but make up for it by being obsessively tidy in a kitchen.) He got into bed wearing a very snazzy pair of briefs and a T-shirt. We settled down like an old married couple, and had a good gossip about the evening.

'I can say this, because they are my parents. They are *awful*, aren't they?'

I considered the question. I'd met worse, but then I didn't

know what they'd done to Pete when he was young, and I wasn't sure that I wanted to either.

'Pretty bloody, yes.'

'I thought my father was going to choke when you started talking about the Labour Party, and how your mother had been a communist.'

'I loved it when your mother asked you how you proposed to me! I think the flying me to Paris for dinner was a bit strong . . .'

We were interrupted by the ringing of my phone, at the bottom of my bag on the other side of the bed. Pete handed it over. I handed it back, saying, 'You answer it. It's either an irate builder in Sidcup who insists upon meeting me, or Christopher pleading eternal love, or Mark lusting for a night of rubber, none of whom I wish to speak to.'

'Olivia Hunter's phone, I'm afraid she's taken a few pills and can't speak properly, may I help?'

I hit him with a pillow, and strained to hear who was calling.

Pete had a leisurely conversation with someone who was obviously Steve. His side of the talk was punctuated mainly with expressions of surprise, until eventually he hung up saying, 'Nicola has had a call from her lawyers. Apparently the police in America have dropped any ideas of his death being suspicious. It seems that he simply fell in the bathroom, and hit his head.'

I yawned, and said sleepily, 'Thank God for that. Has she arranged the funeral yet?'

'I don't know, he didn't say. Do you think we'll have to go? I *do* have a rather beautiful black silk shirt that I haven't worn yet and . . .'

I fell into a deep sleep and heard no more.

The following morning I awoke with that blind panic that

happens whenever you open your eyes and have no idea where you are. I stared wildly around the room for a moment, and then it all came back into focus. Pete was already up, and was leaning against the bedroom wall, looking out of the window, giggling.

'What are you looking at?' I demanded.

'Oh, so snoring beauty awakes!'

'I do *not* snore. I may possibly make rather cute woodland animal snuffling noises, but I certainly do *not* snore.'

'Well, all I can say is that the woodland animals were holding a party last night, then. But do get out of bed and come and have a look.'

I climbed out of bed and joined him at the window. Suzanne was swimming in the pool wearing a bathing cap made up of rubber flower petals, doing a stately breaststroke up and down, keeping her head clear of the water. She reminded me of Margaret Thatcher. It must be freezing out there, I thought, not that she'd notice. The outside temperature was probably still higher than the warmth in her veins.

I grabbed some clothes and headed towards the bathroom, praying that I didn't bump into Michael. When I was dressed I joined them all downstairs for breakfast. Well, tea and orange juice. I count liquids as breakfast, much to the obvious disapproval of Michael, who kept trying to foist some very unattractive looking muesli on to me.

'Keeps you healthy, you know,' he insisted, 'inside and out.'

I shuddered, and resolutely stuck to the tea.

Suzanne tried to make Pete go for a swim, and he looked uncomfortable. She laughed, 'Oh you're not *still* sulking over the time that I pushed you in the deep end as a child, are you? I told you, it's the only way to learn how to swim.'

'Well, it didn't work, did it? I still can't bloody swim, and if I remember rightly the lifeguards had to give me mouth to mouth as you nearly drowned me.' Pete sounded weary, rather than angry, and I gave his hand a squeeze under the table.

'But, you didn't, did you?' Suzanne said coldly, looking with great distaste at her son. I nearly choked on my orange juice and Michael jumped to his feet, rubbing his hands together, and suggested it was time to go to the club. I personally felt it was time to go home, but no such luck.

Pete and I climbed into the back of Michael's burgundy Rolls, and we all glided off to the Marina. I've always thought Rolls-Royces the height of vulgarity, and being in this one merely confirmed my suspicions. It also made me feel rather sick. So it was with huge relief that I greeted our arrival at a windy, desolate car park, where we made our way to where Michael's yacht *The Denial* was moored. I sniggered rather rudely at the name, and Pete had to have a coughing fit. Michael looked doubtfully at my footwear, and I offered to wait in the Yacht Club for them. He escorted me inside and brought me a Bloody Mary, before dragging Pete around his pride and joy.

I sipped my drink and looked around me. It was exactly like being in a set dressed by a very unimaginative designer given the brief: 'Design a yacht club somewhere *circa* 1990 in the affluent south'. We had teak, framed knots, ropes, rigging, and a wheel and bell over the bar. The only good thing about it was that for a change I was by far the youngest person in the place. Suzanne soon joined me, as it was rather windy outside and her hair was beginning to look frayed at the edges.

As we sat over our drinks I could feel depression hovering over me like a rain cloud, ready to descend. Suzanne chatted about the sad lack of discipline in schools nowadays, and the appalling council taxes that they had to pay. She was wearing what was obviously her nautical outfit, which consisted of a lot of navy blue and white. My mobile rang in my bag, and I escaped outside with it. It was the builder, John. I probably sounded happier than I actually was to hear from him, but it was just such a relief to get away from Suzanne. We had rather a silly conversation, and I finally agreed to meet him for a drink. I told him a little of the situation that I was in, and he very sensibly (so I thought) said, 'Well, it sounds awful to me. Pretend that this is an emergency call, and then you and your friend can escape.'

I thought it was an excellent idea, and told him so as I turned around to find that Suzanne had materialised by my side and was eavesdropping.

'Why has your voice gone quiet?' John demanded. 'Is someone listening to you?'

'Umm . . .'

'Is it the witch?'

'How did you guess?'

'Didn't you know I had supernatural powers?' he laughed.

'No, but I do now.'

I could see out of the corner of my eye that Suzanne was looking very interested.

'Well, now let me see, what sort of emergency do you need? Something to get you out of there and back here, quickly. I know. I'm your next-door neighbour calling to tell you that your long lost cousin from Patagonia has turned up and I'm giving her tea, while we wait for you to come back.'

'Why is my cousin a female?' I asked.

'All long lost cousins are. It's a fact. Besides, I've got to flirt with someone, haven't I?'

'Have you?' I teased.

Suzanne by now was practically leaning on my shoulder, trying to hear the other side of the conversation.

'Of course! Anyway, Patagonia is fascinating – it has a ragingly high economy at the moment apparently.'

'Patagonia or Brighton, it's all the same to me. I'm such a world traveller, you know. It runs in my family. Ask my cousin,' I said breezily, watching Suzanne trying to figure out what the hell I was talking about.

'Well, your long lost cousin, whose name, by the way is Petunia, hopes you can get back soon.'

'Petunia!'

'Yes,' he said firmly, 'Petunia.'

I laughed and hung up. Suzanne and I walked back into the Yacht Club, and I began readying myself to make my excuses, but there was no need. Pete, bless him, had already done so, and had even called a taxi so that we could make a quick getaway.

'Yes, Livia, it's the Bar, there seems to have been some trouble so I must get back as soon as possible. Shame, isn't it?'

'Gosh yes!' I said brightly, showering kisses on everybody in my haste to get away.

We had slight hysterics in the back of the taxi, and even though we had to wait half an hour for a train, and it was a slow one stopping at every single station between Brighton and London, we continued to laugh, all the way home.

I was ecstatic to be back. I let myself into my flat after having dropped Pete off (I'd tried to get him to come home with me, but he'd wanted to be by himself) and felt a bit like the Pope entering a foreign country – I nearly kissed the ground. Nicola and Steve were ensconced in the drawing room, looking very cosy indeed. A tray of tea was on the floor in front of the fire, and all the Sunday newspapers were spread over the rugs. I flopped down in a chair and related the grisly details of the weekend.

'They both sound like monsters, thank God you managed to get away early,' said Nicola.

'Not like you though, Liv. Didn't you chew them out?' Steve asked me in surprise.

'It was all too much effort. I took my lead from Pete, really.'

'Where is he?'

'He's gone home, I think he's tired, he's probably gone to bed.' I hoped he was OK, it was so hard to tell. I thought he was getting worse, and I knew he was struggling to pretend that all was normal. I asked Nicola about Stan and she went on to tell me that she had decided to have him cremated in New York, and was not going. She had arranged to have his ashes flown back to her. I was surprised, I mean, the funeral of a huge star like Sam Bentley was going to attract the world's press. I wasn't sure Nicola was going to be able to duck out of it that easily.

'Oh yes I bloody can. My lawyer has arranged everything. I am *not* going, it's as simple as that. The press and everyone else can think what they like. I've made my mind up.'

I couldn't resist asking if Stan had made a will.

'Oh yes. You, my dears, are looking at an *exceedingly* rich woman. So I want to spend some time thinking about what I'm going to do with it all.'

'What did you have in mind?' Steve asked curiously.

'I don't know yet, I'm still working on it. All I know is that I'm damned if I'm going to start some crappy musicians' benevolent society, or fund a sanctuary for stray cats. I want to do something worthwhile with it. Something that makes a difference.' She shook her hair back from her face, and again I marvelled at the change in her. She was strong and determined, and looked transformed since the first couple of times I'd seen her when she'd been unsure of anything, and uncertain of her future.

She suddenly stood up, and said, 'I'm going to pour us all a glass of champagne, we'll have a farewell drink and you can wish me *bon voyage*. I'm leaving today. I do so hope you'll all come out and stay with me. Promise you'll try?'

We nodded, but I could see that Steve and I were thinking exactly the same thing – our bank balances, or rather lack of them.

We sat around drinking champagne and talking about Nicola's holiday while I tried hard not to feel jealous. I mean, I wanted to laze in the sun and not think about anything for a while, too. Pete's illness, Molly's unemployment, my imminent bankruptcy, even poor Mimi's inheritance that Mrs Grieg had absconded with – it all seemed too much for me to cope with at the moment.

Making my excuses, I wandered into the bathroom and had a consoling hot bath. I could hear Steve and Nicola hooting with laughter in the other room, and slid under the water, blocking out the noise. When I finally emerged from the bath, Nicola was all packed and ready to go.

We hugged her, and she pressed a bit of paper with her phone number on it into my hand. Her car was waiting outside, and we carried her luggage out for her. She climbed in the back of the car, put her dark glasses on and retouched her lipstick.

'*Very* rock chick, Monty would be proud of you,' I said, leaning forward to kiss her on the cheek.

She smiled, 'Liv, there's something for you in your bedroom. Thanks for everything, see you soon . . .' She waved at us as the car drove away.

There was an envelope on my bed, with my name scrawled across it. I sat down to open it, and some air tickets fell out, with a note from Nicola suggesting that I might like to bring Pete out for a much-needed holiday. I was hugely touched and had to blink back a few tears of gratitude at her thoughfulness. I ran in to show the note to Steve, and we toasted Nicola with the dregs of the champagne.

'What a lovely thing to do. Pete really does need a holiday, you know. Before it's too late,' Steve said rather pointedly, upending the bottle over his glass.

I knew he was right, but I couldn't bear thinking about it.

'Too late for what?' I replied, tartly.

Steve looked sympathetically at me, and put his hand on my arm. 'Liv, you do know, don't you? You know he hasn't got long . . .'

I was furious. 'Don't you dare start to talk like that! He's on a really good drug combination now, and every time you turn on the news there's some new cure just around the corner—'

'No, Liv. It's his heart. He really needs a transplant, and he won't get one. You know that. I know you do, you just can't accept it. But you have to. He has. We all have to, he really needs us to.'

I buried my face in my hands. I am hopeless at accepting unchangeable situations and have great sympathy with the fabled behaviour of the ostrich. I knew, in my heart, that Steve was right, but it didn't make it any easier.

Chapter Seventeen

I spent the following days making rather half-hearted plans for Nicola's house. I'd gone over there a couple of times to take measurements and plan where everything was going to go. It had been strange being there, and I had resisted any curiosity to snoop. Well, to be honest, I hadn't had much of an opportunity as Rick followed me around with eyes like a hawk. I'd arranged for the work to start, and had lined up builders, electricians, plumbers and plasterers.

I was swamped at home with samples of materials I'd chosen for Nicola's new look. It seemed that every time I opened the door there was another delivery of stone, or tiles, or linen. It was a bit like opening wedding presents, and I had to make endless lists to keep track of who'd sent what.

Whilst not exactly bored with making the plans, I didn't feel my usual enthusiasm. Perhaps I really didn't want to spend my life doing up other people's homes. I missed the buzz of an office, and wasn't sure that I was psychologically suited to working alone. You know how it is, you spend your life moaning about work, and then when you're not there, you find to your surprise that you miss everyone. I had even begun to miss Julian, and trust me here, that's quite a surprising thing to do.

I'm hopeless at keeping in touch with people, and think

it's not a good idea to go back to things. I mean, I'm certainly not one of those people who can go out to dinner with their ex and the new girlfriend – dreadful idea. So, I haven't exactly remained in contact with the people I previously worked with.

I used to have a good laugh with some of them, Beth, for instance. She and I would become hysterical at Julian's temper tantrums and would imitate his voice rising to a crescendo when things went wrong. Julian tended to stomp around the office trying to look butch. He would stop and point at someone, and shout, 'My office. Now.' It became a catchphrase among all the workers and we would scream in a high falsetto voice, pointing to one another, 'Wine bar. Now' or 'Lunch in the pub. Now.' The only person I had to shout with at the moment was Steve. I sighed and went through some paint charts again, trying to find the right colour for Nicola's bedroom. I was glad when the phone interrupted me. It was Mimi, calling from Milan. Callously I put her on to Steve, and had great delight in watching him squirm.

I wandered away from him, and went to faff around in the kitchen. I thought I'd make some tea. I didn't really want any, but it's the sort of thing you do when you don't want to settle down to work. You know, you make a bargain with yourself. I'll have one cup of tea, smoke a cigarette, water the plants, clean the kitchen floor, put the washing on, and *then* I'll make those phone calls. (You do realise after a while that you're not fooling anyone, but it doesn't stop you doing it.)

I finished my tea and went back to work. I'd just got settled into the tedious job of fine costing the materials, when the phone rang again. This time, it was Molly who had a wonderful plan to make money. She was going to sublet her flat to Steve. I reasonably pointed out that she wasn't going to make any money on that idea, as she still had to live somewhere herself. As the words left my mouth, I could see the trap I'd fallen in to.

'Exactly!' Molly squealed excitedly. 'I can move in with you!'

Resistance (as the Borg would say) was futile. Soon we were in deep discussion about the logistics of the move. I very grandly ended up saying that as it had absolutely nothing to do with me, I wasn't going to be humping suitcases around, but that I would cook dinner. And no, we weren't going to be having roast bloody chicken.

I tried to get back to work, but it was useless. I just couldn't settle to it. I phoned Sarah for a chat and learned that the only way to keep cats off furniture was to sprinkle copious amounts of citronella oil everywhere. (*Really* useful bit of information, I said sarcastically.) Then she had to ring off, as she was about to go into a very important meeting. Have you noticed that all meetings are very important? I'd love it if everyone had to attend completely pointless, insignificant, trivial meetings, but they never do. I then called Pete, who sounded a bit down. He said that he was just tired, and that he'd had a bad night's sleep . . . and then told me off for 'fussing'. I said that I was cooking dinner for Steve and Molly, and did he want to come over?

I trailed into the kitchen to find Steve having a shouting match with Connie on the phone. I rolled my eyes at him, and drifted away again. If he was ditching the dyslexic milk-maid and swapping her for the Slav smoulderer, it was definitely a case of out of the frying pan . . .

Joe had offered to help move Molly, so I automatically set him a place for dinner. Steve eventually left with his phone still clamped to his ear, pleading with Connie to let him take his futon and his collection of Beatrix Potter books (don't ask).

I called Monty to see if he'd like to come to dinner too, but he *said* that he was swamped with work, and was hunched over a lightbox sorting out catwalk slides. I personally thought it more likely that he was hunched over a policeman, but didn't say so.

Molly and Joe arrived, and staggered to and from the car under bulging cardboard boxes and tatty looking carrier bags. They dumped everything in the office, which was now to be called Molly's room, and slumped in the kitchen, gagging for a cold drink. Joe was complaining about the amount of rubbish he'd had to carry, and Molly was trying to justify why she'd needed to bring with her a huge pile of unframed pictures, and a lot of blank canvases.

'This move is going to take *days*, I didn't realise I had so much stuff,' Molly wailed.

'You'd better not have too much more, this flat isn't the Tardis, you know. We won't get much more inside.' I glanced despairingly at the cardboard boxes.

'Don't worry, one more trip should do it,' Joe said leaning back in his chair and swigging from a can of Coke. I could see Molly drooling over him, and to be fair, he did look like the Coke man from the TV ads, but he was just so damn young. I caught Molly's eye, and she giggled. I removed anything breakable from her orbit, as I knew that soon she'd be knocking things over. Joe offered to drive back to Molly's to help Steve and then come back here for dinner. As soon as the door had closed behind him, I said to Molly, 'Please stop looking at him like that, and don't say like what? Because you know *exactly* what I mean . . .' I gave a very poor impersonation of Molly looking like a leering female Benny Hill.

'I can't help it! He is *really* fit, isn't he?' Molly wailed.

'Yeah, and he's also just got the vote. Lay off him. He's too young.' I tried to sound wise and as if I was imparting divine advice, but I could see that it cut no ice at all as Molly immediately started to retouch her make-up. Oh well, I'd tried. I started to prepare supper, and made Molly tear up salad leaves. (The only job in the kitchen that she was qualified to do, and even that had its dangers. I saw her once slice a tulip bulb, having mistaken it for a red onion.) The intercom buzzed, and Pete arrived, carrying the ubiquitous bottles. Molly caught my eye, and we both looked at Pete with alarm – he looked bloody awful. I pushed him on to a chair, and he sat down gratefully. At once he started to tell us about Monty. Apparently he'd been 'seen' with a new man.

'Talk about London being a village. Anyway, my informants tell me he's rather divine, any idea who it is?' Pete asked, easing the cork from a bottle.

'I'll put money on it. I bet you it's the laughing policeman,' Molly said, grabbing glasses and passing them to Pete to fill.

'I can't say I blame him at all, our boys in blue are rather gorgeous, aren't they? I wouldn't say no to being handcuffed myself.' Pete sounded rather wistful.

We had a good gossip about the state of Monty's love life. Which was all guesswork really, as he was the master of secrecy where that subject was concerned. He'd always had a string of younger boys around him, but as they all looked the same, they'd become interchangeable in our minds. I do remember one in particular, though. Mike. You couldn't forget Mike, he truly believed that he came from another planet (and so did we). He also collected antique dental instruments. No, he did. Really. He'd gone to buy a round of drinks in a bar one night, and that was the last we ever saw of him, although Steve swore he saw his 'wanted' poster once in a police station in the south of France.

As soon as Joe and Steve arrived, I cooked the pasta. We all sat around the table eating, drinking and talking drivel, the way that old friends can. And despite Pete looking so ill, and the chaos of Molly and Steve moving, it was a lovely evening.

Life could often be dull, and sometimes sad, but like a plain white sauce sometimes there were capers to be found in it. And this was one of them. I looked around the table and realised that I really did love all these people. If only Monty and Sarah had been here as well, it would be perfect. I looked at Molly who was excitedly telling Joe of her plans to start painting again: her hair was coming undone as she bounced in her chair, describing what she was going to do. I saw Joe surreptitiously move his glass away from her waving hands and I smiled. Steve was making Pete laugh, telling stories of when we were at art college together. Steve was describing our infamous party piece.

'. . . You have to remember it was around the time of the three-minute warning. All of our discussions revolved about what we would do in the last three minutes. You know, call your mum, or pray, or whatever. So Liv, Molly and me evolved the three-minute off-yer-face. We had one of those things, what d'you call them?' he asked me.

'A Lazy Susan,' I supplied, smiling at the memory of a very young Steve and Molly at college.

'Yeah, you know, those big plates that you get in Chinese restaurants and things, that revolve. We'd all sit round the table with this big plate in front of us, and we'd set the alarm clock for three minutes. Molly's job was to roll a joint, mine was to pour three tequila shots, slice the lime, and pour the salt, Liv's was to chop out three lines of coke. We'd do them, and swing the plate round for the next person. I tell you, smoking that joint, doing the coke, and then the tequila all in under three was fantastic . . . we usually ended up falling off the chairs. Well, Molly did, anyway . . .'

I remembered it well: we'd managed to elevate it almost to performance art. I think at one time we'd actually applied for a grant, to take it on the road. It seemed so very long ago. It had one good lasting effect though, the smell of tequila or grass still made me feel very queasy indeed. I stood up and started to clear away the plates. I saw Pete glance at his watch, and he began to take out various packets and bottles of pills. I put a glass of water in front of him, and he smiled at me, 'Ta, doll. But I never do, if I can help it. You *know* what fish do in that?'

Everyone laughed, and we watched Pete swallow his pills with a large swig of wine. There was absolutely no point at all in warning him of the dangers of mixing medication with alcohol, but I could see that Joe was very tempted to do so. Half-heartedly I put the kettle on to make coffee, but I was pretty sure there'd be no takers.

The conversation turned towards Mimi, and what Steve was going to do about her. As usual, he managed to be evasive about it. Though he did say that he was going to give her some money as he felt bad about Mrs Grieg hopping it with her heirloom. I snorted derisively. If I knew Steve, the only money that Mimi would end up with would be a tenner now and again.

We were picking at some grapes and goat's cheese when the buzzer sounded. I made Steve answer the door, in case it was Christopher or, even worse, Mark after some latex therapy.

'Relax, it's Monty,' Steve said, opening the door for him.

'Hello my loves. Ooh, *chèvre*, my favourite, although it is of course a *moment* on the lips, a matter of *lifetime* on the hips . . . but I can't resist. Don't, whatever you do, ask me about my evening. Let's just draw a veil over the whole sordid proceedings.'

'I thought you said you were crouched over a lightbox, working?' I said accusingly.

He shot me a glance of complicity. 'Well, it *was* work, of a sort . . . But let's not dwell on it. Anyway, I suppose I'm too late to eat?'

I scraped together a plate of leftovers and pushed it in front of him. Molly poured him a glass of wine, and he raised his glass and said, 'Very good news. Let's all drink to the newest model on the block. Apparently she can walk the walk and talk the talk. She is going to be a sensational hit. I spoke to Thunder this afternoon, and they are collectively wetting their Calvin Kleins over her. The next big thing, or so I'm told. Babaganoush is born!'

We all drank to Mimi, and I for one felt a great deal of relief. Maybe she wouldn't mind about Mrs Grieg so much now, and maybe she'd be too busy swanning off to shows to bother Steve. I saw Pete leave the room, and assumed he was going to the bathroom. Molly was quizzing Monty on Mimi's progress in Milan, and Steve and Joe were absorbed in a near-mystical conversation, as far as I was concerned, about cricket.

I washed up, and poured more wine for everyone. Pete had been gone for a long time, and I went to the bathroom to check he was OK. The room was empty, and I discovered him lying across the sofabed in the office, or Molly's room, as it was now technically called. I went and sat on the side of the bed. He was pale, and his breathing was laboured.

'Pete, are you OK?'

Slowly he shook his head. Oh God, he was ill, what was I going to do?

'Shall I call your doctor? Or an ambulance or something?' I said, getting up. He put his hand on my arm, and I sat down again.

'Get my pills, would you?' he whispered.

I could see the sweat on his forehead, and guessed that he was in pain. I ran into the kitchen and grabbed his jacket. Molly followed me back in, and we wiped Pete's face with a cloth and helped him to sit up so that he could swallow a pill. He sighed, and lay down again.

'Sorry about this . . . I need to sleep, can you get me a taxi?' He was licking his lips, and it seemed to be a huge effort to talk. Molly and I glanced at one another, and she shook her head at me.

'Don't be daft. Stay here. Please. It's not a problem, let's just get your trousers off, and then you'll be more comfortable . . .' I said, stroking his arm.

The boys appeared in the doorway. 'Absolutely typical,' Monty said walking towards Pete and waving Molly and me out of the way. 'You two will always find an excuse to get a man's kit off . . . Don't worry, Pete, I shan't let them near you.'

Pete managed a weak smile, and with a surprising nurse-like efficiency Monty had Pete undressed and settled very quickly. I kissed him goodnight, and we closed the door.

Back in the kitchen, we found ourselves talking in whispers. I felt frantic with worry and concern. I didn't know what I could do for him, but was convinced that I should do something. I said as much, and Monty looked at me gravely.

'Liv, the only thing you can do is let him stay here. Look, I wasn't going to tell you this, but Pete and I had a talk the other day. He doesn't want to burden you, or worry you, but he has come to terms with it, or as much as he can. But you do know, don't you? He hasn't got long . . . Let him live how he wants to live, and die. It's up to him, all we can do is support him. The only thing I know is that he doesn't want to be anywhere near his bloody parents.'

Monty put his arm around my shoulders, and continued: 'The other thing is, he doesn't want a hospital, he doesn't want this dragged out. Let him go when he wants to go. He desperately doesn't want this prolonged, and that's what a hospital will do. He wants to carry on as normal, or as normal as he can be anyway . . .'

'But I've got to do something. I can't just . . . just watch him being ill. I'll go mad or something.' Angrily I brushed a tear away, and was aware of Molly doing the same thing.

'Look, he'll have good days and bad days. The amount of morphine he's on, he won't feel any pain.' Monty sounded grimly knowing. He'd always said that the amount of friends that he'd lost practically qualified him as a surrogate doctor.

Steve had his head in his hands, and I could see that Joe was so miserable he was actually fiddling with a dreaded packet of cigarettes. I stared dully at the table, wondering what I could do. I thought about the air tickets Nicola had given me, and raised the idea.

Molly gave a huge grin, and Steve nodded enthusiastically. I looked at Monty, and he smiled at me. 'That's a brilliant idea – couldn't be better. Why don't we all try to go? Even for a week, it would be fantastic.'

We looked at one another, and then frantically started doing sums on the back of envelopes.

Monty had his diary out, and Steve was bargaining with Connie over the phone to gain access to his summer clothes.

Molly concentrating on her list of figures, said, 'Right, if I borrow a hundred from Monty and make my parents give me my Christmas cheque months early, I'm on.'

'Don't you think I'd better call Nicola first? We can't all just go barging out there, can we?' I said nervously.

Steve came off the phone, 'Good idea, call her now.'

I went to find the bit of paper with her number on it, and looked in on Pete as I passed his door. He was asleep.

After a lot of high-pitched squealing noises from the phone, and two wrong numbers, I finally heard Nicola's voice. I explained the situation to her, and she shouted with delight, even before I'd finished. Once I'd ended the call, I looked around the room at every one.

'Well, she's very happy about it. I said we'd try for next week, is that OK?'

Everyone was smiling, and I felt as though a huge weight had been taken from me. At least I was doing something for Pete, even if it was only arranging a holiday. I dreaded to think what my bank manager would have to say on the subject, but resolved, if necessary, to borrow some money from my ex-boss, Julian. He'd give it to me, just for the pleasure of seeing me squirm asking for it.

Molly was asking Monty if she could get away with wearing a bikini.

'As long as it isn't thonged, darling.'

We laughed, and people started to make their way home. To my great surprise (not) Molly was going to stay with Joe, next door. We all kissed goodnight, promising to call in the morning to check on dates and schedules. I watched Molly casually slip her hand into Joe's, and I smiled. Joe didn't stand a chance.

Chapter Eighteen

Sarah came to my rescue, and generously lent me £500 to go away with everyone in the sun for two weeks. She insisted that she was doing it for Pete, and was only pissed off that she couldn't get any time off work herself. I hugged her, and blessed my good fortune. It was worth it, just to see Pete look so happy about having a holiday. Zena, too, had offered to lend me money, and when I refused she gave me a wad of £20 notes, insisting that I take it and spend it on buying Pete dinner out there. The amount would have probably bought the restaurant, but I gratefully pocketed it anyway.

Molly looked like the cat who'd swallowed the cream, and was being very irritating indeed, swanning around with her arm linked through Joe's and buying a variety of brightly coloured sarongs. I hadn't had time to quiz her on the progress she'd made with him, but one look at her face told it all, really.

I was packing and trying to get Pete to rest (he had stayed with me since the night he'd been ill, and was issuing instructions about how many T-shirts and shorts he needed) when my phone went.

'Well, thanks for standing me up.' I recognised the builder from Sidcup's voice at once and realised with a start that I'd promised to meet him, well over an hour ago. He sounded resigned, and I felt sure he thought we were never going to meet.

'Oh, God, I'm so sorry.' I could feel my face go red, and my armpits prickle with embarrassment. I hate leaving people in the lurch, and had genuinely forgotten all about it. I stammered out an explanation (which sounded lame, even to my own ears and involved me wittering on about packing for Pete and trying to book flights) and promised that I'd call him as soon as I returned. I was sorry that I hadn't met him, he sounded fun. I was actually going to miss his calls.

After a week of tearing around London, borrowing money, booking flights and packing, we finally left Heathrow in a haze of duty-free. But after just a day at the villa our lives had taken on a slow, honeyed rhythm of their own.

Every morning I would wake up in a room flooded in sunshine, with white muslin curtains moving sexily in the breeze. I kept expecting Catherine Deneuve to appear behind them *à la The Hunger*. I would lie very still for some moments, savouring the silence that was punctuated only by birdsong, and the distant harsh cries of the fishermen setting out in their boats. I would then languidly get up, and wrapping a sarong around me, venture out on to the bedroom balcony to look over the garden and down the hill to the sea.

The garden was the most magical part of the villa, it had olive and lemon trees, jasmine and bougainvillaea. In a small field next to the garden sheep and goats (and yes, we could hear the tinkle of the bells around their necks) grazed, as well as a few antiquated beehives. There were wild poppies in the field, a startling scarlet against the backdrop of the pale blue sky and sea. The sea always had a pearly glow in the early mornings, and sometimes a faint mist clinging to it. I would stand entranced, watching the sea change colour and the sun rise in the sky.

Soon, the others would start stirring, and my spiritual (or so I thought) reverie would be broken by Pete, calling from the next balcony, 'Oi, I hope you're wearing some knickers under that!'

We gathered in the morning around a large marble table outside, beneath a grape vine that trailed over a trellis. The leaves and tendrils of the vine grew at an alarming rate, prompting Monty to observe that if we sat there too long we would all look like effigies of the god Pan, with vines in our hair.

Breakfast would have been spread on the table, and we helped ourselves to the bitter strong coffee, fruit, honey and yoghurt. Plans were discussed and then discarded for the day. We would gradually start to wake up (aided by the caffeine hit).

'And tell me, whose feet did I hear scampering down the hall at dawn this morning?' Monty asked in a mischievous voice. 'They were definitely over a size ten ... So whose door were you creeping out of, Joe?'

Joe spluttered into his coffee and tried to change the subject. 'Shall we go and get some fish for dinner tonight? I could pick some herbs and we could bake them on the barbecue ...'

I glanced at Molly, and saw that she was grinning complacently. Well, that was that mystery solved, then.

'Aren't we going to the Dolphin?' (The Dolphin was the local taverna that Nicola had developed a fondness for. The food was pretty awful, but the wine was wonderful.)

More coffee was poured and then the serious business of

the day was planned. Who was doing what where and what should we have for dinner?

Molly and Steve decided to paint in the garden. They were going to attempt some sort of joint show, and had knocked up an improvised studio out of bamboo screens. Steve was accused of overworking his pictures, and he in turn accused Molly of pushing the colour spectrum out of the realms of possibility. They had infused us all with the painting bug, and they (rather patronisingly, we thought) gave art lessons. Joe definitely showed signs of talent, and was encouraged shamelessly by Molly. The rest of us were quite content to stand back and admire our daubs with a feeling of accomplishment and pride, complimenting each other's work only if the compliments were reciprocal.

Nicola spent three hours a day bashing a keyboard. She could be found every morning in her bedroom, linked to her laptop and consulting her diaries. Sometimes she would read out her morning's work for our horrified amusement over lunch.

'December 1979,
Stan took delivery of some dope today, the block was so large, and arrived in a box, that I mistook it for the Christmas turkey and stashed it in the fridge. He spent all day looking for it. Had dinner with David Bowie, he kept asking me if I thought he should have his teeth capped. Stan wanted to invite Basher (the drummer of Stan's band) for Christmas lunch, I said no. The last time he was here he was sick at the table, and then fell asleep in it. Got too stoned to remember what time I'd put the turkey in the oven. It was still raw at midnight, so I cooked egg and chips. Stan gave me a Rolls-Royce for a Christmas present, forgetting that I'd already got

one. Oh well, I suppose at least it's a different colour. Stan bought himself a helicopter, I don't know why, as he hates flying in them. He said he'd forgotten. Went to Elton John's for Boxing Day, I don't care what Stan says about him being a poof, I liked him.'

Joe spent a lot of time working out. He would run before breakfast, then bully all of us unmercifully till we caved in and went swimming with him. We were all very unsatisfactory pupils.

'No, Molly, it is *not* a shark, they don't have them round here.'

'Go on, keep going, you can do it, Liv, no you haven't swum three miles already, you've barely covered three yards.'

'Seaweed is *not* dangerous, and no it *doesn't* sting you.'

'That young fisherman is waving at you, Pete, or is he waving to Monty?'

'Nicola, you *have* to get your hair wet if you want to do backstroke.'

Pete had rapidly become very attached to the garden and spent most of his time pottering around it. Transplanting things, pruning and weeding. He was a mine of information when it came to plants, and loved putting sweet-smelling flowers in all the rooms of the villa. He also fed and watered the animals, which we were in increasing danger of being overrun by.

The cats came with the villa, but Pete had added to them by rescuing a puppy from the village. The cats viewed it with total disdain, whilst the puppy, who'd gained considerable weight in just a few days, was desperate to play with them. He was blind in one eye, and had been christened Pugh. Poor Pugh had constant scratches from the cats, who, if he pestered them too much, would lazily reach out a paw and swipe him across the nose.

One of the goats from the field had started a love affair with Pete, and would follow him around the garden, butting him gently now and again. He also fed the birds, and as it was spring, he had a succession of baby birds crammed in his shirt pockets till he could find a home for them. He would feed them throughout the night, and had to make his room a cat-free zone.

I was queen of the kitchen. I loved being in the large cool room, where I would happily slice tomatoes and baby cucumbers into a bowl, and then drizzle the local peppery, fruity olive oil over them for lunch. Sometimes I would add the regional salty cheese, or maybe some olives, with a squeeze of lemon. Steve often joined me, and when we didn't go to the Dolphin we would concoct huge dinners, usually from the local fish, that we served on the marble table outside, with scented candles on it to keep any mosquitoes at bay.

Steve and Pete vied for the official title of barman, but Pete won hands down with his version of a martini. He believed, like the film director Luis Buñuel, that the only way to make a Martini was to allow the light to pass through the vermouth on the way to hitting the gin (or vodka). He would then put the cocktail shaker into the freezer till it became a bit like an alcoholic jelly. These lethal drinks were rightly named 'the silver bullet'.

A charming elderly couple, Maria and Dimitri, who lived in a cottage a short walk away through the wildflower field, looked after our basic needs. Maria did the laundry, draped the sheets over lavender bushes so that the beds had a heavenly smell. Dimitri would sweep and wash the terraces, and rebuild the barbecues. He had taken a great shine to Pete and Joe, and on our third evening they'd persuaded him to take them night fishing in his little boat, accompanied by a torch and a bottle of ouzo.

Anyway, this particular morning I was standing in the kitchen, languidly squeezing some lemons to make lemonade and marvelling that there was still a whole basket of the bright yellow fruit that I had brought from the village yesterday. The lemons on our trees (we said 'our' the whole time, even though we knew with a sinking heart that we had to go home soon) weren't ripe yet, but they were a visual treat and I would go and stare at them, stroking the unripe fruit and glossy leaves with wonder. I thought that after making up the jug of lemonade I would go for a swim and then try to finish my painting (Steve was rather rude about it, saying that the only good thing was that it didn't matter which way up it was hung). Nicola walked into the kitchen, beaming from ear to ear.

'God, that feels better! I've finally done it.'

'What? You haven't finished the book already?'

'No, no I'm only up to 1980. I've got a whole decade to go yet. No, I've just got rid of a million pounds, and it feels great.'

'What have you done with it?'

'Well, after weeks of wrangling with my lawyer, I finally freed up the money. I think they forget just whose dosh it is! I made a hefty donation with it, and I must say I feel very virtuous.'

I had become used to talking to Nicola about her financial situation, although it still seemed like Monopoly money to me. The casual mention of a million-pound donation to charity seemed amazing.

'Good for you. Do you fancy a swim? I can't believe we've got to go home soon. It's been wonderful, being here.'

'I wish you didn't have to go, are you sure I can't lend you some money?'

We'd been through this many times. I kept refusing and she kept offering.

'Honestly Nicola, you've done enough for us all already . . .' Tempting as the offer was, I did have to get on with my own life.

We walked through the garden, waving to Pete who was trying to lead the goat back to the field and being playfully butted dangerously near the groin area. Pugh followed us, running in excited circles at our feet. He had a fascination with butterflies and would desperately try to catch one, pouncing with his front paws. It was possible to chart Pugh's progress by the cries of 'Leave them alone you little bastard' wherever he went.

We passed the bamboo studio and stood and watched Steve and Molly work for a while. Molly, wearing a blue swimsuit with a bright blue and yellow sarong, had a daub of acid green paint over her face, and was absent-mindedly wiping her paintbrush over her sarong, whilst draping the paint rag over her shoulder. Steve was frenziedly rubbing charcoal into a large portrait he had done of Maria. They both had a furious concentration about them, and were oblivious to our presence. We left them to it, and walked down the slope towards the sea, through an iron gate set into the garden wall, and along the path to the beach. There was a wonderful aromatic scent all around us as our feet crushed the wild thyme that grew there so profusely.

The beach that came with the villa grounds was a small sandy cove protected on either side by rocks. Monty was spread out sunbathing. Nicola and I waved at him, and walked down to stand ankle deep in the sea, letting the waves lap over our feet.

'Have you noticed how well everyone looks?' Nicola asked.

It was true. Already Steve had actually managed to put on some weight and his ribs didn't stick out quite so much. Molly was glowing with health, Joe even more so. Nicola had lost the haunted look in her eyes and I had even lost a few pounds, due to the excessively healthy lifestyle. Pete had stopped smoking so much, so that his breathlessness seemed more under control. I knew that his health was stabilised, rather than better, but he seemed so happy here. It was by far the best thing that we could have done for him. But more than the outward signs of health, we all seemed so much more at ease than we had done in London. The pressure was off, and although we all knew that it couldn't last for ever, a fortnight's respite from the daily grind of making a living in one of the hardest capitals in the world was a great release.

We stood for some time, gazing out to the horizon. I could feel the sand being washed away beneath my feet and knew that this holiday was coming to an end. We had all begged and borrowed time and money to come here with Pete, and soon we would have to go home again.

'Liv, you and Pete could stay on, you know,' Nicola said. I promised to think about it, but felt uneasy at trespassing for so long on Nicola's generosity.

I changed the subject. 'How about that swim now?'

We ran into the water, leaving our sarongs, T-shirts and hats littered across the beach. The water was buoyant and exactly suited our mood. We swam out as far as we dared, then turned back to find Monty performing an elegant side-stroke in the shallows, and splashed towards him.

The three of us walked lazily back to the villa, and drank the cool lemonade in the shade of the vine. Then Molly and

Steve appeared, covered in paint and charcoal, and thirstily gulped some down. The others drifted in and Steve continued to badger us all to sit for him: 'Come on, I've done Maria and Dimitri, and Molly. I nabbed Joe yesterday and Nicola has promised to let me do her tomorrow. That just leaves you and Pete, so, Livia, let me do you this afternoon? And don't say that you'll be preparing dinner, because you know we're going to the Dolphin for some poisoned dynamited goat, so have a shower and come down right away, OK? And we're leaving soon, so it's got to be this afternoon.'

Reluctantly I agreed. Like most people I hated even having my photograph taken, and sitting for a portrait was far worse, but I knew that Steve wanted to do everybody here. He and Molly were really into the idea of a joint show and had been making plans to take their work back to London. I went and showered and came back into the garden. Joe and Monty were making plans to row out to sea, and practise diving.

'What about you, Pete, any plans this afternoon?'

'I have a very hot date with a book and my bed. A siesta is calling me. I'll see you all this evening.'

'Are you OK?'

Pete ruffled the top of my hair as he passed me. 'Yes, I'm fine, I just need a bit of a lie-down, that's all.'

Steve dragged me off to a seat under an olive tree and started to set up some paper.

'I do so wish that you weren't a warts and all sort of painter, can't you at least take off a couple of pounds?' I grumbled, settling myself down on the seat. 'And don't start banging on about artistic integrity, OK?'

Steve laughed and told me to shut up. There was a companionable silence for a while, broken only by the noise of his hand scratching away at the paper. It was quite hot now, and it was very still and silent in the garden. The birds and insects were probably having a well earned siesta, I thought, just like Pete. I shifted slightly in my seat.

'Bloody keep still,' Steve complained.

'This is why I hate sitting for you – you turn into a real bully. I only moved a fraction of an inch.'

Pete appeared behind Steve, with a book in his hand. 'I couldn't sleep, so I came down here. Do you want to do us together?'

'Great idea. Hang on, I'll have to change my position. Sit down next to Liv,' Steve told him.

Pete settled himself beside me as Steve faffed around with some new paper, and started to sketch us. He told us all about the idea that he and Molly had of doing a joint show: his pictures would be shown next to hers, and they were both of the same things. For instance, the charcoal picture that he was doing of us would be entitled 'Heads # 5&6'. Then Molly would interpret it in colour.

Pete was his usual scathing self about art: 'You mean Livia and I will end up as a series of orange triangles and bright blue circles?'

'Well, if that's how you see yourself . . .'

'Please don't start, either of you. All you two do is argue about art, it's too hot! Just agree to disagree, OK?' I said, with mock weariness.

After that we spent a very peaceful afternoon, chatting and reading in the shade of the olive tree while Steve captured us for eternity. The shadows grew longer, and the sun lost its sting. The goats made their way into the courtyard of Maria and Dimitri, looking for more food. The insects started to make their noises again, and we decided it was time for a drink.

'After all, we *are* on holiday, aren't we?' Pete said, leading the way inside, heading for the kitchen and the booze.

Chapter Nineteen

We usually walked down the hill on to the beach and scrambled over the rocks to get to the Dolphin. The other way was much longer, and involved a rough track up through the village. We always walked back home that way though.

We were sitting at the table, idly watching a firefly buzz around the garden trees, sipping silver bullets and waiting for Monty to finish dressing.

'Have you noticed that it's *always* him who's the last to come down?'

'Yeah, but have you noticed that he always looks the best?'

'What does he *actually* do in the bathroom? He's been in it for ages and ages, I think he's got his own personal plastic surgeon in there.'

Monty had finally arrived, and he overheard the last remark.

'Exfoliate, cleanse, moisturise, tone and buff. The knife is not yet for me! A silver bullet? How divine, and are we dining at the Dolphin? Well, let us depart!' He drained his glass in one long swallow and we set out.

This was my most adored time of the day, the heavily scented dusk. Bats started to swoop out of wherever the hell bats sleep, and Molly obligingly squealed. Joe and Steve, who were carrying torches, started to play the light over the swooping dark creatures. The sheep were silent, but the goats, being curious, made faint bleating noises as we passed them. Pete grabbed my hand as we went through the garden gate, and squeezed it, saying, 'This really is about as good as it gets, isn't it?'

I nodded, but he could barely see me, so I squeezed his hand instead. The evening had an end of holiday feel to it. I knew that he was dreading going home and checking in with his doctor, but he seemed so happy and healthy I didn't have any anxiety about it at all. Nicola and Monty were walking ahead of us, and I could hear them discussing her book.

'But Nicola, it sounds positively *scandalous*, are you sure you can get it printed?'

'Well, that's why I'm going to New York, the lawyers there are a damned sight tougher than they are in England. Kiss and tell, that's what I say!'

'Kiss and sell, more like,' he chortled. 'Well, good for you. Are there any pictures?'

'God, loads! You wouldn't like to wade through them with me, would you?'

'I'd love to . . .'

We had reached the village now, and started to climb the steep uneven steps to the Dolphin, stopping every so often (apart from Joe, who, as we pointed out, was a non-smoker, and much younger than any of us) to recover from the steepness of the path. Nico, the owner greeted us with open arms and kissed us all, his gold teeth beaming at us in the light. He ushered us towards the table that overlooked the tiny harbour with its boats bobbing up and down. Nico wiped his hands on his grubby apron, then clapped imperiously for one of his sons to bring us drinks. Soon we had glasses and bottles in front of us and, as I reached for a drink, the emerald ring that I never took off flashed fire in the candlelight. Pete noticed it, and we exchanged complicit grins.

Nico put out plates of olives, bread, cheese, cucumbers and almonds. The Dolphin's cats materialised out of the darkness and started to beg under the table, one very skinny grey one with battle scars over its face pressing against my legs and making demanding noises. I gave it a chunk of cheese, and it quickly ran to the corner with it, ready to fend off any enemies. These cats were certainly not the pampered pets of London; they were scrawny and, I suspected, partly wild. Nico, as well as Maria and Dimitri, scorned our habit of feeding the villa cats, but none of us could help it. Pete in particular had really fallen for the animals, and it was always he who made sure that the sheep and goats had enough water and food. He spoilt the cats dreadfully, making special journeys into the village to forage for suitable food for them. Pugh was devoted to us all, but Pete was his master. I dreaded the day of parting the puppy from Pete.

'Come on then, what are we all having? The fish or the lamb?'

'You know perfectly well it's not lamb, I'm sure it's goat. A tough old billy at that!'

'Don't! Do you remember the dinner from the Ivy?'

'You don't think we could tempt the chef out here do you?'

'Perhaps we'd better stick to the fish.'

'The cats will be happy with whatever we choose.'

We ended up, as we usually did, with a large platter of rather too oily fish and some under-washed salad.

The meal out of the way, we sat back (as much as we

could in the straight-backed wooden chairs) and drank our wine. It really was good – flinty and very dry.

Nico arrived at the table, banging down a bottle of the local brandy and some small tumblers. Once the fiery liquid had been poured we raised our glasses and toasted each other. I had to shake off a slight feeling of melancholy. I guessed it was just the usual end-of-holiday blues. I drank a glass of brandy and poured myself another, determined to shake off this gloomy mood. Pete filled my glass a third time, and squeezed my hand under the table. I saw Molly looking at me with concern, and to my horror felt my eyes prick with tears. Steve was gazing at me now, and soon everybody had stopped talking and watched as two tears ran down my face.

'Livia, what on earth is the matter?'

I gulped and sniffed, 'I don't know really. It just occurred to me that I'm going to miss you all, and this has been the most perfect fortnight of my life, and, oh I don't know! Perhaps I'm just getting hormonal or something . . . But it feels like the end of something.'

Pete called me a daft tart, Molly and Nicola started to cry in sympathy and Joe looked uncomfortable. Steve put his arm around me and gave me a cuddle. Monty looked very worried and said nothing at all.

Now I was embarrassed. I mean this was a farewell dinner, and I was spoiling it by weeping. Oh God. 'Maybe the island is getting to me, you know, Greek tragedy and all of that. I am sorry, I don't know what came over me. Please forget it, I'm just tired and emotional.'

'Ah, pissed as a newt, is that it?' Steve teased.

'Yes, that's it. Now pass the brandy . . .'

The evening continued and I did my best to join in and show a happy face. Two of the local men challenged Pete and Steve to backgammon, and we all placed bets on them.

After the locals had smilingly collected their winnings we decided it was time to walk home, and set out through the village. As the path dropped, we passed open doors and balconies strung with washing and peppered with pots of geraniums. The pale colours of the cottages glowed in the moonlight, and the local people were sitting out having a last glass of wine, or coffee. A black dog followed us for a while, sticking closely to Pete.

'Don't say you've found another stray, Pete!' Nicola groaned.

'No, I've never seen this dog before . . . Go on, boy, go home now.'

'No, he hasn't,' Monty said quite sharply. 'Go on, go home!' He gave the dog a gentle push.

Molly and Nicola were walking arm in arm and singing quietly together. It was an old Beatles number, and their voices sounded soft and low in the dark. Joe bounded ahead with the torch, calling us all 'unfit hippies' as he exhorted us to move more quickly. Pete and Steve were having one of their interminable mock arguments, with Steve matching his pace to Pete's. Monty and I were silent as we climbed through the outskirts of the village.

Where the ground levelled off and gave way to trees and bushes, the air was filled with a dry aromatic smell that I loved. It was made up of pine trees, herbs and flowers. I stopped at some jasmine and breathed in the heady sweet scent. I picked a sprig and tucked it into Pete's shirt. When we had reached the villa I decided to go straight to bed. Monty followed me upstairs, and we could hear the others calling goodnight to us and trying to tempt us back down again with the lure of a last brandy.

'I'll even let you win at Perudo!' Steve shouted.

As I was turning into my bedroom, Monty stopped me and swung me around to face him. He looked very serious.

'Liv, do you believe in omens?'

I knew in a flash that he was thinking about the black dog that had followed us in the village.

'No,' I said firmly.

We looked at each other for a long moment, then wordlessly kissed goodnight. As I undressed and made ready for bed, I thought about Monty's question. I knew that he was a great believer in tarot cards, fortune tellers, astrology and all things mystical. My belief, if I had one, was more along the lines of 'there are more things Horatio, in heaven and earth than are dreamt of in your philosophy . . .' I pushed the thought from my mind and settled down in the supremely comfortable bed that smelt of lavender.

It was the first sleepless night I'd had at the villa, and I was unprepared for it. Usually I had several tricks to outwit that devil, insomnia. Reading, getting up and making a sandwich, counting up ex-lovers (I got to what I thought was an exceptionally high number once and decided to stop before anyone could accuse me of nymphomania) and if the worst came to the worst, a sleeping pill. But like an idiot, I hadn't got any with me. I read for a couple of hours, but was restless and couldn't concentrate. I could hear the owls outside, but the rest of the villa was silent. I decided to try to sleep again. I was getting hot and uncomfortable, and the sheets tangled around my body.

Exasperated, I stood up, and remade the bed. It was the dead of night, and even the owls had stopped their sonorous cries. I decided to tiptoe into Pete's room and look for his sleeping pills. Even if I woke him up, he wouldn't mind.

Gently I eased open the door to his bedroom. In the moonlight shining through his window I could see the white glow of the bed. I could also smell something very sweet. I realised that it must be the jasmine. He kept his pills in a neat regimented line in his bathroom, and I crept towards the door of the bathroom trying not to make a noise. Once inside, I closed it behind me so that when I turned the light on it wouldn't wake him.

Pete was lying fully dressed on the bathroom floor. His eyes were wide open and he wore a look of faint surprise. His hands were on his chest and his lips were pale blue. I knew instantly that he was dead. It seemed that I stayed there for a long time, looking at him. Then, I think I must have started to scream.

Pretty soon the bathroom was full of people. Monty and I sat on Pete's bed, holding hands. Nicola and Molly were crying and sobbing and Steve was desperately trying to revive Pete. Joe had run across to the cottage to wake Maria and Dimitri. Pugh was whining and trying to lick Pete's face. I picked the puppy up and cuddled him.

'Steve, stop. You know he's dead. Please stop,' I begged from the bedroom.

'But he can't be! You saw him tonight. He can't be!'

'You know he is. Come on, leave him alone . . .'

Molly was crying so hard that her tears seemed to be coming from her belly. Nicola was holding on to her, trying to comfort her. Steve eventually gave up, and sat on the bathroom floor next to Pete, with his head buried in his hands. The jasmine I had picked for Pete was lying on his pillow, the small white flowers already turning slightly brown at the edges. I picked the dead flowers up and held them in my hand. Pugh wriggled out of my grasp and sat beside Pete, whimpering. I heard Joe come running up the stairs, followed by a distraught Maria and Dimitri. Joe was panting as he said, 'I tried to make them understand, I think they've called a doctor . . . Is he . . . ?'

I nodded. Maria and Dimitri crossed themselves. Then Maria leaned forward and gently closed Pete's eyes. Dimitri went to the windows and opened them wide; the curtains fluttered in the breeze.

'It is to let his spirit go free,' Dimitri muttered apologetically, adding, 'I will wait outside for the doctor.'

Maria knelt at the door of the bathroom, praying. Suddenly I wished that I could, too. I offered up my own prayer for Pete, wishing him a crowded bar, and animals to look after, and a window table groaning with his favourite food with places set for his friends to join him when they could. I sighed, stood up from the bed and went to put my arms round Molly.

'Come on, let's go downstairs and have a drink.' I led her out of the bedroom, and she leaned heavily on me, Nicola supporting her on the other side.

We sat in the drawing room downstairs. The room looked strange, as if I'd never seen it before, with unfamiliar furniture and objects staring out of the gloom. Nicola snapped on all the lights, and went about the business of preparing drinks, making tea and pouring brandy. Molly was sobbing, and her tears had soaked her face and hair. Steve and Joe came down next, looking grave. Monty was still upstairs and I could hear the murmur of his and Maria's voices.

'Oh God! I've just thought, I'll have to call his parents, won't I?'

'Don't do it now, Liv, do it in the morning,' advised Nicola.

I nodded. The phone lines here were erratic at the best of times, and I dreaded being asked to repeat myself or having to shout to make myself understood. One of the best things about being at the villa had been that none of our mobile phones worked. Now I realised it could be a curse.

Molly was shaking and sobbing still, clutching a glass of brandy to her chest. Joe sat next to her and put his arm comfortingly around her. Steve and I just looked hopelessly at one another whilst Nicola continued to busy herself with handing round drinks.

'The doctor should be here soon.'

'What's the point?'

'What should we do?'

'I don't know.'

Monty came downstairs and poured himself a brandy. 'You know, we'll have to think about his funeral. I mean, where do you think he'd like to be buried?'

The thought of all the legalities involved in flying Pete's body back to England left me feeling daunted.

'Maria has called the priest.'

'Why?'

'I think it's something they just automatically do.'

Abruptly I stood up and started to pace the room, restless and unable to sit still. I picked up a book that had been left lying on the floor, and placed it in the bookshelf. It was the battered paperback copy of the Angela Thirkell novel that I had bought in Brighton with Pete. I put the already fading jasmine between the pages and closed the book. How appropriate, I thought.

We jumped as Dimitri came into the room with a pale faced young man carrying a medical bag. He went upstairs with Monty, and we could hear their voices in muted conversation. I had an overwhelming need to be outside, and I slipped out of the french windows into the garden. Dawn couldn't be far off, and the velvety black sky had taken on a slightly grey tinge. I could hear Molly crying from the other room, and wondered if the doctor could give her a sedative. Steve came outside, and we stood together in silence watching the day break. Our hands sought each other's, and I held on tightly.

'I can't believe he's gone, can you?'

I put my head on Steve's shoulder and he stroked my hair.

'He has though, hasn't he? I mean, I can't feel him here any more.'

'He once told me that he never travelled anywhere without a bottle of champagne. Do you think he's got one now?'

'Bound to, knowing Pete. Come on, let's go back inside.'

The priest had arrived and was upstairs with the doctor, Maria and Monty. Monty called down to us, 'I think you should all come up.'

We trooped upstairs. Maria and the doctor stood aside, and we entered the bedroom. They had lifted Pete on to the bed, and someone, Monty I thought, had placed flowers in his folded hands. His lips had lost their blue tinge and he looked peacefully asleep. I kissed his forehead, and almost flinched when I felt how cool he was. Molly kept repeating to herself 'No, no, no', and the doctor and Joe led her to her room.

Maria had made coffee and we started to discuss formalities with the priest and the doctor.

'Do you think he might like to be buried in the little churchyard on the hill above the villa?' Nicola asked me.

'I'm sure he would, but won't that involve hideous problems? I mean, he's not Greek, I mean *wasn't* Greek, and he was ill, you know, Nicola and . . .'

She patted my hand and the doctor said something to Maria. Maria looked embarrassed and translated for him.

'He says that the burial must take place tomorrow. I am

so sorry, it is our way. You know we have to do this, we have no place for him to stay. We are a small island, it must be tomorrow. Or you fly him home.'

I realised that we in England, who pay people to deal with our dead, do not suffer the same way as in a hot country, where the bodies must be buried quickly.

I nodded, hoping that the priest and the doctor could somehow arrange for a foreigner, and a non-believer, to be buried in their churchyard. I didn't want to have to think about it, I didn't want to have to face all these people and make these decisions. But I knew he would have liked to be buried here, amongst the pine trees up on the hill, looking out towards the blue bay that dolphins skimmed across.

'Livia, I think you should go to bed,' said Nicola. 'I'll arrange what I can and we can talk in the morning, well, in a few hours anyway. Steve, why don't you take Liv upstairs? Monty and I can deal with this.'

I looked at her gratefully. Steve and I shook hands with the doctor and the priest. Maria kissed me, and Dimitri just stood in the corner of the room, twisting his battered cap in his hands. He patted me awkwardly as I walked past, and I tried to smile at him. Monty and Nicola hugged me and we went upstairs. I found that my whole body was shaking.

A few hours later I awoke, with a heavy feeling in my chest. I wanted it to be untrue, and like a child I closed my eyes, willing it to be so. But I knew I had to face the horrors of the day. I got out of bed and dressed.

When I came downstairs I found Monty and Nicola still talking to the priest, a stern-faced man with a luxuriant wavy beard. This was not the jolly face of the local priest in Ireland or Italy who could be found in a bar having a tipple. This was the face of a man who had faced his demons and was prepared to help you face yours. He stood up when I came in, shook my hand and blessed me. He then did the same to Nicola and Monty, and left.

They both sighed, and Monty said, 'Well, thank *God* that's over . . . it was worse than being back at school with the headmaster.'

'What happened?' I asked.

Monty and Nicola looked at each other before answering. 'Well, he's going to be buried tomorrow, if that's OK with you, up in the little churchyard . . .'

I went over to the phone and picked up the receiver to call Michael and Suzanne Aston. I dialled the long, complicated international code. The phone rang and rang, and cravenly I hoped they were out and that I wouldn't have to talk to them. Eventually it was answered by Suzanne. I broke the news to her as gently as I could, telling her that her son had died of heart failure, and that with her permission he was going to be buried tomorrow on the island. There was a long silence, and I started to think we had been disconnected.

'Hello?' I said. 'Are you still there?'

'Yes. I see. Thank you for calling me, Olivia. No doubt you will be coming home soon?' Her voice was chilly and distant.

I stammered something out and she said, 'I would stay in the sun my dear, if I were you. It's terribly cold and rainy here at the moment. I've even had to turn the temperature up on the swimming pool. Well, goodbye.'

I stared at the phone in my hand. Was that conversation imaginary? Or had I just told her that her son was dead and she had started to talk about the fucking weather? Maybe she was in shock, I reasoned. Or maybe not. I ran into the garden, with Pugh barking joyfully at my heels. The goat was straining to see who was coming out of the villa.

'Sorry boy, it's only me.' I stared into the goat's strange yellow eyes, and he turned his head disdainfully away from me. I carried on through the garden and unlocked the gate that led to the sea. Pugh followed and was running in circles up and down the path. I walked into the shallows and watched Pugh braving the small waves with an air of triumph. I turned back to look at the villa, it stood midway up the hill, with the green of the lemon and olive trees framing its apricot coloured walls and soft red roof. The sky was a deep brilliant blue and higher up on the hill stood the tiny white church surrounded by cypress trees. Pete would have a stunning view.

Chapter Twenty

Monty and I flew back to England together. After Pete's funeral Molly, Steve and Joe had decided to extend their holiday for a week and stay on at the villa, much to Nicola's relief, but I thought that the sooner I got back to London and work, the better. Or I never would, and I would end my days cooking fish and picking olives on a small sunny Greek island.

A smiling steward served us champagne which, inevitably, reminded us both of Pete. We had waved goodbye to Nicola, Joe and a very red-eyed Molly early in the morning (Steve was still asleep) and the last thing I saw of the island was the roof of the small church. Then the plane had banked steeply, the horizon dipped and the church was no more. Monty and I clinked glasses as we headed back home.

'Let's go out tonight. I'll come and pick you up.'

'OK,' I said, listlessly.

'Liv, you've got to snap out of this.'

I just didn't have the energy to talk properly. I didn't even have the energy to cry, I just felt blank and rather empty.

'I'm fine,' I murmured.

'No you're not.'

'Yes I am.'

He paused. 'We've got to tell everyone at the Bar about Pete, you know. Shall we go and get it over with tonight?'

'Yes, all right.'

That was a dreadful thought: having to walk into the Bar and announce Pete's death. It had to be done, and really I should have phoned and told them from Greece, but I hadn't.

To our surprise, we had found a will in Pete's room, amongst his papers. He had left his flat in Brighton to me and, rather shockingly, the Bar to Steve and myself, jointly. We had a half-hearted discussion about what we were going to do with it, although it was probably mortgaged to the hilt anyway, but hadn't reached any sort of conclusion. I had promised to try to figure it out once I was back in England, and said that I would go into Pete's office and have a look through the paperwork.

It was a great comfort to return to my flat. I persuaded myself that the first thing I should do was to have a shower. The flat was beautifully clean and tidy, thanks to Sarah who had been popping in to look after it for me – there was even milk in the fridge and some flowers in the drawing room – and after standing under hot water for fifteen minutes I reluctantly dragged myself out of the bathroom and, wrapped in a dressing gown, wandered aimlessly around the flat. It *was* nice to be home, but it felt odd. I made some tea and, curling up in my chair, started to listen to my messages.

The first three were from William Magpie. I fast-forwarded them. Then there was a drunken message from Christopher, 'You haven't taken your mobile away with you, you bitch! I really want to talk to you . . .' I fast-forwarded that one too. The next one was fascinating, and I saved it and replayed it several times. It was from Mrs Grieg.

''Allo, love. It's me, I thought I'd better call you, seeing as you might be worried about me. No need, I'm very comfy 'ere. Got myself a lovely garden, cor! You want to see me roses, coming along a treat they are. Nice little 'ouse too. Don't miss Blighty at all, well, not the bleedin' weather anyway! I saw that friend of yours Nicola in the papers, I thought to meself that you'd gone away with her. Well, I'm an old woman, and I like it in the sun growing things. But you come back to London, do you hear? Plenty of time for you to do that when you're my age. Anyway, ducks, got to go. No hard feelings, I hope. You stick at it and—' The message ran out. The sound of her voice cheered me up no end.

I found that I was humming as I played the rest of my messages. To my surprise, there were quite a few from prospective clients, leaving numbers to call them back. I hastily scribbled them down on the back of an envelope, wishing that I was more organised. Lord Abbingdon (Freddy now, to me) left an invitation to spend the weekend at his house as soon as I came home – 'and do bring dear Nicola, too'.

There were a few messages from friends and then a wonderful cooing message from Zena, 'Darling, are you back yet? It's so sad about *darling* Pete. I've been worried about you. I'll meet you at the Casa tonight, I've just spoken to Monty. Lots of love sweetie, it's wonderful to have you back, you've been gone far too long . . .'

I called Sarah and thanked her for looking after the flat, and begged her to come to the Casa tonight. She agreed.

'Where's everyone else?' she asked.

I explained that they had stayed on for another week, and that I had to go to the Bar to tell everyone about Pete.

'I'm dreading it, Sarah. You know how fond everybody was of him.'

'Don't worry, Liv, I'll come too. I've missed you . . . I'm so sorry about Pete. We'll talk tonight, OK?'

I smiled, it felt like home now. Though I really should turn the central heating on. I was freezing. I peeped outside and saw that Sarah had even tidied up the patio. I looked across to Mrs Grieg's flat, and was shocked to see movements behind her windows. I looked closely, wondering if she'd come home, but no, it was a young man hanging some curtains. Her flat must have been let. I switched on my mobile, but the battery was dead so I put it on recharge and went and sat in the kitchen with some paper and a pen ready to make a 'to do' list. I doodled for a bit, and made some more tea, putting off the evil moment. I hated lists, but invariably made them. At last I came up with this:

Things that MUST be done.

1. Return ALL calls (even Freddy).
2. Make dental appointment. (Very grown up of me, as the mere mention of one has me running to the bathroom for tranquillisers.)
3. Make appointment with Kerrison and discuss £. Take the books from the Bar to him.
4. Decide what to do about the Bar.
5. Decide what to do about flat in Brighton.
6. Make hair appointment. (My hair was looking terrible, as though I was wearing a national health wig – it had also taken on a very peculiar colour, due no doubt to too much sun and salt water and absolutely no conditioner.)
7 Snap out of taking Pete's death personally. Realise that *everyone* is upset about it, not just me. (Hard, this one.)
8. Buy Cadbury's chocolate immediately. (Sadly lacking on the island, and missed sorely.)
9. However tempted, do *not* take drugs tonight. (I suspected that this one was going to be the hardest of them all.)

10. Get dressed and stop moping. (Very, very hard.)

I threw on some old, warm clothes on and ran round the corner to the hairdressers, begging them to somehow fit me in. I think they took pity on me, and I was having colour slapped on to my roots before I'd taken my jacket off. I bribed the young girl who rather grumpily did the hair washing, to go round the corner and buy some chocolate. Then I distributed it around the salon, and settled down to the pleasant tedium of having my hair done.

It was starting to get dark by the time I got home, and I was glad I'd put the heating on. I sat down and methodically made my telephone calls. To my relief, a lot of people were out, so I could leave messages and at the same time feel that I had done my duty. I was operating on automatic pilot, I realised. Coasting through things, not willing to think about Pete at all.

There was a buzz at my door, and I ran to answer it. Monty came bounding up the stairs, saying, 'Well, you do look better, the back to my roots look was definitely not for you, darling! It's good to be home, isn't it?'

I tended to agree with him. He chivvied me into my bedroom and chose clothes for me to wear. 'I don't think the grieving fiancée look is madly you. Let's settle for something that shows off that fabulous tan, shall we?'

He pulled out the contents of my wardrobe and after a quick look through, he made me wear a sleeveless black roll-necked top and a pair of jeans that to my delight not only fitted me, but were a little big. He slung quite a few silver bangles on my wrists, helped me into a leather jacket and we set off for the Casa, to prepare ourselves for the Bar.

'Do admit, it is bliss being in the back of a cab again, isn't it?'

'Yes. Do you think we're Londoners at heart?'

'Well, I got home, and I don't know about you, but I nearly cried with happiness. I do *love* the villa, but . . .'

'I know what you mean. It feels like a dream now, doesn't it?'

The taxi was nosing its way through the crowded London streets, and I felt a pang of excitement. I had missed all this. All this chaos, and crowds, and ideas and gossip. Most of it, I knew, was worthless – but I had still missed it.

We walked into the Casa, and Ben immediately came from behind the bar to kiss us both.

'Zena's in the corner, holding a table for you. She told me about Pete. I can't believe it! Are you OK?'

'Yes, I'm fine.' I discovered that I had trotted out the platitude without really thinking about it, but I was touched by Ben's concern. And I *was* fine. I felt at home, and although I missed Pete desperately, I was in the right place.

Zena was waving to us, and we joined her at the table. There was a bottle of champagne on it already, with some glasses.

'Olivia darling, I *have* been thinking of you.' She hugged me. 'Have some champagne quickly, Ben sent it over . . . I don't think anybody can quite believe the news about Pete. How are you both? Is it dreadful or wonderful to be home?'

'Both,' Monty and I said in unison.

Laughing we raised our glasses in a silent toast to Pete. I could see that this was going to happen an awful lot tonight and I remembered that the last time I'd had too much to drink I'd fallen in with rubber man. I decided to order some food, even if it was just a sandwich, so as not to repeat the last awful experience of drinking on an empty stomach. Monty joined me and we both ordered a steak sandwich.

Sarah arrived and hugged us all. She was wiping tears

away from her face as she sat down, and soon we were talking about Pete. The crowd at the Casa were looking at us curiously, and one by one people dropped by to offer condolences and to share memories of Pete. Soon, the table was crowded with champagne bottles.

'Do have this for Pete, it was his favourite, wasn't it?'

'What's going to happen to the Bar?'

'I'm so, so sorry. He was a grand man wasn't he.'

'I spent many a night on the tiles with Pete . . . God, I'll miss him . . .'

'Soho will be a sorry place without him.'

Out of the corner of my eye I saw the door open and Mimi appear. Damn. There was no escape, however, and soon she was standing in front of us.

'Leevia! Monty! Baba is here! We drink vodka, no?'

I introduced Mimi, or Baba, to Zena and Sarah, and had the satisfaction of watching her eyes narrow at the sight of Zena's impeccable beauty. They were both stunning, but so very different from each other. Zena's was a pampered, coiffed, careful beauty, whilst Mimi's was wild and unstructured. She was also a great deal younger, but Zena had the charm and soft sophistication of a woman born into wealth, and who knew exactly what she wanted from life (practically anything, I would have said as long as it was easy). Like most beautiful women they acknowledged and saluted each other's looks, and after an initial skirmish, got on like a house on fire.

'Where *did* you find her?' Zena whispered to me.

'It's a very long story . . .'

Mimi was banging the table with her fist, calling for vodka. Ben scurried over, bringing a bottle and five shot glasses, and she smouldered her thanks at him, making him blush.

Well, that was a first, I thought. I'd never seen Ben flustered before.

'I 'ave been so busy, zey zinck I vill be famous! Ees good, no? But, oouf! All ze photographers, zey work me so 'ard!' Mimi confided in us, waving her arms around as she spoke. 'And Leevia, you 'ave my lucky charm, no? You keep for me, yes?' I nodded rather guiltily and avoided looking at anyone. I hoped to God she *would* become famous.

Looking away from Mimi's floorshow I saw to my horror that Connie had just come into the club, and watched her make her way over to us. Monty and I rolled our eyes at each other and he muttered to me, 'Oh God, the woman we all *least* want to see.'

Connie came up to the table and said, 'I've just heard about Pete. It's awful, isn't it? I am surprised that you're out celebrating, I would have thought you would have been too miserable.'

Zena smiled sweetly at her and said, 'But you know, Connie dear, thinking never *really* was your strong point, was it?'

I choked on my drink. Mimi was staring at Connie.

'I have seen you! I have seen you in Steve's flat, no? He 'as picture of you. Ees so sad that you are ordinary looking, or you could be model like me! I zink you are tall, but not good enough in ze face, no?' she appealed to Monty.

'When have you been in my flat?' Connie demanded angrily.

I thought it was time to visit the Ladies. Zena and Sarah joined me, and we swept down the stairs, giggling.

'Oh God, Mimi'll eat her for breakfast!' I said.

'Umm, let's not be *too* long. I don't want to miss anything . . .'

Lots of new cards had been added to the board in the loo,

and I was delighted to see that two of them read '*Angie has been kicked out of the Casa, good riddance to bad rubbish!*' and '*Does anyone know of a man called Mark, who's into rubber? What a sad git he is!*'

When we got back upstairs, there was a group of people around our table, and others standing on their chairs to get a better look. Monty was pushing his way out of the crowd, holding our glasses.

'What *is* going on?' I demanded.

'Well, Mimi slapped Connie round the chops, and then called her a cow . . .'

'No!'

I pushed forward and saw that Connie had a handful of Mimi's hair and was red in the face, trying to pull her out of her chair. Mimi was hacking away at Connie's legs with a series of vicious kicks and screaming at the top of her voice, 'She attack me! Get off you *paysan* ! I keel you!'

The crowd seemed to be enjoying themselves immensely and were cheering Mimi on. It seemed that Connie was not very popular.

'Don't you think we should try and stop them?'

'Good God no! I think they're both quite capable of looking after themselves, don't you?'

'My God, Pete would have loved this, wouldn't he?' Sarah whispered delightedly to me.

'I *think* it's time for us to go . . .' Zena said.

I agreed with her, and we headed towards the door.

When we got to the Bar it was fairly crowded, and it was impossible not to somehow expect to see Pete, pushing his way through the crowd ready to hug us and pour champagne. We went over to the bar and I searched for a familiar face to talk to. I saw Jackie, who Pete had left in charge whilst he was away, and waved to her. Her face lit up, and she quickly came forward.

'Hi! It's great to see you! Where's Pete?' Her smile faded as she saw my face.

'Let's go to the office, shall we?' I said.

Jackie followed me downstairs and unlocked the office door. It hadn't changed at all, it was a real mess. The bomb damage had been repaired upstairs, but down here it was still the same chaos. Papers and bills were spread over the desk, the lights were flashing on the phone and a crate of beer propped up the sagging filing cabinet. I could see a postcard that Pete had sent to the staff pinned on the wall and I took it down and read it.

Don't drink the profits, you bastards!
I'll be back soon, this is the most perfect
place I have ever been. Phones are
impossible here – great, huh? Have a
bottle of bubbles on me.
Love and filth, Pete XXX
P.S. It's true what they say about
Greek boys !!!

I smiled and turned it over: the picture was of the harbour, and I could see the Dolphin, where we'd had our last meal together.

'Livia, it's Pete, isn't it? What's wrong?' Jackie's face was white with worry.

I felt that I was probably pretty white too. I took a deep breath and said, 'I'm sorry, Jackie. Yes it's Pete, he's . . . he's dead. I'm so sorry to have to tell you this. I know how fond you were of him and . . .'

She was crying, and had sat down, covering her face with

her hands. I put an arm around her; I could feel her shoulders shaking.

'He sounded so happy! How did it happen?'

I comforted her as best I could, and told her that he had died quickly and, we thought, painlessly.

'What's going to happen here? This was the best job I've ever had! I'm sorry, that sounds thoughtless of me, it's just that I love working here.'

'Well, Jackie, Pete left the bar to me and Steve.'

'You haven't come to close it down, have you?'

Had I? I didn't know. I looked around the office and wondered how the hell I was going to sort this mess out. I felt a twinge of annoyance with Steve: he was out in Greece playing at being an artist and I was stuck dealing with what looked like a lot of unpaid bills, and sobbing staff.

'Look Jackie, I'll be honest with you. I don't know what I'm going to do with this place yet. But I promise you, things can carry on as they are for now, and as soon as I know what I'm going to do, well, you'll be the first person I talk to. OK?'

She nodded, and I passed her a tissue. She wiped her eyes and blew her nose.

'Let's all have a drink for him when we close.'

'Absolutely. Look, you go back upstairs when you've got yourself together. I'm going to stay down here and try and make sense of all of this.' I waved my hand in the direction of the papers and filing cabinets.

'It's not as bad as it looks, honestly, and I've been doing the banking, you know. Here's the key to the safe, all the books are in there. Do you want a hand?'

I shook my head. Jackie went back to the bar, and I opened the safe. It contained account books, payment slips and the float for the night. There was also a large brown envelope addressed to me. I poured myself a brandy from the drawer I knew would have a bottle stashed in it, lit a cigarette and started to read.

Chapter Twenty-One

Dearest Darling Old Slapper Liv,
I really wanted to start this letter with the cliché – By the time you read this I shall be dead, but I thought it was too much.

You know Liv, that I've been ill for a long time now, so please don't be too sad for me. I needed a transplant and I knew I was never going to get one. I am sick of the pain, and the endless amounts of sodding pills I have to take every day, so sick of it, I have thought once or twice of killing myself.

But the main reason I didn't – was you.

That probably surprises you, but it shouldn't. We have been such good friends, that at times I couldn't tell who was who. You know I love you, and nothing will ever stop that.

Don't care too much, Liv, about other people. Most of them, after all, are bastards. Live your own life now, have the Bar with Steve (if he wants it) and have a laugh. You deserve it.

See you soon (but not too soon, I hope!)
Your loving friend, Pete XXXX

After I had read the letter, I cried for the first time since

Pete's death. It was a huge release, and I unashamedly laid my head on his desk and sobbed. He had obviously written it before we had gone to the villa, and it sounded so like him that when I was reading it I could almost hear his voice. It was full of affection and advice, it was funny and loving and it made me sob even more. I clutched the letter to me, and trying to catch my breath I wiped my face. I saw a scribbled PTO at the bottom of the page and turned it over. It simply said 'Stop crying and go and have a bottle of the widow. All my love, Pete'.

I turned the emerald ring round and round on my finger, and then spent more than a little time trying to repair the ravages that crying had done to my face. I found a rubbish bag and stuffed all the books from the Bar into it, ready to take to Kerrison, then shakily applied some lipstick and, still sniffing, made my way upstairs.

Monty, Zena and Sarah were knocking back champagne as if their lives depended on it. They looked sympathetically at my pink and puffy eyes, and pushed a glass towards me. Zena patted me on the hand and said, 'Don't cry any more, Liv, you know that Peter would have simply *hated* it.'

I nodded in agreement. She was right, he would have hugged me and told me stop, and drink up.

There were so many people coming up to our table, offering sympathy, expressing shock and grief, that I started to feel claustrophobic. The table was sticky with spilt champagne, and the air was heavy with smoke. Desperately I longed for my bed, and whispered to Monty that I was leaving. Sarah decided to come as well, but Zena opted to stay.

We managed to extricate ourselves with many a farewell hug and kiss, and eventually got outside. I was clutching the bag full of accounts, and Monty flagged down a taxi. Once we were in the cab he asked me what I was going to do with the Bar.

He was looking at me astutely as he added, 'Well, it's a fabulous location. It *must* be making money, and if he was going to buy the place next door and turn it into a restaurant it would certainly give the Casa a run for its money. But it's an awful lot of hard work, you know, and if Steve's involved, I'll know who'll be doing most of it!'

'I know,' I said gloomily. Steve wasn't exactly renowned for his commitment to anything, and getting him out of bed most mornings was an impossible task.

'Call me in the morning, Liv. I can help with the books and figures, you know,' Sarah said as she kissed me goodnight. We waved to her as she reached her front door and Monty dropped me off next.

I let myself into my flat, dumped the bag full of books down in the hall and went round, flicking the lights on. I had drunk an awful lot of champagne, one way or another tonight and thought I should try and dilute it with some water. I also felt the imminent threat of a headache, so I went into the bathroom to get painkillers.

'That is it, I've had enough!' I said aloud as the hideous lime frosting shocked me for the hundredth time. The bloody colour of the bathroom had to go, it was driving me mad. It also reminded me of rubber man far too much.

I marched into the office and scouted for some paint. I always had some knocking around, and I was determined to do it right this minute. I found a large tin of paint in a dusky mauve colour, almost damson. That would do.

I ripped off my clothes and put on some old painting stuff streaked with all the colours I'd ever used, and in a burst of energy threw the clutter in the bathroom into a large wicker basket. It's a lot of nonsense, by the way, about washing walls down before you paint, it's really not necessary. Painting *over* cobwebs adds interest, I think.

I found a roller, stirred the paint with a chopstick and poured it into the tray. As soon as I started to cover the walls I felt better. It was wonderful seeing the awful frosted lime being replaced with the dusky plummy colour. Limes to damsons, I thought to myself happily. It sounded like the description on the back of a wine bottle – '*A mellow, fruity wine with a hint of jam and damsons, goes well with oriental food and fish*'. With a bit of luck it wouldn't even take two coats if I slapped it on thickly enough.

I made some tea, and sat on the edge of the bath to admire my handiwork. There were just the fiddly bits left to do now, and that required a brush. I went to hunt for one, knowing that I had to finish it now even though I was tired. I buried my head in the cupboard under the sink and searched through years of accumulated rubbish. Blackboard paint (I had no recollection at all of ever using that), tins of beeswax (far too much trouble, I used Sparkle), jars of silver cleaner (what silver?) and an obscure bottle of a foreign liqueur that somehow had managed to find its way in there. Eventually I spied a brush that had stagnated in a glass jar of what presumably had once been white spirit. Trying to clean the brush in the sink, I glanced at the clock in the kitchen: it was terribly late, past two in the morning.

I stretched and yawned. All I had left to do was paint around the skirting boards. I knew from experience that if I didn't finish it now I would quite happily get used to it melting into the background. I could walk past a bit of unfinished decorating for months. I knelt on the floor and quickly whizzed round the boards with a loaded paintbrush, then sat back with some satisfaction and looked at the walls. They were great, a dusty, rich damson. All I had to do now was finish the glass mosaic tiling, but not tonight. Definitely not tonight.

Sleepily I washed my hands, trying to avoid the wet paint, and fell into bed. It was lovely being back in my own bed, was the last thought I had as I settled down to sleep.

The following morning I tried to call the villa, to impart all the news from last night, but infuriatingly could not get through. The bathroom looked even better in the daylight and I promised myself that after the meeting with Kerrison I would buckle down and finish the tiling. I collected all the accounts and set off to see what sort of financial ruin I was really in.

Two and a half very tedious hours later, I knew. It wasn't great, but it wasn't as bad as I had thought. Kerrison had a quick look at the Bar's accounts and promised to let me have his opinion as soon as he could. He thought that Pete had actually nearly completed buying next door (at the moment it was a run-down sandwich shop) and was getting in touch with the lawyers. I had to decide if I wanted to run it with Steve, or sell it. Kerrison's last words rang in my ear: 'If you decide to sell, you must sell it now, as a going concern. It's terrible selling somewhere that's empty, even in that location, you'll lose a lot of money. Try and decide what you want. I'll call you this evening.'

I walked back home, noting that the pale English sun was trying to make an appearance. I stopped to buy some food, well, to be honest, a Kit-Kat, and wondered what to do. Steve, I thought, would want to sell it. I couldn't see him pouring his heart and soul into making the place work – it would mean getting up in the mornings, for God's sake! Then there was the flat in Brighton.

I sighed. I wasn't turning out to be very good at making decisions. But I knew that I wanted to make the Bar work, and I wanted to settle to something that would help me take my mind off losing Pete.

True to my word, I tiled the bathroom in the rest of the boiled–sweet–like tiles. They looked enchanting and I was really pleased with it. I sat on the bathroom floor, wishing that I was convinced of my future. What *was* I going to do? I decided to try the villa again. I dialled and waited, listening to the undersea noises that came down the line. Eventually I heard the phone ring, and Molly answered.

'Liv! God, we miss you! I tried to cook dinner last night, it was awful, we ended up giving it to the goats! How are you?'

'Oh Moll, I'm OK. I just don't know what I want to do. Has Steve said anything about the Bar?'

'No, he's too busy thinking about this exhibition we're going to have. I think it's something for us to focus on, everyone is so miserable here. But we'll all be back next week. Don't think about it till then, OK?'

'It's not that easy, I'm afraid. Can I have a word with him?'

I heard her footsteps and the sound of her voice calling for Steve.

'Liv? Hello, how are you?'

I told Steve about the Bar, and what I wanted to do. There was a silence, and I could tell that he was thinking frantically about what to say. I knew he really wanted to sell it to pay Connie off, and start again. He even had a dream about financing his exhibition with the money. I was sure that Steve had been shocked that Pete had left the Bar to us, but that now he'd had some time to digest it, he was viewing it as a glorious sort of windfall that would get him out of all his troubles. I knew all of this, but Steve was also a nice guy, and wouldn't want to upset me if that was what I really wanted to do. I could hear him struggling with himself.

'The thing is, Liv, I'm not sure that I want to run the Bar . . .'

'Look, Steve I know that really. Let me try and sort things out first and we'll talk again, OK? I can't do anything yet without talking to Kerrison anyway.'

'OK.'

I could hear in Steve's voice a trace of disappointment. I thought I'd better get off the phone, as I was starting to feel emotional too.

'That's the intercom, I must go . . . give everyone my love and we'll talk tonight, OK?'

I hung up. I wished the intercom *had* buzzed, I felt like talking to someone. I called Zena, and left a message for her. Then I tried Sarah, but she was busy arranging a conference, so we agreed to meet later that evening. I sauntered around the flat, convincing myself that I was doing the right thing. I needed some fresh air, and grabbing my keys I went outside.

The sun was shining properly now, and people were starting to look more cheerful. As I walked home, I considered the can of worms I was about to open in taking on the Bar. I knew I was doing the right thing. This was home, and I needed to work. If Steve didn't want to join me, well, I'd have to manage on my own.

I waved at Bert, the flower seller and he motioned me over.

''Allo love, thought you'd done a runner too! Lovely and brown, just got back?'

He handed me a postcard, saying, 'Look what I got!' It was from Mrs Grieg. The picture on the front was of an overblown, magnificent red rose. I flipped the card over and read her message. *'I'm growing them now, not buying them. Keep your pecker up! Love, Mrs G.'* The postmark was from somewhere in Italy I noticed. I handed it back to him, smiling.

I went to the local shops and bought some proper food, not just chocolate, and thought of Molly cooking supper at the villa. A raw fish diet could be very healthy I thought – they *might* all get used to it. I picked up some wine for when Sarah came round later that evening and went back home.

I had just unloaded the shopping into the fridge when the phone rang. It was Kerrison. He told me to get a pen and paper, as he knew I wouldn't remember anything and then he asked me if I had decided what I wanted to do with the Bar. I took a deep breath and told him that I wanted to keep it, and run it. I also told him that Steve wouldn't want to.

'That means you'll have to buy him out. And that means raising a lot of money. Are you sure?'

'Yes. What do the books look like?'

'Very healthy, I'd say. The place next door has been bought, as well, and that gives you considerable scope.' I was encouraged to note that Kerrison sounded quite excited. Well, as excited as an accountant can. We arranged to meet in the morning.

'Just before you go, Kerrison, tell me *about* how much money would I have to give Steve?'

Kerrison told me. I thanked him and very slowly replaced the phone. Then I went immediately to the fridge and opened the wine that I was saving for Sarah.

I poured myself a glass and sipped it slowly, looking around the kitchen. Was I mad? It was a colossal amount of money. I wondered how on earth I could manage it. I went into the bedroom and rummaged through the clothes that I had been wearing last night. I pulled out Pete's rather crumpled letter to me and re-read it. The words on the page translated into his voice once more, and it was as if I could hear him talking to me. Back in the kitchen I finished my wine, staring at the clock, willing it to go faster so that Sarah would arrive and I would have someone to talk over my doubts with.

Sarah always gave good advice, unless it was anything to do with men or cats, on which she had some very strange ideas. For instance, all cat food must be the sort of food that you would happily eat yourself. (I'll gloss over the horrors of this, but with a pinch of queasy imagination you can just picture the sort of food that Sarah has tried herself, and if she didn't like it, well, the cats didn't get it.) And her judgement on men was a little bizarre, too. She only went out with men who drank red wine. Anything else, forget it, they were deemed untrustworthy. (Needless to say, she didn't go out on dates that often.) But her financial advice was sound.

I watched Sarah walk up the street, and went to the intercom to buzz her up. She handed me a bottle of wine and a bunch of anemones, saying, 'They're Greek, you know, I thought they'd be appropriate.'

'Oh, thank you so much,' I said, touched by the thought. 'They're lovely.'

'Liv, I didn't really get a chance to talk to you last night, but it must have been so awful for you, finding Pete, and then having the funeral. Are you OK?'

'Yeah, I'm all right. I miss him so much, though. Sit down and have a drink, I've started already.'

We sat at the table in the kitchen and caught up with each other's news. I opened another bottle and started to make supper for both of us.

'Liv, you know, we *have* all missed you. Have you decided what you're going to do?'

I started to tell her about the plans I had for the Bar. Her eyes widened with surprise.

'But that sounds brilliant! What's the problem?'

I told her about having to buy Steve out.

'How much?' she asked.

I told her. She gave a slow whistle. 'Wow, that's a hell of a lot of money.'

'I know. I was rather hoping that you would be able to come up with some solutions,' I said a bit helplessly.

'I can try, do you have a calculator?'

'In the debris of what is laughingly called my office.'

'I'll go and search. What are we having to eat?'

'Mushroom risotto, and some salad. Is that OK?'

'Mmm, lovely. But don't put too much garlic in, and then if there's any left over I can take it home to the cats.'

'Sarah, when have you and I *ever* had any leftovers?'

She laughed and went to look for the calculator.

I was stirring the hot chicken stock into the rice when the phone rang. I managed to stretch the cord over to the cooker so I could continue stirring the risotto as I answered it. (If you don't the rice won't be cooked and creamy, which is the whole *point* of making a risotto as far as I'm concerned. That, and to see how much cheese and wine you can get in it, of course.)

'Hello?'

It was John, the builder. My heart sank. I wasn't up to making more excuses as to why I couldn't meet him for a drink. It's not that I didn't want to; frankly, I just couldn't be bothered . . . although, there was something intriguing about this man. I mean, he didn't exactly sound like a builder, if you know what I mean. His voice sounded more like an art dealer's (or what I *imagined* an art dealer's voice to sound like, as I didn't actually know any). But I still felt a residue of guilt about standing him up, so I half-heartedly agreed to meet him during the week. I also found myself telling him about Pete.

'I'm so very sorry, this must be a sad time for you,' John said.

I could feel tears start in my eyes, and I concentrated on stirring the risotto. It seemed that sympathy from anyone sparked off self-pity, which turned on the tears. I sniffed, and murmured my thanks.

'This is obviously a bad time . . . I'll leave it for you to contact me, but I really would like to meet up with you. Call me when you feel you can, OK?'

'Yes, I will. I promise.' I sniffed again, and then thought how horribly unattractive that must sound.

'Are you crying or chopping onions?' he asked.

'Both, really,' I said.

'Oh please don't. Let me take you out for dinner, then you could tell me everything properly. Face to face, how about it?'

I felt much better after having spoken to him. Maybe it was because he was unconnected with Pete, but he was certainly easy to talk to.

'OK, I really will call you. Thanks.'

I hung up, and turned to see Sarah looking speculatively at me.

'It's just the builder, you know the one who kept calling me and it was a wrong number, that's all . . . Nothing to get excited about,' I said in a defensive tone of voice, banging plates around.

'Hmm, we'll see . . . Have another glass of wine, you might feel in the mood to call him back,' Sarah said, eyeing me gleefully.

I took the glass, and we sat down to eat.

Chapter Twenty-Two

'Look,' Sarah said, very sensibly, 'let's try and work out your finances, shall we?'

'OK, OK. Shall I make some tea, or would you like a brandy?'

'Tea,' Sarah said firmly.

She spent the next half-hour asking me questions, most of which I was pathetically incapable of answering accurately, and writing down my feeble attempts on a sheet of paper. I was ashamed of my ignorance, and resolved to brush up my financial acumen. I mean, it was ludicrous for a woman of my age to be so woefully unknowledgeable about things.

'Don't worry, most women are,' said Sarah, adding up a column of figures.

'That's no excuse. I will try, honestly. I just get very confused over money and it's all the jargon. It's fearfully off-putting, isn't it? All that stuff about equity, and futures and gilt edged and things . . .' I trailed off, miserably aware that Sarah did all these things for a living, and probably considered me an absolute fool.

'Everybody uses jargon, don't they? I mean, I've got no idea what a stumble glaze is, but I've heard you say it. Really, it's not as bad as you think it is. And yes, you should be more informed. Doesn't Kerrison explain things to you?'

'Well, he does, I suppose. But most of the time, I sort of glaze over and I realise that I'm nodding, but it's going in one ear and out the other.'

Sarah was still adding up figures and waved me away. I cleared the table and washed up, watching her out of the corner of my eye. She was tapping a pencil on her teeth, and narrowing her eyes at the sheet of paper in front of her.

'Right! Now sit down and I'll explain it in words of one syllable.'

'Thanks!' I sat.

'You're welcome. This is approximate, because you don't know exactly the amounts of everything, but . . . if you sell the flat in Brighton, the emerald ring, and either rent this flat or raise a loan on it, you can buy Steve out. It will also give you some capital to play around with. Which you'll need. The Bar has living accommodation above it, or rather it will, once next door has been completed. It makes far more sense for you to have that than this flat. Right, what do you think?'

'Oh God, I don't know. What do *you* think?'

'Livia! It's up to you, isn't it? How much do you want to do this? Because unless it's the most important thing in your life, it's a huge upheaval and an awful lot of work. I wish you had the Bar's accounts here, I could look at them as well, and give you more of an accurate picture. But I can only assume those figures, and that's not enough. I think you should sleep on it. Call me tomorrow and we can go over anything that you're unsure about. OK?'

I nodded. I don't think I'd realised what a huge sum of money I had to raise, it seemed almost impossible.

'Sarah?'

'Yes?'

'Would you be able to do the books and stuff? I mean I'll

need a financial head, won't I? And Kerrison, well, I mean I don't dislike him or anything and he puts up with my appalling filing habits, but he never *explains* things to me properly. How about it?'

Sarah stared at me, and said slowly, 'I'll do better than that. If you decide that it's what you really want to do, I'll come in with you. I'll be a partner. I hate my job and I'd love to do it. I think you may well need me, it's a big thing to take on by yourself.'

I was stunned. And also vastly relieved. I realised that I had been dreading doing everything by myself, and had felt lost and lonely. But with Sarah, it could really work.

'Oh God, yes! That would be fantastic! Are you sure?'

'More sure than I have been about anything. You know, Liv, I work really, *really* hard. Then I go home and I feed my cats. I know you're smiling, but I rarely go out. I don't want to end up being one of those elderly women who have nothing to talk about but their pets. Boyfriends? I can count on one hand the amount of times that I've gone out with a man in the past two years! No, this is the chance of a lifetime for me, I'd love it!'

She was beaming from ear to ear. I gasped. I'd suddenly thought of something: supposing Steve didn't want to sell? Where would that leave Sarah? I explained my thoughts to her.

'Well, I don't think it will happen, do you? Anyway, let's cross that bridge when we come to it. Get the books from Kerrison, get them to me and we'll sort things out from there. As I said, sleep on it.'

We kissed goodbye, and I saw her out.

As soon as I got into bed the phone rang. I snatched it up, rather hoping that it was the builder, but it was a somewhat drunk Suzanne Aston. She was slightly slurring her words, and sounded belligerent.

'Olivia? Just tell me something, I want to know something, and I know that you know . . .'

'Umm, yes, of course. What?' God, she was even scarier drunk.

'I want to know. Was my son a homosexual?'

I hesitated. Not what I'd expected.

'Umm, Suzanne, why don't I call you in the morning? It's quite late, you know. Give me your number and I'll—'

But she was shouting now. 'Was he gay? Was he? Just tell me.'

'Yes. Yes he was.'

I could hear her begin to cry. 'I knew it! I knew it, Michael was so bloody to him as a child. Well, so was I really. We did it, didn't we? We made him that way.'

She was racked with sobs. This was highly alarming. I could never have imagined Suzanne ruining her make-up by crying. Oh God, maybe she wanted to contest Pete's will or something. That was the last thing I needed.

'Look, Suzanne it really doesn't work that way, you know. You didn't make him anything at all.'

Well, the last bit was certainly true. She hadn't made him anything because she hadn't given him anything: no love or security or anything else associated with a happy childhood. It was on the tip of my tongue to say that after meeting her I was surprised that Pete had turned out as well as he had.

'You're just being nice . . . I know we did! Why did he tell us you were getting married?'

I sighed. 'Maybe he told you what he knew you wanted to hear. We all tend to do that, don't we?'

'He never spoke to me, never! He should have told me . . .'

I made soothing noises, and told her that Pete had loved

both of them and just didn't want to hurt them. God forgive me, I thought. She continued to sob.

I took her phone number and promised to call in the morning, then I turned the light off and tried to sleep.

The following morning I set off to Kerrison's and was let into his office by his secretary, Mary. She was a tiny woman with an inordinate amount of teeth and a face that sported several unsightly warts. She flapped around the office trying to locate the books, and finally unearthed them under a pile of tax returns. I thanked her, trying to avoid staring in horrified fascination at the largest of the warts that wobbled on her chin and, I noticed, was sprouting hairs. Controlling a shudder, I took the books and grabbed a taxi to go to Sarah.

Outside her office I paid the driver and stood outside, looking up at the building. I'd never been here before, and I was suitably awed by the size of the towering office block. Built to intimidate, I thought. It was a new structure, with tinted windows and gleaming steel. A gigantic modern sculpture stood inside the entrance hall, a marble figure of what I supposed was a man climbing a ladder. Huge fleshy plants crept around it. The reception desk was staffed with very thin girls wearing telephone headsets who were busily answering calls.

When I said that I was here to see Sarah Bradshaw I saw a gleam of respect in their eyes. I was directed to the lift, told to take it to the tenth floor and turn right. The lift had a camera in it: its little red eye was winking at me, so I waved cheerfully and wondered who the hell was watching it. What an awful job, I thought. Sitting watching tapes all day of people standing silently in a lift – there couldn't be a great deal of job satisfaction there! I noticed that the lift had been expensively painted to resemble coloured marble, but it actually looked like Spam. The lift stopped smoothly and I started to wander down a thickly carpeted corridor. Sarah was walking towards me and beckoning me into an office.

'My God, Sarah! This place is *huge*! Wow, is this your office?'

She laughed as I rushed over to look at the view through the smoked glass window. Taxis and red buses were moving sluggishly, and the dome of St Paul's dominated the scene. Her desk was a slab of black wood held up by four brushed steel columns, the latest state of the art technology shone on her desk and there wasn't a scrap of paper in sight. With a pang of guilt I realised that I didn't really know what the hell it was that she actually *did*. I mean, she spoke about work, and I think she'd explained it to me a few times, but I had never really grasped it. I thought of the office at the Bar, and looked doubtfully at Sarah.

I think she must have read my mind because she laughed, saying, 'It's really not as big time as you think. Did you see the cameras in the lift? They're there to stop us all trying to rush up to the roof to throw ourselves off! Give me the books, have you got time for a coffee?'

I nodded and she spoke into an intercom on her desk. Two minutes later another thin girl dressed in black carried in a tray of coffee.

'Thanks, Jo, please hold all my calls will you?'

I whistled and said, 'Get you! Miss Big. I've *always* wanted to say "hold all my calls" to someone! Are you sure you're ready to give all this up? Because I can assure you there won't be any call holding where we're going!'

She laughed and said, 'You are an idiot, you know! Right, let me just have a quick look at the books, then we can have a chat.'

I watched Sarah bend her head over the rows of figures,

her face utterly concentrated. I'd never seen her at work before and it was quite a surprise. Somehow I'd imagined her to be working as a part of a team somewhere in the City, with sandwiches at her desk at lunchtime and an office full of files and photocopiers. This hushed, plush place was a far cry from all that. It positively oozed money. The thin young girl popped her head around the door and said nervously, 'I'm so sorry to interrupt, Sarah, but Sir Benson is on line one and he sounds absolutely furious, and he really wants to speak to you . . .'

'Tell him I'm in a meeting and can't be disturbed,' said Sarah calmly, without looking up.

I definitely wouldn't want her job either, I thought. I helped myself to more coffee and had another look round the office. Corporate design was crammed in here: the ergo-dynamics, the flow of space, the use of colour, it was all textbook stuff. The only personal touch I could see was a tiny framed photograph of three cats perched on the edge of her desk, probably ready to be whipped into a drawer if necessary.

Sarah glanced up at me and gave a quick smile. 'This looks better than I thought. How long will it take to convert next door? And how much will it cost?'

I told her what I thought and she smiled again. 'Have you spoken to Steve yet?'

I shook my head.

'What are your plans now?'

'I'm going to the Casa. I wanted to talk to you about that. I want to poach Ben, what do you think?'

'I think it's a brilliant idea! We'll need a general manager, he'd be perfect. I thought Pete had tried before with no success.'

'He had. But I wanted to offer him something that he hasn't got at the Casa.'

'What?'

'Well, something like a profit share, or an interest in the place. What do you think?'

'Maybe. But I can think of something that would attract him even more.'

'What?'

'Offer him the flat above! A newly converted flat in the heart of Soho, he'll jump at it.'

'I thought I had to live there?'

She laughed, 'Not if I come in. You'll still have to sell the flat in Brighton, but you could stay in your flat and keep the ring.'

She went on to outline plans until my mind was reeling.

'Please stop,' I begged, 'I really won't remember anything else now. Let me go and chat up Ben, OK?'

I waved at the camera in the lift again, and walked to the Casa. It was a glorious spring day, and the trees were shyly putting out their pale green leaves. Soho was full of people talking into phones with one hand and carrying take-out cappuccinos in the other. Dark glasses seemed to be *de rigueur*. I walked into the Casa, and it had a lunchtime buzz. I decided to have something to eat, and asked Ben if he had the time to join me.

'God, yes! That would be lovely, I don't think I've sat down for twenty-four hours!'

He went to fetch a bottle of wine and when he had sat down I put my proposal to him.

'Are you serious?' he said, watching me carefully.

'Very.'

'Then the answer is yes. It'll be easy, and half the members here would follow me – if that doesn't sound too big headed! Christ, Pete would have loved that, wouldn't he?'

Our food had arrived: the plates of salad so beloved of London chefs – radicchio and rocket abounded. It went untouched as we gabbled about plans. Ben was thrilled that Sarah was going to be involved.

'She's so level headed, isn't she?'

'Meaning I'm not, I take it?' I said with mock seriousness.

He laughed. 'You know what I mean! How long do you think it will take?'

'If we move quickly, weeks rather than months. How much notice will you have to give?'

'None. The second I tell them that I'm leaving, I'll be escorted out of the place and have my keys taken away. They'll be paranoid about me lifting the club membership list to take with me.'

'And will you?'

'Nah! No need, it's all on a database at home!'

I burst out laughing. 'Isn't that rather underhand? I mean, we don't want to get into trouble, do we?'

'All's fair in love and the bar business. Besides, let me tell you a few things about the owners here . . .' and he proceeded to whisper the most wonderful gossip. I was suitably shocked and delighted.

'Have you got any other staff lined up yet?' he asked.

'Well, I'd like to keep Jackie on, if she wants to stay that is, do you know her?' I instinctively liked Jackie. I asked Ben about the rest of the staff.

'Sack them and then reinstate them if they want to stay on,' he said promptly. 'It keeps them on their toes, and lets them know that things have changed.'

'My goodness, I'm seeing a new side of you,' I laughed.

Ben looked speculatively at me. 'Can you keep a secret?'

'Probably not!'

'Well, it'll soon be out anyway, but a hostile take-over bid has been put in here.'

'No! Who?'

Ben leaned forward, and said, 'William Magpie.'

'What! Are you sure? He hasn't got that sort of money.'

'No, but his board of directors have. I think they all rather fancy themselves owning a club. So, you see, it's perfect timing!'

We drank to the success of our venture and I left, promising to keep him up to date with developments.

I walked over to the Bar and had a chat with Jackie in the office. Her eyes filled with tears and she hugged me, delighted with the news. I asked her not to tell anyone yet, and she promised not to.

Then I went next door and peered through the windows of the locked-up sandwich bar. It was a good space and I was looking forward to getting inside it and measuring up.

I walked through Soho, enjoying the spring sunshine and wondering about the others back at the villa. I wanted to know how Nicola's book was getting on, and how Steve and Molly were progressing with the show. I was so glad they were coming back soon, I missed them. I stopped off at Bar Italia and sat outside in the sunshine, drinking a *citron pressé*.

I'd forgotten how prosperous London was. The sun had brought everyone out from the offices and shops, and I was surrounded with the sleek beautiful people of the capital. As usual in England, as soon as the sun peeked out, nobody was quite sure what to wear. There were men sweating slightly in heavy jackets, and women with white legs trying to cover them with long skirts. Oh to be a leg waxer, now that April's here, I thought to myself. I poured sugar syrup into my lemon drink and stirred it, answering my phone. To my delight it was Molly.

'Oh Moll, I was just thinking of you all . . . How are you?' I was unreasonably glad to hear from her.

'Well, we're all OK. Nicola is going to New York for her book. Anyway, I'm calling to say that Steve and I'll be home tomorrow now. The pictures are great, so that's something to look forward to, I suppose.'

Slowly I wandered home through the park, scowling at happy couples. It was a habit, really, and one that I should grow out of, I know. As I walked along the path I thought of all the people I missed. My mother, Pete, and even bloody Christopher. I sighed. Maybe I should phone the builder. Perhaps I needed a spot of new romance in my life. I smiled. That proved how depressed I was, I was usually allergic to the R word . . . it was *so* Mills and Boon, wasn't it? Work was the answer, I decided. I bought myself an ice cream and pondered on what colour the Bar should be.

Chapter Twenty-Three

I was so pleased to see Steve and Molly that I kissed them both on the mouth. Which surprised them as much as it surprised me. They staggered into my flat under the weight of all their canvases: they propped them up around the flat, demanding that I admire them immediately. I thought they were great, but found it hard to look at the charcoal drawing Steve had done of Pete and myself. I could remember that afternoon perfectly, and could even smell the perfumed air of the garden as I looked at it. I closed my eyes to it, and moved on to the others.

I really hoped that they'd do well with them, but didn't hold my breath – I mean, *another* exhibition, of even *more* art was hardly going to set London on fire, was it? Although the press would at least be interested because of the portrait of Nicola, I suppose.

Steve asked me how Nicola's house was getting on. I had the grace to look guilty about it. Most of my time was taken up with the Bar now, but I had overseen most of the work going on at Nicola's.

Molly was stuffing the washing machine with paint-splattered sarongs and swimsuits, and asking about Sarah, Zena, and the Bar. I glanced at Steve, and saw that he was looking nervously at me. We both started to speak at the same time, and then laughed.

'Look, Liv. I've really been thinking about it. I'd so much rather you bought me out, if you can. I want to buy a space somewhere that I can live in and have a gallery, and—'

I was so relieved I gave a whoop of joy, and hugged him. I explained all about Sarah and Ben, and the plans we'd made. The phone rang, preventing further celebrations, and I snatched it up. It was Nicola in New York. I could hear that she was lighting a cigarette, and guessed that she was sitting in a suite in the Gramercy Park Hotel, practically the only place left in New York that you can smoke in. She spoke to us all in turn, and then said to me,

'God, Liv, I'd forgotten what this place was like. Everything happens here so quickly. I've got a great lawyer, Laddie, and we're coming to London soon to see the publishers. The book is going to ruffle so many feathers I can't tell you, but it's the best thing I could have done. Tell me your plans.'

I explained about Sarah and she was delighted.

'Tell Steve to send me my portrait, I think there are a few people here who would be interested.'

We sat down to supper, and it was as if we'd never been away at all. I think we expected Pete to walk in with a bottle of champagne under his arm, and a filthy joke on his lips. Steve raised his glass and we drank to absent friends. I could see that this was going to happen a lot from now on whenever we were together.

After dinner Molly and I taxed Steve about Mimi. *What* was he going to do about her?

I smiled as I watched him squirm. I had known Steve a very long time indeed, and was very, very fond of him. But if there was one thing he couldn't cope with, it was being pinned down and *made* to answer a question. I don't know if there is any truth to be found in astrology, but if you believe in it, then Steve was a classic Pisces person (I refuse to say Piscean, it sounds far too silly, from which you may well deduce that I am an Aries person.) He finds a direct question far too stressful, and will swim around the reeds and weeds of truth and responsibility with amazing agility. But this time there was to be no hiding in the safe shallow waters. Molly (Leo) was out for the kill.

'Right, Steve, she *is* your responsibility, and before you say anything at all, you *have* to do something about her. I know that we all are guilty, in a way, of losing her good luck charm, or whatever she calls a firearm, antique or not, but I think we should find out how much it was worth and all chip in and give her some money. In fact, the more I think about it, the more convinced I am that I'm right . . .'

No surprise there, I thought. Once Molly thought she was right about something, you simply had to bow to the inevitable. The end of her speech was marked by a thump on the table with her clenched fist, and we watched in fascination as her full wine glass wobbled dangerously, then miraculously righted itself. The three of us burst out laughing, and Steve started to gather his bags together to go home. Well, back to Molly's flat.

After he'd left I realised that he had done it *again*. He had managed not to answer anything to do with Mimi at all. I had a sneaky admiration for him, but he was still avoiding all responsibility for her. I determined to tackle him on my own.

Molly was washing up, and eating cold chicken.

'Where's Joe then, Moll?' I asked.

'Oh, he's OK, I think he's gone to stay with his parents

for a while. But you know, really it was just a holiday romance. He was way too young for me, wasn't he?'

I fervently agreed with her. Well, that was a relief, anyway. A lovestruck Molly would be a real pain to have around the place.

'Oh Liv it is nice to be home.' She gave a huge yawn. 'I've got to get to bed. See you in the morning.' She kissed me goodnight.

I looked into the sink. There was a roasting pan, a bunch of cutlery and a roast potato in the hot soapy water. That really was Molly's idea of washing up. She'd once told me that she couldn't ever finish washing up because there was never enough room. I pointed out to her that there would be if you dried the dishes *as well*, but she'd given me a pitying look, and poured another glass of wine.

It was a relief to have Molly back though, for all her appalling kitchen habits. I didn't want to be alone. Not that I had much of a chance to be, anyway. The weeks simply rushed by and I was frantically busy. Busy and sad. I'd love to be able to tell you that the combination made me a nicer and thinner person. It didn't. I ate tons of garlic and parsley mashed potato and still ridiculed happy couples. My days were frantic. I had to be on site at the Bar most of the time and Sarah was making ever more frenetic calls to suppliers and contractors, promising them the earth. Ben had left the Casa and was walking around with the look of a cat who's swallowed the cream. Doug was doing the renovation for me, and I had young Roger following me around all day with rather tedious doglike devotion. My days were so busy that by the time evening came I was ready to fall into bed and practically pass out.

Laddie Bernstein, Nicola's ace lawyer, had arrived in London and had endeared himself to us all. He was a roly-poly man, bald, and always wore a buttonhole, or as he termed it, a *boutonnière*, pronounced in a broad Brooklyn accent. He had a wild taste in silk ties and would often turn up unannounced, clutching a bottle of bourbon. He was a fast-talking, typical New York lawyer, and probably an absolute shark if he wasn't working for you. Luckily for us, he was. He'd been sent over by Nicola, to handle her book while fending off lawsuits left right and centre from irate pop stars.

'Jeez, these guys don't know they're born!' he would announce with relish, rubbing his hands with glee at the prospect of a wrangle with yet another smacked-out rock star.

He had also proved invaluable in sorting out the legalities of Pete's rather informal will, and smoothing the path between Steve and myself over the exchange of money from the Bar.

'Hey you guys, it's only a few dollars, you're both friends, right? Well, let's keep it that way. Who wants a bourbon?'

Zena was planning the party to end all parties for the grand opening of the gallery Steve had bought with his share of the money from the Bar – and which I was designing. His first show was to be the work that he and Molly had done on the island, and Zena was immersed in guest lists and determined that all would go smoothly. She wanted the gallery opening to finish at nine, and then to transport everyone *en masse* over to the Bar. Getting the right form of transport for this magical feat consumed her every waking moment. Laddie was obsessed with her and would whisper, 'She's real class,' every time he clapped eyes on her.

We had all been working so hard that come mid-May it was time we all took a night off: we decided to go to a swish restaurant that had recently opened. It had jumped on the

Moroccan bandwagon, and was swamped with low tables, velvet cushions and fretwork lamps. There was a huge queue outside, but we sailed past them all, being in the company of Zena who, of course, knew the owner intimately.

We were waiting for Monty in the restaurant bar, laughing at Laddie's complaints about the place: 'Jeez, at these prices they can't afford chairs? My ass is sure gonna be sore if I've gotta sit on the goddamn floor.'

Molly had ordered some form of alcoholic mint tea, and was spilling it over Sarah as she waved frantically at Monty who had just arrived.

Monty apologised for being late and kissed everyone, including Laddie (who kissed him back with an air of surprise) good evening.

We were wafted to our table by a slim Arab boy with doe eyes, that Monty made blush by flirting with, and were just settling ourselves when we heard a familiar voice coming from the far end of the room.

'But ees impossible, no? You know who I am?! The chef here is good friend of mine, just say to heem that Baba wishes to eat.' Mimi pushed her way through the crowded restaurant and spied us all trying to hide under our napkins.

She fell on us with loud expressions of joy, that became even louder once she'd spotted Steve. She wriggled on to the cushion next to him, stroking his arm and pouting magnificently.

'I theenk that you are very naughty boy, no? And you 'ave my good luck charm still? Why you not call poor Baba?'

Much to my delight, Steve had gone rather red and was looking embarrassed.

'Yes,' I said, 'why haven't you called poor Baba? You naughty boy, Steve . . .'

Everybody laughed, and Steve tried to move slightly away

from her, which is difficult when you are lolling on the floor at a very low table. Laddie was staring at her, open mouthed. 'Who the hell is she?' he whispered to me.

'A walking disaster area, but quite fun,' I whispered back. He looked astutely at her, then back to me and said, 'Gottcha.'

The evening progressed aided by an awful lot of the alcoholic mint tea, which proved to be lethally strong and strangely addictive. The food was delicious, and we ate every scrap. It had all the best bits of Moorish cuisine, but none of the horrid bits like damp couscous or wet mutton.

'You like food? Yes? Ees my friend Ali! He's so talented, they want heem to do tourist menu. Ha! He say, Ha! I am arteest, not just a cook!'

Sarah and I pricked up our ears at this. We had been trying to find a suitable chef for ages, with very little success. Ben had even been trying to tempt a friend of his away from the River Café, but we just couldn't match his salary. Maybe Ali was worth a try. I'd pop into the kitchen after dinner and see if I could have a word with him.

'Well, the food's just swell, sweetheart, but the seating's hell!' Laddie said. We all agreed, clinking our ruby coloured tea glasses together.

Zena started to tax everyone with the problem of finding suitable transport for the grand opening.

'You see, darlings, I have to get three hundred people in style from the east end of London to the west. *How* am I going to do it?'

'Stretch limos . . .'

'Fleets of taxis . . .'

'Simply hundreds of those sweet rickshaw things . . .'

'Make the bastards walk, it'll work up an appetite . . .'

'Coaches . . .'

'No, no. Horse and coaches . . .'

The mint tea had taken hold on us all now and the suggestions were becoming more and more impractical. We managed to lever ourselves up from the floor and made our way outside. I nipped into the busy kitchen and gave my phone number to Ali, asking him to call me. Monty, I saw, was sliding his phone number into the hand of the waiter.

'You can *never* have too many waiting staff,' he said to me, smiling broadly.

We all split up outside, Laddie squiring Zena to her house on the river before going off to his expensive hotel. Sarah back to her cats, Monty off to a secret assignation, Molly and I back home and Steve to his new flat and studio above the Gallery. He was having some trouble shaking off Mimi though: she was clinging to his arm like a limpet and looking up at him from under her eyebrows.

'Remember what happened last time,' I warned him.

'Liv, help me,' he hissed, 'I can't get rid of her . . .'

'Try harder. And sort out the bloody pistol,' I muttered, leaving him to his fate. He cast a despairing glance at me as Molly and I jumped into a taxi and waved wildly at him. As the taxi followed the bend in the road, our last glimpse of them was of Mimi gesticulating wildly, and Steve cowering away from her.

'Do you think he'll be all right?' Molly giggled.

'I should think so. After all, he's managed before!'

'Yeah, and look what happened then!'

The days before the opening were fraught. I was running between the Bar and the Gallery (we had all spent many, many hours trying to think up a different name, but the old name had stuck) trying to match paint, source furniture and keep everyone calm. Sarah was convinced that we would never be open in time, and I had to keep reminding her that

I really did know what I was doing (I crossed my fingers behind my back when I said that) and that we would be ready.

The best fun to be had however was sitting at home with Ben and Sarah, considering the membership applications that we had received. The arguments were fierce and very funny. We'd had loads of people apply from the Casa, and lots of new ones, too. We agreed that to get in there had to be a vote of at least two of the three of us.

'William bloody Magpie! I don't think so . . .'

'I know he's awful, but he did want to take over the Casa. He just wants to spy, I think.'

'I think over my dead body!'

His application went on to the reject pile.

'There's one here from Allegra.'

'Who?'

'You know, that blonde model . . .'

'Nah, she only drinks mineral water and nibbles on lettuce leaves.'

'Look, look! There's one here from the brunette bitch from hell — Angie!'

'No.'

'Definitely no. Bloody cheek!'

'Oh, look, one from Mr and Mrs Abraham . . .'

'Oh, sweet.'

'Good God! There's an application from Connie!'

There was a unanimous vote on that one — reject pile.

'Heavens! There's one from Mimi!'

We contemplated the dreadful scenes in the Bar, should she become a member.

'Oh, why the hell not? She'll certainly liven the place up, won't she?'

'We don't want her stopping Ali from working though, do we?'

'She'll get in anyway, whether she's a member or not!'

She was in.

One of the first rooms to be finished at the Bar was the office, and Sarah and I decamped to there. It was a far cry from Pete's day, and Sarah had worked like a demon installing computers and setting up phone lines. I noticed that the framed photograph of her cats was nowhere in evidence. She had turned into a whirlwind of activity and usually had a phone clamped to her ear alternately cajoling and bullying contractors, the bank, and suppliers. Nicola called in one day, to catch up on the news. I told her that her house was going well, and that the Bar was nearly ready. I hoped she'd be there for the opening.

'But of course! I wouldn't miss it for the world. I want to make the first booking with you for my book launch, although it's not till next year. But by some sort of twisted marketing, I'm now getting letters from rock stars that I've never met, begging to be put in the diaries!'

I laughed. Her book had generated so much interest that already Nicola had been doing interview after interview for it. She'd been hinting at the salacious details that it contained, and most of the London music scene was holding its breath waiting to find out if they were in or out.

'How's Molly?'

'OK, I think. She's still staying with me, I don't think she's ever going to go home. She and Steve are working very hard on the gallery opening, I do so hope that her pictures sell.'

Nicola laughed. 'Well, I'll buy a couple anyway. And how's Monty?'

'Exactly the same. I'm going shopping with him tomorrow

to buy something for the opening. I'd better go, Nicola, we've just got a delivery of furniture, see you soon.'

The Bar looked great. We had put in a bleached wooden floor that stretched the length of the building, including the restaurant that we'd opened next door. I'd chosen a smoky, petrol blue for the walls, and had found some wonderful steel framed mirrors that reflected the space. The restaurant was quite formal, with the tables covered with linen and fresh flowers. The reception area had a huge bunch of roses and lilies. Sarah had blanched when she saw the bill, but agreed that they looked stunning. It was the first thing you saw when you came through the revolving door, where Jackie would be sitting behind the desk signing people in and out, answering phones and checking coats.

I'd also put in, at huge expense, a really wonderful serpentine zinc bar which snaked its way voluptuously down the length of the building. Glasses were gleaming behind the bar, and Ben was in the process of stocking it. He called us over to try some samples, to choose the house champagne.

'Try this one, it's a good colour, a nice finish and quite biscuity.'

'Umm, but I think this one has more toast in it . . .'

They all tasted great to me, so I left him and Sarah to argue over the merits of the various brands.

I called Doug, who was now over at the Gallery, to ask him how things were progressing. He sounded amused.

'Well, we'd be going a whole lot faster if the wee Russian girl would stop wandering about the place with no clothes on!'

'Oh God, is Mimi still there?'

'Not for the want of your friend Steve trying to get her out! She's a real handful, isn't she?'

That was one way of describing her, I thought. I rang Steve.

'Oh Liv, I really don't think we'll be ready on time, Molly and I just can't decide where to hang everything, and the builders have still got to put a second coat on . . .'

'I think Mimi should put a coat on and things would go much more quickly.'

He lowered his voice. 'Liv you have no idea, I am *exhausted*! She insists on turning up at all hours, and she's distracting the painters and—'

'Tell her to go, you lily-livered coward!'

'I've *tried* . . . She's very, umm, *persuasive* . . .'

'Well, turn it to your advantage, do some sketches of her. I still have a deeply pornographic one that I'm sure would guarantee huge publicity for the Gallery!'

'Do you think she'd let me?'

'I wouldn't think she'd care, would you? Ask her . . . It's not a bad idea, you know. Anyway, keep her away from the builders, and everything'll be fine. I'll come over tonight, after I've finished here, OK?'

I wandered upstairs to the private rooms of the Bar: they still needed dressing, but they were looking good. Ali wanted to do a test run of the menu at lunchtime, so we had invited Monty to join us. I came back downstairs to find that he had arrived and was sampling the champagne downstairs. As I joined them, he lifted his glass and said, 'Well done, this place looks *divine*! I just know it's going to be a *huge* success. I do so hope you haven't turned my application for member-ship down?'

'It rather depends on the outfit we get tomorrow! No, of course not, although there was a lot of opposition and I really had to do some fast talking to get you past Ben and Sarah.'

They laughed, and we moved into the restaurant. Ali was bringing out plate after plate of food. He had cooked one dish of everything on the menu, and we all had to sample it and give comments. I had just got a fork poised over a delicious looking pile of spicy crab cakes when there was a banging on the front door. I left Jackie and Ben ushering the remaining builders into the restaurant to test the food and went to answer it. I found Zena and Laddie standing arm in arm, smiling broadly.

'Hello, you two! Do come in, you're just in time to try the food,' I said, waving them through the door.

'Well, darling, what luck! Let's call it a wedding breakfast, shall we?'

'You can call it what you like, but do come and taste— *What* did you say?!'

I looked closely at them both. Zena was wearing a cream silk dress, with a *real* ivy leaf pinned on to it by a huge diamond stud. And Laddie had an ivy green silk tie, and a white rose in his lapel. They were radiating happiness, and Zena was holding out her hand so that I could see the Tiffany wedding band on her finger.

'When you see a classy broad like this one, you don't take no for an answer. We did the deed today! And no pre-nup agreement either!'

Zena smiled sweetly up at him, holding on to his arm. I dragged them inside and broke the news. Sarah jumped up and kissed them both, and Ben and Monty broke into applause.

'Quick!' I shouted, 'Champagne!'

We had a splendid wedding reception, with the builders toasting Zena and Laddie's health solemnly with champagne. Ali rushed back into the kitchen and concocted a cream and apricot soufflé that he dusted with icing sugar and decorated with rose petals as an impromptu wedding cake. Sarah telephoned Steve and Molly, and they arrived with a packet of confetti. Steve and Molly hugged Zena and slapped Laddie on the back. We sprinkled them with the confetti, and toasted them endlessly. They made an unlikely couple, but were obviously besotted with each other.

'I didn't think it would *ever, ever* happen to me,' Zena whispered, 'but he's such a poppet, isn't he? And so very, *very* rich!' Molly and I exploded with laughter, and Monty was practically having to bite the inside of his mouth to prevent himself from becoming hysterical. There was definitely more to it than that, though, I had never seen Zena so happy. Her customary vagueness was gone, and she hung on Laddie's every word. Reluctantly he stood up, and formally thanked us on behalf of himself and his wife (there was a chorus of catcalls at that) and said that he had to go back to work.

'Me too darling, I think I've solved the transport problem. No, I won't tell you, but I think you'll be *thrilled*.'

Monty jumped to his feet. 'Christ, look at the time, I'm meant to be at the Ritz interviewing Vivienne Westwood. I know the darling is always late but this is ridiculous! I must fly . . . See you tomorrow, Liv, 10.30, fifth floor, Harvey Nicks. *What* an afternoon!' He rushed out of the door.

I went back to the Gallery with Molly and Steve. In the back of a cab we speculated wildly on the afternoon's events.

'But Zena wouldn't even kiss me!' Steve grumbled, 'and now she's *married*!'

'But Laddie's lovely . . .' Molly said.

'I think so too. He's quite sexy, isn't he?'

'Umm, I think so . . .'

'What about me?'

'Oh, shut up,' Molly and I both said together.

The Gallery was looking wonderful, a large white space with a polished stone floor. The lighting was finished, and canvases were stacked against the walls. There was an over-whelming smell of paint drying, and I could see that the builders had rushed to give it a second coat.

'Wet paint!' I warned, but it was too late, Molly had already brushed against it. Steve started to sponge her off with cold water, and I walked around the place, getting a feel for it. By removing some interior walls we had created a large space that would look perfect with the pictures in it. I turned some of the canvases around, and the faces and colours jumped out at me. I didn't think they needed to worry, these were fantastic pictures and should sell well. We tried to lay them out on the floor, marking the walls where they would go. It was a time-consuming job, and we all had our own ideas about the placements, so in the end I decided to leave them to it, and make my way home.

'Liv, before you go. We've got something for you.' Steve had a framed picture in his arms: he handed it to me. I turned it over and saw it was the charcoal sketch that he'd done of Pete and me in the garden of the villa. Pete's face was in the shadows, but you could clearly see the sparkle in his eyes; I was turned towards him, smiling at something (probably obscene) that he had just said. I stared at it in silence for some time. I could feel the tears prick behind my eyelids as I thanked Steve. They both came over and hugged me, and I thought I'd better leave quickly before I boo-hooed properly. As I staggered out of the Gallery with the picture in my arms, looking for a taxi, I thought that I'd hang the picture in the Bar. Pete would have loved that, he had always liked being where the action was.

I checked my messages when I got home: a lot of them were from friends accepting the invitation to the opening.

Suzanne and Michael Aston were coming up from Sussex for it, Frankie was bringing her film crew, and Lord Abbingdon was leaving his stately pile for the night. Well, those four alone would make for an interesting mix, I thought. I listened to the rest, ticking the names off from a printed list (Sarah had organised me somewhat) and saw that every person we'd invited had accepted. The last call was from Christopher, irate that we had refused him membership of the Bar. This was news to me. I realised that Sarah and Ben must have hidden his application, and I smiled as I deleted his message. I decided to get an early night, to be ready for the shopping spree with Monty.

I met Monty as arranged and spent a fruitless hour following him around Harvey Nicks.

'No, not that, darling, it makes you look like a poisoner . . .'

'Umm, maybe . . . It's too long on you though.'

'God, no, take it off immediately, you've gone from a poisoner to a prison warder!'

I was standing in the changing room getting hotter and more bad tempered by the minute, when Monty pushed his head round the door and said, 'Try this on, I've just got to pop and see if they do a top in blue for the woman in the next-door changing room. The poor dear's in red at the moment and it makes her look like a prawn.'

'I thought you were *my* stylist!' I wailed, but he was gone. My phone rang in the bottom of my bag, and with one arm in the new dress that Monty had supplied, I awkwardly bent down to answer it.

'What is it?' I snarled into the phone.

'Are you *always* this bad tempered?'

John.

'I'm in a changing room in Harvey Nicks trying on an

increasing pile of ill-fitting clothes for a grand opening of my new bar and restaurant, *and* my best friend's gallery, nothing fits, and my personal stylist has deserted me.'

'Sounds like you could do with a drink. I could be with you in ten minutes. Meet me on the fifth floor.'

'What the hell are *you* doing near Harvey Nichols?'

'There you go, being rude again.'

'How will I recognise you? I don't even know you!'

'I'm the psychotic axe murderer. You can recognise me by my hunchback and yellow fangs.'

'Don't joke about it, the last time I had a drink with someone I didn't know, I ended up in a rubber catsuit.'

'That sounds very uncomfortable and not remotely sexy. I'll see you in a minute.'

'But, I can't—' He'd already hung up.

Monty came back with an armful of clothes and I told him about the builder.

'Darling, you *have* to go! I'll lurk in the background, and be fatherly. Come on, put some lipstick on and brush your hair.'

I scrabbled around in my bag for some make-up then I decided it was ridiculous getting tarted up for some builder from Sidcup that I didn't even know. I marched off to the fifth floor, leaving Monty helping out all the other women in the changing room, then took quite a lot of detours, to give John time to arrive first.

I looked around the room. There was only one table that had a single man sitting at it. He had his back to me, so I skirted around him, trying to get a good look at him without being horribly obvious about it. He had dark hair touched with silver, a wide smile and glinting amber eyes. He stood up, and handed me a glass of champagne. 'I think you should drink all of that before you say anything at all.'

'Are you trying to get me drunk?'

'Good Lord no! Does trying on clothes always make you bad tempered?'

I laughed, and relaxed a little. As I sipped, I studied his face carefully, and decided that I quite liked what I saw. We ordered more champagne, and soon we were embarked on a very silly conversation. He made me laugh a lot, and was also doing something very disturbing to my heart rate. He kept prompting me to tell him more about my life and I found him easy to talk to. I spotted Monty lurking (as best he could, but it must be said not that successfully) in the background, so I waved him over and introduced them.

Monty shook hands with John and said, 'I've bought you that last dress you tried on. It's perfect. Anyway, I must fly, it was so nice meeting you, John, I'll see you at the opening. Oh, and by the way she's even more bad tempered in the mornings than she is on the phone . . .'

We watched him leave.

'What makes *him* think that I'm going to invite *you* to the opening?' I said truculently.

'Oh, I think you will, don't you?'

Chapter Twenty-Four

I ended up having lunch with John. And alarmingly, I rather felt that it would be only too easy to have dinner *and* breakfast with him as well.

'So is that Pete's ring?' he asked me, and I realised with a start how much he'd learned about me over the course of our phone calls.

'You know lots about me,' I objected. 'What about you?'

'What about me?'

He looked steadily at me, and I felt an unfamiliar giddiness. I discovered that I was making a bargain with myself – if he's not married you can sleep with him, if he is, you pay for lunch and leave right now. That's it, no other dates, no phone calls, nothing. I gathered my belongings together, ready to leave.

'What are you doing?'

'Getting ready to go. Are you married?'

He looked down at the table, and played with some cutlery. Oh God, I thought, a sure sign of guilt. This is where the lies start. The last thing I wanted was another Christopher in my life. (I know, I know . . . I'd already jumped to the conclusion that he was, of course, going to *be* in my life. But this feeling of giddiness had stayed with me, and the truth was that he had deeply touched me somewhere, and yes, I *know* that I'd only known him for five minutes, and knew absolutely nothing about him.) I could hear unknown voices screaming 'warning warning' at me, but nevertheless, I asked him again.

'Well, are you?'

'My wife died two years ago.'

'I suppose that punching the air and screaming *yes!* would be completely inappropriate? Oh God, I'm so sorry to have said that, I really, really didn't mean it. I mean, I did mean it, but only the fact that you weren't married, *not* that she was dead. Oh shit, I'll shut up now, I'm sorry.'

To my relief he was laughing, and he leaned forward and stroked my hand. Suddenly I didn't want to move my hand away.

'That's OK. I know what you meant. Look, I *have* to go to a meeting, shall we have dinner?'

'Oh *yes*. Oh damn, I should have played a little harder to get then, shouldn't I?'

'No, what's the point?'

I went giddy again. I gave him my address and we left the restaurant. Wildly I waved goodbye to him in the street, nearly knocking out the eye of an elderly lady with my elbow. High on air, adrenalin and champagne, I ran back to the Bar.

I was met with gloom, doom, and despondency. Sarah was pleading with the bank to allow us to have an overdraft, Ben was arguing with a lorry driver over a wine delivery and Ali was hurling a box of salad stuff back into the face of a delivery boy, calling it, 'Feelth, not good enough to feed peegs!' I was humming happily and got so much on their nerves that they all begged me to go home.

When I reached the flat I found that Molly had spread every single item of both of our wardrobes over the floor, and was despairingly trying everything on in an attempt to find something suitable to wear for the opening.

'Why didn't you ask Monty?'

'Because I've got no money. Anyway, I wanted to put it together myself and look like a successful artist so that all the people I used to work with will swoon with envy at the opening of the Gallery. Why are you looking so damned happy?'

I laughed and told her about John.

'What – the builder that keeps phoning you, you mean the one that you're so rude to and keep standing up?'

'That's the one!'

'I don't like the sound of it at all. Supposing he's been stalking you? Supposing he—'

'Stop it. You can see him for yourself tonight, he's picking me up for dinner.'

'Supposing he's married?'

'His wife died two years ago.'

'What of?! You see, that alone should arouse your suspicions.'

'Molly, stop it! You can ask him tonight, can't you? Now for God's sake, let's find you an outfit and put this lot away.'

We spent a hilarious afternoon trying on every possible permutation of clothes. At one point Molly was seriously considering wearing a pair of painter's dungarees with a sequinned boob tube underneath.

'People might think that I'd bought it from Voyage or the Cross . . .'

'No, people will just think that you've lost the plot completely! Try on the trouser suit again.'

'But I want to look arty, not like a businesswoman!' she wailed.

'All successful artists look like businesswomen,' I said firmly.

'What about Tracey Emin?' Molly said defiantly.

'Well, no, I grant you that she doesn't. But then you don't wet the bed and exhibit the sheets, do you?' I had a moment's fleeting pity for the cleaners at Saatchi's – should they make the bed or not? Was it art or was it just a mess? Who knows?

We narrowed the clothing dilemma down to two possible outfits, and Molly went to phone Monty to ask his opinion. I dashed around the flat, hurling clothes back into cupboards and wardrobes, trying to make the place look presentable. Molly came off the phone and said, 'Monty says that he's very nice and has got eyes like a lion, and that I've got to wear the trouser suit and that you're to wear something easy to get out of tonight and not to eat too much and don't forget to invite him to the opening.'

'Bloody queens! Of *course* he's coming to the opening.'

'No, he meant John, not himself.'

'Oh, well, we'll see . . .' But I was elated that Monty had liked him at least. I always counted on Monty's judgement on things. Well, most things, actually, from clothes to men. I remembered that he'd never been very keen on Christopher. Maybe this was a good omen for John. I hoped so.

I'd nearly forgotten what it was like to get ready for a date, all that nervous energy, and anticipation. I was ready and waiting far too early, and Molly poured me a glass of wine to calm my nerves. At least that's what she said, but I noticed she was gulping down rather a lot herself.

'Where's he taking you?'

'I've no idea.'

'Probably the cab stand at Warwick Avenue, that's where all the builders eat, isn't it?'

'In that case I'm horribly overdressed, aren't I?'

'Oh, I don't know, they probably get a lot of Jasper Conran clad women in there with their stalkers.'

'Oh do stop, I'm nervous enough as it is. Was that a taxi stopping?'

Molly and I fought each other to get to the window. Zena was climbing out of a black cab, and a minute later the doorbell rang.

'Damn,' I said. I mean, I love seeing Zena, but not when I'm expecting a man I hardly know to pick me up on a first date. As I went to answer the door, Molly hissed at me, 'Make sure that he knows Zena has just got married, you know how men go gaga over her. You don't want him drooling over her, do you.'

I laughed, and opened the door.

'Darling, you're in, thank goodness! I just need to go over a few details for the opening with you. You're looking very glam, is this a bad time?'

Molly explained about the date with the stalking builder.

'A *builder*, darling! Are you *sure*?'

I was just about to accuse Zena of being a sexual snob, and tease her about the validity of marrying into that most slimeball of professions, the law, when the intercom went again. I could feel my heart fluttering as I let John in.

He came bounding up the stairs clutching a bunch of red roses. I introduced him to Molly and Zena, and was unreasonably glad to see that no drooling took place at all. Molly faffed around finding glasses, whilst Zena was doing her social chit-chat thing. Looking closely at him she said, 'Do excuse me, but haven't I seen you somewhere? I'm sure that I have, I never forget a face.'

'Probably on a building site,' Molly muttered.

I looked at John properly. He was certainly broad

shouldered enough for a builder, but I had never seen a builder wearing an Oswald Boeteng suit before.

'I know! Of course, I've got it! You were in the *FT* today, weren't you?' Zena cooed triumphantly.

John laughed. 'Yes, it was an appalling photograph, wasn't it?'

Molly and I exchanged glances. I could see that we were thinking the same thing – what the hell was a builder from Sidcup doing in the *Financial Times*?

'They were *very* nice about you. The merger went through beautifully, didn't it?'

'Yes, according to them I'm going to singlehandedly change the face of the British construction business,' he said.

'What *are* you talking about?' I demanded.

'Darling, I've *told* you to buy something else other than the *Guardian*, and I know you only read the women's page in that. I take it you have no idea who you're about to have dinner with?'

John was grinning broadly at me.

'No, all I know is that he's a very grumpy builder who phones me up, demanding to know where his delivery of lights is. Oh yes, and he comes from Sidcup.'

John laughed. 'I'm a very hands-on owner, and I never said I *came from* Sidcup, I said I was *in* Sidcup, which is a very different thing. We're constructing a new hospital there.'

'Well, who the hell are you then?' I said rather ungraciously.

'We never got round to last names, did we? Allow me to introduce myself, my name is John Llewellyn.'

The name really meant nothing to me, and I smiled politely. John laughed, and went to fill Molly's glass. Zena took the opportunity to whisper to me, 'You know, darling, *the*

John Llewellyn. Think of all those little boards you see outside buildings being put up.'

It was gradually dawning on me that this was no ordinary builder. I could see from the gleam of respect in Zena's eyes that he was, in her lights, a man not to be trifled with. I felt a bit bewildered, I mean, I was prepared to have a fling with a builder, but this was turning into something very different indeed. I looked carefully at him again. I must have been mad to think that this was an ordinary builder. But then again, I had been so flustered by my feelings about him that I hadn't taken notice of much else. The outward trappings of wealth were all there – the handmade shoes, the expensive watch – and I had completely missed them. I felt obscurely cheated somehow, and very off balance.

Meanwhile he was getting on like a house on fire with Molly and Zena and they were all chatting like mad about the opening of the Bar.

'Look, darling I *know* you're about to go out, but do just cast your eye over the positively *final* guest list.'

I took the sheet of rather crumpled paper from Zena and ran down the list. John stood behind me so that he could read the names too.

He whistled in admiration, 'Very "A" list, very impressive, but I can't see my name on it. Anybody got a pen?'

'I shall amend it straight away, darling. Now I must fly. Laddie will be wondering where on earth I am.'

Then followed a conversation between Zena and John, where we discovered that he knew Laddie very well, as he had been instrumental in helping John with some land deal or other in America.

This was getting out of hand, I decided, and thought it best if we left soon to go to dinner.

'Molly thinks that we're going to the cab stand in Warwick

Avenue,' I announced. 'And as it's just round the corner we can walk.'

'I think you'd put the cabbies off their bangers and mash if we turned up with you in that dress. I was thinking of the Ritz, if that's OK with you.'

'Well, it's a little bit common, but I don't mind slumming it.' I grinned.

We waved Zena goodbye, and John asked Molly if she'd like to have dinner with us. He got ten out of ten for that, I decided. Molly got eleven out of ten when she declined. We were just leaving, when the phone rang. I hesitated, but knew that in the end I'd have to answer it. I was sorry I did: it was Sarah, sounding hysterical.

'Liv, oh thank God you're there! I don't know what to do . . . I tried calling Doug, but there's no reply. There's about an inch of water in the kitchens that's spreading into the restaurant, the power has gone in the bar, and we open tomorrow! Liv, you must know another builder! What *are* we going to do?!'

My immediate thought was that young bloody Roger had been up to his tricks again and how exactly was I going to kill him – a stabbing to the heart maybe? Or a slow torture involving electrodes? I told Sarah to calm down, and that I would be right over. Damn, damn, damn, here I was, all ready to go to the Ritz with a lovely new man and I was soon going to be wading through water and trying to find a plumber at eight in the evening. My eyes turned towards John.

I explained the situation. He calmly pulled out his mobile and began issuing orders, saying to me, 'What's the address? Oh, and I think you'd better change, don't you? You won't want to be paddling in those shoes. We'll go straight over there, I'll cancel the table.'

I ran into the bedroom and pulled on some jeans. Molly followed me in, saying, 'God, he's awfully impressive, isn't he? Can I come too?'

'Yes, I think we'll probably need all the help we can get.'

We piled into a cab and rushed over to the Bar. Sarah met us outside wringing her hands in despair. 'I can't find the stopcock, or whatever the hell it's called. I've been mopping for ages, I'm frightened of being electrocuted. My God, aren't you John Llewellyn?'

We waded into the Bar, Sarah whispering to me, 'When I said don't you know another builder, I didn't mean *him*!'

'No, he's the one that I met today in Harvey Nicks.'

'Why didn't you say it was him?'

'I didn't bloody know, did I?'

John was out of sight, doing something mysterious to the water system. Sarah had lit candles, and the whole place was lit by their flames, reflected in the gently lapping water. I had to remind myself that this was a disaster, because in a strange way it did actually look rather beautiful. Two men were knocking on the door, and I paddled across the room to let them in.

'Mr Llewellyn sent us. Blimey, I've heard of a wet bar before, but I've never really been in one.'

John appeared and immediately took charge, dispatching the two men to different parts of the building. He had found two brooms and handed them to Sarah and Molly, giving me a mop and bucket. 'The sooner we start, the sooner we can have something to eat, even if it's only takeaway pizza.'

We swept and mopped till our arms ached. 'Where's Ben?' I asked, as I trailed through the water.

'Gone to see Steve at the Gallery, but they're both coming back as fast as they can,' Sarah panted, heaving a bucket of water outside. John had taken his shoes and socks off and had rolled his trousers up above his knees – always an attractive look in a man, I think. But despite that, I found that I still fancied him. I kept sneaking a look at him out of the corner of my eye when I thought he wasn't looking. I caught him doing the same thing, and we both started to laugh.

'Great first date, huh?' he said.

The water level had subsided and the floors were now glistening wet. The electrician was lying on his back sorting out some cables and John and the other builder were in the kitchen.

There was a loud banging at the door, and Ben and Steve burst through.

'The cavalry's arrived, no need to panic!' Steve shouted.

'Christ! What a mess.' Ben stared around in disbelief. 'What the hell happened here?'

'A burst pipe that knocked the power out, but it's all under control now,' John said, coming through the bar, wiping his hands on a towel.

'Who are you?' Steve asked.

'A friend of Olivia's, John. How do you do?' John held his hand out to Steve, then Ben.

Steve looked curiously disgruntled. 'Well, thanks for the help. I'm sure we can manage now.'

'Well, if you're sure. Liv, shall we go and get some dinner?'

They were staring at each other like two dogs ready for a scrap. Oh God. Men. Honestly.

'Look, I'd love to have some dinner, but there's so much to do here, we're opening tomorrow and this is still such a mess.'

'In that case, I'll stay and help. But you must have something to eat, I'll go and get everyone something. See you all in a minute.'

John started to walk towards the door. I called him back.

'Haven't you forgotten something?' I pointed to his bare feet. He laughed and bent down to put his shoes on.

He had barely got outside when Steve said, 'And who the hell is that? Is that the bloody builder who keeps calling you? Are you mad? What are you doing with him? You don't even know him.'

I was furious. I thought of the interminable dinners I had cooked for Steve and his string of moronic girlfriends, and all the trouble we had gone through with Mimi and Connie and here he was, lecturing *me*! Bloody cheek. Molly and Sarah had melted away and Ben had drifted to the end of the bar, cleaning the floor.

'Are you jealous, or what?' I demanded, facing him with my arms on my hips.

Steve looked away, and suddenly I felt sorry for him.

'Look Steve, he's a new man in my life. That's all. It doesn't alter anything between us, OK?'

Steve was rubbing his head, and he looked about thirteen. A thirteen-year-old boy in a sulk.

'Come on, snap out of it. This is daft. You might even like him,' I said, cajolingly.

Steve gave me a half-hearted grin, and added, 'OK, I'll try. By the way did I tell you that I finally told Mimi about us, sorry, I mean me, losing her pistol? She was fine about it. She's going to be raking it in soon, so she doesn't care.'

Well, that was a huge relief. I picked up a mop and started to clean the floor again. The power came back on, flooding the bar with light. There was a chorus of approval and applause and the builder responsible came forward to take a bow. We were clapping him on the back when John walked back in with a stack of pizza boxes. He began unloading them, and handed one to me saying, 'You look like a bit of a four seasons woman, so I got you that.'

'What, you mean I look like I like a bit of everything?'

'As long as I don't have anchovies,' Molly said, opening a box.

'Oh, give them to me, the cats simply adore them,' Sarah said.

Steve and Ben were already wolfing down pizzas, and Steve grinned his thanks at John.

'You're welcome,' John said.

I glanced at Steve and he mouthed 'sorry'. I called him a twit and cuffed the back of his head. We made the two builders eat some pizza too. A party feeling was developing: Ben opened some wine, and we all sat around eating with our fingers and swigging the wine. I was just licking the last bit of tomato sauce from my fingers when there was another loud banging on the door.

'Who the hell is that?' Molly said.

'Probably Mimi, ready for a little recreation,' said Steve gloomily.

Ben went to open the door and I heard the loud, drunken upper-class drawl of Christopher.

Oh God, what a perfect way to end an already pretty disastrous evening. I wearily stood up, ready to make my way to the door and tell Christopher to go home.

'Problem?' John said to me.

'Nothing I can't handle,' I said.

Ben was blocking the way into the Bar, and Christopher was trying to shove him aside.

'I just want to wish you all well for the place, thass all,' he slurred.

'Christopher, just go home. You're drunk.'

'Livia, Livia, you are still my Livia, aren't you?'

'No. Now go home.'

He lurched against Ben, who stumbled backwards against

me. Steve and John appeared behind us, and Steve started to remonstrate with Christopher.

'Let me in! I just want to talk to Livia. She's such a bitch, you know. Won't even talk to me now. Bitch!' His arms were flailing wildly and Ben and Steve were finding it hard to control him.

John stepped forwards, took Christopher firmly by the shoulders and frog-marched him on to the pavement.

'The lady is not a bitch, and she doesn't wish to talk to you. Now go home.'

He gave Christopher a gentle push on his way. Christopher reeled around and swung a punch at him. John neatly side-stepped it and said, 'Go home.' We all watched Christopher lurch down the road, weaving between cars.

'Thanks. Sorry about that . . . he's a little bit . . .'

'Little bit of a piss artist rather than an artist, isn't he? I've always thought his paintings frightful. You're so much better off without him,' said John. I looked at him in amazement.

'Do you know him?'

'By reputation. He painted my partner's wife's portrait – made her look like someone on a chocolate box. Pretentious little sod. His poor wife . . . Still, she's made her choice, hasn't she?'

Things were definitely looking up, I thought.

We cleared away the pizza boxes and tidied the bar. Molly and Sarah shared a cab home, and Ben persuaded Steve to go up to his flat for a nightcap.

Much to my embarrassment, John peeled off what looked like the debt of a small country from his wallet and handed it to the builders. I tried to pay him back but discovered I only had five pounds in my purse. I offered to write a cheque but he waved away my offer, saying that he had only tipped them, and that he would send me a bill.

The bar was very silent after everyone had left, and we sat at a table, facing each other.

Suddenly I was nervous, and wondered how the hell I was going to get home. Or to his home. Or to a hotel. Or anywhere that he had in mind, really. It's a load of rubbish about not sleeping with someone on the first date, I always think. That's what I was telling myself, anyway.

He leaned forward and touched my hand and I jumped about five feet in the air.

Lust makes me very twitchy.

John laughed and started to ask me about the Bar.

To my horror I felt tears well up in my eyes, as I thought about Pete. John stood up and swiftly walked around the table so that he was sitting beside me. I felt his arm around my shoulder and with a great feeling of relief I buried my head in his chest and sobbed.

He let me cry for a while, and then when I had reached that awful gulping, sniffy phase, he handed me a paper napkin. I saw that I had left great tracks of eye make-up over his shirt, and ruefully apologised. I realised that I must look absolutely dreadful, and stood up to go to the loo to try and repair the damage. He pulled me back down saying, 'There's no point putting make-up back on when I'm going to kiss it all off, is there?' Which he then proceeded to do, quite gloriously, I might add.

A long time later he said to me, 'I shall never be able to look at that table in quite the same light. It would have been far more appropriate to have been in a squishy double bed at the Ritz, and probably a great deal more comfortable, but, all in all, I think we acquitted ourselves admirably, don't you?'

I had to agree.

We lay happily in silence for a while longer, and then,

pulling myself together, I said regretfully, 'I really think that I should go home, the opening is looming. I've still got so much to do, not to mention reassuring Molly that I haven't been kidnapped by the sinister builder of Sidcup.'

He laughed, and guided me towards the door. I locked up and we stood outside in the warm dark night, then walked arm in arm along the road looking for a taxi. I couldn't bear for the evening to end, and was quite content to hold on to him.

Abruptly he stopped and swung me round to face him.

'Look, you're going to be incredibly busy with the Bar, and I've got to go to New York in the next day or so. So we might not have another opportunity to speak properly for some time.'

My heart began to sink. This was when he would start to mouth the usual nonsense about not being able to see me for a while, and that he wasn't looking for commitment, blah blah blah.

'. . . But you've been through a terrible time, and I think we are good together. Now you know that I'm not a sinister stalker or a beastly builder, we could make a go of things. Well, I think so anyway, and I'm rarely wrong about these things. So, let's see each other soon. OK? Very soon. As soon as we can.'

'What did you say?'

'Have you been listening at all?'

'Obviously not. But, yes. I'd like that.'

We kissed again, and with that he packed me off in a taxi, promising to see me at the opening tomorrow.

I sank back into the taxi seat and discovered that I was slightly alarmed. I mean, yes, I really, really liked him, and fancied him, and he had, so far, not put a foot wrong. But a new relationship? Well, that was a different kettle of fish altogether.

I turned in my seat to look out of the back window. John was standing in the road waving at me. I gave a wave back and tried to consider the future. London looked alive and well as it streamed past the taxi window; there were couples everywhere, it seemed, holding hands, laughing, talking, arguing. Did I want to be part of that again? The Bar was going to be such a commitment, would I even have time to have that again?

I twisted Pete's ring round on my finger and gazed out of the window. I decided to talk it over with Molly when I got home, and maybe I'd call Monty or Steve if it wasn't too late. Or Nicola in New York, or Zena and Laddie. I blessed the fact that I had so many good friends and pushed aside the idea of making any decisions that night. Life *could* be peachy, I realised. I had the opening of the Bar and the Gallery to look forward to – with all the guaranteed chaos that they would undoubtedly bring – and now, it seemed, I had a wonderful new man in my life. Why decide anything now? I settled back and watched London, with all its attendant horrors and glories, roll by.

After all, I consoled myself, tomorrow was a big day and I had time to think about it, hadn't I?